Also by Armand Croft:

AMONG
the LOST

Armand Croft

Per me si va ne la città dolente,
per me si va ne l'etterno dolore,
per me si va tra la perduta gente.
[. . . . .]
Lasciate ogni speranza, voi ch'entrate

Through me you go to the grief wracked city;
Through me you go to everlasting pain;
Through me you pass among lost souls
[. . . . .]
Abandon all hope Ye Who Enter Here

Dante Alighieri *The Inferno* (Canto III – The gate of Hell))

To our friends, the cetaceans

Among the Lost

1.

VERA SNEAD, having categorized Thomas Padgett as the largest human being she had ever seen in person, had not again thought of him in the eleven years since she saw him at her identical twin sister, Tamara's, wedding. Vera had wondered at the time why any woman, even one as devoid of taste and good sense as her sister, would marry this brute. Oh, how desperate she must have been. But she was in no position to criticize: she had married the reprehensible Jonathan in her own time of desperation.

But desperation for Vera and Tamara had been inevitable. Fate, not satisfied with making the girls tall, skinny, and flat-chested, had added small, closely spaced ferret eyes looking out from their identical lean and hawkish faces at a world they found distasteful, if their clenched, bitter mouths were any indication. Other than an acidic intelligence, the pair lacked even the tiniest of character traits that might have compensated for their unfortunate appearance.

As she barely remembered Thomas Padgett, she was surprised when he called her one early fall day. He said he had read a letter she had sent to Tamara saying she needed money.

This was true. Six-months earlier Vera had swallowed her gorge and had sent a letter to her detested but wealthy sister, begging her, since she had no children of her own, to help with her nephew's education. She was anxious to get her son, Brian, a slovenly, disrespectful teen-ager, out of the house. She had heard nothing back, as she had expected. In some perverse way she was relieved, being spared her sister's insufferable contemptuous patronizing. There being no money for college, Brian had joined the service.

"But you could still use some money?" Padgett said.

"I'm like everybody else. Of course, I could use more money. What do you have in mind?"

"If I flew up to Buffalo would you talk to me? I have a proposition for you."

"You mention money. How much?"

"Little Byron's education is something we should discuss face to face."

"Brian, not 'Byron.' And he's not little. He's eighteen and six-feet-two."

"Whatever... If you agree, I'll meet you in the entrance of Riverside Park. I understand you have a home in that area. One p.m. on Sunday. That's October 22nd, a week from tomorrow."

"Will Tamara be coming?"

"Good God, no! And leave Brian at home."

"This all sounds so secretive."

"We're family, Vera, and families help each other. And you need it, the way you got shafted by your old man."

Two years earlier their father had died of a heart attack while playing golf. Vera despised the old man so she hadn't bothered to attend the funeral. Her father and her husband, Jonathan, during a heated disagreement over the proper approach to the North Korean problem, had come to blows. In the melee an expensive cut glass decanter containing even more expensive Napoleon brandy had fallen on the floor and broken. Her father had already been furious with her for marrying a lawyer, a species he detested, but this pushed him beyond endurance. He demanded she and her husband leave the house and never return, and he warned her to expect nothing in the way of a bequest.

Vera did attend the reading of the will, in spite of being disinherited. As she had expected he had left the bulk of his estate, seven-million dollars, to Tamara. She hadn't loved the ugly old fool either, but being a much more accomplished ass-kisser, she had convincingly played the part of the affectionate dutiful daughter. Tamara handsomely taken care of, the lawyer had droned on, listing several small bequests to employees and servants, leaving Vera for last. To her the old man had left the sum of twenty-eight dollars and forty-six cents which, according to Jonathan, was sufficient recognition to forestall any legal challenge.

October 22nd, a bitterly cold overcast day, Vera arrived five-minutes before the appointed time. Thomas Padgett had already arrived and was waiting by the sign at the entrance. He was bigger than she remembered, probably six-feet-nine or ten. His coarse features, flat nose, and bristly black hair—like a worn-out shoe brush—gave him the Mike Mazurki look of a semi-retarded thug in an old-time noir movie, but his flashing deep-set black eyes suggested intelligence she wouldn't otherwise have expected from his appearance.

Vera judged from Padgett's weak, gap-toothed leer when he caught sight of her that smiling was not an activity he practiced with any regularity. She reluctantly shook his catcher's mitt-sized hairy paw—he had politely taken his glove off, which she hadn't expected—and allowed him to guide her by the elbow to a bench inside the park.

He appraised her closely. "You look exactly like Tamara, except for your hairdo—it's remarkable." This he said in a scratchy high-pitched voice, much at odds with his size.

"A double blight on humanity, according to our father."

He said, chuckling, "That's hitting it a little heavy, don't you think?"

She stared up at him, her unsaid message being, get to the point. Not only was she cold, she didn't want to spend any more time with this person than was necessary.

"What I'm about to propose will shock you."

She assured him she wasn't easily shocked, and suggested he lay it out for her before she froze to death.

"Tamara is divorcing me. A friend of mine heard her lawyer mention it to another lawyer. Her fortune, now about nine million, thanks to good management, is her personal property which means I'll get next to nothing. Even the house is hers. But you'd know about that, getting the rough end of the stick from the old man's will the way you did."

"Yes?... So?"

"There *is* a way to make it right, for both of us." Padgett inhaled, held it a moment as if uncertain whether to proceed, and exhaled, sending a steamy blast of acrid cigarette breath in her face.

She scrunched her eyes and waved the air in front of her with her mittened hand. She again suggested he get to the point.

"This is all hypothetical, you understand, but what would you say if your sister should have an unfortunate accident?" He studied her intently for a reaction.

Vera looked away, thinking this over. If she was shocked at all, it was how amenable she was to the idea. She had no problem with this creature killing Tamara—and that's what she assumed he meant by an "unfortunate accident." Her concerns were the chances of getting caught, and how dangerous her role in this might be. "I'm assuming, with her out of the way, you inherit everything. So where do I come in? I doubt it's out of the goodness of your heart."

"It's not inheriting anything. I'm not in her will. It will be a divorce settlement." He explained the plan he had concocted. In early November, he said, he and Tamara were taking a Caribbean cruise. When they landed in Puerto Rico, he would humanely dispatch Tamara—Vera interrupted to say this was a delicacy he need not trouble himself with—and bury her in a nature preserve he knew about. This was where she, Vera, came in. He and she would return to the ship where Vera would impersonate her sister. Because there were slight differences in the two women she would stay in their stateroom the remainder of the cruise, claiming migraine headaches. After docking in Fort Lauderdale they would return to Texas where she would familiarize herself with Tamara's routine, her hair styles, way of dressing, and learn her passwords, PINs, and account numbers, all of which Thomas had purloined. After a week or so, however long it took to do a credible impersonation of Tamara, she would relocate to Nevada, where she would establish residency, hire a new lawyer, and complete the divorce. When it was final they would split Tamara's fortune, roughly four-million each after costs.

Padgett assured her he would cover her immediate expenses, her flight and hotel in Puerto Rico, and he would arrange her relocation to Nevada.

"I don't know. It sounds sketchy."

"Not really." Padgett drew his overcoat tighter around him and hunched his shoulders against the cold. "I'll admit there are three critical areas where the plan might go wrong."

"I can guarantee you there are more than three but start with those."

He said, ignoring her sneering, "One, and most critical: she can't be found before her fingerprints are unreadable. You may be identical in most ways, but your prints aren't. Second, someone may link our visit to Puerto Rico in the cruise ship with you being there. This is unlikely as there'll be no record of Tamara and me being on the island. And no one knows we're going on the cruise."

Vera looked away, scowling in disgust at an old lady kissing a small fluffy dog on the mouth.

"Well? What do you think?"

She said, still looking away, "A million details will have to be worked out."

"That's a given, And there's still the third thing, maybe the most important—your kid. What's his name, Byron?"

"Brian—I told you before... He'll be no problem. Like I said, he's in the service, the navy. He's on a carrier in the Far East."

"Yeah, good, that's fine for now, but later, how will he take your supposed death?"

"We're not real close. He'll get over it."

"Will you miss him? You can't see him again, you know."

"Like I said, we're not real close. Maybe I can reconnect later as his aunt... Speaking of missing, won't Tamara's friends miss her?"

"Tamara's a bitch, and the few friends she has, I've managed to alienate." Vera had to close her eyes and look away from the man's ugly leer as he said this. "Nobody will miss her when she supposedly moves to Nevada—this is the story I'll give out. When the time's right I'll say she's gone to live in Europe. You'll be able to live wherever you want, of course."

"If I do this, this cruise thing, you understand we'll have to have separate beds. There can be no physical contact between us."

He assured her with ill-disguised revulsion there was no danger whatsoever of him making any unwanted advances in her direction. This she assumed was the end of their meeting. She rose to leave, anxious to get somewhere warm. "Take this." He handed her a prepaid flip phone. "Keep it charged and turned on in case I have to contact you."

Vera, shivering, teeth chattering with cold, left Thomas Padgett in the park and returned to her grubby second floor apartment in a decaying two-unit building four blocks away. She said she might agree to a second meeting a week later, after she had thought over his proposal.

A twenty-minute scalding shower warmed her up but didn't wash away the grimy sticky feeling of contamination she felt from being involved in something like this. But if what he said was true—and she would examine the plan from every angle for signs of weakness or betrayal—this was her only hope of escaping her squalid life. To do so, however, she would have to hold her nose and endure this repulsive monster.

She slipped into her tattered old chenille robe and poured herself a half glass of supermarket Bourbon. She took a sip, grimacing at the burning in her throat.

She settled in at the cheap chrome table in her tiny kitchen with a pad and pencil and wrote down what she saw as weaknesses in the plan. First, why not do away with Tamara in Texas and bury her body somewhere around Buffalo? Why all this rigamarole with Puerto Rico? Second, what contingency plans did he have if someone realized she was not Tamara? Third, there was Brian. He and she might not be close, but what if he nosed around and found her? He would recognize her immediately. Maybe a pile of money, say, two-hundred thousand dollars from his "aunt Tamara" would dampen any curiosity about his mother's death—assuming he cared one way or the other. And could Thomas guarantee access to, and control over, Tamara's money? Otherwise, the whole exercise was pointless. These were all questions needing answers.

In the event, the second meeting, scheduled for a week later, never took place. Padgett explained they shouldn't be seen together; instead he called her prepaid cell phone from a second prepaid phone:

"I've sent you a package. It should arrive in a day or two. There's a dress exactly like the one Tamara will be wearing, and a thousand dollars in cash for expenses. Make sure you use your own credit card for the hotel and flight. It's not as if you'll have to pay it back. And you need to send me your passport, your wallet, and your iPhone by overnight delivery. Keep your driver's license—you'll need it for the flight." He gave her the address, a UPS mail box in San Antonio, and had her repeat it.

She raised the concerns she had written down.

"I agree," he said, "those *are* vulnerabilities. Now is your last chance to back out."

"No. I'll go ahead. Give me the details."

"You'll need to get a reservation at the Double Tree Hilton in San Juan. It's a nice place, I've stayed there. If they're full up get another hotel in the area. You'll fly to San Juan on November 11th. Take a shuttle to the hotel. Let the staff get to know you, spend a lot of time in the lobby, use room service, compliment the maids on what a good job they're doing—all this so they'll miss you when you don't show up. I know it'll be hard for you, but try for once to be pleasant.

"On Tuesday, November 14th, our cruise ship docks in San Juan. At 12:00 noon you'll take a cab to Café 18, it's on the Avenida Juan Ponce de León—make a note of it. I'll meet you there after Tamara is taken care of. We'll walk to the Puerto Rico Museum of Contemporary Art, the last place we're likely to run across other cruise passengers. We'll wander around a little in the museum, and take a cab back to the ship... Are you writing this down?"

"I am. How will I look like her—clothes, hairdo, all that?"

"There's a photo of Tamara in the package I sent you. Have a hair stylist copy her hairdo exactly. Like I said, you'll have the same dress."

"Shoes, jewelry?"

"Wear white sandals and simple earrings, little gold circles. Don't worry about it. Nobody notices that stuff."

"I still have to know how Tamara's going to be taken care of."

"Your, uh, concern about your sister is touching."

"I don't give a damn about my sister. I need to be sure you're not getting me involved in some cockamamie fiasco that'll get me sent to prison."

"You only need to know her body will be quote discovered four-months later in a shallow grave in the nature preserve, along with your wallet, your passport, and your phone. Final identification of the body will be by DNA. Suffice it to say there will be no dental exam."

"You're saying in so many words someone else is involved."

"Someone very reliable."

"How do you know this person's as reliable as he's led you to believe?"

"He's being very well paid. And I have him saying his name and discussing the gorier parts of the plan on a voice recorder which I'll play for him when the deed is done."

The next day Vera demanded a two-week vacation from her boss at the trucking company where she worked as a secretary. She said she needed time to "decompress." The jerk refused. She had been sure he would—as smart and efficient as she was, she'd become indispensable—but he relented when she threatened to quit. She told her landlady and everyone at work about her trip, saying it was the vacation of a lifetime, that she was going to look up some college friends.

She was able to book a room at the Double Tree Hilton, as Padgett had suggested, and she found a 5:40 a.m. Delta flight from Buffalo to San Juan on the eleventh. As he had ordered, she used her own credit card for the hotel and flight which maxed it out. She wouldn't touch Padgett's cash until she was in Puerto Rico. She didn't want the authorities finding any suspicious financial transactions.

She took Tamara's picture to an uptown hair stylist and said this was a style she'd had a few months before and wanted it again. The resulting match wasn't perfect but it was close enough, especially if Tamara wore a hat.

Vera took special care preparing her apartment, knowing it would be searched when she was reported missing. She threw away all traces of her contact with Padgett, including the pad she had written on lest they find the imprint of her writing. She left the coffee maker on—a cute touch, she thought. She also left an assortment of perishables in the refrigerator and a list of things she planned to do the coming year, which should rule out any suspicion of suicide.

At 3:30 AM on November 11th, Vera Snead took a last look around her apartment and locked the door, not only on the apartment itself but on her entire life up to now. In the cab to Buffalo Niagara International Airport she reflected there was one advantage to squalid poverty: there was nothing she regretted leaving behind.

She arrived in San Juan early that afternoon and took a cab to the hotel. While checking in, she complained bitterly to the manager about having to wait while the incompetent clerk fiddled with her computer. She interrupted his slavish apology to complain about the heat—she had dressed for the Buffalo winter, not for tropical San Juan's eighty-five degrees. After being shown to her room she shot the bellman, waiting for his tip, a cold look and asked what he was waiting for. He muttered something and left. Five minutes later she took the elevator down to the front desk and complained the hot water in the shower didn't work. A second bellman accompanied her to her room and showed her how to use the shower controls. He too departed tipless.

Vera settled in at the little table near the window with a split of California white wine from the honor bar she wouldn't have to pay for. She looked out at the city, chuckling at how easily it had gone. She'd be remembered all right, she'd see to that, but it wouldn't be for being nice.

2.

"Andrew," Karen said, "the Champagne is supposed to shoot out like it does in the movies."

"What, and waste all that perfectly good wine?" MacCrimmon drew the cork slowly with a soft hiss and filled two flutes. He joined her at the balcony railing, handed her one, and tapped it with his own. The two stood shoulder to shoulder, watching the roiling water rushing by the sides of the giant ship. "It's so nice to relax," she said, "after all the confusion of the flight and the embarkation."

"The flight and embarkation were nothing compared to the past three years."

She nudged him in the ribs with her elbow. "I wish we could forget it all, like a bad dream."

"Forgetting—or ignoring—those missteps and idiocies is one reason we keep repeating them. Like Emerson said, 'Bad times have a scientific value, occasions a good learner would not miss.' If our history is any measure, we're very *bad* learners."

"Speaking of our history," Karen said, "I know you don't like to talk about what that horrible count did to me, but—?"

"The count paid for his sins ten-times over, so it doesn't bother me anymore, at least not in the way you think. I blame you less for being raped when you were drunk than I blame myself for being so judgmental and unforgiving... You asked if I was still upset about you and the count—how about me and Consuela? That must bother you."

"Yes, of course it bothers me," she slapped his arm as emphasis, "since you kindly remind me you enjoyed it. I can't complain—I made you do it. You did get her pregnant, like she demanded. If you *hadn't*, she would have taken Maddy to Mexico and we would have lost her for good."

"It did work out. She's due to deliver next month, according to Cindy, her daughter. The child's a boy, much to her disappointment. She had her heart set on another little Maddy. Norman, the man she married, will be a good father."

"Another little half-Andrew running around. How many are there now?—stick to the ones you *know* about. And Alex doesn't count because he's legitimate."

"This will be the third. Dre and Maddy were both by vile trickery, Consuela's by extortion."

Karen smiled at the "vile trickery" remark. "I'd let you sleep with Consuela every day for a year if that's what we had to do to get Maddy. I couldn't love her more if she were my own. But what'll we tell her when she asks why she doesn't have Asian eyes like Alex?"

"We'll wait until she's grown before we tell her about Lena— assuming she asks. We sure as hell won't volunteer it."

Karen said, looking out to sea, "It's hard to believe Lena's been dead a year."

MacCrimmon cast a suspicious look at her for so abruptly bringing up a woman she had despised. But she seemed rosy and jovial, thanks to the Champagne. "Are you still Jealous of her, Karen?"

"She was so beautiful."

Two years earlier Lena Montoya, Maddy's mother, the cause of several of their blowups and separations, had engineered a separation between MacCrimmon and Karen and had seduced him, resulting in pregnancy, the last thing either of them wanted at the time though both couldn't have been happier with the result. A year ago members of her late husband's drug cartel had killed her when she wouldn't tell them where his fortune was hidden. In the aftermath Maddy's wet nurse, Consuela, had absconded with her and only gave her up when MacCrimmon, at Karen's insistence, gave her a child of her own.

He downed his Champagne in one gulp. "Enough of this morbid stuff. Let's go to dinner."

The first night at sea, dining was casual. Karen wore a short sleeveless white linen sun dress that stopped above the knees, showing off her beautiful legs; MacCrimmon wore pale tan slacks, an open-collar white silk shirt and blue blazer. They were early enough to get a window table for two in the cavernous dining room. Later diners had to make do with tables that seated up to eight.

Karen said over the rim of her wine glass, "What do you suppose Alex and Maddy are doing now?"

"Sleeping. It's ten o'clock in San Francisco."

"Do you think they understand, you know, us going away?"

"Alex does. Six-year olds know about time. Maddy has no idea what's going on. She was howling because Alex was."

An old woman, overdressed in a ball gown and gaudy jewelry, swept by them, which reminded Karen of a party invitation they had declined. "Maybe we should have gone to Ilanora's cocktail party." Ilanora Phelan-Nash, one of San Francisco's leading socialites, a woman they had never met, had confronted them during intermission at the opera, introduced herself and her husband, and had extended an out-of-the-blue invitation to an upcoming cocktail party. MacCrimmon had said they were busy preparing for a cruise, but they'd think it over.

"When I called her back," Karen said, "she said it would be an honor to have the man who caught those horrible young men killing the homeless."

"I doubt that. They wanted us for the notoriety factor. Me, the unapprehended serial murderer—according to the media—and you, well—"

"You think they know about me?"

"Judging by Mr. Nash's salacious leer when he looked at you, it's a possibility. He may know someone who was one of your clients in the old days, someone who recognized you somewhere and told him about you. It's likely they invited us to spice up what would otherwise have been another dreary party with the same old people."

"I'm not so sure, Andrew. She sounded genuinely disappointed we weren't coming."

"That's what Nathan said too, so it's possible." Nathan Stohr, one of San Francisco's pre-eminent surgeons, Dr. MacCrimmon's

14

friend and colleague, had said Mrs. Phelan-Nash, beyond being disappointed, had been offended. She wasn't used to having her invitations refused. People went to absurd lengths to be invited to her parties. "Nathan said we would have added a 'decorative touch'—meaning you, of course—which the gathering sorely needed."

"Oh, come off it, Andrew! You'd be the handsomest man there, and you know it."

"That's not saying much if Mr. Phelan-Nash and those other old fossils were my competition."

Karen leaned toward him and whispered, "You really, honestly, think they know about my past?"

"They might," he whispered back. "Three-decades later, you're still recognizing old clients, though I'd wager not many of them would admit patronizing the sleazy Honolulu Sun massage parlor. And if you're recognizing *them*, it's a sure bet they're recognizing *you*. You're as beautiful as you ever were."

"They do seem to pop up all the time. That silver-haired old man in the black suit I pointed out at the opera was one of the men who offered to marry me."

"It's just as well we didn't go to their damn party. I probably would have insulted one of the politicians. It's best we avoid the San Francisco social scene and confine ourselves to our precious little island of sanity at 818 Mason."

Karen tapped Andrew's hand. "Don't look now but there's a giant at the Maître D's desk. He's as big as Alan." MacCrimmon snuck a look over his shoulder. "Maybe an inch or so taller than Alan. Not as wide though." He had once described his nephew Alan as having the same vertical and horizontal dimensions as a standard American doorway. "Rough looking brute."

"The woman who's with him hates him."

He looked at her in squinty-eyed skepticism. "You can tell all this from a half-second's glance, can you?"

"When it's that obvious, yes."

"From the looks of him he'd be easy to dislike. The woman's a sour looking number too."

Half an hour later, Karen, seeing how anxious her husband was to get her back to their suite, taunted him with sweet smiles as she dawdled over her dessert, taking slow miniscule bites.

After dinner she prolonged his agony by insisting they take a slow stroll around the ship. At the fantail they leaned against the railing and looked down at the phosphorescent wake. She pressed her breast against his arm and whispered in his ear, "You like me?" He nuzzled her silky lavender-scented hair and said he liked her very much, so much so that unless they immediately returned to their suite he couldn't be held responsible for his actions. Once the door was safely locked behind them Karen slowly shimmied out of her dress and stood in front of him with her hands on her hips. "Let the games begin."

Afterward, they lay on their backs looking at the ceiling catching, their breath.

"That was satisfactory," he said.

She chuckled in her breathy way at this masterpiece of understatement. She rolled over and straddled him. "What did it remind you of?" She pinned his hands behind his head and waited for his answer.

He prefaced his response with a quick lick to a dangling nipple. "It reminded me of the night we were married, when I was finally convinced we'd always be together, that we belonged to each other. At long last I could let myself believe being with you wasn't some delicious dream that would explode in my face."

"I remember it was that night we hooked pinkies and officially left our pasts behind, your philandering, my, uh, unfortunate—"

"Yes... But this," he said, "what a pleasant way to start the second half of our lives, putting a whole bucket of agonizing missteps and disasters behind us." He gently rolled her over. "Come on. Let's get some air."

He checked the balcony; the coast was clear. They padded out, naked, and leaned against the railing, shoulder-to-shoulder, sipping the warm leftover Champagne they had opened that afternoon.

"I love Alex and Maddy to death," she said, "but it's so nice to have you all to myself like this." They had observed more than once that lovemaking at home wasn't as uninhibited as they might wish.

"I half-expected Alex to come barging in with Maddy toddling along behind him," MacCrimmon said. "He's been interested in our, uh, activities recently." Alex had already caught them a couple of times and as a precocious six-year old he already knew what they were up to. His friend Walter, a twisted obnoxious eleven-year-old, had explained to him in exquisite detail what it was his parents were doing.

The next day, sunning themselves on adjacent deckchairs in the pool area, two pudgy teen-age girls in tank tops and too-tight cut-off jeans approached. The shorter of the two asked, "Are you movie stars?"

MacCrimmon glanced at Karen, smiling behind her hand, and said, "Nah. We're ordinary ol' folks."

"You're the guy that played in that old Hatchcock movie, aren't you?" This from the taller of the two. She corrected herself. "No., no! You're the guy with the mustache in that Hawaii show." The shorter girl, "Deena," informed Karen she was Lucy Liu. This comparison had been made several times over the years. Karen did slightly resemble Ms. Liu, especially the cat-like eyes, but beyond that Karen was much prettier.

"Sorry to disappoint you, ladies."

17

"You're, like, saying that so you can have privacy," Deena said with a saucy toss of her head.

"We do value our privacy, yes."

The girls ignored this broad hint and asked for their autographs. Dr. and Mrs. MacCrimmon looked at each other and said okay. Deena asked if they had a pencil and paper.

"I believe it's customary," MacCrimmon said, "for the auto-graphee to provide the writing materials, not the autographer."

"We'll be right back."

Three minutes later they trotted back. Deena handed over a padded notebook and a ball point pen which exuded fuchsia-colored ink. MacCrimmon and Karen dutifully signed their names, to which MacCrimmon added, "Yours in anonymity."

The two girls puzzled over the signatures and looked at each other. "You're not famous," Deena said.

"Nope. We're plain ol' folks, like I said."

He may have told the girls they were "plain ol' folks," but the ill-concealed gawking by many of the twelve- to eighty-year old males lounging around the pool suggested they were anything *but* plain, especially the distaff side of the pair. Karen, stunning in a black bikini, may have been middle-aged, but thanks to her fanatical diet and exercise regimes, she was as slim and beautiful as she had been as a twenty-five-year-old.

The MacCrimmons hadn't left the ship other than for a couple of hours cycling on Turks and Caicos, always an adventure with Ms. Ting, living proof there was no truth to the old saying you never forgot how to ride a bicycle. They socialized very little with other passengers, and always ate alone at their window table in the dining room. They spent long hours lying naked together, making love, not necessarily vigorously, sometimes joined in the closest possible way two human beings can be physically joined, talking, planning, basking in a feeling of liberation, as if they had been transported to a fresh life, one they could take with them back to San Francisco, a life free of the resentments, the separations, the desperate griefs and rages of the past few years.

The biggest step in this, the second half of their lives, had come when Dr. MacCrimmon swore, his right hand raised to heaven, his left on the copy of Beowulf he always travelled with, he would never again involve himself in other people's affairs, especially those that might put his or his family's lives at risk. In his career as an incurable meddler he had been stabbed, slashed, kidnapped, beaten, shot—twice, and shot *at* too many times to count. Karen had said, enough was enough.

Karen, equally culpable in their many disruptions, promised to see Dr. Kreutzer, their family counselor, at least twice a year. She admitted things sometimes "bubbled up inside her," and she could get "a little goofy." MacCrimmon had raised an eyebrow at this gross minimization. He thought back five-years to one of her more spectacular departures from sanity when she divorced him and married an abusive fundamentalist preacher in Portland. Other examples made up with frequency what they lacked in flamboyance.

The fourth day out, Tuesday, November the 14th, the ship docked in San Juan, Puerto Rico. The MacCrimmons, for only the second time, went ashore to stroll around the old city and to visit the Puerto Rico Museum of Contemporary Art.

3.

11:37 A.M., November 14th, the giant, Thomas Padgett, and his sour, skinny wife, Tamara, joined the queue disembarking in San Juan. Their preparations for the visit to Puerto Rico's capital had been contentious. Tamara had refused to wear the simple white dress Thomas had chosen and had insisted on wearing a gaudy flowery thing Thomas said made her look like a clown. She said if he made any further fuss about it she would stay on the ship. He backed down, even sweet-talked her, a ridiculous performance that had her openly laughing. Sweet-talking, decent conversation of any sort came about as easily to Thomas as speaking Welsh or ballet dancing. To further irritate him she pretended to object to the floppy straw hat she fully intended to wear.

Padgett had told her he had hired a limo to drive them to scenic places on the island's coast where she could take her nature photographs. This was a romantic and uncharacteristic gesture which pleased her but at the same time made her suspicious.

Once free of the shuffling mob on the gangway, the pair walked the few hundred yards to Calle San Augustin where Padgett pointed at a shiny black Lincoln Town Car parked in a taxi space. "This is the limo I hired." He introduced Tamara to Enrico Nelson, the driver, a squatty, swarthy Hispanic.

Threading the cumbersome car through the traffic to state 187 Enrico said in lightly accented English he would be driving them east along the north coast to a nature preserve.

Ten miles east of the city, Tamara broke the tense silence and said in her shrill, cracking voice, "Where are we going, Thomas? What are you up to?"

Thomas feigned injured innocence. "But Tamara, I thought you'd enjoy taking some of your pictures in the nature preserve."

"No, you're up to something—something awful." She leaned forward and tapped Enrico on the shoulder. "Turn around, whatever your name is, and take me back to the ship."

Enrico checked the rearview mirror. Thomas shook his head and mouthed "no." He waited. When she leaned back he bellowed, *"Tamara!"*

She whipped her head around. He hit her a vicious uppercut that stunned her. She flopped back against the seat, her head lolled to one side. He opened a plastic shopping bag he'd snuck out of his pocket as she'd been looking out the window and drew it over her head. He tightened it around her scrawny neck, at the same time compressing her carotid arteries with his thumbs. She revived enough to claw at his hands—he had drawn on gloves in anticipation—and kicked feebly but within five or six seconds she had lost consciousness. He laid her flat on the seat, out of view of passing motorists, and tied the bag tightly around her neck with a length of cord he had brought for this purpose. He removed her white sandals and, after positioning her in the well between the seats, he covered her with a robe Enrico had brought.

"Turn around. Let's go back. But take your time. I can't get to that cafe too early."

Enrico pulled into a side road and turned around. Ten minutes into the return trip, certain she was dead, Thomas removed the bag from over her head, removed her small gold earrings, and with great difficulty wrestled the gaudy dress off her, leaving her scrawny body in a bra—un-needed—and panties. He stuffed the dress in his backpack and replaced the robe over her body.

"You do have my fifty G's, don't you, Hoss?" Enrico said over his shoulder.

"I do… I'll give it to you when you let me off at that cafe. I'll have a courier deliver the last fifty to a UPS mailbox in four months, when her body is discovered."

"How much are you getting out of this?"

Padgett caught Enrico's eyes in the rear-view mirror. "That's none of your damn business! And in case you get greedy listen to this." He pulled his phone from his shirt pocket and played the conversation the two men had had when he had finalized the details. "A hundred G's for two hours work and a phone call four-months down the road I consider adequate compensation."

Enrico, unfazed by the recording, said, "You left out cutting her head off and burying the body. But I'm not complaining, Hoss, and I'm not angling for more money. Just curious, is all."

"Speaking of her head, how will you get rid of it?"

"Put it in a bucket, fill it with concrete, dump it in the ocean."

"Sorry for snapping, Enrico. It's not the money, there's not so much of that. Mostly it's to get away from the nasty bitch. She's made my life miserable."

"I hear ya'. I wish I could get rid of my old lady so easily."

At 12:42 Enrico stopped a block from Café 18. Padgett fished a brick-sized packet tightly wrapped in Kraft paper from his backpack and handed it him. He also gave him Vera's purse which contained her phone, her passport, and her wallet—with her ID and credit cards, all to be buried with the body. "Ball's in your court now, Enrico. Call my cell when the authorities have the body. If all goes well I'll tack on another ten K."

"It'll go well, Hoss… Take care."

Padgett found Vera Snead at a window table in the crowded café, eating a tuna salad sandwich. He hadn't seen her since the meeting in October, and now, with Tamara's haircut, the resemblance was astonishing, down to her sparkling beady eyes and her bitter mouth, clenched as if she'd been chewing lemons.

He pulled up a chair. She showed no surprise at seeing him and offered no greeting. "How did it go?"

"So far so good. We won't talk about it until we get back to the ship." He handed her his backpack. "Her bag, hat, shoes and earrings are in here. She refused to wear the white dress, the one you're wearing, so put on that flowery thing I got off of her. Go to the john and change."

Vera scowled at him. "How appealing—wearing a dress salvaged from a corpse."

"Cut the commentary and go change, Vera—or *Tamara*, I should say." While she was gone Padgett finished off her sandwich.

She returned, wearing Tamara's dress, shoes, and hat. "This is the ugliest dress I've ever seen, let alone worn. I feel like a clown."

Padgett looked around at the other diners to see if they had noticed her. None had. "I'm not happy being seen with anyone wearing that monstrosity either, but we have no choice."

She pointed at the empty plate. "That sandwich was mine."

"I was hungry—*Tamara*."

She handed him his backpack and shook her head in disbelief a man could be so degraded he could kill a person with his bare hands and with the same unwashed hands eat a sandwich.

"What?" he said.

"More bad news, beyond the dress. Tamara's ears were pierced. Mine aren't."

He shrugged. "So? Who'll notice you're not wearing earrings?"

"Nobody, I hope... Tell me, why are we going to this museum? Why don't we go straight back to the ship? I'm ashamed to be seen in this dress."

"Nope," he said, wagging his finger. "We'll go to the museum like I planned. It'll give you time to get used to the role, get both of us used to calling you by her name."

She conceded with a shrug and insisted he go wash his hands.

"Why? I was wearing gloves, uh, *Tamara*."

"Go wash your hands, Thomas."

Over the next thirty-minutes Padgett consumed two roast beef sandwichs and a beer—with washed hands. He paid the check and the pair left the café for the two-block stroll to the Puerto Rico Museum of Contemporary Art.

Thomas , walking behind Vera, watched her take a few steps. "Don't raise your knees so high. You're walking like one of those birds in a swamp, nothing like Tamara. You look like you've got some kind of nerve disease."

"These shoes don't fit."

"And you're wearing that hat like a Mexican Bandit." He adjusted it, giving it a jaunty tilt to one side. He again let her go a couple paces ahead to check her out. "Hopeless. I pray no one from the ship sees you."

"Oh, for God's sake! Take me to that ship if it's so obvious I'm not Tamara... Tell me again why we're going to that museum."

"The idea was to practice walking like Tamara, learning her mannerisms, getting used to using her name, like I said before."

"Why bother if I'm going to be shut up in the cabin?"

"Because, dear *Tamara*, we have to work our way through the crowd getting back on the ship, which means we'll be seen by a lot of people, and in three days we have to disembark. Both are critical times when someone might notice the difference. And there's the cabin steward. You'll be seeing him every day."

She asked, "What are the chances of anyone noticing the differences?"

"Slim but possible... Details, *Tamara*. It's the little fuck-ups that could derail the whole thing."

She rolled her eyes and shook her head at what she saw as his excessive caution and attempted a gliding walk which was even clumsier. "It's hopeless, Thomas," she whined. "My feet are killing me."

"You're twins. How can your feet be different?"

"I worked for a living," she snapped. "That takes a toll. That parasite Tamara never worked a day in her life!"

"Oh, for Christ's sake, wear your own goddamned shoes then."

Vera leaned against a storefront to change into her own white sandals she'd stuffed in Tamara's bag. Thomas waited and again watched her as she walked ahead of him. She stopped at a trash bin to deposit Tamara's shoes. He called to her, "The sandals are different but you're walking much better."

On the steps between the large columns of the Georgian building that housed the Museum of Contemporary Art Thomas looked around. He stopped and grabbed her arm. "Shit!... Don't turn around! Some people from the ship are coming." He said out of the corner of his mouth the museum turned out to be not such a good idea after all. Vera agreed. It would unnecessarily increase the time these people could notice differences.

On the sidewalk, heading back toward the street, Thomas smiled weakly and nodded at a middle-aged man and an Asian woman walking toward them. The man returned a cool nod of indifference, but the woman looked hard, first at Vera, then at Thomas.

Vera looked back over her shoulder at them. "You know those people?"

"Of course I don't *know* them. I've seen the woman on the ship a couple of times—it'd be hard to miss her—but I've never seen the man, at least never noticed him. They recognized me—us, I should say."

"I didn't like the way she looked at me, like she was appraising me."

"Nothing we can do about it now."

The return to the ship was uneventful. The officers at the top of the gangway who checked the returning passengers' electronic room keys passed her off as Tamara without a moment's hesitation. Padgett had her take his arm as they negotiated the elevators and corridors of the giant ship.

He had paid the extra money for a veranda stateroom, thinking Vera would be less likely to go stir crazy in a room with a view than in an interior room where she'd be looking at walls the remaining days of the cruise.

"It's nice," she said, taking in the separate beds. "Give me your backpack. I have to get out of this ugly shroud." He tossed it to her. She pulled her own dress out and scurried to the bathroom to change.

Padgett poured himself two-fingers of Bourbon, downed it, and poured another.

A minute later, Vera, wearing her white dress, joined him. "Pour me one of those... Sit down and tell me how it went." They took chairs on opposite sides of the table near the glass door leading to the balcony.

"How much do you want to know?"

"I don't need the gory details, only the parts that convince me it's going to work, that I'm not going to jail for the rest of my life."

Padgett assured her Tamara had been dispatched cleanly and painlessly. Enrico, he said, would bury her body in the El Yunque

National Forest, a place he knew well from driving people there. Four months down the road he would make an anonymous call saying he'd found a body and would describe in detail where it was. "Four months is long enough that there won't be fingerprints."

"What about dental records?"

"There won't be dental comparisons."

"You mean this Enrico guy is knocking her teeth out?"

"No. Let's say it's a, uh, much more foolproof solution... Best let it go at that."

"You mean he's cutting her head off?"

Thomas looked down at the Bourbon he was swirling in his glass and nodded. When he looked up Vera was wiping her eyes. "I despised the bitch," she said, "but for some reason not having any happy memories of her makes it worse, as if my whole life has been nothing but hate and bitterness... And it's so shocking, so—so final... It seemed kind of dream-like before, like a movie or something, and I was only a spectator. Now I'm a murderer and it's more like a nightmare, imagining her, a beheaded corpse, lying in her underwear in a hole. To make it worse, here I am unloading to *you*!"

"I sympathize," he said—a statement so patently false she had to smile—"but you've got three days to pull yourself together. Fortunately, the worst is over. After we disembark I'll rent a car. We'll drive to Tampa for our flight back to San Antonio—so we avoid people from the cruise at the Fort Lauderdale or Miami airports."

Vera blew her nose and shook her head, casting off her unseemly attack of sentimentality. "I guess you know there's no such thing as a perfect murder."

"Maybe not but there are plenty of good-enough murders."

"Yeah, fine, but tell me again where it could go wrong, where it might not be quite good *enough*."

"I worked out the areas of vulnerability in the very beginning, as you know, and there *are* weak points. The big one is someone noticing you're not Tamara and taking action. But I figure if someone—like that Asian broad—did notice you and Tamara looked different, why would they care? What's it to them?... Your performance is another weak area. You might slip up, say something that gives you away. Or there may be some problem with that kid of yours. But the biggest—permanent—vulnerability is the fingerprint angle. She had her prints taken like everybody else. It's required for a driver's license in Texas, same in California, Colorado and Georgia. If anyone compares your prints to hers— unlikely but possible—the jig is up, so avoid like the plague having your prints taken."

"Don't worry about me. How about her friends—and your servants?"

"She had no friends by the time we left and I let all the servants go. Anyway, you'll be going to Nevada a week or so after we get back—they don't require fingerprints for a DL. There's an apartment complex in Henderson that's perfect. You'll hire a lawyer and file for divorce claiming irreconcilable differences. I'll brief you on all the legal and financial stuff over the next few days. You'll have to practice her signature and memorize all the milestones in Tamara's and my marriage, anniversary, dates we moved from place to place, my birthday, all that."

"No problem with that stuff... Now, that Asian woman we saw at the museum. What if she makes a fuss?"

"Make a fuss to who?... What would she say? They'd think she was nuts."

"You'd better be right... How about Tamara's body?... What if someone finds it or, worse, sees this Enrico person burying it?"

"Either way we're in trouble. I have to trust Enrico on this." He motioned for her to wait while he fetched the Bourbon bottle.

When he returned Vera covered her glass. "How trustworthy is this Enrico?"

"If he screws up he's out fifty grand. And he's been in stir and doesn't want to go back."

"And we get life in prison."

"In Texas it could be a lot worse than that."

"And after the divorce is final?"

"Make sure the final settlement gives me half the money as community property. That way there's no tax obligation. Should be about four and a half mill... I'm leaving the country afterward. I'd advise you to do the same."

Vera, squinting at the Bourbon bottle as if she'd had second thoughts about another drink, pulled it to her, and poured herself half a glass. "Leaving the country," she said, "is exactly what I intend to do." She confirmed this resolution with a deep swig that left her eyes watering and her throat burning.

4.

KAREN STOPPED and looked back at the retreating giant and the skinny sour-looking woman striding along next to him, trying to keep up.

"Marital bliss," MacCrimmon said, "must not strike all couples with equal intensity."

Karen said as if she hadn't heard him, "That's not the same woman that awful man left the ship with."

MacCrimmon smiled at this observation but, impressed by her certainty, he looked after the pair more closely. "Really? She looked the same to me."

"Good grief, Andrew!" she cried, and slapped his forearm. "We followed them from the ship until they got into that car. You, the big detective, didn't notice this woman's shoes are different?—that she's walking differently, and she's wearing no earrings?"

"The lady, if you'll pardon an uncharitable esthetic judgment, doesn't invite a lot of gawking—unlike present company."

Karen watched the odd couple turn west on the sidewalk. "The dress and hat *are* the same—that must be the only dress like that in the whole world."

"One would hope."

"She has to be a twin... What do you suppose happened to the other woman?"

"You're sure she's a different person?"

"Absolutely."

"Twin sisters sharing a cruise maybe."

Ms. Ting let the matter drop but she was unusually quiet during the hour-long tour of the museum and only responded in distracted monosyllables to her husband's comments, including those which were humorous, at least to his way of thinking.

On the steps, leaving the building, MacCrimmon said, "Still thinking of the mystery woman?"

"Something awful happened to her—the other woman I mean. I'm sure of it."

Karen's distraction, her somber look and heavy breathing, and above all, her certainty, convinced him to take her seriously. "Maybe we can poke around a little, see what we can find."

"Yes, we should. And maybe we should notify the authorities. Even if what they're doing is harmless it has to be illegal."

"No, Karen!" he said crisply. "Illegal or not, it's none of our damn business! No more talk of the authorities. I can't afford any more mix-ups with them."

The next morning after breakfast, Karen, late as she often was, bustled off to a cooking class, leaving MacCrimmon lingering in the dining area. Karen's detailed points proving the woman they had seen in the company of the giant was different than the wife, had fermented in his mind. The possible consequences were serious enough he had decided to look into it.

The giant showed up twenty minutes later wearing baggy shorts, sandals, and a loud Hawaiian shirt. The woman was not with him. A half-hour later he left, having wolfed down enough eggs, sausage and toast for three normal people. MacCrimmon followed him to the top deck where he settled onto a deck chair at the far end of the pool, sunning himself and smoking cigarettes. MacCrimmon button-holed a steward, a short smiling Malay, and offered him fifty-dollars if he could get the name and cabin number of the giant near the fantail. He said he would wait at the bar.

Half-way through his second tomato juice the steward returned. He whispered out of the corner of his mouth, "Thomas Padgett, San Antonio, Texas. Cabin 5826." MacCrimmon slipped a folded up fifty into his hand. "How did you get it?"

The steward said with a toothy grin, "I asked him. I got his address and room number from the passenger registry."

He hurried back to their suite to look up "Thomas Padgett" on the web using his Intelius people search. The 48-year old Padgett had been a contractor but had sold his business six-months earlier. No children. He had no criminal record, which was a surprise—he looked like a mafia thug, a large one. He was married to Tamara

Padgett née Vissley, 42; parents deceased. Her twin sister, Vera Snead, also 42, lived at an address in Buffalo; divorced, ex-husband, Jonathan Snead; one son, Brian, 19. Karen was right. They were identical twins.

He googled Padgett's address on La Tapiceria, north of San Antonio. If the mission style mansion was any indication, the guy had money. What the hell was he up to?

MacCrimmon had cleared the history and closed the laptop when Karen returned. "You were right, Love," he called to her as she slithered out of her jeans. "The wife and sister are twins."

Karen stepped into shorts and joined him at the table. She asked him with her clenched-mouth frown of disapproval, "And how did you find this out?" Before he could answer she reminded him of his sacred promise. He explained he had bribed a steward for the man's name and had looked him up on the internet. Her disapproval, melting away in the heat of her curiosity, she asked, "What did you find out?"

"Thomas Padgett, San Antonio, Texas. Wife, Tamara. Sister-in-law, Vera. Identical twins."

"Any idea what he's up to?"

"I'm only guessing here, but he may be using the sister-in-law to get rid of the wife. We have to assume she—the wife, I mean—was the woman he left the ship with. Two hours later he shows up with a woman who has to be the sister-in-law. I can't think of any way the wife would approve of that."

"Definitely not. And another thing, Andrew, the first time we saw the man and the wife in the dining room, it was obvious she hated him. The brief look I got when this other woman passed us, her expression was neutral, the look a woman might have for a brother-in-law or a business partner."

"Probably both, if our speculation is correct—and make no mistake, it's nothing more than idle speculation. It may be something completely innocent."

"Innocent?... Such as?"

He shrugged and shook his head. "Can't think of a thing, not a damn thing."

An hour later, on their way to lunch, rounding the corner to the elevators, Padgett was waiting for them. He grabbed MacCrimmon's right arm and said in a raspy voice, much too high for a man his size, "Why did you pay that steward to get my name?" His deep-set black eyes bored first into Karen then into MacCrimmon. Karen blushed and looked down. MacCrimmon glared up at him. "Let go of my arm."

The man was a head taller than MacCrimmon but he was soft and flabby. MacCrimmon clenched his teeth and pulled back his left fist. Padgett let go and stepped back. "Paying stewards works both ways, *Doctor* MacCrimmon. Again, why did you want my name?"

"Curiosity."

"It killed the cat."

"Yeah, and for every dead cat a hundred criminals were caught because someone was curious. Now, excuse us."

"It'd be a good idea for you to mind your own busin—," he called to them, but the elevator doors had closed, cutting him off.

Karen hugged herself as if she were cold. "That look he gave us."

"There was more than hatred in his look. I saw guilt and nervousness. The guy's up to something bad."

"Stay away from him, Andrew. He's evil."

"He is that."

"Whatever it is, it's serious, probably dangerous, so you stay out of it! You promised me you weren't going to get involved in things like this anymore. As awful as that monster is, he's right—it's none of our damn business!"

He patted her hand and smiled. "Don't worry, Love. Like I told him, I'm curious. You know, old habits, all that. From this moment on we'll forget about it."

And forget about it he did, until 3:15 that afternoon when Karen fell asleep. He hurried into shorts, sandals, and a polo shirt, snuck out, and closed the door silently. He took the elevator up to the top deck to check the pool area. The giant was drinking a beer at the bar. He returned to the elevators, descended to level five, and strode down the starboard corridor to Room 5826. He tapped lightly on the door. "Purser, Ma'am," he cried. "You've got a telegram."

There was no response though he could hear her rustling about. He knocked again. Half a minute passed. She'd probably been given explicit instructions not to open to anyone. "Telegram, Ma'am," he shouted. "It's important. It's about your son, Brian. There's been an accident."

She opened. Her head swayed back and forth. The woman was knee-walking drunk.

She squinted at him with beady close-spaced eyes. "My son?" she slurred. "What happened to him?"

"He's okay, Vera."

She scanned him head to toe. "Wait a minute. You're that, that guy we shaw, sh-saw at the museum."

"What did you do with Tamara, Vera?"

She tried to slam the door, but he blocked it with his foot. "What did you do with her body?"

"Get out!" she screamed. He didn't move. She opened the door all the way, preparing to slam it hard. Wearing only sandals and preferring not to suffer a broken toe, he let it close, but he stayed next to the door, listening. There was a clumping sound and muffled curses. She must have fallen down.

She had responded as a mother. She was the sister-in-law, without doubt. They had likely done away with the wife, as he and Karen had thought.

He returned to his own suite as Karen was rousing. She sat up, yawning, rubbing her eyes with her fists. The coverlet fell away exposing her full breasts—she was sleeping naked, as she had been the entire trip. She watched him stripping off his shirt and kicking off his sandals. "Where have you been?"

Her sweet smile and her fetchingly tousled hair washed all thought of Thomas, Vera, and Tamara from his mind. Fighting his way out of his shorts and boxers—at times like this they always seemed glued to his body—he said, "I took a stroll up to the pool."

"You missed me."

"I guess it's obvious."

5.

BY SEVEN that evening Vera was clear-headed enough to come to an agonizing decision: she would tell Thomas what she had done so he could do what he could to salvage the situation, assuming it wasn't already too late. Her punishment would be severe—she didn't doubt that for a minute—but whatever he meted out was better than the near certainty of being implicated in the murder of her sister.

She tried eating a few bites of the dinner room service had delivered, but she could force nothing down. Instead she lay on her bed with a moist washcloth over her eyes, waiting for Thomas to return.

Vera jerked awake at the thudding of the stateroom door shutting. The bedside clock showed 8:47.

"Why are you lying like that?" Thomas said.

"I have a headache."

"The steward asked if your migraines were any better. I said, no, so I wasn't lying."

Thomas had been drinking. If there was one single good thing to say about the man it was that he got mellow and jolly when drunk. She doubted it would last long after he heard what she had to tell him. "I have a confession," she said. She crawled out of bed and dragged over to the table by the outside glass door. "You better sit down for this one."

Thomas grabbed a glass and the half-full bottle of Bourbon from the cabinet under the TV and slouched down in the chair opposite her. His mouth sagged in a sloppy leer. "What, you had an erotic dream about me?"

Normally she would sneer at such a ridiculous suggestion but she couldn't risk riling him. She said in a neutral tone, "That guy MacMillan, whatever his name is, the one you told me about?—the guy who got your name and cabin number?"

He sat up straight, no longer mellow or jolly. "Yeah? What about him?"

"He tricked me."

Thomas leaned forward and laid his interlaced fingers on the table, like a boss about to fire an incompetent employee. "I sense something bad—real bad—is coming."

Vera leaned back and looked down at her skinny fingers tapping the table. She told Thomas in a weak shaky voice how MacCrimmon had tricked her, and that he now knew who she really was and that he knew they had killed Tamara.

Thomas rose and stalked about the cabin, pounding his fists against his temples and snorting, "Damn, damn, damn..." over and over. He glanced at the Bourbon bottle. "You were drunk, weren't you?" He came toward her, his hands extended to strangle her. She shrieked and lurched back, away from him. He flexed his fingers and drew his hands back to his chest as if restraining independent living things yearning to wring her scrawny neck. He slumped back into his chair, growling curses.

For a long moment he sat pinging his Bourbon glass with his forefinger. "Okay," he said, "there are two possibilities. Either he *has* told someone else what he knows, or he hasn't."

"He's probably told his wife."

He ignored this. A moment later he slapped his massive hand on the table, startling her. He said he had come to a decision. "I know where his suite is. I'll follow him and find out what he's going to do. I may have to take care of him. If so, the wife will be distraught and anything she says will be considered the raving of a grief-stricken widow."

Vera, sensing by his normal conversational tone she was temporarily out of danger, was emboldened enough to ask, "Take care of him? How?"

"That will depend on the circumstances. I'll try buying him off. He's probably got money—his suite is one of those fancy ones up top—so it won't be cheap, a mill at least. Or maybe I'll threaten to hurt his wife."

"And if he's already reported us to the captain or the cops?"

"We're fucked, thanks to you!" He rose, leaned over the table, and shook a finger in her face. "If we go down, I'll have nothing to lose. I'll kill you myself!"

Thomas marched to the cabin door. He said over his shoulder he was going to talk to Fajar, their cabin steward.

Half an hour later he returned. Vera asked him what he had decided.

"I gave Fajar another hundred bucks to put me in contact with MacCrimmon's steward, a guy named Jalak. I met this Jalak and offered him two-hundred if he'd let me know when MacCrimmon leaves his suite tomorrow morning."

"That sounds kind of conspiratorial. What if he talks about it?"

"The deal was a hundred for letting me know, and a hundred for keeping his mouth shut. I told him I'm a private investigator working up a case against MacCrimmon for securities fraud."

"And what are the chances of him believing *that* bullshit?"

"About five-percent, but enough to ease his conscience, if he has one."

At 6:15 the next morning Thomas Padgett woke to a tapping on his stateroom door. He rubbed his eyes and shook his head to wake up. He stumbled over and opened cabin door. Jalak told him Dr. MacCrimmon had left his suite five-minutes earlier.

"This early? Where did he go?"

Jalak said in heavily accented sing-song English, "De fantail of deck nine, pool deck. He go there as sun came up. He write somet'ing." Padgett thanked the man, tipped him another fifty, and reminded him of the need for absolute discretion.

While he dressed he told Vera, hiding her head under the covers as she always did during this operation, he was going up to confront MacCrimmon.

Ten minutes later Thomas Padgett found Dr. MacCrimmon where Jalak had said he would be, sitting at a small table on the deserted fantail scribbling on a legal pad. He checked the area for security cameras but saw none. Uninvited he took the other chair. He said with a forced smile in his wheezy high-pitched voice, "What are you writing, Doctor?"

MacCrimmon closed the book, using the writing pad as a bookmark, and removed his glasses. "What do you want, Mr. Padgett?"

"Right to business, eh? Okay, if that's the way you want it. You visited my wife yesterday and—"

"Your sister-in-law, you mean. Your wife is probably dead. I could be mistaken. A simple fingerprint exam will set me straight. If I'm wrong you'll have my sincere apology."

"I'm admitting nothing, but my wife wouldn't allow—"

"She can't allow anything—she's dead until proved otherwise."

"I started to say, perhaps we can come to an agreement."

"I doubt we'd ever agree on much of anything, Mr. Padgett."

Padgett's forced smile faded. "Let's cut the bullshit, Doc! I'll give you a mill to butt out."

MacCrimmon rose. He gathered up his glasses and book and said, glaring at Padgett, "I wouldn't 'butt out' as you put it for *fifty*-million. You and your accomplice are going down." He had turned and had taken two steps past Padgett's chair when the larger man sprang up, grabbed him by the back of his shorts and his collar, ran him to the railing, and with a single fluid motion, threw him over the port side. Padgett watched him graze a railing on the way down, wave his arms, and splash into the ocean feet first.

"I saw what you did," someone said in a shrill creaky voice.

Padgett hadn't noticed another early riser who must have come on the scene while was he talking to MacCrimmon. The short skinny bald-headed old man on the other side of the fantail who had said this was now struggling to lift a life ring from its bracket. Before Padgett could get to him, he dropped it into the ocean. The old man, seeing Padgett's scowl of rage, tried to run but Padgett caught him. He carried him bodily to the railing and dropped him overboard. Falling, his head hit the steel railing, two decks below. He landed in the ocean on his back, unmoving, and sank within seconds. Padgett saw blood in the wake, fifty yards back.

MacCrimmon was now a hundred, a hundred- fifty yards behind the ship, being tossed around in the wake. He would have at least a seventy-five yard swim to the life ring, assuming he could find it in the chop. Padgett raised his hand in farewell. He looked around for other witnesses but there were none. He picked up MacCrimmon's glasses and the pad he had been writing on from the deck where he had dropped them and threw them overboard. He picked up the book where he found it near the railing. "Beowulf?... Jesus!" He threw that over too.

He sagged into the chair at the table, clenching and relaxing his fists. His breath came in deep gasps, his heart pounded at the enormity of what he had done. He had killed Tamara because she was a vile bitch and he hated her. He hadn't lied to Enrico when he said it wasn't the money so much as breaking free of someone who had been a cancer in his life. Killing MacCrimmon, at least sentencing him to probable death, was much different. He resented his meddling but he didn't hate him and he was sorry he'd had to do it. In other circumstances he might have liked him. Those three or four seconds he had hold of him he had smelled a strange spicy fragrance coming from him that tingled his bowels. To the old man he gave not a passing thought.

Over the next hour he waited at the little table, collecting himself. There were no security cameras in this area, but they covered much of the rest of the ship. If he were seen walking from the fantail this close to the time the two men went missing there would be questions, especially if MacCrimmon's wife raised a ruckus.

By now people were beginning to arrive, individually and in groups. Five minutes later a mob of large boisterous men, maybe a sports team of some sort, came out. He joined them and for the benefit of the cameras, if there were any, he slouched down and moved his mouth as if he were talking with them.

In the elevator he considered going to MacCrimmon's suite and taking care of the woman. If all went well, when her body was discovered, MacCrimmon's absence might be ruled a suicide driven by the remorse of a man who had killed his wife. A prominently placed security camera convinced him this was a bad idea. There were still a couple of days before the ship docked, enough time to deal with her. He had to assume MacCrimmon had told her what he had tricked out of that idiot, Vera. He hoped against hope the pair had kept it to themselves.

Vera was already up and dressed when he returned to his stateroom though it was only 7:30 and she was usually a late sleeper. She sat at the table, hunched over his laptop like a myopic bespectacled rodent. He poured himself a half-glass of Bourbon and downed it.

She squinted at him and pushed her glasses up the bridge of her nose with her middle finger. "That bad?"

He slammed the empty glass down on the cabinet. "A fucking catastrophe. The likelihood of our plan succeeding has decreased by about a third." He told her he had tried to bargain with MacCrimmon but he had not only refused any accommodation but had promised the two of them would "go down." Seeing no alternative he had thrown him overboard.

"Good God! Overboard! Anybody see you?"

"A feeble old man, so he had to go too. But before I got to him he threw a life ring over. I doubt it'll help MacCrimmon much, even if he can get to it. It'll be hours before he's missed, too late for him to be found. The sharks will get him if he doesn't die of exposure first."

"The way you talk about it, you seem kind of sad."

"Yeah," he said, shaking his head. "It was *real* murder, a lot different than taking care of Tamara. But enough of that. The problem now is the wife."

"Listen, Thomas, about the wife."

"Yeah? What about her?"

"First of all, MacCrimmon is not some nobody. He's all over the web. He caught some lunatics killing the homeless in Frisco, and there were some other exploits too."

"Okay, but what's this have to do with the wife?"

"I found his home address, 818 Mason, San Francisco, and, more important, he and his wife have two kids."

"So?"

"I'll take care of the wife. No worries on that score."

"All we can do is lie low and wait. All hell's going to break loose once they realize MacCrimmon and the old man are missing."

"I'd better write my note. I want to deliver it to Mrs. MacCrimmon before she goes nuts and starts throwing our names around."

6.

PADGETT had grabbed MacCrimmon by the collar of his shirt and the seat of his shorts, had bum-rushed him to the railing, and was hoisting him over before he even realized what was happening. He had grabbed for the top rail but his hand slipped away. Falling, his hip grazed the side of a railing two decks below but he had enough time to position himself by helicoptering his arms to land feet-first in the water. As high as the ninth deck was, the impact was like hitting dry land—it drove him fifteen or twenty feet deep. He was desperate for air by the time he surfaced, panting so hard the ship was a hundred yards away before he had breath enough to bellow for help. Padgett waved to him, a taunt that guaranteed, if he survived, he would hunt him down and kill him.

The ship was receding quickly but he thought he saw a life ring fall from the starboard side. A few seconds later someone fell or was dropped overboard. The person struck a railing two or three decks below and went cartwheeling into the water.

He kicked off his remaining sandal—he'd lost the other one when he hit the water—and swam to where he thought the life ring would be. Fighting the heavy chop and the turbulence in the wake, and having to circle the area, he tired badly before he found it. He held it against his chest a minute, catching his breath. Without it he would have drowned within an hour or two, he had no doubt of that. He slipped the ring over his head and snaked his arms in, one after the other. Positioned under his armpits, it held his head and shoulders out of the water at collarbone level. The effort of squirming into it had turned him around. When he re-oriented himself, the ship was at least a quarter mile away. He waved his arms but unless someone was watching with binoculars no one would see him. He clumsily paddled back to see if the other person was still alive but he never found him.

The ship was now a half-mile away. He closed his eyes and consciously slowed his breathing to calm himself enough to take stock. He was wearing only a polo shirt and cargo shorts but the water was about eighty-degrees so hypothermia was not an immediate problem. Sharks, however, might be. If they didn't get him, and he wasn't found in a day or two, exposure and dehydration would probably do him in. His resources were his Swiss Army knife, the plastic electronic key to his suite, his wedding ring, and his wristwatch, which wouldn't last long immersed in sea water. He couldn't see land and he had only a general idea where he was. The ship had left Labadie in Haiti in the night and was on the return leg to Florida. The area was heavily travelled by shipping so there was a decent chance he would be picked up.

All this had happened after he had sworn, his hand raised to heaven, he would never, *ever*, again involve himself in matters like the Padgett affair. He had blatantly broken his promise to Karen. If he died, he jolly well deserved it.

Recriminations out of his system he lay back and drifted in the chop that was getting worse. The time was 7:07. One short hour earlier, he had been peacefully translating Beowulf and swelling in anticipation of making love when Karen woke up.

Six hours he had floated limply in his life ring, completely passive. Only if he were suspended weightlessly in space would he be less at the mercy of earthly physical forces. He was thirsty but not painfully so, and though it was now lunchtime, he wasn't hungry. The water was neither warm nor cold; the weather was fine; the chop had lessened; he had seen no sharks nor any other life, except gulls and frigate birds; he had no pain, either from grazing the railing on the way down or striking the water; and his life ring showed no sign of imminent disintegration.

In the beginning, watching the ship disappear in the distance, appreciating how dire his situation was, he had been apprehensive—terrified, to put a finer point on it. But as one's sense of smell goes dead in the continuing presence of a scent, so had his terror abated. He still knew intellectually he might die, but he had pushed his likely fate and the fear that went with it to the back of his mind.

His concern, beyond his own situation, was Karen. Her mental state, to put it charitably, was fragile. Cloistered in the sanctuary of their home with him to lean on, where there was love, comfortable routine, and freedom from outside stresses, she was perfectly content and stable. But once that stability was breached, as it had been during their many separations, she tended to "decompensate," as the psychiatrists called it; twice she had suffered outright psychosis. Because of the bizarre bond between the two of them, almost as if they had grown together anatomically, when separated they may have been technically alive (and in a couple of times in Karen's case, barely that) but their lives were reduced to days of joyless monochromatic tedium, twenty of the twenty-four hours consumed by leaden aching for the other.

But their previous separations had been only in space and the hope of being reunited had always hovered over them for the very good reason that, even after separations that had seemed permanent—divorces in a couple of cases—they always *had* been reunited. Death, however, allowed no such hope. If Karen believed he was dead she would likely fall completely apart and might harm herself.

Imagining her agony, seeing her in his mind's eye weeping, pounding the sides of her thighs with her little fists, marching around in desperate distress, his rage at Padgett rose again. "I'll live," he bellowed to the warm Caribbean air. "I swear to God I'll live, so I can hunt you down, and when I find you, you dysgenetic, misbegotten motherfucker, you are going to die!"

The hours wore on. As improbable as it might seem for someone in his situation, he was bored. As frequently happened when he was bored his mind idly played over his life, a life that at times like this seemed nothing more than a chain of absurdities: thinking he had killed his grandmother; getting kicked out of kindergarten; marrying a prostitute; time after time risking his idyllic life by injecting himself into squalid crimes that were none of his business; and this, the ultimate—letting his guard down and getting chucked into the ocean.

But in the roulette wheel of memories the little ivory ball first fell on Lena Montoya, a major player in a whole tangled web of absurdities and the cause of many of his problems with Karen. He saw her as clearly as if it were yesterday, this brilliant and beautiful woman, who, for reasons he never understood—or believed—had fallen in love with him while he was a bartender in a little town near Death Valley—an absurdity in itself.

Poor Karen had been rabidly jealous of her and had been certain up until Lena's death he would run off with her. Nothing he said or did would convince her otherwise. He and Lena *had* had their moments. It was during one of Karen's numerous departures—one Lena had engineered—that Maddy was conceived.

It had been exactly a year since Lena, this woman who hated and desperately feared the water, had drowned, thrown in her own swimming pool by three members of her late husband's now-extinct cartel, men who were convinced she knew where he had hidden his gold. Imagine their surprise when they found she couldn't swim—and they couldn't rescue her because they couldn't swim either.

These thoughts of swimming prompted him to clumsily paddle around in a circle to demonstrate his helplessness, as if he'd had any doubt. He shouted up to Lena, in heaven or wherever she was, "You must be getting a good laugh out of this one!"

He caught motion out of the corner of his eye. He whipped his head around. A hundred yards away several large creatures cavorted. He couldn't make out what they were, only that they weren't sharks, thank God. Probably dolphins.

He relaxed back in the life ring in drowsy languor. Thinking of relationships brought to mind Ellen Fong, his first girlfriend, a pretty, flat-chested, delicate waif he had been in love with when he was a student at Cal. How sweet and innocent, how non-absurd it had been. He shuddered remembering his over-the-top reaction when she left him to marry someone else. In blind grief and rage he'd thrown his office chair through the front window of his third-story apartment. Even now, decades later, he felt a twinge at the suffering that, in his youthful folly, he'd been certain would never

46

go away, pain so terrible death had seemed the only anodyne. Alexander "Dad" Sutherland, his maternal grandfather, drawn into the fracas to pay for the damage to the apartment, had somehow smoked out his plan to do away with himself. Suicide, Dad had agreed, was indeed an effective analgesic though a bit permanent. But murdering a man, he had warned him, was a despicable thing to do. Dad had dismissed his own argument—that he wasn't killing a man, only himself—by saying he was a callow, mentally disturbed, youth planning to kill the person who would one day become a fine man, and that was *murder*, not suicide. In a rare instance of actual physical contact, unheard of in their household, Dad had put his arm around him—the scent of his Old Spice aftershave came back so strongly it was almost as if he were wearing it himself—and said gently that in rare cases people had healed from heartbreaks like this. As it turned out, Ellen's father had forced her to leave him. He had refused to allow a daughter of his to marry a *loh-fahn*.

Matthew—and a worse younger brother would be hard to imagine—had found the whole episode hilarious. He said he'd expected nothing less from a dork who read Darwin and played the baritone horn in the high school band. Seeing him moping around, he said something like, "You moron, there're a billion more women in the world and all of them but the ten-year olds have bigger tits than your little Chink." A real sweetheart, Matthew. He was a dirty football player, too, so bad his own teammates called him "MacCriminal."

He blew a salty raspberry at the jerk his brother had been, probably still was. He hadn't spoken to him in decades.

A brisk zephyr blew seawater in his face, rousing him from his reveries. He lazily paddled with his right hand around in a half-circle to face away from the wind. He didn't want saltwater in his mouth, it would make him even more thirsty.

Hours of listless drifting passed. Evening came, the time he and Karen customarily had a glass of wine on the balcony. If he died, and if she recovered, and he hoped she did, who would she drink wine with? There would be someone, there was no doubt about that, for the sake of the kids if for nothing else. A widow as beautiful and wealthy as she would be, men from twenty to ninety would gather like hyenas at an elephant's carcass. Who would it be? What would the man be like who nuzzled her silky black hair and inhaled the spicy scent of lavender, unchanged in the thirty-years he had known her? And who would caress her full breasts, and run his fingers over the satin skin of her perfect thighs? In whose ear would she murmur words of love in her low sensuous contralto? And who would Alex and Madeleine call "Daddy"? Would he be younger, handsome and sexy? Or would he be older, more stable and paternal?

He hadn't fully felt loneliness and despair until now. But neither had he been as determined to live, a sentiment he bellowed not once, but three times at the sun, now half engulfed by the limitless sea.

He awoke, bobbing up and down in a swell, to a loud rushing noise. It took him a moment to orient himself in the dark. A huge brightly lit cruise ship, fifty yards away, amidships to him, was passing by. He raised himself as high as he could and shouted to the several people on balconies, "Help! I'm overboard! Tell the captain!... Help!" One of a trio of young men looked toward him, the only person who seemed to have heard him. "Help me! Tell the captain!" The young man looked away and laughed, a silly high-pitched drunken giggle that carried over the water. He frantically repeated his shouts but in fifteen or twenty seconds the ship had passed. He watched until it was a mere speck of light on the horizon. Again floating in the dark, what had been mere loneliness morphed into complete desolation.

He passed the rest of the night in tense wakefulness, listening beyond the continuous lapping of wavelets against his life ring for strange noises. From a young age he had been uncomfortable being outside in the dark. It wasn't fear exactly, more free-floating anxiety and a hunger for light. He had once spent a pitch-black moonless night sitting in a lawn chair at the top of the driveway of his mountain home, hoping to conquer his fear. But when the sun rose, he had judged from his relief his "apprehension" of the dark was worse for the experience. Whatever he called it, it was an aspect of his personality he had never admitted to anyone, even Karen, thinking it a sort of silly cowardice that would diminish him in her eyes.

Toward dawn, relieved at seeing the first blush of light, he dozed. He dreamt of Karen. She was in a massive stone and steel kitchen in a castle somewhere, wearing a chef's toque, taking one of her signature lemon meringue pies out of a wood-burning oven. She was telling someone, he couldn't see who, that the meringue was as high and firm as it was because she made it with the whites of duck eggs she bought specially at Whole Foods. He called to her, begging for water and a piece of pie, but she ignored him. A strange man he didn't recognize came in. She gave him a wedge of pie on a pewter plate and the two walked out arm-in-arm, smiling at each other. He tried to follow, to tell her he was alive, but his legs and tongue seemed made of stiff wax and neither would move.

He woke, weeping at this vision of loss that had seemed more real than any waking life experience. The psychological defenses— rationalization, repression, and outright denial, among others— of a man not terribly emotionally expressive had failed him during sleep when truths hit much harder than they did when he was awake and fully armored. The castle he saw not as an actual castle, of course, but as a symbol of the home of someone rich and powerful, the kind of man who would replace him; the kitchen, her happy resumption of the domestic duties she loved, epitomized by her famous lemon meringue pie; and in the sweet smile she gave the faceless man, he saw she had healed and was happy. The grief at the prospect of never seeing her again was a heavy ache in his chest and belly, so agonizing it hurt to breathe.

But it was a new day. He wiped his eyes—stinging them with the salt crusted on his hands—and chastised himself for his girlish self-pity. He paddled a quarter-circle turn to look at the sun peeping over the eastern rim of the Caribbean. "*Eos rhododactylos*," he shouted, Homer's "rosy-fingered dawn," the epithet the poet used so frequently in the Iliad. But with the sun came the first of the sharks.

7.

IT WASN'T large as sharks go, four, maybe five feet long, and it wasn't a great white or a hammerhead but otherwise he had no idea what kind it was or what its intentions were. It cruised around him, checking him out. He lay back in a position to kick it away, but it circled behind him. He went upright. It was better to sacrifice a foot or leg than to have it bite his trunk, maybe perforate his bowel or a kidney. He fumbled for his pocketknife but decided against using it. The blade was too short to kill the beast and its blood might attract other sharks.

He paddled frantically, trying to rotate fast enough to face the shark as it circled him but, before he could react, it darted behind him and bit his right calf. He kicked at it and it retreated. Out of the corner of his eye he saw what he thought in the first instant were larger sharks, ten, twelve feet long, coming toward him, but they weren't sharks, they were dolphins. They looked superficially like killer whales, the same grey throat and neck, but they were slender. At their approach the shark swam away. He had known of cases of dolphins protecting humans from sharks but it wasn't clear if that was what had happened. Had the shark feared them? More likely it had found the taste of human flesh not to its liking, at least the taste of this human, and had swum away in disgust. He flexed his leg and felt the wound on his calf—it was positioned in such a way he couldn't see it beyond the life ring. He felt four puncture wounds, each about a half-inch in length. They didn't seem very deep and bleeding wasn't extensive enough to show up at the surface where he would have been able to see it.

The seven dolphins swan closer and cavorted in front of him. One of them glided close enough to touch. It had to have had

previous pleasant experiences with humans. He stroked its head and thanked it for its timely appearance. The dolphin sped off, but immediately returned and rose out of the water to appraise him more closely, as if to say, "Do my eyes deceive me or is that some idiot human floating around in the middle of the ocean?" He again stroked the dolphins smooth head, which it seemed to like. Lacking fluency in any of the cetacean languages he resorted to singing, that universal communicator. He bellowed in his rich basso one of the old folk tunes he sang to Alex and Maddy what seemed a century ago:

Oh, Shenandoah, I long to hear you
Look away, you rollin' river
Oh, Shenandoah, I long to hear you
Look away, we're bound away
Across the wide Missouri.

He had to laugh at their reaction, leaping out of the water, darting around, as if the song excited them. The larger, more forward of the pod, probably the leader, prodded him gently with its snout. Taking this as a demand for an encore he sang, "Spanish is a Lovin' Tongue," and finished with Tom Paxton's, "Last Thing on my Mind."

The dolphins dawdled in the area another few minutes and departed as quickly as they'd come, leaving him lonelier than before. How much better off we humans would be if we had half the gentle playfulness and happiness of these creatures, these models of perfect behavior placed before us as examples of what we *could* be, with nary a greedy psychopath or warmonger among them. But humans have never adhered very consistently to standards of decent behavior.

A darker thought came to him. In his extremity would he kill one to survive. It wasn't likely to be a real-life decision, having only a pocketknife with a three-inch blade, but it was something to think about.

Late morning a small raft of trash floated by driven by the wind, including a half full 1.5-liter plastic bottle. The stale water with a finish of chlorine was nectar, better than any Champagne he had ever tasted; so good, in fact, he forgave the miscreant, whoever it was, who had thrown it into the ocean. He scavenged a thick red plastic shopping bag to cover his head, protection from further sunburn, and he wadded up another bag and stuffed it in the pocket of his shorts, to be pulled out and held open to the sky if it rained again. He had no use for the Styrofoam cup, pieces of a Styrofoam cooler, and two empty plastic bottles.

The day was hot and the water glassy calm. He splashed his face to cool it—he was sweating heavily, and the last thing he needed was to sweat out more fluid. The life ring was a tight fit and was chafing his sides. At the risk of losing it he slipped out of it and swam a few yards to loosen up muscles that had stiffened due to his immobility. He returned to the ring and positioned it under him, to lay on it, to check the shark bite. The punctures were larger than he had thought. The wounds were blue and puffy white, not likely to heal well immersed as they were in saltwater.

He spent an hour floating outside the life ring, his left arm hooked through it.

At lunch time—his watch had stopped but the sun was directly overhead—after many attempts he grabbed one of the numerous little fish clustered around him as if he were a sanctuary in the oceanic vastness. It was an odd little flat silver thing, at most three inches long. He rested it on the life ring, scrubbed away the scales, gutted it with his pocketknife, and cut it into six tiny, bony, scaly, fishy bites. It was not at all like the sashimi he loved and it did little to sate his hunger, in fact it only intensified it.

A rapid thumping noise to the north interrupted his grabs for more of the little fish. A helicopter! It was a mile or more away, too far to identify as Coast Guard but it probably meant they were looking for him. As futile as it was he bellowed and waved his arms. It continued north, flying back and forth, until it was out of sight.

In his logical mind he recognized the improbability of him, this tiny speck of waterlogged humanity, ever being found in this aqueous desert. Hungrier than ever, thirsty, still aching from the dream of Karen, and now teetering on the verge of lethargic hopelessness, he remembered Byrthnoth's line from the *The Battle of Maldon*:

> *Hige sceal ðe heardra   heorte ðe cenre*
> *Mod sceal ðe mare   ðe ure mægen lytlath*

[Our minds must be firmer, our hearts keener,
Our spirits all the greater, as our strength wanes]

The perils of a tenth century English thane facing a horde of marauding Vikings with an undermanned army was not much like those of a man floating helplessly in the ocean but the message was appropriate.

Odysseus too had been in a situation seemingly as hopeless as this after Poseidon in a fit of rage had destroyed his raft, leaving him clinging to the wreckage, as Padgett had left him clinging to a life preserver. But while the goddess Ino gave Odysseus a magic scarf granting him temporary immortality until he was saved, in his situation the dolphins were the closest analogy, a bit of a stretch, and Athena had guaranteed Odysseus fair winds until he found land. Who would be his Athena—would there *be* an Athena? "If you exist," he bellowed to the sky, shaking his fist, "if you're any kind of goddess at all, forget the goddamned wind and send a helicopter! I refuse to die in this miserable geological tub of tepid saltwater and I'm tired of waiting!"

To calm himself, he lay back, closed his eyes, and let his breathing slow. In the drowsy meditative state that followed, music came to him, *The Dance of the Blessed Spirits*, Gluck's masterful dance scene from *Orfeo ed Euridice*. Long ago in another desperate time he had chosen this piece to accompany his departure from life—assuming when the time came he would be in a position to choose. He waved his hand, conducting the sweeping theme for strings, hummed along with the flute solo, and again conducted the strings as they reprised the original theme. He roused, feeling better than the salt-encrusted derelict he was—enough better that he bellowed out "Kentucky Sunrise," a jaunty bit of circus ragtime. His affection for brassy circus music was another character flaw he admitted to no one.

Late afternoon he jerked awake after dozing briefly. His sleep had been disturbed by a febrile dream in which he had begun to rot before he officially died and was bobbing along in the ocean, paralyzed and helpless, as sea creatures nibbled on his bloated carcass. This scenario suggested the line in Revelations about the sea giving up her dead. Disturbed by this revolting image he shouted at the sea around him, "How 'bout giving up the living, you bitch!"

The day wore on. His thirst, which had plagued him from the beginning, had passed from discomfort to an agonizing obsession. He thought of little other than lakes and rivers, even puddles and gutters, constantly fighting back the urge to drink sea water.

Toward evening the sharks returned, this time three of them, all about the same size. Or they might have been dolphins—his mind was fuzzy. Whatever they were, they circled him, as the earlier one had. In what would be a corny *deus ex machina* in a novel or a play real dolphins returned. They ignored what he thought were sharks, and they showed no aggressive behavior toward them but the sharks—if that's what they were—retired and were seen no more. Perhaps they had picked up a telepathic warning that this sorry pickled primate was a toy of the dolphins alone and was not to be harmed or shared.

The dolphins swam closer. He saw something in the leader's mouth—a fish, a decent sized one. The leader bumped against the life ring and offered it to him. He grabbed it, the dolphin released its hold, and darted away. What had happened took a moment to register. This dolphin had *given* him a fish! Unless it had somehow sensed he was in desperate straits why would it do such a thing? It was dream-like in its improbability. Maybe it *was* a dream. Maybe *he* had caught the fish.

The fish, still feebly writhing, was a plump greyish-tan creature, about ten-inches long, weighing maybe a pound. It might have been some kind of seabass but he knew nothing of Caribbean fishes. He clutched it to his chest, not knowing how prevalent Indian giving was in the dolphin community, but they all merrily cavorted around him, arching and twisting in and out of the water, showing no intention of taking it back.

He scraped the scales away with his pocketknife, carved fillets from the backbone and wolfed them down, more for the water than the flesh. He finished by picking out the tiniest of morsels from between the bones. He left only the head and the guts. He estimated he had imbibed about a cup of water with the meat, enough to somewhat blunt his ferocious thirst.

He thanked the dolphins and sang to them but they showed no interest in his dry croaking version of "Mona Lisa" and swam away.

He watched with special melancholy as the sun went down. As bad as he felt and as weak as he was getting it would likely be his last sunset. "No *Götterdämmerung* for the likes of me," he said in a hoarse whisper, "no gods in this twilight. More like the twilight of a damn fool, a *Dumkopfdämmerung*."

Night fell, several hours passed, and even his fear of the dark dulled, replaced by vague indifference to everything but his burning thirst. In spite of the water from the fish, his strength was rapidly failing and his mind was wandering in weird directions.

Had the dolphins really given him a fish?—or had he found it floating in the water? Had there been a fish at all?

Time passed, how much he didn't know. The worsening swell had roused him from what had been merciful oblivion. A raft! Right next to him. They would have water. He croaked, "Hallelujah!" Someone hauled him aboard. It was crowded, tilted, bobbing crazily in the waves. French people, piled on top of one another, were screaming and falling off while one man tended a jury-rigged sail. Someone behind told him to leave his life ring on. Unseen hands pushed him to one side. He looked back. All the people were gone. They must have been washed overboard. Where the people had been, Karen and a young man were now sitting side by side on a blanket. The man fiddled with her hair while Alex and Maddy played at their feet, speaking a language he couldn't understand. He tried to call to them but his words came out as strangled groans they didn't hear or perhaps they were ignoring him. He tried to approach them but they were behind a glass partition. He pounded on it and screamed their names, but they didn't look up.

The person behind him whose face he couldn't see pushed him down a long teak-decked corridor. It must be a ship, not a raft. It had to have come next to him when he was asleep. Next to a swimming pool Lena Montoya lay on a chaise lounge, naked, sunning herself. "This can't be! You're dead, Lena."   "No, Andrew. Gus was wrong about that."   "But Gus and I put you in the ground in that Palm Springs cemetery."   "That was all a dream, Andrew. We're going to be together, you and I."   "But I want to be with Karen."   "There is no Karen. Her real name is Christine. She was lying to you all those years. She was married to another man all the time. She tricked you, you poor simple fool. She only wanted your money."

A wave smashed him in the face, filling his mouth, stifling his howl of grief. He looked for the raft but it must have sunk. He paddled around to turn his back to the wind. Exhausted by the effort, he lay back and closed his eyes.

When he woke the full moon was shining down on him. He called to it in disconnected syllables, "Lu-na... lu-na-*tic*... Se-le-ne... Le-ne... Le-*na*." The raft came back. Lena had heard him calling. She helped him climb out of the water back onto the same raft where he had seen Karen and led him into a closet-like room. He felt for her in the inky darkness. He grasped her hand but her flesh came away in his fingers. He surreptitiously wiped his hands on his life ring so as not to offend her. Stumbling along a woodland path, through an opening in some bushes he saw Karen and the young man, their heads together, laughing. He called to them, but Lena ordered him to follow her. "I'm thirsty, Lena." "I know you are, Andrew. There's beer here. Follow me." She led him down a narrow corridor to a counter covered with frosty mugs of beer. "Drink up, Andrew." "You died in the water, Lena, and I'm going to die in the water too. That's an interesting coincidence, isn't it?" "Nobody's going to die, Andrew. Drink up." He gulped sea water out of his cupped hands. "This beer is salty, Lena." "It's good for you, Andrew, have some more."

Another wave hit him hard in the face. He looked around. Lena, Karen, the raft, they were all gone. They'd left him behind.

"Lost!... I'm lost... *Lasciate ogni Speranza*...."

8.

MID-MORNING, the two fishermen who had found the man floating in the ocean, by working together managed to drag him over the gunwale. They slid the life ring over his head and laid him on the slimy fish scale-encrusted deck.

"*Deað*," the man mumbled slowly, "*deað oferswyðeð*."

"He's a Russian," the first man, the captain, said in Spanish.

"No, Beto, I know a little Russian. That's German."

"Whatever he is he's about done for. Look at that sunburn, those cracked lips. See if he'll take some water."

The second man, Jorge, fetched a plastic bottle of water from the cabin and poured an ounce or so on the man's lips. He licked it and gave out a breathy groan. Jorge held his head up and poured a sip in his mouth. Most of it dribbled out but he swallowed a little, and with each dose he swallowed a little more. He droned, his eyes still closed, "*Semninga bið þæt ðec, dryhtguma, deað oferswyðeð* [Thus it is, noble lord, that death prevails]."

"Definitely German," Jorge muttered to himself. He rotated the life ring to read the ship's name, Miesterdam. He called to the captain, "You want to keep the life ring, Beto?"

"No. If that *cabron* Abrantes finds out about it he'll think we stole it, or worse, we were smuggling or dealing with foreign ships. Throw it back in."

"What in the name of the blessed Virgin is a German doing floating around in the ocean?"

"Must've fell overboard from that ship, the Misterdam or whatever it is.... Let's take him below." Beto took MacCrimmon's arms and Jorge his legs. They half-dragged, half-carried the heavy man to the companionway, bumped down the steps, and hoisted him onto a bunk covered with filthy rumpled blankets stinking of fish.

Back on deck, Beto said, "We have to pull in the nets, Jorge. It's too rough today to catch anything and we're shipping water."

"What'll we do with the German?"

"He's in bad shape. He needs to go to the hospital. Who knows, maybe the German consulate will give us a reward. Or maybe he's rich and *he'll* give us a reward."

An hour later, after docking, they enlisted the help of two fishermen mending nets to haul the German out of the cabin and up to the shack of the harbormaster. They told him how they had found him floating in the ocean, that he was a German, and he needed to go to the hospital. The harbormaster said they could take him in his car, a '56 Chevy he had converted to a short bed pickup using a hacksaw and salvaged lumber.

The five men had carried him into the parking area when Teofilo Abrantes, the Chief of Police of the City of Mariendo, drove up. He called to them, leaning out of the driver's side window of his police car, "What do we have here, Silvio, a drunk?"

Silvio, the harbormaster, repeated the story the two fishermen had told him. "I'm taking him to the hospital. I called ahead. They'll be waiting for us."

Abrantes gave the men a sweeping wave with the back of his hand which they took as permission to carry on. Beto, watching him drive away, muttered, "Lard ass son-of-a-dog!"

Silvio slowly drove the mile and a half to the local hospital while Jorge, given leave by Beto, rode in the bed to support the German's head and to keep him from falling out—the bed sloped down and there was no tailgate.

Two orderlies and two nurses met them at the loading area that served as an emergency entrance. The six of them loaded the German onto a gurney and wheeled him into an examination room. Jorge and Silvio, the harbormaster, were ushered out, and the male orderlies removed the man's soggy, salt-encrusted clothing. They put the electronic key to his stateroom, his pocketknife—a Swiss Army model one of the orderlies eyed greedily, his gold ring, and his watch in a manila envelope. They washed the crusted salt off his body, being especially gentle with the sides of his chest where the life ring had chafed him badly. They had wrestled him into a tattered patched hospital gown when Dr. Chavez, the local surgeon and head of the hospital, poked his head in and asked what was going on. He listened to the story while he examined the man. He said he was dangerously dehydrated and told the nurses to start IVs with normal saline in both arms. The man fluttered his eyelids and mumbled, "*Deað... deað oferswyðeð.*"

A nurse said, "The fisherman claims he's a German."

"I don't know what language he's babbling," Chavez said, "but it isn't German—could be Norwegian, Polish, something like that. Does he have any identification?"

An orderly showed him the electronic key from the Manila envelope. "Only this card."

Chavez examined it. "'Andrew MacCrimmon.' The name sounds English, or maybe Canadian or American. Have Donato take care of him. He speaks English."

Dr. Sergio Donato, apprised of the situation, arrived an hour later. He told the nurses to put this special patient in one of the hospital's two private rooms. Twenty-minutes later, adjusting the flow of one of the IVs, he said to a man entering the room, "You got here quickly, Captain Abrantes."

"I was at the dock when he was brought in. Who is he, Doctor? What's the matter with him?"

"He's badly dehydrated and suffering from exposure."

"Will he live?"

"Yes. Once his fluids are replaced he should recover. He has wounds on his right calf, probably a shark bite. They are suppurating and will need treatment. He was fighting us, and he's very strong, so I had to sedate him. He was saying something in a foreign language I didn't understand and he called in English for someone named 'Karen,' his wife I imagine. He went on and on about being on a raft. I judge from his accent he's American. I was assigned to care for him because I speak English."

"Does he have any identification?"

Dr. Donato, washing his hands in a small sink in the corner, said over his shoulder, "His name is Dr. Andrew MacCrimmon according to a plastic card he had in his pocket, an electronic key on a ship called the 'Miesterdam.'"

"When will I be able to question him?"

Dr. Donato dried his hands, neatly folded the towel, and hung it on the rack. He turned to the policeman and crossed his arms. "Question him?—about what?"

Abrantes shrugged and spread his hands as if the answer were obvious. "What's he doing here? Where did he come from? How does anyone fall off a ship with a life preserver?"

"Catching the scent of a spy from the sea, Captain?"

Abrantes said, looking at his watch, "It's possible, Doctor... But duty calls." He had missed the irony in the question.

Doctor Donato, watching the fat man lumber away, mumbled, "Buffoon."

Late that afternoon a nurse changing the IV bottles heard the patient say, "Am I on the raft? Is Karen here?" The nurse, who had no English, finished switching the bottles and rushed to the nursing station to inform Dr. Donato the *Yanqui* was speaking.

Dr. Donato hurried to the room of the man whose name he now knew. "Dr. MacCrimmon, can you hear me?"

MacCrimmon asked, his eyes still shut, "Am I on the raft?... Karen... Is she...?"

"Not here, Doctor. You're in hospital."

MacCrimmon tried to rise. Dr. Donato pushed him back. He held the struggling man by his arms and called for help. Two nurses held the patient down by his shoulders and an orderly sat on his legs while the doctor injected a sedative into his IV line. A minute later, when he had relaxed, Donato ordered him to be put him in soft bed restraints.

Dr. MacCrimmon woke early the next morning. He struggled to rise but looking down, seeing his restraints, he relaxed and lay back. "I'm alive," he said to the ceiling. "I'm breathing, beating-heart, pillow-pounding alive!" For long euphoric minutes he ignored the pain in his right calf, the stinging of the chafing on his sides, and the headache likely caused by drinking seawater and basked in the simple joy of being alive. "Karen," he mumbled, "I didn't die. I promised you I'd survive."

He looked around the shabby room, paint peeling, a single straight chair in one corner, in another, a small sink. A lazily revolving ceiling fan did little to move the air, already hot and sticky though it was early morning. Two IVs were running, one in each arm. He licked his rough cracked lips. He was thirsty, but normal-life thirsty, such as he might be from working outside, nothing like he had been.

He called out, "Where am I?"

A nurse appeared and said something in Spanish. MacCrimmon, recognizing Spanish, indicated in Spanish he had no Spanish. "*Un momento*," the nurse said and scurried away. Ten minutes later a gangly pimply teen-age boy appeared, the only available English speaker. "De nurse, she say jou wait. De doctor, he come one hour," a unit of time he emphasized by shaking his little finger.

"Where am I?"

"De doctor, he weel say you avryting."

He whispered, "Untie me. I have to, uh, pee pee."

"De nurse come."

The nurse returned . Seeing from his grin and twinkling eyes further violence was unlikely, she released his ties and handed him a jug to pee in.

An hour and a half later, after a breakfast of rice and black beans and several glasses of a delicious fruit juice, a slender balding man of medium height, wearing a stethoscope around his neck, tapped on the doorjamb and entered. MacCrimmon saw a resemblance to his late friend, Father Gus Paredes, the same over-sized glasses and large teeth, and the same kindly expression. The man introduced himself in a pleasant baritone with only a light Hispanic accent. "Well, Dr. MacCrimmon, you're much better this morning."

MacCrimmon squinted up at him. "My vision's a little fuzzy."

"Reflected glare from the water. It's like a mild case of snow blindness. You'll recover."

MacCrimmon tried to sit up but Dr. Donato gently pushed him back. "Rest, Doctor. You've had a very bad time."

"Where am I?"

"Mariendo."

"Mexico?"

"The northeast coast of Cuba."

"Cuba!... Oh, God!"

Dr. Donato said softly with a wry grin, "That eminent person hasn't been seen on this island in over fifty-years."

MacCrimmon chuckled at this. "Or anywhere else, if the world situation is any indication... How did I get here?"

"To answer that I would have to know where you came *from*. Two fishermen found you floating in the ocean."

"You sound like an American, Doctor."

Dr. Donato looked back at the doorway and tapped his lips with his forefinger. "Speak softly, Doctor MacCrimmon. One never knows who might be listening and I'd rather not remind people... I *was* an American. Born in Miami, college, med school, all in Miami."

"How did you end up here?"

"I came back as an idealistic young healer—to help my suffering people, I thought. I was arrested as a spy, of course. But after a time, the authorities conceded a person *could* indeed be stupid enough to come back here. They released me and sent me to this backwater where I could do no damage. But the taint of being

American lingers, like having a venereal disease or being a child rapist."

MacCrimmon had listened to the doctor's account with politely hidden impatience but he now moved on to more important matters. "When can I be released? I have to get home."

Donato grimaced at the question. "There will be certain bureaucratic difficulties, I'm sorry to say, immigration issues, all complicated by the local police captain, Teofilo Abrantes, who is, unfortunately, stupid, vicious, and paranoid. These are undesirable traits in anyone but especially in a policeman."

"But surely the American consulate can be notified."

"That is up to Abrantes. I would advise you to be extremely deferential to the man. In addition to his other deplorable qualities he is vindictive."

"I *must* get home, Doctor, or at least get word to my wife. She will be frantic."

"I don't want to discourage you, Doctor MacCrimmon, but it will take time... Now, if you're not too tired, can you tell me what happened, how you ended up in the ocean?"

MacCrimmon did so.

"So, if I understand you correctly, you suspect this man, Padgett, of murdering his wife with the help of his wife's twin sister. When you told him you would report him to the authorities, he threw you and another man overboard but not before the second man tossed you a life preserver, and you floated in the ocean for two days. The currents, which flow westerly must have brought you here."

"Yes. And I was bitten by a shark—"

"Yes. I thought those were shark bites. The wounds will need debridement."

"—and a dolphin gave me a fish, which probably saved my life, you know, because of the water in it."

Dr. Donato, chuckling softly, patted MacCrimmon's wrist. "Yes, of course—a dolphin gave you a fish... A strong word of advice, Doctor. Do *not* tell this story to Abrantes. If you'll forgive me for saying so, it's a bit, uh, fanciful."

"And the exact truth—at least I think so. I was getting a little crazy."

"Yes, of course. *I* believe you but an unimaginative man might not... But continue... After the dolphin gave you the fish, what happened?"

"All I remember are wild hallucinations about being on a raft."

"Yes. You were raving about this raft, Gericault's *Raft of the Medusa*, which you described perfectly. Now, Doctor, listen to me carefully. Abrantes will certainly question you. I beg you, keep the story simple enough for a stupid man to believe and, above all, forget the story about the dolphin giving you a fish. Say you got in a fight, the man insulted your wife, something like that. You were thrown overboard, floated two days, and were picked up by fishermen."

MacCrimmon nodded agreement. He said he'd had a good deal of experience dealing with stupid vicious policemen. "Do you have internet?"

"Limited to the island, slow, unreliable, and heavily censored. No help there."

"I'd like to get up, walk around—" he rubbed the bristles on his face, "—shave, shower, maybe return to the civilized world."

"Are you sure you're strong enough?"

"Only one way to find out." He slid out of bed and stood unsteadily a moment. He straightened up and spread his arms in triumph.

Dr. Donato laughed at his broad grin. "Very good. I'll see you are given a razor. The shower is down the hall—the facilities here you'll find are much different than what you are used to." Again serious, he touched MacCrimmon's shoulder and whispered, "When you've finished I'm afraid you'll have to confine yourself to this room. There's already a great deal of suspicion about you."

MacCrimmon whispered back, "Could you notify the American consulate?"

"I'm sorry, Doctor. That's out of the question." He grimaced, showing large yellow teeth, and drew his left hand, blade-like, across his throat.

Standing was one thing, but walking, MacCrimmon found, he did not do well—his legs were still accustomed to floating in saltwater. A nurse who saw him stumbling helped him down the hallway to the shower room. Washing in the weak tepid drizzle was painful, especially where the life ring had chafed him, but it was not half as painful as shaving his badly sunburned face with a dull razor.

Donato looked in again after he had settled in. He handed him his wedding ring and watch and laid his knife and key card on the chair. "Feeling better?"

"Much better."

"Your clothes, what's left of them, are being laundered."

MacCrimmon slipped his watch on and checked it to see if it was running—it wasn't. "Tell me about this town, Doctor, this hospital."

"Mariendo is on the northern coast of the island in Holquin province, about 50 kilometers, roughly thirty miles, from Holquin itself, the closest major city. We're five-hundred miles from Havana. We have thirty-thousand inhabitants, mostly farmers, fishermen, and miners. The hospital is fifty-beds in large wards. You have one of the two private rooms. As you may have observed, we are short of almost everything—anesthetics, antibiotics, syringes, blankets. But we make do and considering our limitations, we do a pretty good job."

"Doctor, how do I go about thanking the fishermen who rescued me?"

"They came by last night to ask about you. I took the liberty of passing on your thanks."

Several nurses and hospital personnel, many of whom had probably made a special trip, peeked in to get a glimpse of the big handsome *Yanqui*. Likewise, based on the people peeking at him, Dr. MacCrimmon concluded Cubans were a handsome people and if there were indeed food shortages the people he'd seen didn't look malnourished. Slim, yes, but that was preferable to the other extreme suffered by far too many of his own countrymen.

9.

MID-AFTERNOON Captain Abrantes, the local police chief Donato had warned him about, arrived, accompanied by a tall, emaciated, scholarly looking man of middle years who said he was the English translator. Judging by his sweating and tremor he was a nervous and reluctant translator.

Abrantes was much as MacCrimmon had imagined him, a gross-featured man who twisted his mouth in a cruel sneer when he spoke. He was overweight, a generally reliable sign of corruption in an area of food shortages. His uniform was too tight and displayed the expected food stains down the front of his shirt.

Abrantes, typical of the arrogance of stupid, self-important men, didn't bother introducing himself, assuming the interviewee would automatically know someone of his eminence. He got straight to the point: how, the translator asked, did he end up in the ocean? MacCrimmon told him the story Donato had suggested, that a man had insulted his wife, a fight followed, the bigger man threw him overboard. A second man, who saw it happen, threw him a life ring. He floated in the ocean two days until he was rescued by two fishermen. Abrantes followed with a flurry of Cuban Spanish directed at the translator. The translator summarized: "The captain wants to know, what is the name of this man who threw you overboard?"

MacCrimmon, knowing the quality of a lie was directly proportional to the amount of truth in it, said, "Thomas Padgett." He volunteered the ship was the Miesterdam, a cruise ship, and this happened about six hours out of Labadie, Haiti, on the trip back to Fort Lauderdale.

More rapid Spanish. The translator, more nervous than ever, said, "The captain says you have your story worked out very well."

Looking coldly at Abrantes, MacCrimmon said in what he hoped was Spanish intelligible enough for this cretin, *"Es completamente vero."*

"The word is *'cierto,'* Doctor, not *'vero,'*" the translator said, "but I think he got the point."

As Abrantes rambled on, MacCrimmon interrupted to ask when he could be released to the American consulate. The question angered Abrantes. The translator said, "The captain thinks you wish to report what you have seen."

"'Report what I've seen'?... You mean the national secrets I found hidden in a hospital room?"

Abrantes blustered something. In response, *Señor* Gomes—the translator had admitted his name—said, "The captain thinks you are not taking this seriously."

"Tell that stupid bloated dullard I'm taking it *very* seriously! My wife will be frantic, may harm herself if she doesn't get word I'm alive!"

Gomes translated. Abrantes grimaced in rage and shook his fist at him, all the time bellowing what MacCrimmon assumed were curses. Gomes said, "I know the Spanish words for 'stupid' and 'bloated' but not for 'dullard' so I used *'zoquete'* instead, which means 'blockhead.'"

"You told him that?—every word?... Why in the hell would you do that?"

"The captain insists each word be translated."

"Oh, good *God!*" he groaned. He slapped the thin patched blanket and lamented to the ceiling, "Now my goose is cooked."

A brief interchange between Abrantes and Gomes ensued. "The captain wants to know what cooking a goose has to do with anything."

MacCrimmon closed his eyes and shook his head at the futility of dealing with these morons.

"The captain says you will have to come to police headquarters," Gomes said. "In the meantime you must surrender all personal property."

"Such as?"

"Your clothes. The knife you had in the pocket of your short trousers, your identification card, and of course the ring and watch you are wearing."

MacCrimmon had already noticed Abrantes eyeing his watch. "My wedding ring? And the Rolex my grandfathers gave me when I graduated from medical school?... Not on your bloody life!"

Gomes, tiring of MacCrimmon's truculence, said sharply, "The 'bloody life' you talk about is your own, *Señor Doctor*. It could become a very unpleasant life."

Abrantes, impatient with all the talking, grabbed MacCrimmon's left hand and went for his watch.

MacCrimmon's punch, delivered from where he was sitting up in bed, was not as hard as it might have been had he been standing but it caught Abrantes square in the nose. He staggered back, squealing in rage. Blood leaked between his fingers and flowed down his face. He clenched his fists but seeing MacCrimmon was ready for him, he instead tried to draw his pistol but it hung up on the holster. He jerked it free and pointed it at MacCrimmon, screaming threats and curses but he must have thought better of shooting him. He bellowed something at Gomes who in turn whispered to MacCrimmon, "He is more angry than I have ever seen him. For a doctor you are a very stupid man. That indiscreet act will cost you dearly."

MacCrimmon, still panting in rage, glared at Abrantes, who had stormed to the doorway and was bawling something. "What's he hollering about now, Gomes?"

"He says to hell with Dr. Donato's orders. You are going to police headquarters immediately, at this moment." He added in an undertone, "And the ring and watch you think so much of—they will be taken from you anyway."

That evening, once Abrantes and his underlings had finished with the prisoner, they threw him in a small, windowless cell, steamy hot, filthy, smelling of stale urine and feces. The only light came from a fly-specked 25-watt naked light bulb hanging by its cord from the ceiling. Abrantes shouted something in the distance and somewhere another prisoner howled monotonously.

MacCrimmon crawled up off the filthy floor and sat on the raised concrete platform he assumed was the bed. He was woozy, aching all over from the punishment Abrantes had given him with his fists and a length of rubber hose, administered while two of his underlings held him. At one point the worst of them, the thuggish one, had relaxed and MacCrimmon had given him a good shot to the underside of his chin with an elbow which cost him four more blows. They had confined the beating to his body and legs, sparing his head and face. Beating a prisoner must be illegal since they had left no obvious evidence.

They had, as Gomes had warned him, taken his watch—gently, so as not to damage it—but in jerking off his wedding ring they had dislocated his left ring finger. Now, groaning in agony, he pulled hard on the crazily bent-back last joint of the finger until it snapped back into place.

An hour later, a young guard brought him a beaker of water and a plate containing maybe a half-cup of watery beans enriched by a single half-inch square piece of pork fat. The guard shook his head, no, as he handed him the plate. From this MacCrimmon assumed it was somehow tainted. But the guard nodded a millimeter or two when he handed him the water.

He drank half the water, about ten-ounces, and saved the rest for later. The plate of food he left in the corner near the stinking hole he assumed was for bodily wastes. He lay back, using the wadded up filthy blanket as a pillow.

A few minutes later, as if alerted by the smell, a rat appeared from the hole. It gave MacCrimmon a suspicious myopic glance—reminding him very much of Vera Snead and Tamara Padgett—and quivered its nose at him. The rat sniffed at the plate of food and disappeared back into the hole. He too must have found the meal tainted, probably by the same poison that had done away with many of his compatriots.

MacCrimmon, unlike most people, had no problem with rats as long as they didn't bite him and stayed out of his house. He admired them for their ability to adapt and thrive in such varying environments as houses, ships, and sewers—in this last case, New Orleans and Venice were good examples. And it wasn't the fault of the rats that fleas, in their campaign to transmit the plague around the world, found them such a convenient mode of transportation. During his medical training he had made friends with a few laboratory rats, albeit those of the albino persuasion. This fellow, a plump amiable specimen, he named Teofilo, after the captain of police, though the rat would likely be offended at this choice of namesakes.

Most of that night he writhed in pain from his beating and the throbbing in his finger. What few snatches of sleep he did manage were too shallow to dream of Karen or anything else.

That morning a different guard, the rough looking brute he had elbowed in the jaw, brought his breakfast, again a fresh beaker of water and a plate of watery black beans, this time without the square of pork fat. He slid it roughly under the bars, slopping about a third of the beans out on the cement floor. *"Espiar."* he said. MacCrimmon looked up. The word, similar to espionage, must mean spy. The guard gave him an ugly taunting leer and poured the water out on the floor, washing the spilled beans toward the waste hole.

A few minutes later the rat, Teofilo, appeared. He glanced at MacCrimmon and sat back on his haunches. Holding the spilled beans in his little hands, he ate them one by one. When he finished he waddled to the hole without a look back, perhaps returning to Mrs. Teofilo and a clutch of squeaking ratlings.

That Teofilo had eaten the beans, MacCrimmon took as a sign they were edible. About a half-cup had survived on the plate. These he ate with his fingers; cutlery must be a luxury he was not worthy of.

Later that morning he heard a commotion in the distance, two men arguing. Dr. Donato appeared two minutes later, his lips clenched in anger. The surly guard opened the cell door and let him in. Donato smiled at him, patted his shoulder, and nodded thanks. The guard flickered a smile in return.

"You need to have two of those shark bites debrided. I was supposed to do it today in the hospital but I'll have to do the best I can here. Abrantes objected even to that."

"How did you get him to agree?"

"I threatened to call the police colonel in Holquin. Abrantes has already been reported for several offenses so he relented." He guided MacCrimmon with a hand on his shoulder back to the platform. "Lie on that thing, Doctor. Move that filthy blanket out of the way. I have to cut away the necrotic tissue around two of the wounds and drain the pockets of infection. I used up all my local anesthetic on another case, unfortunately, so it will be painful."

MacCrimmon lay on his stomach as directed and rested his right cheek on his folded arms. He felt cold on his right calf as Dr. Donato scrubbed the area around the wounds, and searing pain as he snipped away the infected tissue. He clenched his teeth and scrunched his eyes but didn't cry out. Donato had finished and was bandaging the wounds when the guard entered and said something. Donato shrugged and handed him the gauze pad on which he had placed the necrotic tissue he had cut away from the infected bites. He whispered, "Abrantes is anxious the contaminated tissue is properly disposed of—a fastidious streak no one would ever have expected."

While he splinted MacCrimmon's left ring finger by taping it to his left middle finger—MacCrimmon had explained they had dislocated it when they pulled off his wedding ring—Donato whispered, "I understand you punched Abrantes in the nose."

"I have a volatile temper."

"And it will probably cost you dearly, but what you did was long overdue and much applauded."

"Will he kill me for it?"

"No. He dare not kill you—it would be murder. In the regional prisons they suffer no such compunctions but they can't get away with it at the local level. Abrantes has lost face. He will punish you in some awful way—how, I do not know—but he will not kill you, though in the end you may wish he had."

MacCrimmon grabbed his hand and shook it. "If I survive and return home, is there some way I can repay you for your care, and even more, for your kindness?

"Yes, there is." Donato pulled his hand away and glanced significantly at the guard watching them. Knowing he understood no English, he said in a normal conversational tone as if giving medical advice, "Ignore me completely. The captain has claimed you are a *Yanqui* spy so any contact with you, other than basic medical care, and especially if I received anything that could be seen as payment I would be suspected of treason. Unfortunately, mere suspicion is all too often enough to presume guilt—as you will probably find out for yourself."

That night after his usual dinner of a half-cup of beans, this time enlivened by a spoon of rice, Gomes appeared, looking more nervous than before. "Doctor, you said your wife would worry about you if she didn't hear from you?"

MacCrimmon, surprised he would remember this, said, "That's true, Señor Gomes. If she hears nothing she will assume I'm dead, and she will likely harm herself... Perhaps you too love someone, and have someone who loves you, and the two of you are close, as my wife and I are."

"No, Doctor," he said in his flat, expressionless tone. "I have never been blessed with love, from anyone. But I have come to offer you paper and pen so you can write a few words to your wife telling her you are alive and you will be coming home shortly. Say you are being treated well and make sure you address it legibly."

He stared in astonishment at the nervous man. "That's very kind of you, Señor Gomes. I will never forget this."

Gomes smiled weakly in return and slid the sheet of paper and the pen under the cell door.

MacCrimmon wrote:

> Karen, my dear Love;
>
> I am alive. I am recovering from being in the ocean.
> I will be home shortly. I can't say where I am, only that
> I am being treated well. Kiss Maddy and Alex for me.
>
> Love,
>
> Andrew

He folded the paper in thirds and addressed the outside in large block letters.

Gomes, waiting outside his cell, nodded and took the note. MacCrimmon again thanked him for this exceptional act of kindness. Gomes acknowledged his thanks with a strange pitying look and shook his head. It was an odd reaction, MacCrimmon thought, but Gomes was an odd man.

The next morning, MacCrimmon woke as the guard arrived. In spite of his aches and pains, the howling of the prisoner in the next cell, and the light they left on twenty-four hours a day, he had slept better than he had since the last day he lay in bed with Karen. The guard slid his breakfast under the bars. Mixed with usual watery beans were white flakes of something he couldn't identify—his vision was still a bit blurry. He picked the tin plate up off the floor and looked more closely at it. Mixed with the beans were soggy shreds of the note he had written to Karen.

10.

THE AFTERNOON of the November 16th, the day Thomas Padgett threw MacCrimmon and the old man overboard, the Miesterdam's safety officer, William Dawson, questioned him. Dawson said three of the stewards had admitted knowing of the contact between him and MacCrimmon. Padgett readily admitted this. He said he was upset at MacCrimmon for paying a steward to get his name, a violation of his privacy, and he had taken him to task for it. Dawson had asked him why MacCrimmon would want his name in the first place. He said it must have been an imagined or unintentional slight, like maybe he caught him staring at his wife. He hadn't knowingly done anything to offend the man and he certainly hadn't thrown him overboard. He said MacCrimmon appeared unstable. Maybe he fought with the old man and they both went over the side. Dawson said this was unlikely to the point of absurdity.

Later, when Padgett talked it over with Vera, she asked if the wife had come up in Dawson's questioning. "Not a word about her. She must not have said anything."

Vera said with a contemptuous poof! that MacCrimmon's wife was one of those beautiful women who was all fluff and no fiber. She said she had written a note to her early that morning, warning her if she said anything of her suspicions to anyone, her children would be killed. She had included her address, 818 Mason in San Francisco, which she'd found on the internet, to add weight to the threat. Vera said the woman was too frightened they would hurt her little brats to ever cause trouble. "You can forget her, and without MacCrimmon's testimony they've got nothing. There's the possibility it was only MacCrimmon all along. Maybe he kept it from her, and she doesn't know a damn thing anyway."

"She knows more than a 'damn thing' now, you stupid broad!... What in the hell were you thinking? If she still has that note she may have your fingerprints, the most critical threat of all. We'll never be safe as long as she's alive and she has that note." Padgett marched around in a circle shaking his fists. "These bonehead stunts of yours—it's like you're *trying* to get us caught."

"I'll get it back somehow."

"Always let me know what you're doing. This is your second major fuckup. We can't afford any more."

Disembarkation, two days later, went off without a hitch. No one paid the slightest attention to Vera. Some people did gawk at Thomas but being a giant, and a gruesome one at that, this was nothing new.

They took a cab from the dock to the Fort Lauderdale airport where he rented a car for the drive to Tampa. With only five-minutes to spare they made the late afternoon non-stop flight to San Antonio on Southwest he had arranged weeks earlier. At 7:30

that night they retrieved his Mercedes from the long-term parking lot and drove the thirteen miles northeast to the Padgett home on La Tapiceria.

Vera didn't say so, but when Thomas pulled his Mercedes into the driveway of his Mission-style mansion he saw by her gawking she was impressed. "Nice, isn't it?" A hint of a smile was all she conceded.

They dragged the luggage in, deactivated the alarm system, and turned on the lights. He took Tamara's—now Vera's— luggage to the downstairs spare bedroom and suggested she tour the place before she unpacked. She returned a few minutes later. "Why did the two of you need five bedrooms?"

"We didn't. But we needed a big house, and when you buy a big house you get a lot of bedrooms." He told her of an exception to this rule he had read about in a trade journal: a winemaker in California's Napa Valley had built an 11,000 square foot house complete with a fifty-foot indoor swimming pool that had only two bedrooms.

"You could go days without seeing each other in this place," she said.

"Yes, we could—and we did."

She came out after unpacking and asked if there was any food. He asked her if pizza was okay. She said, yes, pizza was fine. He phoned an order.

The next morning he set Vera up at the table by the pool and gave her a list of PINs and passwords to memorize, and a pad of paper, a pen, and three examples of Tamara's signature. "This has to be perfect," he said. "I already got caught once forging her signature. It was nothing important—I wanted to see if I could get away with it. I couldn't."

Vera worked for two hours until the words and numbers blurred and danced before her eyes. She told Thomas she needed a break.

It may have been November but the day had turned quite warm. She tested the water in the pool with her hand. Thomas noticed. He said the water temperature was a uniform eighty-degrees all year round, thanks to a solar unit on the roof. She asked if she could take a swim. She said she swam at the YWCA pool in Buffalo. It was the only exercise she liked. He said he had no objection.

Vera came out a few minutes later wearing one of Tamara's one-piece bathing suits. Thomas poured a cup of coffee and took a chair under the overhang, out of the sun.

Vera swam well, unlike Tamara who only occasionally went in the pool on the hottest days of summer, confining herself to the shallow end, flopping around like a dying fish. He lit a cigarette and contemplated Vera. She and Tamara looked almost exactly alike when dressed—butt ugly—but in a bathing suit there were differences. Vera was firmer and she had nicer legs, and where Tamara had had no tits at all, Vera at least had a little something, maybe because she'd had a kid. Vera had been a working girl which had kept her in decent shape, while Tamara, as Vera had remarked, had been a "lazy parasite" all her life. In his wide experience, slender women like Vera with not much upstairs could have nice bodies well into their sixties. But beyond Vera's appearance, inside, under her hard, bitter shell, there was something smoldering, he could feel it.

Watching her do a backstroke, difficult as it was to believe, he felt a little stirring below his equator. This couldn't happen. Too much was at stake. He retreated into the house.

At lunch time, Vera checked the refrigerator but found nothing. "What do you eat around here?"

"We had a cook. She did all the shopping. I let her go, and the maid, too."

"Somebody's going to have to shop unless you order pizza every meal."

"It won't be me. I don't do shopping."

"I'll go. Where's a store?"

He told her. He said she could take Tamara's Mustang. "It'll be a good test to see if you can get money out of an ATM with her bank card."

She returned an hour later with two bags of groceries and plopped them on the kitchen counter. "Piece o' cake. I put in a card, punched in four numbers, and, *voilà*! Out came two-hundred dollars."

For lunch she whipped up tuna salad for sandwiches, heavy on the mayo the way he liked it, slathered it on sour dough bread, and topped it off with a thick layer of crunchy lettuce. The sandwiches were very good and went well with the Lone Star beer she had bought. He told her so, and she smiled at the compliment.

Nibbling daintily at her own sandwich, she said, "I hope you don't mind—I bought a bottle of Jack Daniels. I could never afford it before."

He shrugged his permission. "I like Maker's Mark myself but, sure, go for it. It's Tamara's money, don't forget; in fact it's *your* money, as soon as you get her signature down pat."

She wiped her lips with her linen napkin tented over her forefinger. "You said she had nine-million?"

"All invested in stocks, bonds, REITs, ETFs, MFs, commercial real estate. It brings in about half a mill a year.

That afternoon Vera worked another two hours outside on the table next to the pool, memorizing important dates and putting names to people in photographs in case she ran across them. She was an unusually bright woman so by the time she quit she had pretty much mastered the basics.

That evening he barbequed the New York steaks she had bought while she made a salad and green beans. She set the table outside, including wine glasses. He picked one up, examined it, and looked at her with a raised eyebrow. "I bought a California Cabernet," she said. "I know diddly about wine, but I saw a 93 next to it, probably some kind of score. It was higher than the ones around it so I took a chance on it."

During dinner, one of the best he'd had in a long time, Vera remarked what a joy it was to cook on gas burners. Thomas admitted ignorance in this area. He said he could work the coffee maker and the toaster but that was the extent of his kitchen skills. The wine, as it turned out, was a perfect complement to the meat.

After dinner and cleanup—aided by a dishwasher, an appliance she hadn't owned in years—the pair sat outside in comfortable padded chairs and sipped bourbon. Vera returned to the money topic. "So, this half-million flows in automatically?"

"Yeah. Rents, dividends, stock sales, maturing bonds, they all go into the pot."

"But it must vary from month to month."

"Nope. It's set up so that each month forty thousand is automatically deposited into our joint checking account. That's the only time I have any discretionary spending. And Tamara set it up so that any month the balance goes over a hundred K the excess goes into her savings account which I have no access to."

Vera slowly scanned the house and pool as if appraising it. "A house this big and fancy must cost a fortune to keep up, I get that, but what did she do with the rest of the money?"

"Re-invested it. I didn't care. Up until six-months ago I had my own contracting business. When it went belly up and I had to sell it, and I had no income of my own, that's when I came up with the plan to do away with her."

An hour later, both a little tipsy, Padgett said, "You know, this is the first normal conversation we've ever had?"

"A place like this takes some of the edge off."

"Yeah, edges," he said with a wry chuckle. "With Tamara, every comment had an edge, some nasty retort. There was constant tension in the air, like if I didn't lock my bedroom door, she'd sneak in and stab me with a butcher knife while I was sleeping."

"I've been accused of that myself—the sharp retort, I mean, not the butcher knife thing." She poured another two fingers of JD. "You slept in separate rooms?"

"For the past five years."

"Why, in the name of God, did you ever marry the bitch?"

"Good question." He clicked his glass lightly against his lower teeth, taking time to answer. "I didn't have a lot of choices—I'm no Adonis, as you can see—and neither did she."

"Tell me about it," Vera said with a grunt. "I married *Jonathan*!"

"In the beginning I cared for her, a lot. She was sexy, she had a real strong drive, if you know what I mean."

"I know exactly what you mean. I'm her twin sister, remember?"

"Unlikely I'd forget. Anyway, in the beginning she was nice, treated me well, but that tapered off. And after she inherited your father's money she didn't need my income anymore. From then on she was intolerable. Life with her was hell."

The next days passed pleasantly. Vera memorized names and faces and practiced Tamara's signature, which like her handwriting in general, was rounded and childish. Vera wouldn't have been surprised to see little hearts dotting the i's. Her own writing tended to be square, upright, and business-like. But her forgeries were getting close. The rest of the time she cooked and cleaned up and did the shopping and, in spite of the cold weather, she swam every day. Thomas was away a lot, on business he said, and while he was home he caught up on the yard work—he had let the maintenance people go with the others.

At dinner the fourth night, a nice pot roast, Vera, now Tamara by mutual agreement, asked, "When did you want me to go to Nevada?"

The question caught him by surprise. He liked having her here. He had never eaten this well, even when they'd had a cook, and there was a calmness about the house, a tranquility he had never had with Tamara. Away from her hardscrabble life in Buffalo, Vera was becoming a nicer person. Beyond that, she had nice legs, and much of the time she chose not to wear a bra, a practice he approved of.

"You want to leave?" he asked in what he hoped was not too plaintive a tone.

"No, not at all! But you said I'd only stay a few days... But if I could stay a little longer I was thinking it might be good to really get into being Tamara. Someone is bound to see me, a neighbor, one of her acquaintances. The more I look like her and the more people get used to seeing me the better."

"Yeah, I agree, good idea. Anyway, rushing off and starting a divorce right after a cruise might raise some suspicions. Maybe we could have someone come in a couple times a week, you know, to clean the bathrooms, vacuum, that kind of stuff—temporarily, of course, until you're ready to go." Vera said that sounded good to her.

The next morning at ten the door chime sounded, startling Vera, cleaning up in the kitchen. She looked through the peephole at a large stout African-American man and a younger slender

Hispanic man. She panicked—what if these men knew Tamara?—but she calmed herself and opened. The large man said they were FBI agents. His name was Whitley, the Hispanic man, Andrade. They flashed badges and IDs. She smiled and invited them in. "What's this about, gentlemen?"

"Are you Mrs. Tamara Padgett?" Whitley asked. She said she was. "Is Mr. Padgett at home?" She said he was. She offered them coffee, which they declined, and suggested they wait outside by the pool while her husband finished showering. Fighting the urge to run she sauntered down the hall to his bathroom and knocked. Hearing what she thought was the shower she entered. He was naked, shaving at the sink with the water running.

"Sorry!"

He turned to her, making no move to cover himself. "What's up?"

She turned her head away and closed her eyes, but not before she saw he was endowed in direct proportion to his height. "FBI agents are downstairs. They want to talk to you.

"Shit! Tell them five-minutes."

Both agents were taken aback by Padgett's size, even Whitley who was a big man himself. The men shook hands and took their seats. Whitley explained why the FBI was involved and said they were talking to him because he was a material witness in two suspected homicides. "As you know, a Dr. Andrew MacCrimmon and a Mr. Hans Jeliksen are missing and are presumed to have gone overboard from the Miesterdam on Thursday, November sixteenth. There are suspicious circumstances involving you and Dr. MacCrimmon."

Padgett repeated almost verbatim what he had told Dawson, the shop's safety officer. Yes, he'd had words with the doctor, but he hadn't thrown him or the other man overboard. The two agents traded grim looks. They didn't believe him.

For the next ten minutes the agents alternated questioning him from different angles, but he always returned to the exact wording of his original statement, denying he'd had anything to do with the disappearance of the two men. "Someone must have seen what happened," he said. "Maybe it was caught on CCTV."

"Nope. No witnesses, no physical evidence, no motive."

Padgett smiled and spread his hands as if their problems were none of his concern.

Whitley rose and smiled back. "We'll have to dig all that much harder. Have a nice day, Mr. Padgett."

In the entry, on their way out the door, Whitley paused and tapped his lips with his forefinger. "Oh, yeah, I forgot to mention something. One of the IT geeks at our field office discovered a Mrs. Vera Snead had been reported missing by the management at her hotel. It seems she's Mrs. Padgett's sister. She hadn't been seen in four days and they said all her things were still there. This was exactly the same time you and the missus were in San Juan. Quite a coincidence, eh? Would you happen to know anything about that?"

Padgett paused a moment and snapped his fingers as if suddenly recollecting something. "Yeah, that *was* strange. Tamara and Vera and I were supposed to meet in San Juan, kind of a family reunion, but she never showed up. She and Tamara have had their differences so we figured she'd had second thoughts and had flown back to Buffalo."

"No, Mr. Padgett," Whitley said. "She didn't *'fly back to Buffalo.'*"

Padgett said to the retreating men, "Good luck in getting to the bottom of this."

Whitley stopped, turned back, and examined him as if he were a venomous reptile. "Oh, we *will* get to the bottom of it, Mr. *Padgett*, and we won't need luck to do it. Something will turn up that ties all this together. It always does."

Padgett had tried to keep the taunting tone out of his voice but he had failed.

Vera rushed over to him as soon as the men were gone. "I didn't catch everything you guys talked about, but did he say Vera—I—was reported missing?"

"It caught me like a punch in the face at first. But I realized it's all circumstantial. The body will be identified as yours. What motive would Tamara and I have for killing her poor sister?"

"Maybe," she said with the bitter scowl that had softened in recent days. "But the so-called 'circumstances' are piling up pretty fast." She marched to the kitchen and returned with half a glass of Bourbon. She took a large sip and, as if emboldened by the liquor, said as a harsh command, "Contact this Enrico person, Thomas! Tell him the job's finished, that he'll get his money, but tell him *not* to find her body, *not* to report it."

"What in the hell are you talking about?"

"It's obvious, Thomas... Think about it, for Christ's sake!... What a blunder! And it was in front of us all the time!"

"What was 'in front of us all the time'?"

"Why dig up the body at all?"

Vera had to smile at the brute's open-mouthed look of shock at this basic question. He went silent and furtively looked around as if seeking an answer in the kitchen appliances. "Which do you think the Puerto Rican authorities would devote the greater effort to, Thomas—a beheaded tourist or a missing person?... And if she were found, there would be a funeral where I might be recognized by coworkers or by Brian."

Thomas slumped onto a dining room chair and pounded the table with his giant fist. "I'm a fucking idiot... You're absolutely right."

"We're *both* idiots. We should have thought of this from the very beginning. Thank God we thought of it in time. Something else occurred to me. Say there was a letter to Brian, sent before the cruise ship docked in Puerto Rico, telling him of my meeting with his aunt, my estranged sister, Tamara, in San Juan, in two days."

"What, are you crazy?... The postmark would be about a month too late."

"See you in an hour." Vera slipped into sandals, picked up Tamara's keys and dark glasses from the bureau in the entry, and left by the garage door.

An hour later she returned. She called to him, where he was drinking a beer in the kitchen, "Give me twenty minutes, Thomas." He lit a cigarette and waited. Another cigarette later she joined him. She showed him a small envelope addressed to:

> SN Brian Snead
> USS Abraham Lincoln (CVN 72)
> Unit 100349
> FPO AE 09520

The letter inside written in Vera's spinsterish hand said:

> Sun, Nov. 12
>
> Dear Brian;
>
> I'm writing from the Double Tree Hilton in San Juan, Puerto Rico. I took a vacation after slaving away at Arvil trucking all these years. In 2 days I'll be meeting your Aunt Tamara to try to repair the separation between us. Write me how you're doing, and I'll let you know what happens with Tamara.
>
> Love,
>
> Mom

"Why did you cut out the area where the stamp goes?" Thomas asked.

Vera showed him a larger envelope of a cheaper grade of paper, this one without an address. A first-class stamp with the underlying square of paper from the smaller envelope was scotch taped to the right upper hand corner. "Follow me, Thomas," she said, and led him outside. She stepped in wet soil in a garden bed, placed the smaller envelope on the paving, and stepped on it, leaving a footprint over the still legible address.

Thomas crossed his arms and looked at her as if she'd gone crazy. "You mind telling me what the hell you're doing?"

"Read this." She showed him a second letter which read:

> To who it might concern.
>
> I found this envlope under some trash. It might have fell out of a purse or pocket. I see your one of our fighting men so I took the truble to send it on you. Good Luck.
>
> A frend

At Thomas's stunned look of incomprehension, she said, "Have Enrico fly to Dallas. Say you'll meet him there—you might be seen here in San Antonio. Have him copy Brian's address on the larger envelope in his own hand. Take some gloves so he doesn't leave fingerprints on either the envelope or the letter. Have him re-write the note exactly as I've written it on the piece of binder paper I folded up inside, then have him put his note and the smaller envelope in the larger envelope. Tell him to post it when gets back to San Juan."

Thomas grinned broadly as the fog cleared. He shook his head in wonderment at the woman's cleverness. "So, this backs up the story I told the Fibbies about planning to meet Vera. *And* like you say, the cops in San Juan aren't going to waste too much energy on a missing person. *And* we eliminate one whole potential complication by not having Enrico find and report the body. With MacCrimmon dead and them having no body, no witnesses, and no physical evidence, there's only one problem."

"The MacCrimmon woman, you mean? We can only pray she doesn't have the note anymore. Besides, if she did have it she would have already given it to the cops."

He gently stroked her cheek with his massive hand. "That's damn good damage control, m'lady."

She smiled sweetly. "Why, thank you, Thomas."

11.

MacCRIMMON knew something was up as soon as "Thuggo"—the name he'd given to the brutal guard—opened the cell door. Instead of the usual insults, he beckoned with his finger to follow him. On the way down the corridor to Abrantes' office he gave him none of the usual slaps to his head or shoves in his back. Two stern-looking men in clean well-pressed army uniforms watched him enter. Abrantes, looking sheepish, hung in the background. The older, sterner of the two, a trim distinguished-looking man in his sixties with a cold military bearing, ordered Thuggo to manacle the prisoner's hands. During this operation MacCrimmon saw the date on the calendar behind Abrantes' desk: *Diciembre* 6. He'd been in the Mariendo jail since November 19th, two and a half weeks. Seventeen days without a shower or a change of clothes; his food, inadequate and often contaminated— once with human feces; his drinking water, foul—twice Thuggo had pissed in it in front of him; and twice Thuggo had beaten him with a stiff rubber hose. His only companion had been Teofilo. The rat had become so accustomed to the bedraggled human he had twice sniffed his fingers.

The two officers, who must have been Abrantes' superiors, had barely glanced at MacCrimmon when he came in and they had ignored him as if he weren't there when he asked who they were and what was happening. The younger officer spoke sharply to Abrantes whose shame-faced response both men found unsatisfactory—this much MacCrimmon could tell without understanding a word of what they had said. The junior officer snatched a file from Abrantes' hand and motioned for Thuggo to take MacCrimmon by the arm and follow them. Outside MacCrimmon scrunched his eyes shut and turned his head away from the unaccustomed blazing sunlight. Thuggo dragged him to an ancient transport van and opened the rear doors. MacCrimmon paused on the top step and turned back. "*Mierde pendejo cabron*," he hissed, the only Spanish curse words he knew, and spat the mouthful of mucus and saliva he'd collected full in the man's face. Thuggo clenched his fists and bellowed something, but at a sharp command from the younger officer he backed away, cursing. The officer pointed to a bench along the side and closed and locked the back door.

An hour, maybe two hours later, MacCrimmon heard a metal door clatter open and close again. The van stopped, a guard opened the door. He stepped out into a large dark steamy-hot, warehouse-like space built of concrete blocks. Two thin young guards wearing over-sized military fatigues led him down a corridor to a small office. The older, sterner, of the two officers, a general, he heard someone say, took the chair behind the desk; the other officer stood behind him to one side. At a finger flick from the grim general one of the guards punched MacCrimmon hard in the right flank, over his kidney. He hunched over and let out a sharp groan. The standing officer, a thin, handsome man in whose sparkling eyes, as difficult as it was to believe, MacCrimmon read both compassion and humor, spoke for the first time. He translated in excellent English what the general had said: "The blow was punishment for cursing and spitting at an officer of the law... If that brute hadn't been such a disgusting pig, the punishment would have been much worse." He had added this last on his own, MacCrimmon was sure of it.

The general turned the questioning over to the younger officer, who introduced himself as Colonel Ramon Ximenez. "The general wants to know why a dangerous spy such as yourself would turn up in a backwater like Mariendo."

MacCrimmon ignored the irony in the question. "Where am I, Colonel?"

"Holquin Provincial Prison. Holquin is the capital of the province... Again, how did you end up in Mariendo?"

MacCrimmon repeated his story about being thrown overboard and two days later being rescued, near death, by two fishermen. The ridiculous spy story, he said, was concocted by Captain Abrantes. He had punched the captain in the nose for trying to steal his watch. Colonel Ximenez looked away a moment, chewing his upper lip to keep from laughing at MacCrimmon's exaggerated dead pan delivery of this farcical statement. He translated for the general, who nodded gravely.

MacCrimmon stared ahead, expressionless, not making eye contact with either man. He didn't trust either the colonel's ironic tone, which he might be faking to lure him into an indiscretion, or the general's supposed ignorance of English.

"You see, Doctor," Ximenez said, "we received an anonymous phone call saying a castaway had been arrested in Mariendo. This was a local matter—we had no interest in such a thing and said so. The caller said the person was a notorious spy. At this point we had to act—at a development like this the general himself had to become involved. It turned out it was a hoax. The only reason the caller made this accusation was to force us to investigate. You must have made a friend, Doctor."

It had to have been Dr. Donato, getting me out of Abrantes' clutches.

"But as you said, Doctor, the accusation is ridiculous. You are no spy. But what you are is a terrible embarrassment to us."

"Why is that, Colonel?"

"You are dead, yet you live."

"Your definition of living must be different from mine."

"Whatever the definition of 'living,' you are officially dead. You made that fool Abrantes the laughingstock of the entire region after word got around you had punched his nose, something half the population of Mariendo would love to have done. He lost face, though I would think losing a face like his would be a blessing to everyone, including himself."

MacCrimmon resisted—barely—the temptation to laugh or smile and looked straight ahead.

"He didn't dare kill you, which he would love to have done, so he did the next best thing—he proved you were already dead."

MacCrimmon, showing animation for the first time, asked, "How did he do that?"

"He sent your wedding ring, your knife, the key to your suite on the ship, a sample of your tissue for DNA testing—some stuff a doctor removed, and a box of ashes he claimed were yours to the U.S. Embassy in Havana. He said in his report that your body was too chewed up by sea animals for identification and in the interest of public safety you were cremated immediately."

"Assuming the embassy people believe this—"

"They would have no reason not to."

"—the news will be passed to my wife, my family."

"Presumably."

MacCrimmon pounded his manacled hands against his chest and threw his head from side to side. "I'll kill him for this!" he screamed. "I don't know how, but I'll kill that piece of shit for doing this!"

The general rose and bellowed for the two guards, who came in and roughly grabbed his arms.

"Doctor," Ximenez said softly, "I know how upset you must be, but calm yourself, for your own good... You must understand the general's position. What, he asks, are we do with a living dead man?"

MacCrimmon dropped his chin to his chest and took deep breaths. Tears came as he imagined Karen's distress when she was told of his death.

Ximenez gestured to the guards to release him and gave him time to recover. "The solution is simple, Doctor. The official story will be that you faked your own death, that you yourself provided these materials, and that you are indeed a spy."

MacCrimmon mumbled, "Yes, of course, I am an international spy who faked my own death so I could report on the contents of a village hospital room."

"So, you admit it," Ximenez said, for the benefit of the record and the general, though he himself, as he had said several times, thought the idea was ludicrous.

MacCrimmon sniffed and clumsily wiped his eyes with his manacled hands. Looking directly at Ximenez he said. "What Abrantes has done—with your help—will cause my wife inhuman suffering and may cause her death. Without her I have no reason to live, so, yes, I admit being a Goddamned spy! Shoot me, please, the sooner the better!"

Ximenez translated a summary of what they'd talked about to the general, leaving out, MacCrimmon guessed, the more lugubrious, melodramatic elements. The general seemed satisfied with his confession and being oblivious to the truth of the matter, or more likely, indifferent, he motioned for the guards to take the prisoner away.

The two guards marched him to a shower room where his manacles were removed and he was allowed to shower in tepid water. He saw in a scrap of mirror hanging in the shower how thin his face had become. His beard, now a half-inch long, had grown out grey. A bald-headed dwarf on a tall stool behind a counter issued him baggy underpants, thin black cotton trousers, and a pajama-like shirt to replace the rotting shorts and polo shirt he'd been wearing since he was taken from the hospital.

From the shower room the guards marched him down a short corridor into the main building where the cells were located, another two-story warehouse-like structure which housed, he guessed, about five-hundred prisoners. His cell was on the first floor, the fourth in a bank of twenty or thirty identical cells. It was a space about ten-feet by ten-feet, a cramped, airless, steamy hot room furnished with two sets of metal bunk beds catty-corner to each other, a crude metal toilet in one corner, and a small table near the bars. "*Espiar*," the guard said, as if warning the other prisoners he had a dread disease.

A scrawny old man whose wiry grey hair sprung out of his skull as if he'd suffered an electric shock stared at him a moment through oversized glasses. He crawled out of his lower bunk and held out his hand. "Rubio," he said. MacCrimmon smiled weakly, said his own name, and shook the man's hand.

"You speak English," the old man said with a heavy accent. "You are Irish?"

"Scots." It was better not to broadcast being an American. That would come out soon enough.

His other two cellmates, a thin young man with numerous garish tattoos—probably a common criminal—and an over-weight balding middle-aged man, glanced up but otherwise showed no interest in him.

Rubio opened his mouth to say something but MacCrimmon closed his eyes and shook his head to discourage any further conversation. He climbed up to the unoccupied bunk, the top one above Rubio, his by default. He lay on the filthy blanket, his arm over his eyes, imagining Karen hearing the news of his death. There had to be some way to get word to her. There must be someone in this miserable shithole who could call her, email her, maybe send her a letter, or at least notify the embassy he wasn't dead.

An hour later two different but identically dressed guards appeared. One of them piped in an adolescent voice, "*Tres-siete-ocho.*" "Three-seven-eight," Rubio whispered. "You must only answer to this number, never to your name." MacCrimmon said he hadn't noticed a number had been assigned to him.

The guards led him to an office where his fingerprints were taken and blood was drawn, skillfully he had to admit. Why they needed his blood, he couldn't imagine. Someone, a nurse maybe, rattled off a flurry of instructions, not one word of which he understood.

Walking back, he stared at some of the other prisoners, all thin and sallow, unshaven and filthy. One of the guards slapped the back of his head, a warning, he assumed, not to look at the other prisoners. The meaner of the two young guards pushed him roughly back into his cell.

A half-hour later lunch was served, a plate of soupy ground meat stained red by what might have once been a tomato, mixed with some kind of curd. Rubio said, "Picadillo, a classic Cuban dish. We get it three times a day."

MacCrimmon internally closed off his nasal passages and breathed through his mouth so as not to smell the nauseating mess and ate it all to keep his strength up.

"You must think this is a bad place." Rubio said,

MacCrimmon didn't trust Rubio or his other cellmates any more than he did Ximenez or the general. Any one of them could be a plant, reporting unguarded conversations. He said non-committally he didn't have a standard of comparison.

"The big prisons closer to Havana are much worse."

That afternoon the same guards reappeared and called, "378." This time he was ushered into a different small, hot, office, this one smelling of stale sweat and mold. A lean, balding, horse-faced officer in an ill-fitting, sweat drenched uniform introduced himself as Major Sanchez-Rios. He said in passable English, "I have questions about your spying."

MacCrimmon had decided within minutes of being accused as a spy he would not play their stupid game. He would not admit it, he would not deny it. He was also determined to avoid the wiseass remarks that had gotten him in so much trouble over the years, nor would he be impudent or impolite.

"You are accused of spying, *Señor.*"

"Yes, Major, that's what Captain Abrantes said. He's in charge of the police in Mariendo."

"I know who he is, *Señor*... Do you deny the charge?"

"No."

"So, you are a spy?"

"That's what he said."

"But what do *you* say?"

"If I denied it, whom would you believe, me or him?"

His lips trembled in anger. "Don't play slippery with me, *Señor*! It will go hard for you."

He said calmly, "How much harder can it go for me, Major? I'm stuck here for what may be the rest of my life. I've been declared dead, so my wife may die of grief and—"

The major chuckled and waved his hand as if this nonsense was a foul-smelling gas he was dispelling. "Come, come, *Señor*. That is not how women behave. They are much stronger than men. Your wife will marry someone else in six-months."

"I hope you're right, Major. My children will need a father."

The major rose, circled around behind him, and slowly paced back and forth. "You interest me, *Señor*. Tell me about yourself, where you were born, your education, how you ended up here."

MacCrimmon gave him a three-minute summary of his life, from age five to being plucked out of the Caribbean by two fishermen.

The major returned to his chair. He leaned back and pressed his laced fingers across his chest. "So, you're a doctor. And on this cruise ship you discovered a murder, but you're the one being punished. Ironic, no?" Not waiting for an answer, he asked loudly and abruptly, as if to shock MacCrimmon into a disclosure, "Where did you do your spying?"

"My 'spying,' as you call it, is nothing more than looking at things, places, people. And I had no access to anything other than my hospital room and the Mariendo jail so if I were reporting to some mythical superior I would be a disappointment."

The major scowled and waved his hands. "Yes, yes—tell me what you saw."

"When I regained consciousness, I spied on the hospital room where I was confined. And the people walking by in the corridor, of course. And when I went to the jail in Mariendo, I spied on Captain Abrantes and Thuggo."

"Who is Thuggo?"

"The thug who beat me up and threw my food on the floor—and pissed in my drinking water… Oh, and Teofilo."

"Who is this Teofilo?"

"The rat who shared my cell and my food with me."

"A rat. Of course. And what did you find in the Mariendo jail?"

He leaned forward and said in a confidential whisper, "Captain Abrantes is a mean and stupid man."

The major called the guards and told them to take him back to his cell. As the guards were dragging him away, the Major said, "You were right about spending the rest of your life here—and it will not be a long life."

MacCrimmon smiled back at him. "I hope you're right."

Over the next week MacCrimmon adjusted to the routine. He ate the slop they gave him and did not comment on it. Once a day he was allowed an hour in the exercise yard, a half-acre square bounded by buildings on two sides, and on the other two sides by a chain link fence topped by coiled razor wire. He kept his eyes down and looked no one in the face.

In his cell on even days he did pushups on the floor and pull-ups on the bunkbed railing; on odd days, he did sit-ups and squats. An hour or more a day—however long it took his head to fill to the bursting point—he learned Cuban Spanish from Rubio. He knew little Spanish but it was enough to recognize that *Cubaño,* as Rubio called it, with its silent terminal s's, slurred consonants, among other idiosyncrasies, was different from the way Lena Montoya had spoken Mexican Spanish. Lacking writing materials his lessons were entirely conversational, and Leandro—Rubio's first name— being an ex-university professor, was a hard task master.

MacCrimmon hadn't asked but Rubio must have sensed his curiosity about why he was here. "Participated in a pro-democracy demonstration," he whispered. Regarding his other cellmates— MacCrimmon hadn't said a word to either of them—Leandro said the young boy was a thief and the pudgy middle-aged man was guilty of "economic sabotage." He had illegally tipped two of his employees in his clothing factory as recognition of their exceptional work.

Every other day MacCrimmon underwent interrogation with the major. Prisoner 378 had been accused of being a spy so it was up to the major to provide some basis for the accusation. The major knew he was no more a spy than the general or the man in the moon so the frustration with his impossible task often bubbled out as anger—he even slapped prisoner 378 in the face for what he had thought was an impudent reply. 378 had merely said there was a triad of questions one considered when investigating a crime—did the perpetrator have the means, the motive, and the opportunity to commit the crime—and he had blandly pointed out he'd had none of them. Far from being angered by the major's bitch slap, 378 had said without a trace of irony that he recognized the hopelessness of the major's task and he would like to help him any way possible, short of incriminating himself. This angered the major even more.

MacCrimmon suspected the interviews were being recorded, and the major was coming off looking rather badly while he himself had said neither anything which might substantiate their accusations nor anything offensive.

On his way back to his cell from his last interrogation, a squatty brute of a fellow pushed his shoulder and hissed, "*Yanqui espiar!*" MacCrimmon ignored this taunt from an obvious provocateur. The general and his minions, whoever reviewed the recordings, must have felt a change in tactics was in order. He glanced at his guards who were looking blankly into the distance. "*Traidor,*" the man bellowed. The idea he had "betrayed" Cuba was so ridiculous he had to laugh. This angered the man. He went into a fighting stance, bobbing his closed fists around. MacCrimmon knowing what was coming, let his hands fall to his sides, giving the impression he was passively accepting whatever was coming. The brute curled his lip and moved his right shoulder, telegraphing his punch. He pulled his fist back to strike. MacCrimmon hit him on the right cheek with a lightning quick left jab, which surprised the man. He followed with a hard right from the shoulder to the man's nose. The brute staggered back, holding his hands over his face.

This was what the guards and the general had been waiting for. Dr. MacCrimmon was hauled before Colonel Ximenez. He asked, "What is your excuse for this?"

The way he asked, he tried to give the impression he didn't know the man he had hit was a provocateur. All the more reason not to trust him—as a high ranking official the colonel certainly would have known about a plan to provoke him. Prisoner 378 said he had no excuse. He should have let the other prisoner hit him.

Colonel Ximenez said he had no choice but to sentence prisoner 378 to a week of solitary confinement for fighting.

It was a hellish week in the six-foot by six-foot-square windowless, airless room, empty except for clouds of mosquitos and a thin feces-stained mattress. His only light was a single weak bulb which the guards turned on and off arbitrarily. For his listening enjoyment the guards played loud repetitive music twenty-four hours a day. His only distraction was studying the

Spanish-English dictionary Ximenez had allowed him at the time of his sentencing but reading it was only possible during the hours the light was on.

His term served, Dr. MacCrimmon was escorted back to his cell on Monday, December 25th.

12.

SATURDAY, December ninth, was a day of celebration for Thomas Padgett and Vera Snead. Both the local and national news outlets had reported that, following the notification of the family, the second man lost overboard from the Miesterdam had been identified as Dr. Andrew MacCrimmon of San Francisco. His body had washed up in Cuba, and the identity of his remains had been verified by DNA analysis. Dr. MacCrimmon was known for—"

Padgett clicked off the TV. He didn't want to hear MacCrimmon's biographical details or speculation about his killer. He had been uneasy about what he had done from the beginning and it was worse now that it was certain he had killed him.

Vera, still looking at the blank TV, said, "We should know soon whether the wife is going to make trouble. I was wondering if I should go out to Frisco and take pictures of her little darlings as a reminder to the lady to keep her mouth shut."

"Absolutely not! The cops, the FBI, have nothing on us, Vera. Let's make damn sure we don't *give* them anything."

"Whatever," she muttered, and took a sip of Bourbon. "At least with him dead we're one step closer to getting away with it."

That evening Thomas suggested her impersonation of Tamara had been so effective they might try it out at a restaurant he and Tamara had gone to three or four times.

Thomas vetoed her first outfit. "You look too good. I'm not saying you should wear the clown dress, but cover your legs, maybe with slacks." He pointed at her chest, "And she didn't have tits like yours."

Vera smiled and cocked an eye at this backhand compliment. She returned to her bedroom and changed into a pair of Tamara's slacks and a loose silk blouse that made her look flat-chested.

By the pool that night, after several drinks beyond their now customary nightcaps, Thomas congratulated her on how well she had done. The Maitre'd at Giuseppe's had greeted Mr. and Mrs. Padgett by name, passing Vera off as Tamara without the tiniest flicker. But Vera's eyes were closed and her head bobbed; she was too drunk to acknowledge his compliment.

"Why is it—," he belched into his fist, "Why is it you have tits and Tamara didn't?"

"Tits?... Oh, yeah, those... Uh, I got 'em when I was pregnant with Brian."

"Fascinating. Can I see them?"

"You want to see my li'l ol' titties?"

"Yeah."

She shrugged her indifference. "Why not?" She concentrated so intently on her clumsy attempts to unfasten the buttons of her silk shirt she drooled. She succeeded and spread her shirt open.

She did have tits, small cone-shaped ones, about the size and shape of those meringue cookies, not bad for a forty-two year old woman. He reached toward her, but she closed her shirt tightly and said, "No touchy." She was drunk, she said, but not that drunk. With that she crawled out of her chair and staggered off to bed.

The next morning at breakfast, Vera scrunched her eyes shut and pressed her fingertips against her temples. "God, what a headache!"

Thomas, grey and haggard, was in no better shape. "We have to watch ourselves. As drunk as we were, something might have slipped out."

Vera took a deep draught of orange juice and blotted her mouth with her napkin. "Speaking of 'slipping out,' did I really show you my tits last night?"

"Yes, you did."

"Why?" she asked. "Why in the world would you want to see them?"

He gawked her, squinty-eyed, to see if she was joking. "Why do you think? Because you turn me on. Why else?"

"I?... Turn you on?" She chuckled in disbelief. "I've never 'turned on' a man in my entire life, Thomas."

"Well, you turn *me* on."

At this, yet another proof most men were both stupid and crazy, she shook her head which brought on a wave of pain. She grimaced and scrunched her eyes shut. When she recovered she said in her executive secretary voice, "What we're doing here is all business, Thomas, so don't get any ideas." Still, when she leaned back in her chair, holding her mug of coffee in both hands, she was smiling.

That day and the following Saturday and Sunday they were cool and business-like with each other, as if they had both exposed areas of embarrassing vulnerability.

Monday, the eleventh of December, Thomas flew to Dallas to meet Enrico, as they'd planned. He met him at the arrival gate and led him to a semi-deserted café. "You got her buried all right, Enrico?"

"Piece of cake. Her head's in fifty-feet of water."

Thomas had him put on latex gloves. He showed him the sealed letter, explained what it was, and watched him copy the address to the outer envelope.

"Why is the stamp taped on, Hoss?"

"The idea is, the guy who finds the letter is too cheap or too poor to buy a stamp, so he used the one on the envelope he supposedly found on the street."

"Clever. You want I should copy this note on this other paper?"

"Yeah, exactly as she wrote it."

"'She'? The woman's still with you?"

"Yeah, she is. Hard to believe two twins could be so different."

Thomas examined the note Enrico had copied in his messy scrawl. He pronounced it satisfactory and supervised him as he folded it and stuffed it into the envelope. He again told him to mail it as soon as he got back to San Juan. He looked around. Seeing no one was watching, he pulled a brick-sized package wrapped in a kraft paper grocery bag from his back pack. "Sixty K, Enrico, for a job damn well done."

Enrico thanked him for his generosity and arranged the package in the bottom of his own backpack. "You're sure about me not finding the body, Hoss?"

"Yeah. We never should've planned on finding it in the first place."

"It didn't seem to make much sense." Shaking Thomas's giant hand, Enrico said, "Any more projects, keep me in mind. It was a pleasure doing business with you." He waved over his shoulder and lumbered away to his waiting area.

Thomas had finished much sooner than he had anticipated. Not relishing a three-hour wait he splurged and bought a return ticket on Delta loading in twenty-minutes.

Thomas got home two hours earlier than scheduled. Opening a beer at the kitchen sink he saw Vera swimming. She was nude. He watched her swim laps, sidestroke. When she changed to backstroke he pleasured himself.

Five minutes later, she climbed out of the pool. He rushed to the entry, closed the door loudly, and dropped his backpack with a bang. He was fetching a second beer from the fridge when Vera came into the kitchen wearing a robe, rubbing her short hair with a towel.

"You're home already."

"I finished with Enrico sooner than I expected. I got an early flight. Everything went smooth as silk."

Vera tossed the towel on the kitchen table. She fetched a lowball glass from the cabinet and poured two-fingers of Bourbon. She leaned back against the counter and held her glass at chin level, smiling.

"What's up with the lop-sided grin?"

"I saw you watching me."

"Yeah? It'd be hard not to."

"So, I really *do* turn you on?"

"That's an understatement. It's like when Tam and I were first married. But if you *saw* me, why did you keep swimming?"

"It was strange—it was exciting being watched. I haven't thought about you-know-what in years. All of a sudden it's like something's crawling around in my belly. It's a completely new feeling. It was never that way with Jonathan."

"He was your first?"

"And last."

"You mean in all those years you never, uh—"

"Nope, not once."

"It's about time for a change, isn't it?"

"Give me a few days to think about it."

"Take all the time you need."

The next morning Vera came to breakfast wearing makeup, an effort she had never wasted on him before. She had done her short hair in a special way and had topped it all off by wearing a loose grey silk sweater without a bra. She was still no beauty; nevertheless, there was an elegant sexiness about her, an exotic Egyptian look, like those pictures in pharaohs' tombs. "Remember about a month ago," she said, "when we talked about me going to Nevada?" She smiled at his immediate look of panic.

"You want to go?" he said leaning toward her as if to hear her more clearly.

"No, of course I don't. But our plan called for the divorce. I wondered if you wanted to go forward."

"There's no rush on the divorce—we can do that any time down the line... But, uh—"

She had to hide her smile in her napkin. The big oaf was blushing. "What, Thomas?"

He looked down, drawing designs on the tablecloth with the handle of his spoon.

"Yes, Thomas, what is it?"

"It's that, uh, I don't want you to go, Vera."

Vera feigned shock. "Wow! I don't know what to say." She looked up at the ceiling as if seeking the source of this miracle in the ornate light fixture. "I'm shocked. It's almost like a marriage proposal."

He flashed a boyish grin, grotesque coming from him. "I don't need a proposal, we're already married. All but the honeymoon."

She reached over and took his hand. "What a relief. I was afraid you'd send me away. I never want to go, Thomas. It's been heaven living here."

He bent down and kissed her fingers. "Maybe we can hire a cook, and someone to help with the cleaning."

"That would be nice."

That afternoon, an unusually warm day for December, Vera came to the pool wearing a robe. She slipped it off, letting it fall to the ground. She stood naked a moment, and dove in. Padgett, watching from the doorway, came out and took a chair next to the pool. He smoked a cigarette watching her swim laps. Seeing her up close this way he was able to add a firm little butt to her growing list of charms.

She stopped, suspended, treading water, and called to him, "Come in, Thomas."

"Sure thing." He stubbed out his cigarette. He stripped off his T-shirt, slipped out of his shorts and boxers in a single motion, and jumped in feet first. Vera swam to him and tried to duck him, but he was too big and strong. He picked her up and held her, squealing, over his head as if she were a trophy and let her slip down facing him. He put his arms around her and pressed her to him. She clamped his erection between her slender thighs and pressed her open mouth against his. He fumbled around, but she said, no, she wasn't ready, it had to be in bed. They hauled out of the pool and she led him by the hand to his bedroom, dripping water along the way. She had him lie on the bed and told him she'd be right back. She returned from the bathroom with a tube of lotion. "Use this," she said, "and go gently and slowly. It's been a long, long time."

As the days passed Thomas realized he had awakened a slumbering wolverine. Vera's enthusiasm for the new arrangement exceeded even his own; a few times he'd had to plead exhaustion.

While a disinterested outsider might still consider Vera mirror-smashing ugly, Thomas no longer saw her that way. As well as he was eating, as tranquil as the house was, as happy he was in general, he wondered if his feelings for Vera were more than mere lust. If so, it would introduce complications.

But their pleasant equilibrium didn't last long. Two days before Christmas, a nasty rainy day, a heavy-set, middle-aged woman, her short-cut blonde hair matted down with the rain, came to the door. "Oh, hello, Mrs. Padgett," she said, drawing her head back in surprise. Nervously, as if she expected a beating, the woman offered up with both hands a nicely wrapped package about as large and heavy as a dictionary. Vera took it and stood staring at the woman. "Oh, stupid me," she said smiling. "Come in— and thank you."

The woman's smile faded. She looked at Vera suspiciously and made no move to enter the house. "Is something wrong?" Vera said.

"Yes, I'm sure there is."

Both women turned to look at Thomas trundling down the hall from his office in his clumsy caveman style of walking. He grinned when he recognized the woman. "Marcia. So good to see you again."

"I dropped by to wish you Merry Christmas, Mr. Padgett, and to tell you I found a new job. It's okay, but it's nothing like Padgett Construction."

He stepped back and invited her in with an expansive arm motion.

"No, Mr. Padgett, thank you. I have to be going." She cast a questioning look at Thomas and hurried back down the walkway.

The front door closed; Vera clicked the deadbolt. "I need a drink." On the way to the kitchen she dropped the package Marcia had given her in the trash. She leaned against the counter holding a half-glass of Bourbon against her chest. "The bitch knew immediately I wasn't Tamara."

Thomas, chewing the knuckle of his right thumb, nodded agreement. "It's your New York accent."

"So, what do we do, Thomas?"

"The problem is, you don't look like Tamara anymore, you don't sound like her. You look happy, your makeup is way better, you do your hair better, you dress better even though they're the same clothes, and you're healthy and fit. The dead giveaway, though, was being pleasant to her. Tamara hated her. She found out we'd been, uh—"

"Yeah, I get it."

"Another thing—Tamara never answered the door. It was always Pilar, the maid."

"Why did she come here?—and what will we do?"

"Why did she come?... Beats the hell out of me. Maybe she heard Tamara was getting a divorce and she thought the two of us might start up again. Her coming was so unlikely I didn't think to warn you about her... What'll we do? That's a tough one. We'll probably have to reconsider the Nevada divorce thing."

Vera took a long sip of Bourbon and grimaced at the burning in her mouth and throat. "Do you have this sickening feeling in your gut that the whole plan is beginning to crumble?"

"Snap out of it, Vera, for God's sake! We knew there'd be moments like this and we knew we'd have to work around them. I'll figure something out. But one thing's for damn sure—we can't afford many more fuckups like this. As step one, do *NOT* answer the fucking door!"

13.

HUMAN BEINGS do adjust, always have adjusted, to the most trying of circumstances, and Prisoner 378 was no exception. The weeks passed and by February the morbid depression that had settled over him during and after the holidays had lifted somewhat. He imagined—and hoped—Karen had survived and was over the worst of her grief.

His lessons in Spanish with Leandro had progressed well enough he could carry on a simple conversation. He passed a few words with his middle-aged cellmate, though these were few and only in private as the man was loath to be seen talking to an American spy. He wasted no time or breath on the young thief who was nothing more than a sullen mute.

He continued his exercises to keep his strength up but the number of reps he could do steadily diminished as he lost muscle mass, about twenty-five pounds, he estimated. Food was always on his mind; he was constantly hungry. He asked Rubio why some prisoners ate better than others. Rubio said these were the lucky few who could afford to pay the guards for such things as milk, cheese, sausage, meat, and fresh vegetables. Prisoner 378 was penniless so there was no hope in that direction. He had to make do with the slop served to him three times a day.

His interrogations every other day with the major continued but being unable to shake Prisoner 378 the major had become increasingly frustrated, sometimes slapping, even punching him. MacCrimmon bore these attacks with no change of expression, and there was never any question of striking back, but his very

111

forbearance was seen as taunting by the major and angered him even more.

More than the brutality, what bothered him was the tedious repetition of the same questions over and over: "Who do you work for?—Why did you come to this part of the island?—Who did you spy on?—Were you sent specifically to spy on the prison?" MacCrimmon answered as he always did, with some variation of, "I'm retired, I don't work for anybody; the Caribbean currents brought me here; I spied on the hospital people and Abrantes' jail." As far as the prison went, he said, that was an accident over which he'd had no control.

Between bouts of questioning the major complained constantly to Prisoner 378 that he was being pressured from above to get results. Prisoner 378 sympathized with him but said he couldn't embarrass his own country by being convicted of spying. He reminded the major that the general, or whoever was in charge, could manufacture a confession and testimony any time he wanted and force him to sign it. Who would know? The major huffed in indignation and said this suggestion was preposterous. He shook a length of rubber hose in criminal 378's face and reminded him Cuba was a nation of laws!

February became March, and MacCrimmon endured the ridiculous situation of being verbally and physically abused one minute by the major, the next minute being asked questions about American baseball. The major, it turned out, was a baseball fanatic and he deemed it a rare privilege to be able to talk directly to a man who lived in a city whose team, the Giants, had won three world series championships in five years. MacCrimmon liked the Giants, watched them on TV when he could, and went to Oracle Park once in a while, but he was no expert. The major refused to believe a man as fortunate as prisoner 378 wouldn't know the batting averages or the names of half the players on the Giants team. MacCrimmon, being a sensitive, caring person, and not wanting to disappoint the major, supplied the Giants with players named after political figures, such as the "Golden Polish Infield" of Lewinsky, Kopechne, and Palinsky, and the famous battery mates, Delco and Duracell, and the 143-dollar outfield of Sanders, way out in left; Manchin, in center; and Limbaugh in right—far-right. He wanted to tell the major about the Rice-a-Roni bullpen of Suso, Condoleezo, and Jerry, but he dared not. Even *he* might catch on.

A week later the major threatened prisoner 378 with the rubber hose for making a fool of him with those idiotic names that weren't baseball players at all. "But Major," 378 said with a look of offended innocence, "everybody in America plays baseball. We're all baseball players." The major suspected 378 was toying with him, and threatened him again but, as he hadn't yet hit him with the hose, he didn't this time either—and he never would.

All in all, the major wasn't a bad sort. He admitted he was a family man with three kids and a wife. And his questioning according to Rubio could have been much, much worse.

A more ominous change was the increasing attention he was getting from a prison gang leader, Humberto Llerena, a tall, hulking, brute with a glossy shaved head. Llerena, Rubio said, was a patriot and it galled him to have among them a creature who spied for the arch devil, America. At first he and his cronies merely spat and cursed him when he walked by in the exercise yard, but gradually the affronts escalated to shoves, having his feet stepped on, being pinched on the arm by a weasely little guy with missing front teeth. They couldn't openly beat him—there were at least nominal rules against fighting—so MacCrimmon bore the torment with a show of indifference: he would rather suffer a thousand beatings than go to solitary again.

Rubio had noticed Llerena's antipathy toward 378. Back in their cell he had whispered a warning to MacCrimmon to avoid him at all costs. He was a very bad man imprisoned for smuggling. For years he had bought off the authorities and had operated with impunity, but when the new general came to power, Llerena and many like him were arrested along with the corrupt officials whose palms he had greased. Still, he had a substantial fortune, and lived about as well in the prison as was possible. Though it had never been proved, he was suspected of having killed two prisoners who had been enemies on the outside. But attempts had been made on his life too, several of them. It was thought one or two had been ordered by prison higher ups who feared his power, both inside the prison and outside.

Another month passed and the insults from Llerena's thugs ramped up—punches to the back, spitting in his face, a superficial stabbing to his arm by the sharpened handle of a toothbrush. Leandro advised him never to complain about these attacks. If word got out, and Llerena were punished, it might go very badly for him. MacCrimmon assured him he'd never had any intention of complaining.

In early April events took a surprising turn. For days tensions had risen between Llerena and another thug named Rene Clemente, a shifty-eyed muscular bloke whom Llerena tormented mercilessly. One day, unable to tolerate Llerena's goading any longer, Clemente attacked him from behind, repeatedly stabbing him with a shard of glass with a shirt wrapped around one end as a handle. Most of the wounds were clumsily delivered superficial punctures of his shoulder and back, but one wound was a gaping four-inch laceration of his scalp. Llerena's minions pulled Clemente away and the guards hauled him off. Llerena stood a moment, dazed. Blood rushed from his scalp in pulsating waves. He closed his eyes, his head wobbled, and he sat heavily on the ground.

MacCrimmon knew from his professional experience it was possible to bleed to death from a serious scalp wound—he had done autopsies on auto accident victims who had suffered injuries much like this. If no one intervened Llerena would likely die. MacCrimmon was sorely tempted to look the other way but the pull of being a doctor proved stronger than his dislike of the man. He pulled off his shirt and cried in his limited Spanish for everyone to get out of the way. He pressed his shirt over the wound and ordered Llerena's lieutenant to press it tightly. The man balked, seeing the flooding gore, but MacCrimmon, in that special voice of authority that allows doctors to put their fingers in the cunts of queens and to berate with impunity sadistic despots for their unhealthy eating habits, ordered him to do what he was told. He turned and shouted in Spanish for someone to fetch the doctor.

A nervous minute later a guard reported the doctor had been last seen, drunk, leaving the prison. MacCrimmon would have to do what he could himself. The larger vessels that had been transected needed tying off and the wound needed suturing. He had one of the onlookers who knew a little English ask if anyone could supply a needle and thread. One old man said he had such things. A guard accompanied him back to his cell. A minute later the old man returned and handed MacCrimmon a needle—fine for sewing rough prison clothing but a million-dollar lawsuit if used by an emergency room doc in the U.S.—and a long hank of coarse black cotton thread. Lacking soap, MacCrimmon asked if anyone had a match to sterilize the needle, but matches were contraband so if anyone had one he wasn't admitting it. MacCrimmon told the English speaker to explain to Llerena he couldn't clean the wound properly or sterilize the needle and thread so there might be superficial infections. Llerena looked up at him in dull-eyed incomprehension.

MacCrimmon washed the wound with water and pulled the flap of scalp back. Through the pooling blood he identified two small arteries pumping with rhythmic vigor. These he tied off. He had the lieutenant reapply the shirt and put pressure on the wound while he tried to thread the needle, but his hands were too gummy and slippery with blood. He gave it to the old tailor to do the honors. He pinched the wound together and placed individual sutures at quarter-inch intervals. After each stitch he had the lieutenant blot away the blood, still seeping out of the now-sutured laceration. When he finished he called for more water. He cleaned his hands, wet the shirt, and washed off the wound. A few droplets of blood still exuded but the main bleeding had been controlled. Llerena, who had borne what must have been ferocious pain without a word or a tremor, looked up dumbly at MacCrimmon, now struggling back into his wet, blood-soaked shirt—prisoners were punished for damaging or losing state property. MacCrimmon cocked his head and, admiring his neat suturing job, said, "Frankenstein."

In the ensuing weeks Prisoner 378 was left alone; there was no more tormenting. Llerena had shown no outward gratitude for having his life saved but every three or four days a guard brought a paper sack with a sausage, some cheese, and powdered milk. These he shared with his three cellmates.

The prison doctor was impressed with what Prisoner 378 had accomplished under the most unsanitary conditions, but Llerena did in fact develop a few small infections around some of the sutures but these healed once the stitches were removed. The scar would be noticeable but not at all hideous.

Llerena may have ignored him—he was miffed at being called "Frankenstein," one of the other prisoners told him—but many of the other prisoners took to calling him *"Yanqui espiar,"* not in a nasty way, but in an ironic, affectionate way, asking him who he was spying on today. He got a big laugh when he said he was the president of the Unites States and he was going to have them all released. Some of the prisoners came to him for medical advice and treatment, though there was little he could do. He did reduce an index finger a guard had dislocated, and he lanced some abscesses with a razor blade a guard let him use. Abscesses were common because of the poor diet, unsanitary conditions, and the prevalence of insects.

Early May there was another big change. By this time he had been a prisoner in Holquin Prison for five-months; it had been six-months since he went over the side of the Miesterdam. He had lost thirty pounds by his most recent estimate. His hair had not been cut that entire time and his grey beard, unshaved since the second day in the Mariendo Hospital, was now about three-inches long, the length of his forefinger.

Prisoner 378 would no longer be interrogated by the major—the major himself informed him of this. His case had been turned over to Colonel Ximenez, the acting commandant of the prison. The general was the official commandant, but he was seldom on site, having several other prisons to oversee.

The next day the guards escorted 378 to the grander but still primitive office of Colonel Ramon Ximenez. The colonel dismissed the guards and motioned with a waving finger for Prisoner 378 to take one of the four metal chairs facing his utilitarian metal desk, which, prisoner 378 opined to himself, looked like it had been purchased at an Arkansas DMV surplus sale. The colonel leaned forward, laced his fingers and planted his forearms on the desk. "We put a stop to that farce being played with Major Sanchez-Rios. No one in his right mind thinks you're a spy. But this begs the next question: if you're not a spy, why are you here?... You are a terrible embarrassment to us."

MacCrimmon leaned forward and said with more animation than he had shown—or felt—in a long time, "You said early on that I was an embarrassment. I'll tell you what, Colonel. Send me home, by plane, by fishing boat, I don't care. You have my word as a gentleman I will say I was rescued near death and cared for until I recovered and was returned home."

"Believe it or not, that is an option we considered. While I believe you're an honorable man and would keep your word, your pathetic physical state puts the lie to that idea. But that was only one of several options. Your final disposition is working its way up the ladder now. The final decision will be made in Havana."

"What's that disposition likely to be?"

The colonel leaned back in a sprawl and raised his forefinger. "Option one we have already discussed. He raised two fingers in a "V". "Option two. We shoot you. You disappeared in the ocean, you were never here, case closed. The problem with that is, a good many people know you *were* here and word would get out, it always does. According to a news report from Miami you are a person of some notoriety in San Francisco. If word got out we had liquidated an innocent castaway, especially one as notorious as you, the world would be outraged. Believe it or not, we *do* care about world opinion... Option three"—he raised three-fingers— "we continue the spy farce and exchange you for Cuban prisoners in the U.S."

"Ridiculous," MacCrimmon said chuckling.

"The absurdity of the suggestion is a good measure of our frustration." The colonel leaned forward, over his desk, and said softly, "Doctor MacCrimmon, there is a fourth option."

"Why are you whispering?"

"Here is a test to see if you are indeed the honorable man you claim to be. If you betray me, both of us will be killed."

"Betray you?" MacCrimmon shook his head in confusion. "How could I do that?"

"Suppose I helped you escape."

"'Escape!'... What kind of idiot do you think I am? With talk of escape you'd have a reason to kill me."

The colonel said with a bitter smile, "We don't need 'talk of escape' to kill you, my friend, if that's what we wanted to do. But, if you want to go home, it is the only option. And you will have to trust me as I trust you."

"Say I agree. How will it be done?"

"I have no details. I only know it will require a great deal of thought and planning... You are wealthy, I assume."

"I am—or was. I've probably been declared dead, so all my funds will have gone to my wife. However, I have another source, a secret one. And if that fails, I have relatives who will advance me the money, but that would entail abasement I would prefer to avoid."

"How much would you commit to this endeavor?"

"A million dollars. Cash, gold, whatever you want, in a numbered account. Delivery would be your option."

The colonel smiled and said he was satisfied with this sum. "You understand this will take time. The arrangements must be made with the greatest care and secrecy... And what security do I have that you will keep your word?"

MacCrimmon said in a level tone in which no ambiguity could possibly be read, "My word needs no security, Colonel. And for my part, how do I know you're not recording this to use as a pretext for having me terminated?"

Colonel Ximenez rose and extended his hand across his desk. As MacCrimmon shook it, Ximenez said laughing, "Why, I hadn't thought of that, Doctor. Thank you."

One of the two guards marching him back to his cell, a stout chap named Escarra, a little less objectionable than the others, winked at him, he was sure of it. Not trusting Ximenez completely and Escarra not at all, he didn't acknowledge it.

The guards had no sooner locked him in than Rubio began one of his long, meandering discourses. MacCrimmon liked the old man, but he could be garrulous and this was not a good time. He excused himself; he said he had some thinking to do.

Lying on his bunk, his eyes closed, this little spark of hope illuminated how deeply he had been mired in what Bunyan had called the "Slough of despond." Or as Dante said it,

> *Per me si va ne la città dolente,*
> *per me si va ne l'etterno dolore,*
> *per me si va tra la perduta gente.*

He *had* passed through the suffering city, if the prison qualified as a city. It *was* a place of eternal pain, if there ever was one. And not only had he walked among lost souls, he was one of them.

Two days later an edict came down from on high: foreign journalists were visiting the next day to investigate reports of prisoner abuse. "All prisoners are to shower and clean themselves up," the edict stated. "You are to wear the clean clothes provided to you. If they should ask you questions you must be very careful how you respond."

In each cell the guards placed the more presentable prisoners in the front and, as MacCrimmon was judged one of the more presentable—he had showered and tied his long wavy brown hair in a neat pony tail—he and the middle-aged man sat at the small table next to the bars while Rubio and the young thief were consigned to the shadows of their bunks.

Midmorning a group of ten or twelve men came through, four of whom were prison officials, including Colonel Ximenez; the rest, a hodge-podge of slender-stout, tall-short, old-young men speaking softly in a German which, by the accent, MacCrimmon guessed was

Swiss. He tried to inconspicuously read his Spanish-English dictionary but a young man noticed him and called to him in clumsy Spanish, "*Señor*, what are you in here for?"

He resisted the impulse to answer in German; instead he said in Spanish, "I am a thief, *Señor*. I rob tourists once too many time."

"How do you find the conditions?"

"It's not heaven, *Señor*—it's a prison—but it's not hell either."

Ximenez explained to the gentlemen that Prisoner 378 was a con man who had been able to gain the confidence of tourists because he looked like an American.

The next day MacCrimmon was ushered to the colonel's office. He said with a wry smile, "'Not heaven and not hell,' eh?"

"You realize, colonel, I could be on my way home now. All I had to do was tell them in German, which I speak fluently, that I was an American castaway being held illegally. But that might have caused you embarrassment and it might not have worked. If not, it would have meant trouble for both of us. You should take it as a demonstration of the value of my word."

"Impressive," he said. He leaned back, smiling, fiddling with a pencil. "You are a most interesting character, Prisoner 378. Tell me about yourself, your background, education, what you did for a living."

It was the exact same question Major Sanchez-Rios had asked him when he first arrived. He answered exactly the same way.

"This business on the ship," the colonel asked, "this creature who threw you overboard, he will get away with it?"

"Not if I ever get home."

"What will you do to him?"

"Kill him."

The colonel raised an eyebrow. "So many people toss this threat around, sometimes for the weakest of reasons. Have you ever killed a man?"

"Yes. Several. Four I shot with bullets, one with blanks; one I stabbed; one I threw off a nineteenth-story balcony; and one I killed with a rock—he was an accident, I was aiming for his friend. If I get the chance I will add Abrantes to the list."

"Abrantes?" he said, jerking his head up in surprise. "Oh, but of course, Doctor, you wouldn't have heard... For his gross mishandling of your case, he was fired and sent to a remote mountain mining village as chief of a two-man department. This was in spite of his uncle, who is an influential power in Mariendo. Tragically, two months later he was murdered. The assassin has not been caught."

MacCrimmon looked down, cursing softly. "I had hoped to do it myself. I suppose that means the watch my grandfathers gave me when I graduated from medical school is now lost for good."

"His effects are probably in storage somewhere. Let me see what I can do—as a gesture of good faith... You may go now, but the next time we meet, explain to me how I would get access to this million dollar sum you casually throw out."

"Before I go, Colonel, what if someone were to anonymously call the US embassy and tell them I was here. If you, or someone you trust, could do this I'll pay you the same million."

"if that were possible," the colonel said, "I would have suggested it. But the minute your embassy notified the officials in Havana, you would be disposed of to avoid the scandal and the embarrassment."

14.

THOMAS and Vera passed Christmas day the same as they would have spent any random weekday in October or June—no tree, no gifts—and New Year's was notable only for the skull-splitting intensity of their hangovers.

The holidays behind them, these two non-celebratory people settled in as a married couple. But unlike most married couples, they had little in common. She read thrillers and magazines, he read the newspaper; she liked PBS, he, shoot-'em-ups; she liked soft rock, he, country-western. But for all their differences there was a strong adhesive uniting them which neither would have predicted: sex. The first weeks were a true honeymoon. Sex in every room of the house at any hour of the night or day; sex from behind while Vera was cooking; sex in the morning, Vera climbing on before Thomas was awake; sex in the shower; sex on the dining room table.

But with time enthusiasm waned, as it did with most couples, and their old differences and antipathies resurfaced. Sex became something done in the dark by two people who couldn't stand to look at each other in the light. To Vera, Thomas was again a loathsome brute whose only virtue was his priapism, someone she used as a fleshy, body-temperature sex toy with smoker's breath; and to Thomas, Vera had become the second iteration of the bitter shrew he had dispatched and buried in Puerto Rico, a creature whose only point of attraction was at the juncture of her skinny thighs.

Thomas was spending most of his time out of the house, looking for investment properties, he said. Vera too spent a lot of time away from home, shopping, getting to know San Antonio, a city she liked more and more. In fact she liked the city well enough she was willing to endure Thomas, at least in the short term, enough for her to deflect talk of the move to Nevada, a topic Thomas was pursuing more often as their relationship deteriorated. Vera had other plans that did not include Nevada. These she did not share with Thomas.

Weeks passed and the inevitable encounters with acquaintances occurred, even with some of Tamara's old friends, and no one had been in the slightest suspicious. They grew increasingly confident Tamara was indeed behind them.

In mid-March. Thomas took a call on the phone in his office. He brought the handset out to Vera, reading in the living room. "It's Brian," he whispered. *"Damn!"* she mouthed, and snatched the handset:

"Hello, Brian. This is your Aunt Tamara. I don't believe we've ever spoken. Where are you?"

"I'm on leave in Buffalo, taking care of my mom's stuff. Her disappearing, leaving her hotel and never coming back, it's bogus, not like her. There's something fishy about the whole thing. What I'm calling about, I got this letter from her she must have dropped in the street—it showed up a month after she disappeared. Somebody forwarded it. She said you were on the island at the same time. You have any idea what's going on?"

"We were supposed to meet, Brian, but she never showed up. We've contacted the San Juan police, but they've come up with nothing."

"It's, like, really strange."

"What is?"

"Talking to you, it's like talking to her. Your voice is exactly the same, the same pauses, the same New-Yorky way you say R."

"Well, we are identical twins. By the way, Brian, how are you doing, with the service and all?"

"How do you know about that? You never gave a shit about me or my mother all those years."

"That was a sad misunderstanding. But about that letter she sent you—what did it say?"

"Only that she was meeting you. I turned it over to the FBI. They said it may be connected somehow to a double murder on a cruise ship—that's the fishy part. How in the hell could Mom be mixed up in anything like that? The cops found a whole bunch of fingerprints on it. They're sorting them out now, trying to find the person who sent it."

Vera poured a glass of Bourbon, drained half of it, and reported the conversation to Thomas. "It's bad," he agreed. "Enrico was in stir so his prints will be in the database. But we can only hope he had enough sense to wear gloves when he mailed the letter, and that the prints are Brian's and the mailman's, whoever."

"Didn't you remind Enrico?"

"I didn't think it was necessary." He rescued the handset she was dangling over the tile floor between her thumb and forefinger. "What was it like talking to your kid?"

"Like I said, Thomas, we've never been close."

Over the next couple of weeks, as cracks formed in the plan they had so recently congratulated themselves on, Vera made alternative arrangements. At first nothing big, a new bank account in the name of "Vera Vissley," her maiden name, an identity she proved with her birth certificate. She had brought it from Buffalo hidden in her cosmetics case for an eventuality of this sort. She would gradually write checks to this account to be used in an emergency if the plan was blown and Tamara's assets were locked. The Tamara scam would eventually come to light, there was little doubt about that, and Vera Snead would someday be pronounced dead, but it would be a while before they traced her back to Vera Vissley. By that time, she would be long gone overseas with a new identity.

The bank account had gone so smoothly she took the next step: she rented an apartment, again under the name Vera Vissley. She found a quiet second story one bedroom on Sunset, closer to downtown. Using her new Amazon account, she ordered a folding card table, a simple kitchen chair, and a lamp. She told the concierge to put the packages in her unit when they arrived. She also told him to make the unit available for the phone company for a landline and internet service. She planned to spend no more than an hour or two there at any one time—Thomas might get suspicious—so she didn't plug in the refrigerator, didn't bother with sheets and blankets, and kept only the most basic items in the bathroom. She did keep two of Tamara's business suits in the closet along with a few pieces of underwear and two pairs of shoes.

The next day, after Thomas left on whatever his errand was, she returned to the apartment, changed into Tamara's blue business suit, and visited Charles Schwab on Broadway, a mile from her apartment. She needed a large investment house so she could do business anywhere in the country. She opened an account in the name of Tamara Padgett. Thomas had all of Tamara's passwords and secret questions and PINs for the Southwest account, so he was probably keeping track. When the time came she would relocate to a distant part of the country and would move all the investments *en masse* from Southwest to Schwab where Thomas could no longer monitor them, too late for him to do anything about it.

A lovely early April day, Vera settled into her hard little chair at the rickety table, booted up her new laptop, and logged into the Southwest Investments website using the password Thomas had given her. Breathing hard, her fingers trembling, she liquidated a small investment account, a hundred K and change Tamara had established soon after their father's death, and transferred the entire sum to her new account at Schwab. A message popped up saying the transfer had been successful and the funds should be available in a day or two. She gave a wiggle of joy and relief. Manipulating in seconds a sum that, six months earlier, would have taken her twenty-years to save, gave her a thrill she could only describe as sexual.

That same afternoon Thomas received another call from Brian:

"You're married to my mom's sister, so you'd be my uncle, right?"

"Right... I guess you want to talk to my wife."

"No, I'll talk to you."

"Yeah? What about?"

"Bad news. They found mom's body."

"What?! Vera's dead?"

"Murdered. Robbed. Her wallet was empty. Some kids found her in a shallow grave in the woods in some nature preserve."

"How do they know it's her?"

"Whoever offed her left her ID, passport, all that stuff, with her body. They couldn't get no fingerprints; she was too far gone. But they kept some stuff for DNA, just in case."

"Was she, uh, mutilated in any way?"

"'Mutilated'? You mean like cut up?... I seen the X-rays and nothing was missing."

"X-rays?"

"Yeah, they took X-rays of her whole body. Standard Procedure they said."

"Thorough of them... Did you see the body?"

Yeah. They wanted an ID from someone who knew her. I said it could be her, but she was a mess so I couldn't be sure."

"Yeah, I imagine. How are you taking it?"

"You mean, like, am I sad?... Yeah, sure I am, I guess. But me and mom, we weren't real close."

"You going to have a funeral?"

"No. I already had the body cremated. We'll have a memorial service in Buffalo. I didn't figure you'd come so I wanted to tell you she was dead. I'll let you tell that woman who says she's my aunt. I doubt she'll be too upset."

Thomas hung up the moment Vera pranced in the front door. She was grinning for some reason. As soon as she saw the look on his face her smile vanished. "What?"

"Brian called. Some kids found Tamara's body."

"And?"

"I don't know if it's good news or bad. First of all, that fucking Enrico didn't cut her head off."

"So they can do dental comparisons?"

"Maybe, maybe not. They took full body X-rays. I don't know if those are good enough for a dental comparison."

"So they might go back later?"

"No. Brian had her cremated."

"Wow! That's initiative I never would have given him credit for. But they identified her officially as Vera?"

"From her IDs, all that, yeah. But they took samples for DNA, just in case."

"But that's great news!"

"Probably. But two things still stick in my craw. That goddamned Enrico. And those fucking X-rays."

That night something, maybe the equivocal news about the discovery of her sister's body, seemed to have aphrodisiacal powers. She was a screaming tigress.

The next morning Thomas called Enrico:

"You probably heard, they found Tamara's body."

"Yeah. About her head, Hoss. She was looking right up at me. It was too much. I planned to do it when I quote found the body."

"I'll need some of that money back. You didn't do what you said you would."

"Yeah. Uh, about the money, Hoss. I have to tell you, I'm in a bad bind. I need you to help me out."

"So, you didn't do what you were supposed to do, and now you're blackmailing me?"

"Ooh, Hoss, blackmail, a nasty word. Let's call it a loan between friends."

"A 'loan'? You lying fucking weasel."

"Bad choice of words, Hoss. I was going for fifty, now let's make it a hundred. Care to go for two?"

"I have you recorded."

"Yeah, you do. But you'd go down for murder one with special circumstances. Me, I'm an accessory, but all I did was bury the body. Come on, Hoss, think about it... A hundred K you can easily afford and we both skate. Put it in a locker at the Miami airport and send me the key."

"Yeah, so you can bleed me dry every time you want money?"

"No, no, Hoss... This is it. I got in way over my head with some bad dudes."

"As if I'd believe you, you lying sack of shit... And I'm not flying to Miami. It's the San Antonio Airport or you can go fuck yourself."

Vera, waiting in the hall outside the office, asked what he had said.

"He put the bite on me for a hundred K."

"What'll we do?"

"The deal is, I put a hundred grand in a locker at SAT and send him the key. He comes whenever he wants. No way to watch for him. Even if we did, he'd probably send someone else for the pickup. We have to get him where he lives."

"You mean go to Puerto Rico and kill him?"

"I mean *you* go to Puerto Rico and kill him. I'm a tad, uh, conspicuous."

"No, Thomas. That's where I draw the line. I won't kill anyone. Pay the son-of-a-bitch."

"You're saying you won't do this?—knowing it could ultimately cost us millions?"

"I won't kill anyone, Thomas, even if I have to go to prison."

He looked at her hard. "Okay... It looks like we have no choice. We pay the asshole. But since you're not pulling your weight in the homicide department I'll let you pay the hundred K, say, out of that account you liquidated today and sent to your new Schwab account—what's the number? 319-7363?—from your apartment on Sunset."

"Good God!" she screamed in wide-eyed shock. "How do you know that?"

Thomas observed that, when surprised, Vera's beady close-spaced eyes and narrow snout gave her the look of a frightened rodent. "You're not the first person to confuse *looking* like a dullard with *being* a dullard."

"But—"

"You don't need to know how."

"What are you going to do?"

"It's not what *I'm* going to do—it's what *you're* going to do."

Recovering her poise, Vera crossed arms and said with her customary sour grimace, "And what is that?"

"You are going to convert all the investments and this house from your *separate* property to *community* property. You may take your half, the half we agreed on in the very beginning, and go wherever the hell you want. We can't divorce right away, that would bring up nasty complications and troublesome questions, but I have no intention of marrying again, and I can't imagine anyone, no matter how desperate, wanting to marry *you*. I'll keep the house, but I'll compensate you for your half of the equity."

She said defiantly, "And if I don't?... Everything's in my, well, Tamara's name."

"You will suffer an unfortunate car accident, or maybe drown in the pool, or maybe die in a mugging—that would be a coincidence, wouldn't it? Remember, Tamara had no will, so if you die, since we had no kids, I'd get everything. We'll start the ball rolling tomorrow."

"I have to leave here?"

"Before the ink dries on the paperwork."

Vera slouched off to the kitchen, poured a full glass of Bourbon, and dragged out to one of the chairs overlooking the pool. Thomas poured his own drink. Passing the kitchen window he saw Vera's shoulders shaking. Hard as it was to believe, she was bawling. She had sniffled and wiped her eyes when he described the killing and the beheading of her sister but this was a whole different level. He shambled out and took the chair next to her. More out of curiosity than sympathy, he asked, "What's your problem?"

"I don't know if it's the same with other people, but I only appreciate something when it's taken away."

"What are you bawling about, Vera? You're still getting four and a half mill, closer to five when we throw in your share of the equity in the house."

"Good God, Thomas! How dense can you be?"

"Pretty dense, I can't deny that. Dense enough you'll have to clue me in."

"I love it here." She described 'here' by waving her glass in a wide arc. "I've never been happier in my miserable life... And I love San Antonio. Oh, yeah, I know, you think the Alamo and Riverwalk are touristy... But I didn't realize how much I'd miss it."

He rose and gently pried her drink glass from her hand. As violently as she was waving the glass around, there was a good chance she'd drop it, and the only way to find broken glass in a pool was to step on it.

Looking off into the distance, she said in a flat meditative drone, "Is there any situation in life more hopeless than being an ugly middle-aged woman?"

Being a *sour, deceitful*, ugly, middle-aged woman was worse, but Thomas kept this thought to himself.

She took her drink back from him. "Where will I go, Thomas?... I'll be alone. No one will ever want me."

"It's not my fault you tried to cheat me."

Ignoring this as a minor irrelevancy, she turned to him and put her hand on his arm. "You know what, Thomas, what I'll really miss?—the sex... Thirty years of my life without it, I get a taste of it, and it's over."

"You had a husband, didn't you?"

"Jonathan?" Him she dismissed with a huff of contempt and a violent wave of her drink that sloshed bourbon out on her slacks. "Jonathan was a eunuch. He was so preoccupied with his cases and his shenanigans, most of the time he couldn't get it up, and when he could, it was about as romantic as lying under a garbage bag full of lard."

He had to laugh at this. The woman could be funny.

She squeezed his forearm and asked in a pleading voice, "Where will I go, Thomas?"

With the talk of sex and feeling her hand on him, and seeing her uncharacteristically vulnerable, his first choice of a destination would have been the bedroom. Instead he reminded her they had a lot of business to finish and that would take time. If she closed her new investment and bank accounts, gave up her apartment, and paid off Enrico, he said maybe she could stay after all.

An hour later, sitting in bed, their backs against the headboard, Thomas snuffed out his cigarette and poured them each a fresh drink. Vera clicked her glass against his. "Okay, Thomas, how did you do it?"

"You mean track you?... Why, it wouldn't be prudent of me to tell you that, now, would it?"

15.

BY MID-JULY Prisoner 378's questioning had taken a turn for the worse, at least this was what Rubio had concluded from the bruises on 378's arms. By the painful way he climbed into his bunk, his legs and back must have been beaten as well, but 378, discreet as always, said not a word about it.

Otherwise 378's routine was unchanged. His Spanish lessons had progressed to the point where he could converse reasonably well on all but esoteric subjects. His exercises he'd had to give up because of his weakness, caused not only by the chronic shortage of food but, as he had discovered doing his morning business, he had round worms, *Ascaris lumbricoides*, if he remembered correctly from medical school. On the bright side, he was no longer persecuted by the other prisoners. In spite of his nickname, after the Llerena episode, word had gotten around that he was no more a spy than the colonel himself.

Two days later the guards again roughly hauled him to the colonel's office for interrogation. The colonel dismissed the guards and closed the door. "Those bruises," the colonel said, "are they painful?... I'm sorry about having to do that but if I was too easy on you questions would be asked."

"I understand, colonel. I'm feeble, and as easily as I bruise, I think I'm getting scurvy. I'd appreciate some orange or lemon juice."

"I'll see to it." He motioned to 378 to take a seat. "Dr. MacCrimmon, we are ready to plan in earnest. But first I need you to tell me how you will get access to your funds and how they will be made available to me."

"Yes, of course. First, getting the funds. My investments and bank accounts may have gone to my wife or they may be in probate, either way they won't be available. My next option is borrowing money from my brother and nephew, a path I would rather not tread, but I will if necessary... And there's, uh... " Prisoner 378 paused.

The colonel prompted him, "And path number three—you were about to say?"

"I have access to gold, a lot of gold, which I could sell if I had to, but I'd much prefer not to."

"How much gold?"

"Five-hundred and twenty pounds."

The colonel whistled at the amount. "You are indeed a man of surprises, prisoner 378. But as enchanting as it is to ponder that much gold, I'd prefer cash."

"How do you plan to collect your money, Colonel?—an associate, I assume."

"Oh, no, Doctor. In person. I have a nephew, a son of my brother, who is getting married in Tampa in September. Because I am a loyal and trusted member of the military I am being allowed a one-month's leave."

"In that case, I'll have my financial consultant establish an account. You can withdraw the money personally, or if you start a bank account, you can transfer funds."

"One-million dollars, you said."

"Yes, that's the sum we agreed on. I'll need easily remembered numbers, your birthday for example, for the account."

The colonel wrote out on a scrap of paper a string of numbers for MacCrimmon to memorize. He handed it to him and shouted in exultation, "One million dollars... imagine it!... A *million*!"

"Yes, colonel. But I would advise lowering your voice unless you were referring to the number of blows you're planning to give me. And I assume you'll be staying in the U.S?"

"Of course. With a million dollars I can afford to."

"Now for your part. How do we do this?"

"You, prisoner 378, are going to commit suicide."

"I've considered it enough times."

"You are going to slit your wrists with a contraband razor blade. Your body will be hauled away to the mortuary. You will be certified dead—again—this time for our records, and your body will be released to my cousin, Eddy, for transportation to a place called Playa el Salto.

"Who's 'Eddy'?"

"Eddy Sayas-Rivera, my sister's son. You will ride in a coffin marked *'Peligro! Cólera infeccioso!'* in case you are stopped by a patrol. Eddy will, of course, have all the proper paperwork signed by me."

"And I'll ride in a coffin?"

"Yes, a coffin. From Holquin it is about three-hundred miles, seven or eight hours."

"Why so far away?"

"Eddy has friends who have a boat there. And security there is slack, by Cuban standards. And it's better to drive a car the extra miles and cut down the miles by boat, which lessens the danger of being caught."

"If we're driving that far, why not take me to the embassy in Havana?"

"You want to remain incognito, right?"

"I don't want the people who did this to me to know I'm alive."

"Your anonymity would be lost at the embassy. More important, the car would be stopped ten times by the police before you got close to the embassy, and if by a miracle you did reach it, the high authorities in Havana would accuse you of some crime and your embassy would probably hand you back to us. The greatest American heroes are not to be found in your state department."

"Okay. Playa el Salto. Then what?"

"You will have to swim in the dark to a boat about a hundred yards offshore."

He closed his eyes. His heart pounded at the memories of two nights drifting in the ocean in the dark.

"Doctor, are you listening?"

He opened his eyes and raised his head. "Yes."

"You will be given flippers and a snorkel. The boat will pick you up."

"How about the *Guarda Frontera*?"

"In the kinder, gentler Cuba we no longer attack boats and shoot the people in them. The emphasis is now on preventing people from embarking in the first place—that's why you have to swim out to the boat. Once you reach the twelve-mile limit you will no longer be pursued."

"You said 'close to the keys.'"

"You will have to swim to shore, to a beach on Key West."

"How far?"

"A mile at least. You'll have a life jacket and a paddle."

"Currents? Rip tides?"

Colonel Ximenez shrugged and said he knew nothing of these things.

"I'm weak, Colonel."

"If we were to land you, and the boat and crew were detained, someone would talk, they always do, and my life would be forfeit. But a boat straying into U.S waters will simply be turned away."

"Colonel, I need protein—eggs, meat. I'm too weak to swim a mile."

"I'll see what I can do."

Two days later Escarra alone roughly pushed Prisoner 378 to the colonel's office. On the way Escarra said out of the corner of his mouth, "The colonel says from now on you can be handled by one guard, me."

The door closed, MacCrimmon took a seat. Colonel Ximenez said some additional elements of the plan had been worked out. "The suicide is arranged, and the guard Escarra has been bought."

"So I understand. Can he be trusted?"

"Oh, yes. He is corrupt and cunning, but most important, he is deathly afraid of becoming a prisoner here, so he will not betray us. But now, some details. First, the suicide. When the time comes, we will give you a plastic bag of pig blood. You will make some scratches on your wrist with a razor blade, then drain the blood all over yourself, and play dead. Escarra will come to fetch you for questioning but you won't respond. He will discover you in your bunk. He'll remove your cellmates and prevent anyone from getting close, including other guards. I will hurry to the scene and have you carried to the morgue, where the doctor, who will have been paid off, will certify your death. We're negotiating for a coffin now. By the way, I'm fronting everything, so I'll have to hit you up for expenses."

"Agreed. But where did you get the money? The expenses must be significant."

"Wealthy prisoners sometimes come to my attention. I show them, shall we say, special consideration."

"I see... What comes next in the plan?"

"Eddy is making the arrangements for the boat. That's the biggest expense, that and the extra gas."

"When do I go?"

"August 11th. There is no moon."

Ximenez reached into his filing cabinet and pulled out a sack. He laid out on his desk three eggs, a stick of dried sausage, and two oranges. "I am supposed to be interrogating you so we might as well spend the time profitably. Do you play chess, Doctor?"

"Yes, but very badly."

"Good. I play badly as well." He scratched his chin and said with a droll quizzical look, "I've never understood why, either. Top of my class in university and language school but I can't get the hang of the game." He pulled a chess board and a box out of another drawer of the filing cabinet and arranged the pieces while MacCrimmon wolfed down a raw egg, a bite of sausage, and an orange. The board prepared, the colonel suggested prisoner 378 should prepare himself for defeat.

The game progressed with a shocking incompetence, slightly greater on the colonel's side, a disadvantage he attempted to remedy by cheating. As great a chess imbecile as MacCrimmon was, he did know how the pieces moved and could count how many had been taken, so the colonel's 'fool's gambit,' as it were, failed. Their one accomplishment was ending in a three-piece stalemate, Ximenez' king on a,8, while MacCrimmon's king was c, 8, and his last pawn on d,6.

Ximenez leaned back and, grinning broadly, proclaimed himself the winner.

Prisoner 378 cried in high indignation, "That's bullshit, Colonel! It's a stalemate! Why are *you* the winner?"

"Because I could have you shot."

MacCrimmon, peeling his second orange, nodded, conceding defeat. He congratulated his adversary on the persuasiveness of his argument. But squinting menacingly he said, "You better hope I never get you on a basketball court, Colonel."

As the time to leave drew closer, MacCrimmon thanked Leandro Rubio for being a good teacher, a guide through the perils of prison life, and a good friend when he needed one badly. "When will you be released, Leandro?"

"I'm still awaiting my court date. It could be months."

"Do you have family?"

"I do. A dear wife, a daughter—," with a dubious look he rocked his extended hand back and forth, "—and a beautiful granddaughter, the joy of my life... And you, *Señor*, you have said nothing of your family."

"I too have a dear wife. If she is alive, she and my two beautiful children are waiting for me."

Rubio whispered, "When do you think you will get out?"

MacCrimmon whispered back, "The colonel is convinced I am a spy. It may be years, if ever."

Rubio closed his eyes, shook his head, and smiled knowingly. "No, *Señor*. You will be out of here much sooner than that. You smell of oranges. The colonel would never give a spy an orange."

Five days before he was to leave, MacCrimmon had his last meeting with the colonel. "The last pieces are in place, Doctor. Eddy has hired the boat and bought the extra fuel. He will drive you to a deserted area of shoreline. You will wait until complete darkness. When the boat flashes three times, swim out to it. The trip to Key West will take about seven hours. Eddy has all the details."

The colonel leaned back, looking steadily at MacCrimmon, drumming his fingers on his desk.

"What, Colonel?"

"It is unlikely we will see each other again, my friend."

"I would hope that is not true. You can always reach me at the email address I gave you. Contact me when it's convenient; I'll fly anywhere to meet you. I can't imagine anyone I'd rather have as a friend."

The men rose and shook hands. "God protect you, Doctor."

"And you, Colonel Ximenez."

16.

THE MORNING of August 11th, Escarra led Prisoner 378 to the colonel's empty office and closed the door. He gave MacCrimmon a single-edged razor blade, a quart Ziploc bag containing blood, and a clean shirt. "Hide the blood in the shirt."

When he returned Prisoner 378 to his cell, Escarra said tauntingly to Rubio and the others, "The colonel says your friend the spy is being moved to *Combinado del Este*." He said to MacCrimmon, "Get your things together. I will be back in an hour."

Rubio watched him depart, shaking his head. "Oh, *Señor*, that is terrible news. Some say it is the worst prison in Cuba."

"No, Leandro," Prisoner 378 said, patting the old man's arm, "I won't be going there." He asked that he not be disturbed and climbed up on his bunk.

Half an hour had passed. While his cellmates were distracted eating the mid-day meal, MacCrimmon gritted his teeth and made three superficial horizontal cuts on his left wrist. When enough blood was oozing to be credible, he opened a corner of the container of pig blood. Making as little movement as possible, he leaked it over his wrist and side.

Escarra returned fifteen minutes later and called his name. Prisoner 378 didn't respond. He shouted his number again and threatened him with a beating. Seeing no reaction he entered the cell. He climbed up and shook the inert prisoner. He pulled the blanket away. Seeing the blood, he checked his neck for a pulse. He shouted to Rubio and the others, "Everybody out! 378 is dead. He cut his wrists!" He shouted to another guard, "Get the colonel, 378 committed suicide!"

Five minutes later the colonel arrived. "What's going on?"

"It's 378, Sir. He cut his wrists." The colonel checked the corpse, verified he was dead, and ordered the body covered. He had Escarra and two other guards lift the body onto a gurney and told them to take it to the morgue.

Before they wheeled the body away, Rubio, weeping quietly, said, "*Señor* Colonel, may I say a prayer for him. He was a good man. He was my friend."

The colonel gave permission with an impatient flutter of his fingers. Rubio knelt next to the gurney, folded his hands against his chest, and mumbled a prayer. The colonel, seeing the old man was too weak to rise on his own, helped him up.

The trip on the rumbling gurney—one wheel was crippled—took about thirty seconds. Metal doors banged; the gurney stopped. MacCrimmon's eyes were closed and his face covered but he recognized the morgue by the chill and the smell. The prison doctor, breathing alcohol fumes and emanating the odor of an old man who didn't bathe frequently enough, pulled the sheet back. He checked MacCrimmon's pulse and did something else—he couldn't see what. The doctor said, "The prisoner is dead, exsanguination." Someone replaced the sheet over his face and he waited.

Half an hour later he heard voices, doors opening and closing, and a long clunking noise followed by what sounded like the whine of a cordless screwdriver. Another clunking noise, and hands lifted him, shroud and all, and placed him in a narrow wooden box that smelled of fresh pine. The top was replaced and screwed down leaving him in complete darkness.

He felt the box being carried by hand, not on a gurney, and being slid into what he assumed was a van of some sort. He vaguely heard voices, a door slammed, the engine roared, and the vehicle moved.

Ten, perhaps fifteen minutes later, he heard the crunching of gravel and the vehicle stopped. Someone opened the rear door and again he heard the cordless screwdriver. The top was pulled away—none too soon, the air was getting foul. After he had adjusted to the bright light he had two immediate impressions: the nauseating viscous stench of rotting meat, and a broadly grinning round face sporting a single gold incisor. The face said, "Welcome to freedom, *Señor.*"

"You must be Eddy." The man said he was. "I need to stretch my legs, Eddy."

"Okay, *Señor*, but not too long. Patrols come by once in a while."

"Army?"

"No, *Policia National de Carreteras.*"

"What is that godawful stink?"

"Rotting cat. If we are stopped, the smell and the sign on the coffin will keep the police from opening it."

MacCrimmon clambered out of the coffin and slid out the back of the vehicle. He introduced himself formally and shook hands with Eddy, whose round body complemented his round face. If there was indeed a food shortage in Cuba Eddy was not one of the sufferers.

While he stretched, MacCrimmon examined his remarkable conveyance, a Cadillac ambulance from about 1952. Someone had painted it lime green with latex house paint, sparing only the pink left front fender; the hubcaps, the painter had done in a tasteful glossy black.

Eddy had pulled off on a gravel road in a forest of lush trees and undergrowth MacCrimmon couldn't identify. He breathed in deeply the hot humid air, heavy with the smell of mold and the cloying scent of sweet flowers. This was the first time he had been outside in nine months, other than the dusty gravel exercise yard in the prison.

He ambled fifty yards down the road, rotating his arms and breathing deeply. When he returned Eddy pulled a bucket of water and a sponge from a compartment in the front for him to wash the blood off his body. That done, he immersed his shirt in the bucket and scrubbed the seven-inch blotch of blood. It faded, and while it would be identifiable as blood if one looked closely, it wasn't conspicuous. He was buttoning the sopping shirt when Eddy told him to hurry, they had to get going. He helped MacCrimmon back in the coffin and handed him a spoon and a plastic container of black beans. He said he could sit up but he should be prepared to lie back down at a moment's notice.

The Colonel had said it was 575 kilometers to Playa el Salto, 360 miles, MacCrimmon calculated. It would take a little over eight hours, barring delays, which would get them to the beach about eight o'clock.

They had driven three-hours when Eddy said there was a traffic backup, probably a random checkpoint. He pulled over and replaced the top of the coffin and screwed it on. Twenty-minutes later Eddy stopped. MacCrimmon heard raised voices and someone opened the rear door. A flurry of curses followed. Whoever it was must have caught a whiff of the rotting cat. The door slammed shut and someone pounded on it as if punishing it. Someone else shouted something and Eddy drove off.

MacCrimmon expected him to stop and remove the lid but he drove on, mile after mile. MacCrimmon pounded on the lid and kicked and bellowed but Eddy couldn't hear him over the loud salsa music he was playing.

Half an hour passed. MacCrimmon, breathing rapidly in the foul air, was within minutes of passing out when Eddy stopped. MacCrimmon used his last bit of strength to slap the top of the coffin. Seconds later Eddy removed the lid. MacCrimmon took great gulps of fresh air.

"I'm sorry, *Señor*, I forgot—"

MacCrimmon hissed, panting for breath. "Imagine... coming all this way... only to... suffocate in... a fucking coffin!"

"The music, *Señor*, it is—"

"Loud, yes, very loud!"

MacCrimmon sat up and peeked through the ragged dusty curtain covering the window. They had stopped at a gas station. Eddy meekly suggested the doctor should lie down in the coffin. He replaced the top but left a two-inch crack for air. He said they would be on their way again as soon as he filled the tank.

Over the remaining five hours Eddy twice stopped for bathroom breaks, food, and gas, but the trip was otherwise uneventful. From the little he saw, Cuba was a lovely country, one he would like to visit with Karen if the politicians could ever sort things out, and those psychopathic Castros were replaced.

Two miles east of Playa el Salto Eddy stopped opposite the beach where he said *Señor* MacCrimmon must wait for the boat. He handed him a snorkel and a pair of black fins. He waited as MacCrimmon tied his Huaraches together with a long string to hang around his neck as he swam. He looked up and asked Eddy why he was grinning. Eddy held out a small lumpy white envelope. MacCrimmon opened it. The Rolex watch his grandfathers had given him fell out. It was running; it was 8:30. It would be a two or three-hour wait. MacCrimmon pounded Eddy on the shoulder. "Tell that cousin of yours when he gets to the U.S. we're going to have the biggest party in the history of the world."

Eddy lamented he couldn't attend. He said he had best get going—the ambulance was a bit conspicuous. MacCrimmon thanked him, shook his hand, and waved as he drove away.

He crossed the street to a beach littered with large rough boulders. He selected one that shielded him from the road and sat behind it in the sand to wait.

A few people wandered by, but no one paid any attention to the emaciated, bearded, long-haired tramp in the damp blood-stained shirt. Dark came, he was alone. He lay in the sand and slept.

It was 10:30 and pitch dark when he woke. It was still a little early but he sat up and scanned the sea. He was still so sleepy he had to force himself to keep his eyes open and to concentrate. He dared not look away for more than a few seconds for fear of missing the signal.

By 12:00 it was clear the boat would not be coming. He curled up in the sand and slept, too tired to consider the consequences.

He woke before sunrise, thirsty and ravenously hungry. He had no money—the boat not showing up hadn't occurred to anyone—so he couldn't buy food, and he dared not beg for any. His only option was to wait here and hope they came this night.

A little after noon he asked a passing ten-year old boy in his accented Spanish if he had water or if he could get some. He said he was very thirsty. The boy ran back the way he had come as if terrified. MacCrimmon knew he should flee but he didn't have the energy. He lay back, waiting for whatever or whoever would come.

A thin, dark, hawk-faced woman, holding the hand of the boy who had run off, approached and gave him a one-liter bottle of water. While he drank she looked him over. "You are an escaped prisoner, aren't you?" He couldn't risk offending her by lying. He admitted he was. "My husband—Miguel's father—is in prison... Are you waiting for a boat?" He admitted this as well. "Take your shirt off. Anyone could see it's prison clothing. Give it to me." He obeyed. "This blood on it—is it yours?" He shook his head. "Pig blood." She smiled at this. She wadded the shirt up and stuffed it in her bag. "Pretend you are sunbathing, *señor*."

"Do you have food, *señora*?"

"That is always a problem... I will return later. I'll see what I can do."

At 5:26 the woman returned alone. She looked around but no one was watching. She handed him a small paper sack. "I'm sorry, *señor*. We are very poor."

He thanked her, but she didn't leave. She looked down at him as if she were waiting for something. "Yes, *señora*?"

"If the boat doesn't come, God forbid, you can stay with Miguel and me."

He thanked her again, and this time he asked her why she would risk so much for a total stranger.

"If you are here tomorrow morning the police will certainly get you. It's a wonder they haven't captured you already. The thing is, *señor*, I'm lonely. My husband has been gone eight years. If you stay with me there is a chance they wouldn't catch you for some time. In the meantime I would have a man in the house."

"Come by tomorrow morning, *señora*. If I'm here I will accept your offer."

The sack contained a cheese rind, a crust of dried bread, an orange, and a three-inch length of dried sausage. He gobbled down this meager repast and lay back, thinking he might sleep an hour or two

He woke at 10:05. As he had the previous night he forced himself to scan the horizon, all the time fighting off the desire to sleep.

At 11:15 he heard a distant boat motor, and within seconds, he saw three quick flashes. He walked to the surf, slipped on the fins, and waded into the ocean. He found after only eight or ten strokes he was even weaker than he had feared—he could barely flip the fins against the pressure of the water. He aimed for the vague outline of the unlit boat and began the laborious swim, hoping all the time that a patrol boat wouldn't come by or that the people in the boat wouldn't lose patience and depart without him. Ten exhausting minutes it took him to reach the anchored boat, a distance he could have covered in two minutes when he was healthy. He tried climbing the ladder on the stern but was too weak. Two pairs of hands dragged him over the transom. They left him lying in the bilges, panting, exhausted. A moment later he heard the anchor being winched up. The boat turned and slowly worked its way north.

Once he caught his breath he climbed onto one of the benches on the side of the boat. It was a broad-beamed sturdy-looking craft, twenty-five, maybe thirty-feet long, with an enclosed cabin. Six square fifteen-gallon gasoline containers, three to a side, were secured with wide yellow woven straps.

The stout middle-aged captain, a rough-looking unshaven *hombre* in a filthy T-shirt, smoking a cigar, cast a two-second disapproving glance at him as if he were a great inconvenience—which he was. He said a patrol boat had come by the previous night and they'd had to stay well clear.

The deck hand, an amiable young lad called Pedro, spoke no English, but thanks to Rubio's teaching MacCrimmon understood him well enough. Pedro said the boat would cruise at 20 knots, about 23 miles an hour, once they got beyond the twelve-mile limit. The trip to Key West would take about six-hours if the weather wasn't too bad.

MacCrimmon asked him if they had any food. He said they did. He brought him from the cabin a hunk of stale bread, a smoked sausage, and a bottle of water.

He finished this simple meal and asked Pedro if there was a bunk. He led him below where two small bunks were arranged on each side of the bow in a "V." He took the starboard, less filthy of the two. An hour or so he lay awake, unable to sleep because of the rhythmic pounding of the boat against the water, thinking of the woman and her son and imagining what it might have been like living with them. Exhaustion ultimately prevailed and he slept.

Pedro woke him at 6:15. It was getting light but sunrise was still another hour away. They were about a mile from the drop off. Pedro said the captain had seen how tired he was and knew he couldn't make it from this distance, so he was moving in closer to the beach. Pedro helped him on with his life jacket and his fins and gave him two hand paddles. Five minutes later, now maybe half a mile from shore, the captain signaled to him, a forefinger to the bill of his greasy cap. MacCrimmon thanked the men and jumped feet first into the warm water. He rotated to orient himself and watched the boat cruise away. He waved a paddle at Pedro; Pedro waved back and shouted, *"Buena suerte en América!"*

MacCrimmon turned toward shore, paddling and kicking. With increasing light and visibility it was apparent the captain had understood the currents well enough to drop him off to the southwest so he would be carried to the northeast, insuring he wouldn't miss the beach.

Paddling and kicking for three minutes, and resting a minute, he made slow progress. Two-hundred yards from shore he was so tired he considered letting himself drift off to sleep. He slapped himself in the face with a paddle and floundered on.

It took him thirty minutes to reach a small white sandy beach. He was too tired to stand; instead he crawled slowly, laboriously, on hands and knees to the soft sand above the tide line and collapsed. He was home in America, nine-months since he boarded the Miesterdam.

Part Two

17.

MacCRIMMON unfastened the life vest and lay back on it, using it as a pillow. He closed his eyes and breathed deeply, paying back the oxygen he owed his body from the swim. Several people passed, joggers, early morning walkers, all studiously ignored the bum in ragged prison pants.

An hour later, as the sun came up, a man knelt down next to him. "You okay, old timer?"

"No, I'm not... I need food... and water."

"This life jacket, you come off a boat?"

"They dumped me... a half mile offshore."

"Who did?"

"The people helping me escape from a Cuban prison."

"'Cuban prison,' eh?

"Long story."

"Can you stand?"

"With help." MacCrimmon opened his eyes and looked up at the man. Mid-forties, maybe, muscular, about his own height, good strong tanned face, full head of prematurely grey hair. He introduced himself as Bryce Alberti. MacCrimmon used Malcolm Sutherland, one of his several aliases. Alberti helped him up. MacCrimmon put his arm over the man's shoulders and the two trudged up the beach. He left the life vest, paddles and fins behind for some lucky kid. Alberti led him across the street to an open-air café roofed in palm fronds.

A waiter said to Alberti in an aggrieved lisp, "Thith perthon can't come in here. He hath no thirt."

Alberti said softly but harshly, "He escaped from a Cuban prison! You give him what he wants!"

"Anything I want?" MacCrimmon said, as if he'd won the lottery.

"This story," Alberti said, squinting one eye, "it may be true, it may not, but it's at least worth a breakfast."

MacCrimmon knew he shouldn't overdo it with food so he confined himself to three eggs, scrambled, six links of sausage, and two glasses of milk. When it arrived he looked at it in wonderment. "Mr. Alberti, this is the first decent meal I've had in nine months."

"Call me Bryce... Are you up to telling me your story?"

He said he *was* up to it—if he could do it between bites. He went through the events of the past nine months, episode by episode. Alberti stopped him at certain of the more alarming incidents and repeated what MacCrimmon had said, as if his own repetition was verification. "This giant threw you overboard? And you know his name? And you floated in the ocean for two days? Jesus Christ!"

But as the improbability of it all suddenly hit him in the face, Alberi leaned back and shook a finger at MacCrimmon's nose. "If you're shitting me..."

"I'm not." MacCrimmon finished the story.

Alberti laughed out loud at the part where he almost suffocated in a coffin.

MacCrimmon suggested the humor of the situation might have diminished significantly if Mr. Alberti had been the pre-corpse in the coffin.

"Do you have family?" Bryce asked.

"I do. In San Francisco. But I want to remain incognito until I'm in a little better shape."

"'Incognito,' huh? I'm assuming you're not really this Sutherland cat. If you're lying about this how can I believe anything you say?"

MacCrimmon looked around to see if anyone could overhear. "If you swear never to divulge my real name I'll tell it to you—you can get verification on your phone."

Alberti waved this away as unnecessary. "We can do that later. I can be a little pushy sometimes. Do you have any money? A place to stay?"

MacCrimmon unfastened his Rolex and offered it to him. "My grandfathers gave me this when I graduated from medical school."

"'*Medical* school'? Alberti said, chuckling, "This is getting better all the time."

"I'd sooner starve than sell it, but I'll let you hold it if you'll loan me some money. I'm a multi-millionaire. I'll pay you back double whatever you loan me."

"Keep your watch, Doctor."

Ten minutes later MacCrimmon finished eating. He leaned back and patted his flat belly.

"Feeling a little more energetic?"

"Food is an effective restorative." Food, yes, but what he didn't mention was a far greater restorative, the kindness and bluff energy of this stranger.

Bryce walked MacCrimmon, now stuffed to his back teeth, to a clothing store called the "Blue Pineapple," three blocks away on Duval, where he outfitted him in loose cotton pants, two Guayabera-style shirts, underwear, and a pair of sandals.

No, MacCrimmon said to the clerk, he didn't want his old pants burned. He would take them with him, as a *memento mori*.

Outside on the sidewalk Bryce examined MacCrimmon, his forefinger pressed against his chin in a theatrical pose of appraisal. "Half human, I'd say. But only half."

Bryce hailed a cab and the two rode to his hotel on Palm Street on the west side of the island, a boutique place in the tropical colonial style with wraparound white painted verandas on both stories. Bryce showed him into his first-floor suite. "Take a shower, uh... What's your real first name, not your last, only the first?"

"Andrew."

"Take a shower, Andrew. Afterwards we'll come up with a plan of battle."

Thirty-minutes later, passing over Stock Island east of Key West in Alberti's Cadillac, MacCrimmon asked if he might be told where they were going. In the flurry of packing and checking out of the hotel and retrieving his car and Alberti's twice-normal speed of living life he hadn't had a chance to ask. "Fort Lauderdale, my friend. You need some time to come up to speed in twenty-first century 'Murica."

"How did you happen to be on that beach at that particular moment, Bryce?"

"South Beach is my favorite. I go there every day, like a religious ritual. Every day the sun rises and says, 'Bryce, me lad, here's another day—squeeze it dry.'"

"You're lucky to have juicy days... You're here on vacation?"

"Business."

"May I ask?"

"Yeah... Same secrecy as your name, agreed?"

MacCrimmon symbolically locked his lips and threw the key out the window.

Bryce, accompanying himself with flamboyant hand gestures, explained he was a sort of commodities trader. "Someone has, say, some nice stones and wants to trade them for money. I find someone who has money but wants the nice stones."

"And ownership of these 'commodities,' past and present?"

"I'm flexible on that, Andrew." He asked rhetorically with a big grin, "I mean, who am I to judge?"

"Do you ever deal in gold?"

"I'd love to, but it usually comes in such small quantities it's not worth my time."

MacCrimmon chewed on his inner lower lip to stifle a smile, thinking there must be a God after all. Bryce noticed. Not only did he drive fast, he spent a great deal of time looking away from the road. "What's that smirk all about, Andrew?"

"Did you ever notice, Bryce, how words for some concepts, say, goodness, kind of hang together... 'Gold,' 'God,' 'good,' 'dog.'"

"Or 'friend,' 'fiend.'"

"As a sunny optimist I prefer 'friend,' 'find.'"

"You lost me with all the words but 'gold.' Do you have some?"

"Let's speak theoretically here, Bryce. Say a guy had, oh, about five-hundred and twenty pounds of the stuff."

Bryce declaimed to the smartphone on his dashboard, "14.6 Troy ounces times 520 pounds times 1300 dollars." An executive secretary-type voice said, "9,869,900 dollars." Bryce shook his head in disbelief. "You have this gold, don't you? And if you're lying, I'm gonna stop this car and beat the shit out of you."

MacCrimmon laughed out loud. The last time he had laughed like this was a century ago playing chess with Colonel Ximenez. "Yes, Bryce, I do. Now you're the second person on the planet who knows I have Juan Enrique Montoya's gold. But I won't bore you with the story."

"Like *hell* you won't bore me with the story. We have about two and a half hours left to drive and you're going to fill every damn minute with this story or I'll tie you up and drag you behind this car!"

"Your lurid threat has terrified me out of my wits so I guess I have no choice. But remember, you asked for it, and if—"

"Tell me about the gold, Andrew!"

"Yes, okay... I had taken a road trip out of desperation and I was in the desert outside of Lone Pine when—"

"Wait a minute, Andrew... Why 'desperation'?"

"I'd found my wife, Karen, in bed with her personal trainer. I didn't know it at the time, but he had drugged her and was raping her."

"What did you do to him?"

"He ran away naked. I shot at him as he ran down the alley behind my house but I missed. I did hit the apartment house across the street. And I demolished his Ducati with a sledgehammer."

"Tell you what, Andrew, we'll devote an hour—at least—to this story over drinks tonight, but for now, let's get back to the gold."

"Okay... I was mugged by three Mexicans; left to die in the desert; rescued by a tavern owner; out of gratitude I agreed to tend bar for him while he and his wife went on vacation—"

"Slow down. Tell me about the *gold*, Andrew! The *gold*!"

"Yes, the gold... In the tavern I met Magdalena Alconchel Ruiz de Castilla, otherwise known as Lena Montoya, the runaway wife of the Mexican drug lord, Juan Enrique Montoya, whose gold I now own. She'd come in for a glass of wine. She took a fancy to me."

In spite of multiple threats of violence to his person MacCrimmon told in his own plodding, discursive fashion the story of his two-year friendship with Lena Montoya, of having a daughter with her, her murder by members of her late-husband's cartel who were looking for his hidden fortune, and his own hunt for the murderers.

"I found the guys who had murdered not only Lena but my dear friend, Father Gus. They were holed up in a little dump outside of Mecca—not *that* Mecca—a dusty little town in the Coachella Valley in south-eastern California. They got the drop on me, but I managed to dispatch the worst one with a KA-BAR combat knife. A lady friend shot the other one."

"No, no, *NO!*" Bryce shouted, violently shaking his head and pounding the dashboard. "This is the most preposterous load of bullshit I've ever heard in my entire life!"

"I'm getting to the gold. Do you want to hear this or not?"

"Yeah, okay," he said with a disgusted wave of his hand. "Go ahead, get on with it. But I know you're lying to me."

"When I went back to the place to clean up I noticed this twisted pile of junk metal behind the barn. What I thought was rust was brown paint with sand thrown on it. They'd forged the gold into long bars that looked like construction materials. They'd mixed it with steel and aluminum to mask it from metal detectors. God only knows how many people were killed looking for it while all the time it was right there in plain sight."

"Where is it now?"

"Safe."

By the time they pulled into the building where Bryce had his twelfth story condo, MacCrimmon had filled him in about Karen and the kids, and further details about floating in the Caribbean and his life in a Cuban prison.

Bryce's beautifully laid-out two-bedroom unit looked north through floor-to-ceiling windows over the canal and the brick-paved Riverwalk. The glass, chrome, and black leather furnishings, the trendy dried weeds in glass vases, the monochromatic prints on the walls, and the lack of any personal photos or mementos, gave the place a cold impermanent feel, suggesting it had been left entirely in the hands of an interior decorator.

Bryce interrupted the tour, saying he wanted to talk more about the gold. MacCrimmon said that was fine but he was very hungry and very tired. Could they talk about it over an early dinner?

Bryce agreed. He took him to a steakhouse on Las Olas, the fancy east-west thoroughfare cutting through Fort Lauderdale. MacCrimmon asked between bites of the first of two filets how the gold would be handled. "Do you back an armored car up, weigh it, give me a check, and haul it away?"

"It's a facetious question—you know damn well it's more complicated than that. The armored car and armed guards, yes. But there's the weighing, the assaying, temporary storage, not to mention finding a buyer. And there's the problem of transportation to some place like, say, Key West where a buyer from, say, the UAE might have his large yacht... To cut to the chase, ten per cent."

"Five," MacCrimmon said, his mouth full of partially chewed meat.

"Here I rescue you from certain death, take you in, feed you, treat you like long lost son—"

"Father... Long lost father."

"Whatever. And you try to cheat me?"

"'*Cheat*' you, you miserable thief!" MacCrimmon laughed so hard he sprayed meat fragments on his plate. "Five per cent is half a million dollars!"

"Okay, eight per cent."

"Six."

"Seven, my final offer."

"Done." MacCrimmon wiped his greasy right hand on his napkin and reached over to shake hands.

On the sidewalk after dinner Bryce said Andrew still looked like a bum so a visit to his barber was in order.

MacCrimmon told Tony, the barber, to trim his beard neatly to an inch and a half, but he told him to make sure the scar on his left cheek was still covered. His hair, he said, he wanted in a neatly clubbed ponytail, ala Thomas Jefferson.

The shampooing, rinsing, cutting, and blow-drying completed, Tony twirled the chair around for him to see the results. "You have a beautiful head of hair, Sir."

MacCrimmon was shocked by the change. "And you, Tony, are a magician."

Walking back to the condo, Bryce commented on his appetite.

"I'm eating for two, more likely five-hundred."

Bryce stopped and turned him by his shoulder to look him in the face. "What are you talking about?"

"Is there a place you could get a doc to write a prescription?"

"Yeah. I know a doc in a walk-in clinic who's handled a couple delicate surgeries for lady friends who, uh—"

"I get it. I need a prescription for Albendazole, 400 mgm."

"What for?"

"Worms."

That evening, sipping sixteen-year old Lagavulin—among his other virtues Bryce was a connoisseur of single malts—he asked MacCrimmon, "Don't you want to call your wife?"

"More than anything in the world, but I want to meet her in person. I have to maintain my anonymity—if I called her, her reaction would give me away to everybody she talked to."

"Why is your anonymity so important?"

"The guy who threw me overboard can't know I'm alive. He'd try to kill me again to prevent me from testifying against him. And they might threaten my wife. And if it came out I had escaped, the Cuban colonel who arranged it would be in big trouble."

"So, you'll go to the cops?"

"Oh, no. I'm going to kill him—him and that bitch that helped him."

"Wow! Hardcore!"

MacCrimmon, nodding over his drink, said he'd like to go to bed. The ordeal, and the frenetic pace of the day had worn him out.

He woke at 9:30 the next morning after twelve-hours of dreamless, death-like sleep, but he luxuriated in the fragrant clean sheets and soft bed another half hour. He saw when he did his morning business the single dose of worm medicine had done its job. His infestation had been worse than he had thought. He showered, dressed, and announced to Bryce, outside on the balcony drinking coffee, he was ready for the day.

At breakfast at another place on Las Olas, Bryce told him he would need an ID, which he could arrange through a colleague, as well as clothes and accessories—a wallet, toiletries, and the like. And, he said, looking with disgust at MacCrimmon's teeth, a trip to his dentist. MacCrimmon assumed the dentist was another of the people Bryce had a personal relationship with.

That afternoon, after a much-needed teeth cleaning, and decked out in less flamboyant duds, he weighed himself in the building's gym. "And?" Bryce asked. "One-sixty," MacCrimmon said. "Your normal weight?" "Two-oh-five." "You've got some heavy eating to do, my friend." MacCrimmon tried curling a ten-pound dumbbell but couldn't. Normally, he curled forty pounds with each arm. Bryce patted him on the back. "You'll get there, ol' buddy."

That evening Bryce clinked glasses with MacCrimmon and said in a cold, all-business tone, quite different from his usual amiable chatter, "I'm going to need some hard confirmation of these fantastic stories you've been telling me, Andrew. You're looking a hundred per cent better, and I think you're up to it now. And I want you to understand I am inclined to believe you, but I have to know for sure… Let's begin with your real name."

"You deserve that and a lot more, Bryce. Open your laptop." They repaired to a glass table near an east-facing floor-to-ceiling window. "In the search bar type in 'Andrew MacCrimmon.'"

Bryce did so. For several moments he silently moved his lips, reading the entries. "It's all here!… Lost at sea… Presumed dead… Caught killers of the homeless… Accused of vigilanteism…" He turned and said to MacCrimmon, looking over his shoulder, "Sorry I doubted you, man. I had no idea."

MacCrimmon wandered over to refill his snifter. Bryce, scrolling down, read another entry. He called over. "Didn't you say your wife's name was Karen?"

"Yes. Why?"

Bryce slumped back in his chair. "Jesus, Andrew, I'm so sorry."

What?… What is it?!" MacCrimmon rushed over, slopping Scotch out on his arm and on the carpet. Bryce rotated the laptop for him to read: "On July 9th, Ms. Karen Ting, widow of Dr. Andrew MacCrimmon, wed Dr. Arnold Ohrman in a ceremony at City hall. The bride wore…"

18.

THE ROOM went dark, his knees weakened. He stumbled but caught himself against the back of a chair. He closed his eyes and took slow deep breaths. When words and the ability to speak them returned he said news this bad should be dealt with in private.

He wished Bryce goodnight, and staggered into his bedroom. He collapsed on his bed, unable to move, as if the exhaustion, the despair, the hopelessness of the past months had returned as one massive paralyzing blow. One cruel sentence on a web page had emptied his life of all meaning and direction as quickly and completely as air leaves a popped balloon. All he had endured had been for nothing.

Bryce crept in a moment later and left a glass and a bottle of Glenmorangie on the nightstand. "Thought you might need this."

Grief over a death is usually pure and, in healthy people, fades with time. But the griefs Karen had caused him had always been contaminated in some way: by disgust when she married Reverend Pete and when she slept with the Count of Bassigny; rage when he found her in bed with Pavo Makkonen; and now betrayal. Karen, this woman who claimed she'd die without him, hadn't waited a

161

year to remarry. He should have known. He'd had a warning, a premonition, of this. In every dream, every hallucination while he floated in the ocean, she had been with another man.

Playing it over and over in his mind he wondered if this had really happened. Something this awful was a violation of natural law, as if gravity were reversed. It had to be some mistake. But as the hours passed and his logical mind rejected this comforting delusion, rage set in. He muffled his face with his pillow, howling curses and calling her vile names.

His anger too passed, leaving him empty, as if he had been gutted, "eviscerated," he'd called it on another occasion when she left him to live with a lawyer.

The next morning, after a couple hours of troubled sleep, he showered, shaved, groomed himself, and dressed with particular care so as to give no outward sign of distress. On the way to join Bryce on the balcony he returned the unopened bottle of Glenmorangie to the bar.

Alberti looked up from his newspaper. "You okay?"

"I'm fine."

"You're awful pale for somebody who's fine. The only person I ever saw whiter than you was a corpse."

"The corpse probably felt better than I do right now."

"You were close to her?"

"Some people—including me—thought we were abnormally close."

"What are you going to do?"

He looked away to the north as if the answer lay out there somewhere in the big yachts and fancy shops. He shook his head. "I'm not sure. After I've dealt with Thomas Padgett and Vera Snead, I'll figure something out."

Bryce poured a mug of coffee, pushed it across the table to him, and went back to his paper. A minute later he looked up. "It just occurred to me—what about the gold? Did you lose that like everything else?"

"The gold?" MacCrimmon asked, struggling to remember what the word meant. He cared no more about the gold at this point than he did about the seagull shit on the balcony railing. "No, Karen doesn't have an inkling it exists. Only you and I know about it. If I have no resources left I may have to move it sooner than I planned."

"I'll get started on it... In the meantime, are you ready to do business?"

"I am. And, uh, excuse my distraction... What's on the agenda?"

"First, let's get you a Florida drivers license. It's not perfect but it's good enough to get you on a domestic flight and to set up a bank account, which I'll bank roll. How much do you need?"

"Short term, fifty thousand."

"I can do fifty... Long term?"

"A Million and a half."

"Can't do that. Do you have other sources?"

"Yeah. My nephew and my brother I haven't spoken to in twenty-years."

"There's a transaction I'd love to witness." He rose and took MacCrimmon's elbow. "Come on, Andrew. Let's get breakfast."

MacCrimmon shook his head, no, and mumbled with a sickly smile, "I couldn't eat a thing, Bryce."

"Oh, yes you *can*, Andrew! You're going to eat a big breakfast, a big lunch, and a big dinner. You've got forty-pounds to gain. Let's go, amigo. Chop chop!"

Over the next three days, as Bryce had insisted, MacCrimmon had eaten well. He found his protein-hunger trumped his grief and anger. He had already gained a couple pounds and felt stronger.

Bryce had bought him a laptop and a pre-paid phone, and on the third day, the Florida driver's license arrived by messenger.

163

Using that and Bryce's fifty-thousand he opened a bank account with Wells Fargo under the name "Malcolm Sutherland." He withdrew nine-thousand cash for contingencies.

Saturday morning, he joined Bryce on the balcony for his last few hours before his flight out that afternoon.

"What's next for you, Andrew?"

"I'm flying to LA and on to Paso Robles, to talk to my nephew and brother for the money I owe the prison commandant who arranged my escape. From there I'll go to San Francisco, talk to my lawyer and financial advisor, see where I stand."

"Are you going to let your ex-wife know you're alive?"

"No... First, I have to get myself in decent shape so I can at least get my daughter back—Karen's not her mother. No judge would award custody to a scarecrow like me. My son's probably a lost cause."

"How about those assholes that caused all this trouble?"

He pounded the balcony railing and said through clenched teeth, "They'll die. I'm not sure when or how, but they're going to die!" A breath later he said softly, "But in a weird way I'm grateful to them."

"How so?"

"Without my hate for them I wouldn't have the tiniest reason for living."

"Good God, Andrew," Bryce said with a grunt of disgust disturbingly close to a sneer, "How can any woman gut a man like this."

Unsure whether Bryce was criticizing him for weakness—and there was no other word for it—or Karen for cruelty, he chose not to respond.

After lunch, waiting for his cab on the sidewalk in front of the building, Bryce made him promise to keep him apprised of what was going on. When the cab arrived, as they shook hands, Bryce said, "I've never met a man I liked so much so quickly."

"And I've never met a man I owed so much to," MacCrimmon said. "We'll see each other again, soon."

That evening, exhausted after the six-hour flight from Miami to L.A., MacCrimmon spent the night in a hotel near LAX. He connected to the hotel's wi-fi and looked up Thomas Padgett on his Intelius people search, which fortunately hadn't been cancelled. There was nothing to indicate he had moved from his place on La Tapiceria, north of San Antonio, nor was there any mention of a divorce. That must mean the sister-in-law was still there impersonating Tamara. Her name, he remembered, was Vera Snead. He looked her up. Sure enough, "Vera" had been declared dead, the victim of a robbery and murder. The body, discovered last April in a nature preserve in eastern Puerto Rico, had been identified by documents buried with her. The son had had the body cremated and a memorial service had been held in Buffalo.

He was glad to see this. Having the two of them together would be much more convenient than chasing around the country after one or the other.

Before he went to bed he wrote a short note:

Hello, Thomas,

I know you killed Tamara and MacCrimmon and the other man. I have the proof your "wife" is not who she says she is. I saved a glass with "Tamara's" (Vera Snead's) fingerprints in case I might need it. The price for my silence is a million dollars. I'll be in touch.

He had handled the hotel letter paper and envelope with a handkerchief so as to leave no fingerprints. He would have the desk clerk stamp and mail it.

He looked up Vera's son, Brian Snead, and found a Facebook account. He opened a new gmail account with the clumsy but arresting username, "witness_to_mayhem," and sent a message to Brian's Facebook inbox:

> Talk to Aunt Tamara. She knows a lot more about your mother's death than she's letting on. Visit her. She has interesting things to share.

The next morning MacCrimmon caught a flight to San Luis Obispo. At the airport he wolfed down two roast beef sandwiches and a quart of milk and faced his next hurdle: buying a car. He would love to have retrieved his BMW from 818 Mason but that would advertise his return.

He took a cab to what the driver had assured him was the biggest dealership in town, Central Coast Toyota. Of several choices, among them a Camaro convertible that sorely tempted him, he chose a practical, inconspicuous, dark blue 2008 Toyota Camry with 75,000 miles on it. The dealer wanted nine thousand. He offered eight, cash. The salesman was reluctant to accept cash but MacCrimmon said it was that or no deal. The young salesman relented. At MacCrimmon's insistence he entered the Camry's VIN in the NMVTIS webpage which showed the odometer reading was correct and the car had not been in any accidents. In fifty-minutes Malcolm Sutherland had become the proud owner of a car he hadn't bothered to test drive.

On his way out of town he stopped at a gas station on Monterey Street. While the tank was filling he bought a pine-scented deodorizer to hang from the rear-view mirror to neutralize the stink of stale cigarette smoke.

Twenty miles north on US-101, ten miles south of Paso Robles, MacCrimmon stopped off in San Lazaro, the town where he had grown up. He bought two dozen roses at a florist-cum-book shop on Palma Avenue. He'd been patronizing this shop since he was eight-years old when he bought his first book, the "Golden Book of Natural History." The young clerk said the original owners, the Armstrongs, had died decades earlier. And, no, she said, they didn't sell books any longer.

He drove two miles east of town to Pine Bluff Cemetery where his parents and grandparents were buried. It was a peaceful place, situated on a high bluff looking east over the Salinas river, a place of many terraces, levels, and winding blacktop and shale roads shaded by live oaks and grey pines. He thought the German word, *Friedhof*, "house of peace," would be more appropriate for this tranquil setting than the cold words "cemetery," or "graveyard," the last with its images of full moons and howling wolves. He had been coming to this place in times of despair since high school, when he peddled his bike here, but in the last years it had always been something to do with Karen. But as bad as those incidents had been, none were as permanent or as empty of hope as this one.

He distributed the roses on each of the graves and sagged down on the wet grass, resting his back against a large live oak tree. He hadn't wept in Fort Lauderdale but here, among the sprits of people who had loved him, it seemed okay, as if they and the place itself granted him permission. He did weep, though an onlooker might have said the weeping had only come at the end after a series of agonized howls that had gone on and on.

An old lady, veiled and dressed in black, leading a small girl about Maddy's age by the hand away from a nearby fresh grave, looked at him apprehensively, as if she feared he might attack. She must have heard his lamentations and had taken him for a maniac escaped from the State Hospital a few miles to the south. He clambered to his feet and with a bandana he wiped the tears from his eyes and the slobber and mucus from his nose and mouth. He smiled at the little girl and she waved back at him the way little girls wave.

He felt better. Karen would never hurt him again. When she put herself in a position to be raped by a trainer or a French count or suffered one of her other bizarre flights from sanity, Dr. Ohrman could deal with her. Life might never be the same without her, but after six months, a year, however long it took to heal, life would be a hell of a lot more stable. At the same time, the less reptilian side of his mind hoped she was happy and the kids had adjusted well.

To enter his brother Matthew's hilltop estate west of Paso Robles one was required to stop at a tall arched gate of vertical steel bars where one pushed a button and announced one's name and purpose. Matthew had considerately provided a turnaround for those sorry individuals denied admittance. Not wishing to announce his name, and definitely not his purpose in coming, he said his name was Cameron MacCrimmon and he wanted to visit his brother, Alan. The gate swung open. He drove a hundred yards up a curving driveway to Matthew's mansion, a huge L-shaped two-story Mediterranean-style Villa that looked more like a hotel or a resort than a home. He climbed the wide tiled steps to a covered entry and rang a bell that sounded like Big Ben. A short, plump, Mayan-looking Mexican maid answered. "I'd like to speak to Mr. Alan MacCrimmon."

"What name, Meester?"

"Andrew MacCrimmon."

Five minutes later Alan came thundering down the long hallway, his shower shoes slapping on the terra cotta tiles. "What the hell is this?" he bellowed. "Who are—" He stopped and squinted. "Is it?"

"It is, Alan."

He lumbered to his uncle, engulfed him in his massive arms, and pounded his back."

"Easy there, big boy, I'm a bit frail."

Alan pulled back to look at him. "You're alive! You're really *are* alive. But what happened? You look like a skeleton."

"Cuban prison."

"'Cuban prison.'" He smashed his ping-pong paddle-sized hands together in a blow that would have crushed a human skull. "That's one we never thought of. But come in." He led him down the hall to a giant kitchen done in a rustic Tuscan motif. Alan seated him at a huge pine table, much like the one in the Mason Street home Papa Mac had fashioned out of timbers from an old Scottish mill. Moved by some mysterious force, as he so often was, Alan bellowed to the house, "Uncle Andrew's *alive!*" That established, he ambled over to fetch beers from the double refrigerator.

Alan, six-feet eight, looked to be down to about two-eighty, twenty pounds less than he'd carried when he last saw him four years earlier. This was before Alan had broken contact with the family for reasons no one had ever understood. His already leonine features were a little more lined now and he was greying around his temples. Shorts, a T-shirt, and shower shoes, his uniform for as long as he had known him, no longer looked appropriate.

"Where's Matthew, Alan?"

"In Washington talking to those clowns in the defense department." Matthew's company, the gigantic outgrowth of the welding shop their grandfather, Malcolm "Papa Mac" MacCrimmon, had established in the twenties, manufactured sophisticated weapons components.

Alan popped the caps on the beers and returned to the table. "Tell me everything, Uncle Andrew. All I know is what Cam (Alan's younger brother) and Roger (Roger Fineman, Cam's partner) told me at your memorial service, some giant threw you overboard, and the FBI was looking into it."

"Memorial service?"

"Yeah, in January. Huntington Park. Must have been two or three-hundred people there. We all gave tributes. Everybody was crying. Cam and a bunch of guys from his orchestra played some music. Afterward, we went to a reception at the house. That little Madeleine is about the most beautiful little kid I've ever seen. Alex, too, and he's growing like a weed. But tell me, what happened?"

He gave him the five-minute summary. He had more pressing topics on his mind.

"Jesus! What a story. And this Cuban colonel helped you escape?"

"Yeah. For a promise of a million dollars, which I don't have. That's one reason I'm here. Can you loan me a million until I unload some assets?"

"Sure, of course. How about the million you gave me when you sold the Santa Rosa land? It'll take a little while to get it together."

"Did you see Karen?"

"I did. I hesitate to mention her—I know how you feel about her. Again, all I know is what I got from Cam and Roger. They said she went nuts when the FBI guys brought the stuff proving you were dead—this was early December. She tried to commit suicide with pills. Roger found her in time and called 9-1-1—he was staying in the house to help. After she came around she was completely unhinged, talking to you, begging you to come home. He said she sat by the hour in that window seat in your bedroom, watching for you, thinking you'd show up. He said once or twice she made herself up and waited outside for you."

"Watching for me?" At the thought of her suffering, thinking he was dead, he closed his eyes and looked down. He said he needed a minute.

"She got to be too much for the housekeeper, an old Italian lady," Alan said.

"Renata," he said, wiping his eyes.

"Yeah. They had to put her in a mental health clinic, some fancy place in Marin. She was enough better by Christmas they let her come home... When I saw her, a month later at the memorial service she didn't seem crazy anymore but she projected sadness; it was like a kind of aura, like nothing I'd ever seen."

"Howso?"

"Some sad people are simply not happy. She was way beyond that. You could tell life was a situation she would much prefer not to be trapped in. But she had made solemn promises to Roger and Cam never to harm herself again—promises you could tell she regretted making. The way she moved and acted was like she was slogging through soft sand and each day only brought her another dune to climb.

"I didn't hear anything more until I saw on the web she'd married her psychiatrist." He took a long swig and banged his beer bottle on the table. "This guy must have done a hell of a job washing all thoughts of you out of her mind." He looked up, shaking his head. "It seems so strange she would marry so soon after being so broken up earlier, like maybe he hypnotized her or drugged her."

MacCrimmon, smiling, said that was unlikely.

"There must be a million legal issues, Uncle Andrew. Where are all your assets?"

"I have to talk to my lawyers and financial advisor about that— I may have nothing left."

"I hope to God Karen didn't hand everything over to her this psychiatrist. And how about the kids? Little Madeleine isn't Karen's. Whose is she?"

"You're *really* out of touch. Her mother was a woman I met when I was in the desert. It's a long story."

"She must be a beauty."

"She was—she's dead... Look, Alan, promise me you won't tell anyone, and I mean *anyone*, even your dad, that I'm alive. I don't want to upset Karen or—"

"It may sound a little bitter, but I doubt she'd care one way or the other."

"—or the kids. And I don't want Padgett, the guy who threw me overboard, to know I'm alive. I want to be able to find him when I've gotten back into decent shape. I'll contact you about the money... By the way, why *are* you out of touch?"

"Personal stuff I won't discuss. Let it go, Uncle Andrew."

Later that afternoon Alan prevailed on his uncle to stay overnight. He barbequed steaks himself, and while they ate, he insisted he expand what had been a sketchy account of what had happened. Alan, like Alberti, laughed his grizzly bear roar at prisoner 378 almost suffocating in a coffin in the back of a 1952 Cadillac ambulance. "Good God, Uncle Andrew, the fixes you get yourself into."

"I'm a cat on its thirteenth life."

After an uncomfortable silence during which Alan twiddled his thumbs and Andrew picked at the label on his beer bottle, Alan asked, "Where are you going?... What are you going to do?"

"Before I think about any kind of new life I have to get strong and healthy again. That'll take a month at least. When I'm presentable I'll get Maddy back. I inherited Maddy's mother's estate in Palm Springs so I may go down there. But first I have to see if I still own it."

The next day Alan asked him as he was climbing into his car if he had a place to stay and enough money.

"A hotel, until I get my legal affairs straightened out. And, yes, I do have enough money, for everyday expenses."

19.

DR. MacCRIMMON reached San Francisco a little before noon. He checked into the Grant Hotel, a modest boutique establishment on Bush between Powell and Mason, two-and-a-half blocks down the hill from his old home. Before he unpacked he called Harley David, his best friend. The big PI was the only person he completely trusted. But the message on his machine said he and his wife, LaRita, were on an extended trip to Asia.

Late that afternoon he walked to the building on the corner of Montgomery and Bush where his financial advisor, Martin Wrassle, had fourth floor offices. He wore a flat cap and dark glasses but to further prevent recognition by Martin's office people he ignored the angry shouts of his secretary and marched directly into Martin's office. He closed the door behind him and waited. Martin ignored him, refusing to acknowledge this person who had rudely burst into his office.

"Hello, Martin."

Martin pushed his glasses up his nose with his forefinger and squinted up at him. Two seconds later his secretary charged in. He dismissed her with a backhand flick of his fingers. "Andrew, you're alive," he announced in a midwestern drawl to which he added the nasal harshness of ripping canvas.

The qualities that made Martin such a good financial manager were his lack of such human frailties as a sense of humor, religious and political passions, and, as in this case, susceptibility to shock or surprise.

"Well, I am and I am'nt... My assets, Martin?"

"Yes, you're assets." He explained everything was tied up in probate. He was quick to point out that all the assets *he* managed would pose no problem. He said the trouble was his tangled ownership of various properties, specifically the difficulty in determining his share of the equity and the liabilities of the apartment houses he owned with two partners. "One property in Palm Springs is especially troublesome," he said. "Title was never awarded after Ms. Montoya died and left it to the priest. He too died, but before doing so he left it to you, who also died, or so we thought. It would have taken many more months to work all this out, but now, of course, it's moot."

"No, Martin. I want probate to continue. I want to remain dead. Please swear you won't tell anyone I'm alive."

Martin's minimal sense of curiosity didn't rise to the level of asking MacCrimmon where he'd been or why he wanted to remain dead—he accepted this bizarre quirk with the same bland indifference as he did everything else—but he did say mildly that it wasn't necessary that he swear it: simply saying it was enough.

"What can I do for money, Martin?"

"There a cash account you can dip into that's in both your and Karen's names. Neither of you ever looks at it. Right now it stands at—," he clicked keys and looked at his monitor, "—one-hundred-thirty-eight-thousand dollars and change."

"Can you wire-transfer it to a Wells Fargo account in Florida?"

"All but a thousand or so to keep the account open."

MacCrimmon gave him his account information and signed the transfer.

"I need to set up an account a man named Ramon Ximenez can draw from. I'm borrowing a million dollars as we speak. He'll need an ATM card. He engineered my escape from a Cuban prison." He gave him Ximenez's birthdates to use as the account number. Martin accepted this information without comment.

Their business completed, Martin told him he could leave by the back door, avoiding the office.

"Why, Martin," MacCrimmon said grinning," a back door? Entertaining the ladies, are you?"

"No, Andrew," he said with no change of expression, "I've never been inclined in that direction."

Walking down the stairs he had the feeling that, even with this cold fish, he was among friends.

MacCrimmon walked two blocks up to California and turned east to Tadich Grill, an old-fashioned Croatian seafood place with mahogany booths and waiters who wore tuxes. Tadich had been in The City since gold rush days. He ordered two servings of salmon and a glass of merlot, and another glass when the second course of salmon arrived.

By the time he had paid his bill it was late enough that whoever lived at his old home was probably back from work. He caught the California Street cable car up the hill to Mason and worked his way the half-block down to 818, his three-story Italianate Victorian. He banged the massive Cladagh ring door knocker which, as usual, set the whole house reverberating. A plump young Indian woman in a Sari opened. She was married—the red dot on her forehead told him so. "Yes?"

"My name is Malcolm Sutherland. I used to live here. I know it's an unusual request but I wonder if I might look at the interior from the entry, to see how it's changed."

"This *is* unusual."

"If you'd feel more secure, I can come back when your husband's here."

She appraised him a moment. She must have seen neither a rapist nor an axe murderer in this emaciated but nicely dressed stranger. She stepped aside. He stopped in the entry where the piano had once stood. The oriental carpets were gone, replaced by small shag rugs leaving most of the oak parquet flooring exposed. The paintings too were gone, only the darker colored squares on the walls indicated where they had once hung. The oak bookcases along two walls were empty. God only knew where his massive and very valuable book collection had got to. The furniture was gone, replaced by a cheap wicker love seat and armchair and a pressed-board coffee table. A flat screen TV stood in front of the fireplace. How many nights he and Karen had made love on quilts while cozy fires blazed. The place still had the faint smell of wood smoke from the faulty flue he'd never gotten around to having fixed.

The scene suggested a Gypsy encampment in a gutted London men's club. But there was no damage, at least any he could see. "You've kept the place up well."

"The woman made us pay a heavy cleaning deposit and said we would have to pay for any damage."

"How long are you staying here?"

"Until we can find something better. This house is like a tomb. But the rent is cheap. The woman was anxious to rent it."

"What happened to all the furnishings?"

"I don't know. The woman must have sold them."

He thanked the lady for her courtesy and trust and bade her good evening.

Trudging down the hill to his hotel, thinking over what he had seen, he was not so much surprised Karen had cavalierly disposed of the books and art he had been collecting since he was in his twenties, but that he cared so little. Without her and the kids those things would have been nothing more than troublesome impedimenta. Without her and the kids nothing else mattered.

That evening he was oh so tempted to cross the street to Uncle Vito's, his favorite pizza place. He had fantasized obsessively about an Uncle Vito peperoni pizza with sausage all those months he was in prison. But he dared not—someone would surely recognize him.

That evening he called his friend, Lieutenant Gino Antonelli of the SFPD. A woman answered:

"Dr. MacCrimmon," she said. (Silence) "Hello?"
"Yes. I thought Dr. MacCrimmon was a man."
"He was my father."
"Oh... Is Lieutenant Antonelli there?"
"He'll be back soon. Who's calling?"
"Last time I talked to him, Gino said you were in Boston."
"Well, I'm here now, for good."
"I'll try later. Thank you."

The last he heard, Dre, his twenty-eight year old daughter, was a resident in pediatric oncology in Boston. She had been estranged from her family after nearly getting her throat cut in one of his cases gone terribly wrong. She had broken her engagement to Gino and had taken up with a surgeon back east. She and Gino must be back together which was fabulous news. He couldn't talk to Gino now, though—he would tell Dre and she was notoriously indiscreet. So much had happened while he was away.

MacCrimmon's intention had been to drive to Palm Springs as soon as he had money enough to get by. Whipping himself back into shape would be easier where it was warmer and there was a pool. More important, it was a different world, far from the memories and turmoil in San Francisco. But thinking back to what Alan had said about Karen being psychotic with grief, that she had talked to him and watched for him to come back, there was enough doubt about her situation that he felt obliged to make sure she and the kids were all right, that she hadn't hooked up with this man in one of her attacks of lunacy as she had when she'd married the execrable Reverend Pete.

Early the next morning he drove to Dr. Arnold Ohrman's home in the 300 block of 30th Avenue in the Outer Richmond District. The house was a two story stuccoed neo-eclectic with both a flat-roofed portion and a gabled roof, painted chocolate brown with white trim. A wide set of brick-paved steps led up to a large covered porch. He parked the inconspicuous Camry twenty-five yards down the block across the street and watched.

At 7:22 Karen, in jeans and a sweater, and Alex, in his school uniform, marched out the front door and down the steps to her Lexus SUV parked on the street. She strapped him into his bumper seat in the back and drove off. Alex must still be enrolled at Notre Dame de la Victoire, four blocks from the Mason Street house. It was a long drive to make twice a day. He was shaking too badly and was too far away to see Karen clearly, but he saw Alex had grown and had become lankier in the nine-months he'd been away.

At 8:46 a man in a Volvo station wagon he couldn't see very well backed out of the garage. He had to stop and get out to move a recycling bin at the base of the drive. He turned and surveyed the street, looked right at MacCrimmon, and returned to his car. He was a trim, good-looking man, six-feet or so, early-fifties, long wavy brown hair going grey. MacCrimmon clamped his eyes shut and held his breath to quell the nausea that welled up as he imagined this man fondling Karen's breasts, putting his penis in her. He rested his head on his crossed arms on the steering wheel until the fiery wave of pain had passed.

At 9:03 a stout grey-haired old lady led Maddy by the hand down the steps. Maddy too had grown. It was folly but, unable to resist the temptation, he left the car. Faking a limp, he crossed the street and slowly walked toward them. He stopped and said to the old lady, "What a beautiful little girl. Your granddaughter?"

"No, she belongs to the doctor's wife."

Maddy pointed a pudgy finger at him and said, "Da-da," much to his and the woman's astonishment

"I wish it were so," he said smiling down at her.

"No, Madeleine," the old woman said, "he's *not* your Da-da. The doctor is Da-da." She jerked her arm and snapped, "Come on."

MacCrimmon stood rooted, watching her. Ten feet further on Maddy looked back and said again, "Da-da."

He wasn't sure how he would go about it, but he would get his beautiful little two-year old daughter back. He had squandered his daughter Dre's childhood. It wouldn't happen again. Not for long would Arnold be her Da-da.

Karen returned at 9:17. She parked in the drive, but left the car running. She hurried into the house as if she'd forgotten something. A moment later she reappeared and drove away. This time he followed. She drove a block south and pulled into the parking lot of a market on the corner of Clement and 31st Avenue. She walked slowly in, studying a list, paying no attention to him as he followed behind her. She stopped near the mouth of the third aisle, squinting at the labels of bottles of pasta sauce. This was odd. She had always shunned bottled sauces in favor of the ones she made from scratch. He hurried down aisle four, back around to the far end of aisle three, and slowly sauntered toward her, looking from side to side at the shelves. Passing her, he glanced down at her, and she glanced up at him. He continued on, strolling slowly. When he was out of her sight, he hurried out the door to his car. He wanted to drive away, to escape, but his hand shook so badly it took several tries to insert the key in the lock. Once inside he had the same problem with the ignition.

Rather than try and drive, and risk killing himself and maybe some innocent person, he closed his eyes, let his hands drop to his lap, and waited for his pounding heart and rapid breathing to slow. Karen was thin, though not unhealthily thin, like him. Her hair was greying, but beyond that she looked older, more than the nine months that had passed, more like five years older, probably vestiges of her grief over his death. But she had been brisk and business-like and appeared to have settled into the domestic duties she loved so she had likely recovered. As intensely as she was concentrating on what she was shopping for, he couldn't get a measure of her happiness. All that said, she was still heart-stoppingly beautiful.

Likewise, it was impossible to accurately assess the kids' adjustment, but neither seemed distressed.

From what he had seen, there were no more ambiguities. He pulled out of the parking lot and headed east on California on his way to the Bay Bridge and Palm Springs, leaving Karen to her new life.

20.

EARLY EVENING MacCrimmon arrived at the estate southwest of Palm Springs, a mission-style mansion with adjoining stables set in a flat ten-acre plot of sand, scrubby bushes, and rocks. It had belonged to the late Lena Montoya but now belonged to him, at least he thought so.

He didn't have a key and Isabella Soares, the caretaker, hadn't answered the door. He walked around the north side of the house, clambered over the concrete block fence, and took a deck chair near the pool, the same pool where Lena had drowned two years earlier.

He closed his eyes. Drained emotionally after seeing Karen and exhausted after the seven-hour drive, he dozed.

He roused. Time had passed, how much he didn't know. He slowly comprehended through the fog of sleep that someone had spoken.

"Put your hands where I can see them!"

Now fully alert he raised his hands and shouted over his shoulder to the woman standing behind him, "It's me, Isabella, Andrew."

"Saying that is a good way to get yourself shot, asshole."

He saw by her shadow she was moving around to face him. "It really is me, Isabella. I'm not dead—unless you shoot me."

She faced him and squinted down at him. She dropped her big .45 to her side, the same gun she had pulled on him the *first* time they met. She knelt in front of him and felt for the scar on his left cheek under the beard. "Good God in heaven, it *is* you. Stand up! I have to be sure."

He stood and smiled at her. "Hello, Isabella."

She set the .45 with a clatter on the glass table next to her and threw her arms around his neck. She said through her weeping, "All my prayers were answered. I prayed and prayed it was all a mistake, a bad dream... God, Andrew, you'll never know how I cried when I saw on the news they'd declared you dead." She leaned back and grabbed his upper arms, tightly, as if she were afraid he would disappear again. "You're skin and bones. What happened?"

"Go pour us a glass of wine. I'll tell you the story."

Isabella returned with glasses of a nice Cabernet and they took seats at the glass table. He rotated the .45 with his forefinger to aim away from his heart and gave her the ten-minute version. She interjected, more than Bryce and Alan had, with comments, attacks of weeping, curses, and dire threats to Padgett and Vera.

He said he had come to Palm Springs to heal. She said he couldn't have come to a better place—she would be his nurse, his drill sergeant, his coach, his cook, and his friend. He said with the agenda he had worked out he would need all of those and more.

She told him to hold that thought and disappeared into the house. She returned with the bottle and re-filled their glasses. She leaned back, hugging her wineglass against her chest, and said tentatively, "It's, uh, touchy as hell but you know what I have to ask, to get it out of the way."

"I'll save you the trouble. She remarried."

"I know that much. For someone who was so lovey-dovey she didn't waste any time."

"I did see her. I walked past her in a market. She didn't recognize me—that's why I had kept the beard and long hair in the first place. I glanced at her for a second. She's thin, and looks older, but she seems to have adjusted. The kids look great and her new husband looks like a decent man. They have a nice house in a nice neighborhood."

"And it's eating at you like cancer, isn't it?"

182

"It'll pass... When I'm half-way human again I'll talk to her, see about joint custody of Alex, and offer her a visitation setup with Maddy if she wants it."

"Does she know you're alive?"

"No, of course not."

Isabella leaned forward and again the take-control, no nonsense MP she'd been in the army, she said, "Tell me about this agenda."

"I have to get myself in shape so I can find and kill Thomas Padgett and Vera Snead for what they did to me, to Karen, to all of us. After that, assuming I don't get caught, I have to get Madeleine back."

"How do you plan to get yourself in shape?"

"Heavy weight workouts, aerobics, and a diet heavy on protein."

"Swimming?"

"Laps every day as long as the weather is warm... The next step is to set up a home for Maddy. Karen rented out our place in The City and sold all my belongings so I'll have to start from scratch."

"She sold everything? All the books and paintings?"

"That's what the renter said. All I own is in that bag over there."

She glanced over at his medium sized gym bag.

"My assets are tied up in probate—they still think I'm dead, and we'll keep it that way. And for your information I am now Malcolm Sutherland. And don't ever, *ever* call me 'Mal.'"

"If you need a home for Maddy, how about this one?"

"You said you hate kids."

"Not Alex and especially not Maddy. Anybody who didn't love that little angel should be taken out and shot. I'd love to have her here." She leaned across the table and tapped his forearm. "It's settled. Once you're back in shape and you've gotten Maddy, you've got a house here if you want it."

"Comforting thought. In the meantime I want to make Thomas Padgett's and Vera Snead's lives as miserable as I possibly can."

Isabella saluted him with her wineglass. "I personally want to shoot this giant son-of-a-bitch for what he did to you!"

"Nope. He's mine. I might let you have the witch."

She slammed her hand down on the table as if swatting Vera like a fly and jumped to her feet. "You stay here and finish the wine. I bought a pizza that would take me a week to finish. You're going to eat the whole damn thing or you'll have me to deal with."

Tall, slim, broad-shouldered Isabella marched off fondling the big model M1911 Colt .45 she called "Baby." She looked exactly the same as the first day he met her, two years ago, when he came down after Lena's murder to help Father Gus settle her affairs. He had entered with a key Gus had given him and was standing in the entry when Isabella stepped out into the hallway, aimed the .45 at his chest, and demanded to know who he was. He told her his name and suggested his right to be here was unequivocal but doubted the same could be said for her. Knowing his name and recognizing him from Gus's description she dropped the gun to her side and introduced herself. She said Gus had hired her as a housekeeper. Gus may have been a priest, a skinny, balding priest with a skull face, but he had an eye for the ladies. As attractive as Isabella was, Gus had found the decision to hire her not a difficult one. Isabella had apologized for threatening to shoot him and had told him over coffee she had been an MP in the army. She'd had a troubled childhood but the service had straightened her out.

He had later asked Gus why a woman as attractive and capable as Isabella would work as a housekeeper. Gus confided she had murdered her husband. He had beaten her so badly she'd had to be hospitalized. When he came back for an encore, she shot him. What should have been justifiable homicide became second degree murder because she shot him in the back on the front step of the friend's house where she was staying. She spent eight years in the women's prison in Chowchilla before Bruce Solomon, Andrew's lawyer for criminal matters, had this injustice reversed and she was released. But being an ex-con had limited her employment opportunities.

Her coolness under fire and her military training had proved itself when he had crept onto a place outside of Mecca in the middle of the night, looking for the men who had killed Lena and Gus. In the melee that followed, he had dispatched one of the murderers with a KA-BAR combat knife Isabella had given him, but the other man got the drop on him and was squeezing the trigger when Isabella shot *him*. She had ignored his strict orders to stay in the car and had waited in the dark for this sort of eventuality.

But problems arose shortly thereafter: She fell in love with him. She had been an excellent housekeeper up to that point; she had kept the place spotless, paid the bills, and was a good cook into the bargain, but after he'd made it absolutely clear he was unavailable, she took to the bottle in her distress, and for a while the house suffered. But she had recovered and, judging by the current state of the house and grounds, she had recovered completely.

Half an hour later, he had finished half of one slice of Isabella's pizza. He pushed his plate away. "I can't eat, Isabella. You'll have to give me a couple days to get my appetite back."

"No, sir! Not eating is unhealthy." She held up one finger. "You've had your one day, Andrew. It ends tomorrow at sunrise."

The next morning he awoke from the two decent hours of sleep he'd salvaged between nightmares to the smell of frying bacon. He threw on shorts and a T-shirt and staggered out to the kitchen, yawning. Isabella had laid out a platter with four eggs, six slices of bacon and four pieces of toast. "Your fast is over," she said. "You look like you might live. I wasn't so sure yesterday." She ordered him with a forefinger pointed pistol-like at his nose to finish every bite. She wiped her hands on her apron and joined him at the table for her own breakfast—a single slice of bacon and one piece of toast from his plate.

Isabella said she would do the shopping but she needed to know the details of his dietary regime. Dr. MacCrimmon said this breakfast was a good start. The next month or so, he'd be eating a diet heavy on fish, chicken, lean red meat and complex carbohydrates, with whey protein smoothies, one in the morning, one at night. He would try to stuff down six or seven thousand calories a day with at least three-hundred grams of protein.

"Wine and beer?" she asked.

"Not only acceptable but mandatory."

She said she'd make a grocery run first thing.

Mid-morning MacCrimmon enrolled "Malcolm Sutherland" in a gym called World Fitness, a small but well-equipped establishment a mile and a half north of the estate on South Palm Canyon Drive. He planned to do upper body weights one day, lower body and core the next day, followed by a day of rest.

From there he drove downtown to Ray's Sporting Goods where he bought four pairs of exercise shorts, exercise gloves, and two pairs of cross trainers.

At Nature's Own, a health food store, he bought ten-pounds of vanilla-flavored whey powder and a bottle of 500 caps of creatine, 2500 mgm.

His first run late that morning, he described to Isabella as "pathetic." He had run only half a mile before he gave out and had to walk back, exhausted. Swimming had gone a little better. He swam ten slow laps, but he'd had to keep moving. If he had stopped, having no body fat, he would have sunk like a cannonball.

For lunch Isabella laid out a sirloin steak she had pan fried with sides of mashed potatoes and broccoli and a bottle of Anchor Steam, one of his favorite beers. Her own lunch was a one-inch square of meat, a teaspoon of potatoes, and half a pound of broccoli. She said she'd been eating like a rabbit which must mean she had rodent blood somewhere in her ancestry. He didn't correct her—rabbits weren't rodents—for fear of sounding pedantic which always irritated her; she was sensitive about not having a college degree. He would put up with any number of linguistic and zoological errors for cooking like hers.

Two days later MacCrimmon asked Isabella, "Ready to get after Vera and Padgett?"

"What do you have in mind?"

In his current condition, he said, he was in no shape to permanently deal with the pair but in the meantime he wanted to keep them in constant anxiety, as he had said earlier, making their lives as miserable as possible.

"When do we start?"

"Right now. I'm going to have you call Vera."

"Sure. What do I say?"

"Ask for Vera Snead. If she answers, say you're Rebecca Shaw from the San Juan Double Tree Hilton. Ask her when the hotel is going to get their money. If a man answers, demand to talk to Vera, and go through the hotel business again."

He fetched his laptop and prepaid phone from his room. He opened the file where he stored their phone numbers and addresses, put the phone on speaker, and punched in numbers. He handed it to Isabella. A man answered:

"Hello."

"Mr. Padgett, I need to speak to Vera Snead. I know she's there. This is Rachel Shaw from the Double Tree Hilton. Ms. Snead owes us a lot of—"

Isabella handed the phone back. "He hung up."

"I heard."

"He has a horrible voice, high-pitched, raspy."

"Only one of his many charms."

The next day, Isabella, at MacCrimmon's direction, left a long meandering message on Padgett's machine, claiming she was Vera's landlady, asking if she wanted to keep her apartment. She said people were interested in it and she needed an answer. She offered to ship her things to San Antonio, for a fee, of course.

That same day MacCrimmon left his own message, saying in a disguised voice that he was Hans Jeliksen's son, Erik—a name he had found on his people search. The family was filing a wrongful death lawsuit. His lawyer, he said, had assured him there was enough circumstantial evidence to win the case. (Jeliksen was the old man who had thrown MacCrimmon the life ring without which he would have drowned, the man Padgett had chucked overboard for his efforts.)

Thursday, August 30th, Isabella put out a special dinner to celebrate MacCrimmon's first full week in Palm Springs: a one-pound slab of broiled salmon on a bed of buttered fettucine and, to lubricate his gullet, sixteen-ounces of Zinfandel in a water glass. While he ate, they went over his progress. He had gained five-pounds in Palm Springs which, added to the four he had gained after landing in Key West, pushed him to almost 170 pounds. It already showed in his arms and legs. He was running a mile now, and swimming twenty laps. His weights were progressing well, but the trainer had advised him to stick to lighter weights for a while. In his haste to improve, his form was suffering—he was straining.

"The physical stuff is all great, Andrew, it's amazing how disciplined you are, but how about up here?" She tapped her temple. "Are you sleeping better?"

"A little, maybe."

Isabella slouched back and said over the rim of her wine glass, "It's still eating you alive, isn't it?"

"I don't want to talk about it, Isabella."

"What do you think will happen the first time you meet her at that shrink's house? What will her reaction be?"

He rocked the last of the wine in his big glass and stared down at it as if reading a portent in the purple turbulence. "I don't know. Friendly, I hope, for the sake of the kids. In the past she's gotten furious with me for getting into scrapes like this. That may be one reason she married this guy, like when she married the deplorable Reverend Pete, up in Portland."

Isabella shook her head and wagged her forefinger in disagreement. "Nope. You're way off. Less than a heartbeat after she sees you, realizes you're alive, she'll have her arms around your neck and you'll be back together."

"Nice thought but she's *married*!"

"'*Married*'?... Good God, Andrew!" She closed her eyes and gritted her teeth. "For someone so smart you can be so damn *dumb*!... Have you thought through the legal aspects of all this?"

He admitted he hadn't thought much about it because he didn't care. Without his family, the belongings, the investments, the properties, none of it mattered. What did matter was, first, killing Padgett and Vera for ruining his old life and, second, building a new life with his little daughter, free of all the dreary emotional baggage.

"All the assets, the property, everything is yours, Andrew, because you're alive. She can't do whatever she wants with your house—note the words, '*your* house.' And she can't do what she wants with your marriage. You're her legal husband, not this headshrinker."

"No, not true. Once you're declared dead, the wife is a widow and the new marriage is official. Besides, she's a loyal person. Once she committed herself to this guy, that was it."

He didn't hear her clearly but he thought she muttered something like, "any pimply high school boy understood women better than he did."

Four days later, Labor Day, Dr. MacCrimmon took an extra day off. He said he was stiff and had been cramping up. Isabella said she wasn't surprised—in his haste to improve he was over-training. After lunch she ordered him to strip off his T-shirt and lie on a pad from a chaise lounge.

She excused herself and bustled into the house. She returned wearing shorts and a T-shirt, carrying a bottle of baby oil. She knelt beside him and squirted warm oil on his back. "Madame Isabella of de magic hands," she said in a baritone Transylvanian accent, "iss going to loosen up dees muscles." For twenty minutes, using her palms and elbows, she pushed and kneaded the stiff sore muscles of his shoulders, back, and hamstrings, and milked his arms and fingers. When she was satisfied his back was sufficiently softened up, she ordered him to turn over.

"I can't Isabella. You know damn well why!"

"Oh, that!... In those nine months, did you, uh—?"

"No, of course not, I seldom thought about it... Until now."

21.

AT 9:37 P.M., Monday, August 26th, Thomas Padgett received this phone call:

> "Mr. Padgett, I need to speak to Vera Snead. I know she's there. This is Rachel Shaw from the Double Tree Hilton in San Juan. Ms. Snead owes us a lot of—"

Thomas Padgett hung up.

Vera saw him sliding his jaws from side to side, a sure sign he was upset. "What now, Thomas?"

"It's the Double Tree in San Juan. They called looking for Vera. They want their money."

Vera drifted over to the counter. She poured another two-fingers of Bourbon and took a sip. Finding enlightenment in the spirits, she said, "What the hotels probably do in cases like this is contact the closest kin to get their money. The bill could only be, like, six or seven-hundred dollars. Call them, Thomas. Find out how much it is and send them their money."

Thomas congratulated Vera. Once again there was much cool-headed wisdom in her words. He called the Double Tree Hilton, talked for thirty-seconds, and hung up. "They've never heard of any Rachel Shaw. They said Vera Snead did have an unpaid balance,

$872.68 cents. And they reminded me Vera Snead had been murdered."

"Who called you? What was her voice like?"

"Low, sexy, clear, like she's educated."

"First, that email that person, that 'witness_to_mayhem,' sent to Brian. Now this... This is getting creepy. And if Brian comes here because of that email, and if sees me, we're done."

"The five-grand I sent him to cover expenses seemed to satisfy him. And like I told you before, I said you were broken up about your sister and I didn't want to upset you any worse with malicious stuff from some anonymous email. But we should have a contingency plan in case he does show up... When he called he said you talk exactly like his mother, something about a New York 'R.' Say it, a-r-r."

"A-a-h."

"No, Vera, a-r-r-r, like a pirate."

"A-a-a-h."

"Say 'rose.'"

"Wose."

"Twenty-million people with speech impediments. Pathetic... I'll have to think about it."

The next day Vera listened to a long, incoherent phone message supposedly from her landlady, addressing her by name. Vera knew right away this couldn't be her landlady. She played the message for Thomas. "That voice!" he said. "That's the same woman who called about the Double Tree."

Vera smiled which, Thomas gently suggested, might be inappropriate under the circumstances. Vera disagreed. "Don't you get it, Thomas? Somebody knows a little bit, somebody who might have put it together from the news accounts. But they're fishing, because they don't know what really happened. If we get any more of these, we won't respond. If we have to, we play innocent."

Thomas said he didn't see any alternative. He also said whoever was doing it knew a whole hell of a lot for someone who had mined the news accounts.

Later that morning, Enrico called Thomas. This was the first they had heard from him since Vera paid him his one-hundred thousand way back in April:

"Thank you for the hundred K, Hoss. It got me out of a bad scrape. Problem is, I need another fifty. Sorry, I promised no more, but, you know, shit happens."

"Fifty, huh... Go fuck yourself, Enrico. Do what you gotta do."

"You really want to go down for murder one?"

"Well, you see, Enrico, here's the deal. We have passports and we'll be out of the country safe and sound, and you'll go back to stir."

"No, here's the *real* deal, Hoss. I talked to a lawyer, *muy* confidential of course, 'cause it's a matter of time until this thing breaks open. I told him exactly what happened, you know, me being the driver and burying the body. He said if I gave information that led to the case being solved I'd get at most a misdemeanor, maybe a suspended sentence."

"You're a lying sack of shit, Enrico."

"I didn't tell him no names—not yet."

(long silence)

"You still there, Hoss?"

"Yeah... Fifty, you say?"

"Yeah, fifty. I could have made it a lot more."

"And you swear to an all-seeing God this is the last?"

"Swear to God."

'Okay. Give us a couple weeks. It takes time to put together that much cash with the feds looking into every cash transaction over ten-grand. The same setup as last time. San Antonio airport, we send you the locker key."

Thomas had put the phone on speaker so Vera had heard the entire conversation. "You're going to pay that weasel, Thomas?"

Thomas grinned broadly. "Oh, yes, I'm going to pay him—pay him but good. I'll tell you about it when it's set up."

Thomas, as a sop to the city authorities, had hired ex-gang members, guys who claimed they were cleaning up their lives, as gofers, carpenters, concrete workers, on some of his construction projects. That afternoon he called the two he remembered as being the shadiest, Jesus Villa, a skinny, heavily tattooed psycho with a buzz cut, and a portly, heavily tattooed half-wit named Roberto Armas. Armas's phone was not in service, but Villa said he knew him and would go to the dump where he lived and talk to him. Villa said he could speak for Armas in that they both badly needed money. Thomas set up a meeting the next morning at a little Mexican café downtown called the Arroyo.

That afternoon Thomas was pleasuring himself watching Vera swim laps nude, a little game they played, when the phone rang. He ignored it. Vera, seeing what he was doing, crawled out of the pool, and straddled him, doubling the number of participants in the game.

An hour later, showered and already half-drunk, Thomas played the message in his office. When he came out Vera asked him what it was.

"The son of the old guy I threw overboard is threatening to sue for wrongful death. He says they have enough circumstantial evidence to win."

"That's BS, Thomas. He's trying to shake you down."

"Probably, but if it did go forward a lot of bad stuff could come out."

Thomas was concerned enough with the call he got slobbering drunk and slept all night in the deck chair where he had passed out.

The next morning the two ex-gangbangers showed up at the Arroyo half an hour late, as they had so often done when they worked construction for him. Padgett's first question, asked through a jackhammer headache, was, could they find a classy, attractive woman to help them? Villa said with the right money you could hire the virgin Mary herself.

"What kind of money we talking, Jesus?"

"What does she have to do?"

"Here's the setup. You two and the woman fly to San Juan." At Armas's open mouthed gawp of incomprehension he said, "It's in Puerto Rico, Roberto. It's an island." He went on to explain to Villa that the woman would hire a limo to take her to visit her relatives in Vega Baja, a town about twenty-five miles west of San Juan.

"Why is she taking a limo?"

"To show her relatives how rich she is. Scout the area out. Find a deserted picturesque area."

"What's this pitcher—, whatever?"

"Picturesque, you know, a beautiful scene. Have her tell the limo driver she wants to take a picture. When she gets out, you pop the guy, collect the woman, drive back to San Juan, and fly home."

"That's all the broad has to do? She don't have to fuck the guy or nothing?"

"All she has to do is make an appointment with the driver, direct him to Vega Baja, and tell him to stop when they get to the place you pick out."

"If that's all she has to do, I know a really classy thousand-a-night hooker from when I was flush who might do it. How much will you pay her?"

"Ten-grand, plus expenses."

"That should do it. How about us?"

"Ten-grand up front, forty more when the job's done. You never mention my name, understood?"

When he got home, Vera said a Sergeant Renee Flores with San Antonio PD called. She said she was the liaison between the cops and the FBI."

"What did she want?"

"My fingerprints. She gave me seventy-two hours to report to the northern substation."

Thomas pounded his fist into his palm. "Shit!... What next can go wrong?"

"I'm not finished, Thomas... I called San Antonio PD and asked to talk to Sergeant Flores. There is no Sergeant Flores. It was another crank call."

"'Crank call,' Vera?... The assholes told us they know about the fingerprint angle. That's the one piece of evidence that can sink us."

The next day, when Thomas met Villa and Armas at the Arroyo, Villa said his hooker had agreed but she wanted to fly home later, take a vacation, so she'd need her money up front. Thomas agreed. He told them to rent a car in San Juan and check out the area the day before, to make sure it was isolated enough that they could hide where Enrico couldn't see them. He said the choice of weapons was up to them. If it was a gun, they'd have to get one in San Juan because of airport security. He gave them Enrico Nelson's card. "Tell the woman to make the reservation on-line. Never, ever, mention San Antonio or my name to anyone... Can you get to the airport all right?" Villa said his sister was a secretary and she flew all over with her boss. She said she'd help them with tickets and to get on to their flights.

Thomas handed over three envelopes, ten-thousand for the woman, ten-thousand for them, and three-thousand more for expenses.

As soon as he got home, Vera handed him the letter MacCrimmon had sent from the hotel at LAX. The mailman had delivered it ten minutes earlier.

"It has to be that goddamned Enrico," Thomas bellowed, shaking the letter in the air as if he were summoning the rain gods. "I told him we'd give him his money. Why is he doing this?" Getting no answer from his Bourbon glass he threw it against the brick fence.

Vera reminded herself to warn the gardener so he wouldn't cut himself. She suggested to Thomas the wording didn't sound like it came from a semi-literate Puerto Rican limo driver. "And why would he send it from a hotel in LA, Thomas?"

"Who else would it be, Vera?"

"It could be anybody... Look, the person who wrote it said he'd be in touch. Let's wait and see what he—or she—says."

She asked if he had any news from the two psychos he had sent to San Juan. He said it was too soon yet.

Labor Day arrived. As there had been no further communication from whoever was harassing them they had settled back into their normal life which, by this time, had evolved into a reasonably satisfactory marriage, one vastly better than either of them had known with their previous spouses. They even went out once or twice a week, to movies, restaurants, and took in some of the tourist attractions.

What catapulted their marriage from mutual detestation to the satisfactory was their sex life. Thomas had been looking after himself for the first time. He didn't exercise but he had cut back on his smoking and overeating and his libido was all the better for it, guaranteeing he was ready almost any time and any place.

Vera, not having to work, had put on about five pounds in the right places, and with all her swimming, thanks to the warm weather, she had firmed up even more. And her nude sunbathing had tanned her a warm *café au lait* color. Having a natural sense of style and being able to afford hairdressers and nice clothes for the first time in her life, she had made the best of what little nature had dealt her, enough that her exotic stylishness had drawn looks a few times when she was shopping or strolling. The attention paid by other men conferred authenticity to her attractions which Thomas had feared were a mere idiosyncrasy of his taste. More than once their mutual attraction had been strong enough they'd had to cut short excursions to rush home to bed.

They both loved San Antonio and most of their planning involved staying here. So far law enforcement had only scraps of circumstantial evidence, not enough to worry about. The calls and that letter suggested someone knew a lot, but they had not shown they had enough to pin Tamara's death on them, nor had they threatened to go to the cops. That said, they realized there was a good possibility they would be discovered. Accordingly, they had converted most of their assets to liquid investments, stocks, bonds and cash. Thomas, to prepare for flight if it became necessary, had bought Maltese passports at a cost of two-hundred-thousand dollars, in the names of Randall and Mary Peterson, good for travel almost anywhere.

Enjoying early afternoon drinks by the pool, Vera suggested a good way to cap off the Labor Day holiday would be to hear of the demise of their good friend, Enrico Nelson. Thomas agreed. He called Villa's number. A woman answered. Thomas asked for Jesus:

"He's not here."

"Who are you?"

"His wife."

"When will he be back?"

"Never... Who are *you*?"

"I was his boss. I had a job for him."

"Well, Mr. Boss, Jesus and that imbecile, Roberto, went to California for good. He left me two-thousand dollars and told me to get a divorce. I heard him tell his sister twenty thousand no risk was better than fifty-thousand and going away for life. Do you know what he meant by that?"

22.

ISABELLA held open the French doors leading to the patio for MacCrimmon, carrying the lunch tray loaded with grilled chicken, roasted potatoes, salad, and a bottle of wine. He set it down on the table by the pool, and Isabella, lips pursed, fussily laid it all out.

During the meal, she was quieter than usual and was fiddling with her fingers, folding and unfolding her napkin.

"Something bothering you?"

"Yeah." She dropped her napkin in her lap. "I've been so incredibly happy with you here. I'm going to be awful, *awful* lonely when you go back to Karen."

He looked up at the sky, shaking his head. "Why, O why, are you bringing this up again, Isabella?... How many times do I have to say it? Karen is married to someone *else*! The only way I could '*go back*' to her is by entering some kind of kinky *ménage à trois* with her and her husband. We've been over this several times."

"The minute she sees you, she'll leave him." Her lips quivered and she blinked at tears welling.

He reached across the table for her hand. "Not with me she won't. I don't carry on with married women, Karen or anyone else. She feels the same way. When she married him, she married him for good. That's the kind of woman she is."

Isabella jerked her hand away. She wiped her eyes and looked at him a long moment, shaking her head in amazement. "You poor, poor, idiot!... What you know about women wouldn't fill a thimble."

He admitted they were an exotic species whose behavior wasn't easily understood, at least by him.

He left Isabella to her moping and finished the meal by denuding with his teeth a chicken tibia, called by *hoi polloi* a drumstick. He pushed his plate away and complimented her on the meal. This she acknowledged with a weak smile.

He patted his belly, as he now habitually did , testing to be sure all those calories were going to the right places and not into belly blubber. So far they hadn't. He last weighed in at 180 pounds and his weight workouts had improved proportionately. He was now jogging four miles and swimming half a mile.

As he healed physically his maniacal hatred of Thomas Padgett had softened somewhat. Was it such a good idea to kill him and probably spend the rest of his life in jail? The more he thought about it the more inclined he was to torment him to the breaking point and, when he and the woman were ready to crack, turn the whole thing over to law enforcement. Once that was done he would have no reason to hide his identity. Yes, Karen would find out he was alive, as she would have in a few weeks anyway, but more important, none of them would have anything to fear from Padgett, once he was in custody.

The next day, after his workout, having decided he no longer needed to disguise himself, he drove to Palm Springs Hair, a mile up the road from the gym, and had them shave off his beard and cut his hair.

Twenty-minutes later the "hairdresser"—no plebeian "barbers" in this shop—finished and rotated his chair to face the mirror. MacCrimmon saw a slender version of the man he had been ten months earlier.

Isabella, seeing him shorn and shaved, was at first shocked, as if his new face meant a new man, a stranger. She came close. Her already large brown eyes were larger and sadder. She ran her fingertips over his cheeks and lips and dropped her forehead to his shoulder. "No man should be this handsome."

Isabella came out after cleaning up the lunch things to remind him it was massage day—they always came on the days of his most vigorous workouts when he was most stiff and sore.

As time passed, and he had gotten used to the massages, he had focused on the therapeutic aspect and was able to turn over on his back without embarrassing either of them. This allowed her to work on his quads and chest muscles.

Today, after the usual twenty-minutes of prodding, squeezing and kneading, she straddled him. Out of the corner of his eye he saw her T-shirt fall in a heap next to him. He felt oil dropping on his back as she oiled herself. She lay on him, at first unmoving. She slathered more oil on her front and slid slowly up and down, massaging his back and flanks with her small hard breasts. When she finished she laid her cheek on his shoulder blade. He heard her weeping. Hot tears fell on his back. She ordered him to close his eyes and keep them closed. She clambered to her feet and scurried off, picking up her T-shirt on the way.

He opened his eyes when he heard the French doors close. He rose, washed the oil off under the outdoor shower, and went to the kitchen for a much-needed glass of wine. There was no sign of her. He assumed she had retired to her suite at the back of the house.

At dinner time Isabella still hadn't appeared. Having no idea what was bothering her, he left her in peace and made do with a frozen pizza, a bottle of Syrah, and a pint of ice cream.

That night he awoke from a troubling nightmare, the one in which he had begun rotting while he was still alive—he'd had it a few times before. Unable to fall back to sleep, he slipped on a T-shirt and tip-toed out to one of the padded chairs on the patio. As a rule, he disliked the dark but he made an exception for desert nights. The moon was in its last quarter and a light breeze brought whiffs of alkaline dust and the pleasant medicinal smells of brittlebush and chaparral.

He looked back at the sound of the French doors opening. Isabella crept over and slumped down in the chair next to him. "Tell me about your pain, Andrew."

He was surprised by this abrupt demand and by her odd behavior earlier. Isabella, up to now so clear-headed, had been acting as weirdly as some of the crazier women from his days as a philanderer. "Why do you bring this up now, Isabella? You know I don't talk about that kind of stuff."

She reached over and pinched his upper arm, hard. "Yes, you *are* going to talk about *'that kind of stuff'*!... I cook for you, clean, do your laundry, I do the shopping, I pay the bills, all so you can mope around for your precious *Karen*! I know, I'm only a lowly *housekeeper*, but that doesn't give you the right to treat me like a piece of furniture! I have to know what you're feeling!"

He fought off the temptation to rub where she had pinched him and said levelly, looking straight ahead, "You have to understand, there is no one more selfish than a person in pain, it's the ultimate solipsism."

"Oh, don't start with the philosoph—"

"Okay, okay," he said, shaking his head in surrender. "What do you want to know?"

She laid a gentle hand on his forearm and apologized for pinching him. "That first moment, Andrew, when you found out she was married to someone else—what was it like?"

"Have you ever been punched in the face, Isabella?"

She said with an angry huff, that anyone who knew anything about her late husband wouldn't need to ask that question.

"It was like that. Everything went dark, my knees went weak. I couldn't breathe, I couldn't speak... All night I thought over and over, this can't be happening, it had to be some kind of mistake. She was the light in the distance I aimed for those two nights of terror floating in the ocean; and in prison, through all the privations, the bad food, the beatings, the constant urge to slug somebody, that fatuous major with his endless questions, the guards, inmates who harassed me as a *Yanqui* spy, it was her image that kept me going. And after they dumped me off the boat a half mile from Key West and I was so tired all I wanted to do was slip out of the life vest and sink into the ocean, I saw her on the beach, beckoning, and I would swim another five yards... All for nothing."

"But you carried on."

"Well, let's say I let myself be pushed along by momentum, an autopilot, as if my tough old grandmother had come back to life to make sure I brushed my teeth and changed my underwear and I said 'please' and 'thank you.'"

"But what was it like when you saw her in the flesh?"

"I was shaking so badly I didn't see her clearly. The pain was a thick heavy ache that filled me from the bottom of my belly to the top of my throat. When I saw her husband, and I imagined her with him, naked, seeing them making love, I was nauseated to the point of vomiting.

"But when I saw Maddy, and she said 'Da-da,' I had a purpose again, even if it was only temporary. Momentum took over and I came here to heal... And if I haven't thanked you adequately, it's because there aren't words strong enough."

She squeezed his hand in reply. "And now?—what's it like now?"

"The worst of it, the acute pain, has lessened."

"But what was this 'acute pain' like?"

"At times it was so intense it left me breathless, sick to my stomach. At its worst it had me screaming her name into my pillow until my throat hurt... Now it's the heavy ache I talked about and, paradoxically, a sense of emptiness as if someone with a meat axe had hacked a fifty-pound organ out of me, the one that contained the centers of hope, pleasure, and the reason for living."

"You said 'temporary' purpose in living. You're not going to do anything awful are you?"

"I thought about it, hard! But now that I've reached an equilibrium—thanks in large part to you—I've been considering whether Maddy would be better off in a happy household with her mother, brother, and Arnold, than with a morose bachelor. I've decided to re-evaluate after another ten pounds. I'll be at 195, a level I've bounced down to occasionally during other times of turmoil; it's the low border of normal."

Isabella moved out of her chair and glided onto his lap. She was a tall girl and didn't fit comfortably, unlike Karen who was petite and melted into him almost as if he were pregnant with her.

She put her arms around his neck and whispered, "Are you angry with me for what I did this afternoon?"

"No, not at all," he whispered back. "That's the first intimate contact I've had with a human being in ten-months. I hadn't realized how much I missed it."

"I was afraid to face you. I was worried you'd think I was a cheap slut."

The next day he stretched his run to two-and-a half miles out but walking back after running out of gas a half mile from home, he realized he couldn't announce his return to the world. If the news he was alive got back to Cuba, his escape would be placed squarely on Colonel Ximenez. He also decided to delay notifying law enforcement about Thomas Padgett. But in the meantime, another call to the execrable pair was in order.

At 10:30, 12:30 Texas time, showered and shaved, with Isabella listening in, he called Thomas Padgett:

> "Mr. Padgett, I assume you got my letter, demanding a million dollars."
>
> "Who the fuck is this?"
>
> "Is the money now available?"
>
> "Go fuck yourself!"
>
> "I have a witness who saw you throw those two men overboard. He hadn't wanted to get involved, but he changed his mind at the prospect of a hundred-thousand dollars, which, incidentally, we'll tack on to the million."
>
> "Who are you?"
>
> "I'll tell the FBI to check Vera Snead's fingerprints against the late Tamara's there in Texas and Vera's own in New York, and have her son, Brian, talk to her. They might be able to do dental comparisons. Three homicides, Thomas— that should ensure a death sentence, but not before you languish in prison a few years. Oh, one thing I forgot. Your

accomplice in murdering Tamara is being most helpful. He hasn't given me his name or supplied details yet, but he indicated for another hundred-thousand, also tacked on, he would cooperate fully."

"Look, whoever in the hell you are, I don't have—"

"A million dollars in seven days. I'll be in touch."

Isabella asked about this accomplice.

"Padgett left the ship at about 10.00—Karen and I *saw* him. He showed up at the museum about 12:30, not enough time to kill Tamara and bury her many miles away in the nature preserve where they found her body. And we all had to return to the ship by 2:00, so someone had to have helped him."

"Do you think he'll pay?"

"What choice does he have?"

"How will you collect the money?"

"I won't... I'll make him give it to charity."

Isabella, laughing, threw her arms around his neck and kissed him lightly on the lips. "You, Dr. Mac, are a special piece of work."

Over the next several days Isabella's topless massages continued. MacCrimmon was at first uneasy with this level of intimacy, but this he dismissed as irrational—he was single and unattached. Neither did he object to Isabella sunbathing nude. She claimed it had been her habit before he came. Anyway, she said, being a doctor, he wasn't likely to get all crazy seeing her skinny ol' body.

Skinny, no; slender, yes. To her shapely little breasts she added long muscular legs and a firmly rounded derriere.

Sunday, September 23rd, the anniversary of his first whole month in Palm Springs, he cracked the 190-pound mark, five pounds short of his goal.

This day Isabella massaged him fully nude. When she finished with his back, breathing so hard she could only speak in whispers, she ordered him to close his eyes and to turn over. He obeyed on both counts. He felt her sit up and adjust herself. Slowly, very slowly—it had been months for him, years for her—she guided him into her. They climaxed together within seconds. They lay several minutes in the afternoon sun, unmoving, in delicious languor. He helped her up and, under the warm outdoor shower, they washed away the oil from each other's bodies.

That evening, after dinner, he reminded Isabella he had to call Thomas Padgett to check on the progress of his million dollars— the promised seven days had passed:

> "Ah, Vera. You're still with Thomas. You must have a happy little *ménage*, mustn't you?"
>
> "Who is this? What do you want?"
>
> "My million-dollars. Didn't Thomas tell you? I must say, Vera, secrecy between mates can be a worm burrowing in the very guts of a marriage."
>
> "Spare me your idiotic nonsense. What do you want—I mean *really* want? You don't expect us to turn over a million-dollars."
>
> "Oh, but I *do* expect it. If you disappoint me, my next call will be to the FBI to clue them in on the MacCrimmon-Jeliksen murders. While I'm at it I'll throw in the details of your murder of your sister, Tamara."
>
> "If you do that, you won't get your million."
>
> "I don't need the million. You're going to donate it to various charities. I've worked up a list."
>
> "Donate a million dollars to charity? Dream on!"
>
> "Oh, yes. You see, I wouldn't *have* your filthy money. Think of it this way, Vera—you do a good deed and feel good

about yourselves; or *you* go to the slammer for life and *Thomas* gets the needle... I'll call again with directions on how to donate the money."

The days following were a honeymoon of sorts for Isabella and MacCrimmon. They slept together, and during the day they did what honeymooners do, much of the time outside in the sun, slippery with oil, but no rooms in the house or the stalls in the adjoining stables were out of bounds.

His energy surprised them both. But what surprised him more was how much his mood had lifted, so much so he groaned in embarrassment at his string of maudlin emotional outpourings.

Neither spoke of love. MacCrimmon was far from ready for that kind of commitment. Isabella understood this. The uncomplicated affection between them, which she said was deeper than anything she had ever felt, may not have been love but it was the next best thing. He described it as love without hate lurking under the surface.

Likewise, neither said anything of the future. Each was content to float along in the current, satisfied with the pleasures each day brought—or as St. Matthew supposedly said, though probably not in English, "Sufficient unto the day was the evil thereof," and as Bryce Alberti had said, "squeezing each day dry."

Privately, MacCrimmon had reconsidered his decision to leave Maddy with Karen and Ohrman. He no longer thought of himself as a "morose bachelor," and as capable as Isabella was and as compatible as they were, he could do a lot worse for a mate and Maddy could do a lot worse for a mother.

Midweek, he noticed on the calendar the date for the wedding Colonel Ximenez said he was attending had passed. He called Martin Wrassle to check on the colonel's account. Martin said he hadn't dipped into it, in fact he hadn't heard a word from him. This was troubling news.

Not knowing the first name of the Colonel's nephew, MacCrimmon started in on the list of nine people with the name "Ximenez" in Tampa. The fourth one he called, a man with a pleasant baritone voice named Michael, said, yes, he was the nephew of Colonel Ximenez, and, yes, he had recently gotten married. MacCrimmon said he was friend of the Colonel's and hadn't heard from him. The nephew said his uncle hadn't attended the wedding, and they'd heard nothing from him in weeks. He said they were all worried about him.

Not half as worried as I am.

Ramon Ximenez had been detained in Cuba—there was no other explanation for him giving up a million dollars. It was no longer necessary to remain incognito so when he returned to San Francisco he would rescue his assets, beginning with the Mason Street house, which was his separate property protected by an iron-clad prenuptial agreement.

23.

THOMAS PADGETT considered himself an honest man. He had killed Tamara out of necessity and, as violent and reprehensible as it might have seemed in the eyes of some, there was nothing dishonest about it. As for dealing with MacCrimmon and Jeliksen, he saw nothing dishonest in protecting his interests. He had promised Vera Snead half of Tamara's money and he would keep that promise, even after she tried to cheat him out of the whole amount. What greater proof of honesty could there be?

Among honest people a sizeable proportion can't comprehend that others aren't as honest as they are. Thomas Padgett was *not* one of them. He had deep mistrust of everyone, especially Vera Snead. When her absences from the house had stretched into hours he had hired a private detective to follow her. When she rented the apartment, he'd had the detective break in and install a keylogger on her computer. He wasn't savvy enough to track her himself but the detective was. He reported back every transaction. These details he did not share with Vera—he may have been smitten, at least with parts of her, but he trusted her about as much as he would trust a rabid dog not to bite.

Along these same lines, when he set up the plan with Jesus and Roberto to kill Enrico he had assumed they would try to cheat him somehow, but he'd been certain the promise of forty-thousand dollars, to be earned by popping another psychopathic degenerate as bad as they were, would overcome any temptation to take the easy money. He had been badly mistaken.

After talking to Jesus's wife, he had gone into a rage compounded partially of the disbelief and outrage honest people feel when they're cheated after entering an agreement in good faith, but mostly it was the humiliation of being outfoxed by a pair of semi-retarded lowlifes who, between the two of them, didn't have wits enough to open a combination lock. By his standards, though, the rage was only of moderate intensity, limited to getting bed-wetting drunk and tearing up the mail before it could be read.

Over the next couple of weeks they heard nothing more from Enrico—he had not followed up on his demands for more money—nor anything from the asshole who was harassing them. Enough time had passed they had again settled into their comfortable routine.

On a fine mid-September Sunday, they had dressed in their finest and were leaving for a fancy lunch at Giuseppe's when Thomas got a call. He suspected the worst and put it on speaker:

"Mr. Padgett, I assume you got my letter, demanding a million dollars."

"Who the fuck is this?"

"Is the money now available?"

"Go fuck yourself!"

"I have a witness who saw you throw those two men overboard. He hadn't wanted to get involved but he changed his mind at the prospect of a hundred-thousand dollars, which, incidentally, we'll tack on to the million."

"Who are you?"

"I'll tell the FBI to check Vera Snead's fingerprints against the late Tamara's there in Texas and Vera's own in New York, and have her son, Brian, talk to her. Maybe they can do dental comparisons. Three homicides, Thomas—that should ensure a death sentence, but not before you languish in prison a few years. Oh, one thing I forgot. Your accomplice in murdering Tamara is being most helpful. He hasn't given me his name or supplied details yet but he indicated for another hundred-thousand, also tacked on, he would cooperate fully."

"Look, whoever in the hell you are, I don't have—"

"A million dollars in seven days. I'll be in touch."

As soon as he hung up, Vera, seeing the look in his eye, fled to her room and locked the door.

Padgett's howls of rage and the noise he made throwing the patio furniture around had brought the police who said a neighbor had called to report a disturbance. After they left he confined himself to smashing glassware.

That evening, after three-hours of silence, Vera tip-toed down the hall and peeked around through the patio doors. Thomas lay sprawled out in one of the two surviving patio chairs, his head thrown back, breathing through his open mouth with the sound of a poorly maintained outboard motor. The wrought iron patio chairs were bent and overturned; the glass top of the patio table was shattered—glass that was supposedly shatterproof; the seat cushions were slashed and the stuffing spread around like snow, much of it in the pool; and, as a final touch, the shards of what she guessed had been ten or fifteen glasses were scattered over the patio and undoubtedly in the pool.

The calls and letters had destroyed the tranquil life they enjoyed in San Antonio and had kept them on edge, never knowing from minute to minute if whoever was doing this would notify the law. His rage was directed at this person, whoever it was, who had disrupted the plan he had worked out so carefully, had put so much time and work into, the plan he had been so convinced was foolproof. And whoever it was had a perverse sense of timing, knowing exactly when he was most vulnerable.

After his anger had cooled Thomas said there were two una-voidable facts: the plan was blown and law enforcement would soon have what they needed; and if they wanted to survive they would have to leave the country, which neither of them wanted to do.

Over the next two days while Thomas wandered the house, staggering drunk, Vera and the maintenance crew cleaned up and hauled away the wreckage. Vera chose new furniture at a patio furniture company a few miles away, less for esthetics than resistance to destruction. For a generous tip, they delivered four heavy steel chairs and a heavy wooden table that same day.

That evening, Thomas, now half sober, slumped down in one of the new chairs and launched into a slobbering, semi-coherent protestation of contrition for what he had done and gratitude for her taking care of the mess.

Vera forced three cups of coffee down him and pulled one of the new heavy chairs around to face him. She leaned forward and tapped his knee to get his attention. "Can you think rationally now, Thomas?"

He nodded and said he thought he could.

"What are we going to do? This guy knows everything."

Thomas took a couple of deep breaths, feeding his befogged brain with the extra oxygen he needed to think clearly. "Yes, he does... I see it this way, Vera: if this guy, and his female accomplice, are the only people harassing us, it might be worth our while to pay them the million."

"What if they keep asking for more?"

"That's the problem, of course. In the meantime, we have a week to figure out what to do."

"Another thing... I couldn't be sure—the call passed so fast it was hard to tell—but think I've heard that low rumbling voice before, that smartass tone too, like the whole thing's a joke. And I'm pretty sure I heard someone in the background laughing."

"If you say so. I didn't pick up on any of that."

Four days later Brian called from the airport. He said he had rented a car and needed directions to their house. Thomas, silently grimacing in frustration, said they would be glad to see him and gave him vague, contradictory directions. He would have to stop and ask someone how to find their house, which would give them time to plan.

In the twenty or thirty minutes they estimated it would take him to arrive, "Tamara" put on heavy makeup, and dressed extravagantly in floppy slacks, a loose grey silk sweater and several chains of gold. She presented herself to Thomas for his opinion. He said she looked like a Kansas City hooker who'd escaped from a Turkish harem, which was a good thing—she was about as different from Vera as it was possible to be. "But there's still the problem of your speech impediment."

Vera contended a regional accent was technically not a speech impediment but she agreed it was a problem.

"What if you had laryngitis? We'll wrap a scarf around your neck. Talk in breathy grunts and avoid R's like the plague."

Vera agreed.

Brian rang the bell an hour later. Thomas answered. Vera's breath caught when she saw Brian at the open front door. He had left home for the navy a slouching, petulant teen-ager. He was now a tall, good-looking young man, handsome in his naval uniform. Fortunately for him, nature had averaged out his father's bloated moon face and his mother's rodent-like snout into pleasing regular features.

Brian shook his uncle Thomas's hand and kissed his "Aunt Tamara" on the cheek. She pointed to her neck and said in a breathy croak, "Lawyngitis." She recognized her mistake and blushed through her clownish makeup, but Brian didn't notice—or pretended not to notice.

Over drinks by the pool at the new table—Bourbon for them, beer for Brian—he said he had gotten a Facebook posting from someone named "witness_to_mayhem" who suggested he talk to his aunt because she knew more about his mother's killing than she had told the authorities. Vera showed with an open-handed gesture of innocence she had no idea what this person was talking about.

Thomas stepped in. "There was some indication from the hotel people your mom was seeing a man, probably the person who did her in. That must be what this person meant."

"That's bullshit!" Brian cried. "Mom never saw a man in all the years I was at home. She sure as hell wouldn't pick up some guy in Puerto Rico!"

Vera's eyes filled. She was proud to bursting of the fine young man her son had become, and now for defending her honor. In all the turmoil of the past year she hadn't realized how much she missed him. Thomas noticed. "Your aunt is still upset at what happened to your mother, as you can see." Vera nodded agreement.

Brian's cool glance at his "aunt" suggested he wasn't impressed. "The FBI has the envelope those letters came in," he said. "They lifted several sets of prints. And there was enough saliva on the flap from the little envelope for a DNA test. It was a woman's and said it matched my mom's perfectly." At this he cast another cool look at his "aunt." "They said there are some other things about the envelopes that may be helpful."

"Such as?" Thomas said.

"They wouldn't say."

"Why is the FBI involved in a local Puerto Rican matter?"

Brian scooched his heavy chair around to face Thomas. "That's what I asked those agents I talked to, guys named Whitley and Andrade. They said there might be a connection between my mom's killing and those two guys who got thrown off the cruise ship. Like maybe you threw them overboard because they knew something."

Vera saw by the trembling in Thomas's lips he was on the verge of blowing. She grunted and pointed at Brian's empty beer bottle. She rose to fetch him another, but purposely tripped and fell to the pavement. Both men jumped to their feet. Thomas rushed around to help her up. She mouthed "Thank you," and limped off to the kitchen.

Thomas returned to his seat. Having cooled down, he admitted he had had words with the younger of the two men who had gone missing. "I had stared at his wife—she was an incredibly beautiful Asian woman. He didn't like it, and he said so. But I sure as hell had nothing to do with him going overboard."

Brian, as if he hadn't heard him, said, "Whitley said there was no one else on that ship who could have thrown the doctor overboard—he was real strong."

"Look, young man," Thomas said heatedly, "if you have some accusation, make it!"

"No. I got what I needed." He looked at his watch and rose. He passed his "aunt," limping out with another beer. He waved it off and said he had to catch his flight. In the entry he looked back and said, "The guy was right—you both know a helluva lot more than you're letting on."

The front door had closed when Vera sobbed into her hands. "He's so different, so strong and confident. I can't believe he came from me and Jonathan."

"I thought you said you and he weren't close?"

"I never would have believed I'd miss him this much."

Thomas slapped the table hard, startling her. "Leave off your damn blubbering, Vera. That goddamned kid's yet another problem."

Vera, ignoring him, said through her weeping, "Dow I'll dever see hib agaid."

Oh, for Christ's sake," Thomas said, shaking his head and rolling his eyes. He pushed himself out of his chair and lumbered over to the bar to refill his glass.

He brought the bottle back with him and banged it down on the table. "We have to assume they have Enrico's DNA profile, but he must not be in the database or they would have identified him already. Ditto with the prints. Your DNA doesn't matter, of course, being the same as Tamara's. I wonder what the other evidence they could be talking about."

Four days after Brian's visit Vera took a call. She was taking all the calls now to spare Thomas—and the furniture—from any further maniacal rages.

"A follow up on the call I made to Pagett to see if you've collected my million dollars for charity."

"When was this?"

"A week or two ago. He didn't tell you?"

"Who are you?... Never mind. I *know* who you are. In answer to your question, no, we need more time."

"Nope. A million dollars or I call the FBI. Need I remind you—you'll go to the slammer for life and Thomas will get the needle. Don't disappoint me."

Thomas, sipping Bourbon at the pool, called over his shoulder, "Who was that?"

"MacCrimmon."

Thomas lurched out of his chair and stood, facing her. "What did you say? MacCrimmon? He's alive?"

217

"Yeah. I thought I recognized that voice and that wiseass tone of his. He *is* alive, Thomas."

"He *couldn't* be... They had DNA evidence of his death!"

"He's alive, Thomas. He said he called you earlier demanding a million dollars for charity."

"I didn't bother telling you because I thought he was bluffing again, like all that other stuff. It seems he isn't."

24.

SATURDAY, October 5th, after six weeks in Palm Springs, MacCrimmon had reached 195 pounds. His workouts and running were close to normal; he was now a slightly thinner version of his pre-immersion self. His optimal weight was 205, but he would add those last ten pounds more gradually with much healthier food.

That night at dinner he told Isabella he was going to San Francisco to check on Maddy's situation and take care of business. She nodded with a look of sad resignation and finished her meal in tense silence, picking at her food.

Isabella's wild lovemaking that night, more like fighting with a violent mental patient than sex, left bleeding furrows in the skin of his back. She climaxed with a bestial scream and lay on him, the semi-passive participant in this melee, sobbing, clutching him painfully with her already bloodied fingernails. He may not have known much about women but he recognized despair when he saw it—and felt it.

At five the next morning, time to leave, Isabella, barefoot and wearing the long T-shirt she wore as a nightgown, hugged his arm on the walk to the front step. He kissed her goodbye and released her, but she grabbed him and pulled him to her in a desperate bear hug. She said through her convulsive weeping. "You won't be back, Andrew."

He smiled and kissed away her tears. "Of course, I will, in two, maybe three days."

She backed away and said with the certainty of holy writ, "No, Andrew. You won't ever come back." Without another word, she marched into the house and slammed the front door behind her. He shook his head in befuddlement. She was flattering him when she'd said his knowledge of women would fill a thimble.

MacCrimmon arrived in San Francisco early Sunday afternoon. At a rest stop on I-5 he had called the Grant Hotel on Bush, where he had stayed before, to book a room and to arrange to have the Camry parked in the garage across the street.

That evening, refreshed after a long nap, he had a long-awaited pizza at Uncle Vito's on the corner. Angel, his usual server, a jovial middle-aged Mexican, stared at him in disbelief. "The newspaper, it say jou are dead."

"In this one rare instance a newspaper seems to have made a mistake, Angel... A small pepperoni with sausage and mushrooms and a half-carafe of house red, if you please."

Angel clasped his hands as if praying. "*Gracias a Dios.*"

The next morning MacCrimmon walked the mile down to Embarcadero Number Two. He took the elevator to the seventeenth-floor law offices of Bruce Solomon. The receptionist gave a little squeal of surprise at seeing him. He silenced her with a finger to his lips. "Is his majesty in?"

"He got here a minute ago. Go right in."

Bruce's reaction like everyone's so far, was shocked disbelief. He recovered and let out an uncharacteristic whoop of joy and grabbed MacCrimmon's outstretched hand. "Andrew, you miserable son-of-a-bitch! You're alive!... Karen must be ecstatic."

"I haven't seen her yet."

"What?... Why in the hell not?"

"It's complicated... What I need you to do is inform the courts, or whoever you inform in a case like this, that I'm alive and well. Have probate stopped so I can access my funds. But don't, under any circumstances, tell anyone I'm alive. It will come out soon enough with the court proceedings."

"Sure, no problem. Look, I'm petitioning the court to invalidate your death certificate on the grounds of fraud. That will make Karen's marriage to this psychiatrist void."

"It was fraudulent, of course, but hold off on that, Bruce."

"What?" Bruce shook his head in confusion. "You're kidding."

"No, I'm not. Like I said, it's complicated."

Bruce shrugged. He was well aware of the bizarre workings of Dr. MacCrimmon's mind and he also knew from bitter past experience not to question him. He circled around to his desk chair. "Sit down, Andrew." He said with the expectant grin of a little kid awaiting ice cream, "Tell me where you were all those months. Knowing you, this has to be good."

"Be glad to." Dr. MacCrimmon gave him the ten-minute version. Bruce, like other warped individuals, found the coffin episode amusing.

Bruce said he had a client coming so he had to cut it short but he promised to join him for lunch.

With time to kill, MacCrimmon wandered out to Justin Hermann Plaza and took a bench looking toward the gigantic Villaincourt Fountain. An unfriendly critic had once described the structure as looking like a pile of giant hollow square dog turds. He shook his head to clear his mind of this image before he called Isabella:

"Did you see her, Andrew?"

"No, not yet.

"But you will see her, and talk to her?"

"I was planning on it. Why?"

"Will you tell her about your time down here, with me?"

"Sure."

"Sorry about that scene, you know..."

"It was colorful."

"Will you call me later, after you talk to her?"

"I'll call you tonight from my hotel."

Bryce Alberti, when MacCrimmon called him that evening, said he had company but he could talk:

"Have you ever dealt with the Cubans, Bryce, I mean through diplomatic channels?"

"Not through diplomatic channels, no. What do you have in mind?"

"I need a negotiator to go to the Cuban consulate in Miami. I need to ransom a man I think is being held prisoner."

"'Ransom'? No chance in hell, Andrew."

"Offer them up to four-hundred pounds of gold, starting much lower, of course... Fifty—pounds, that is—will go to you as intermediary and fifty to Ramon when he and his family are safe in the U.S."

"Whew!... Not as idiotic as I first thought. Gold is more valuable to governments than its simple dollar amounts. And fifty for me?... That's a mill, Andrew."

"If you're willing to do it, I'll fly out to Fort Lauderdale. But contact them first. If they won't even consider it, there's no point in me coming."

"I'm in! ... Call me before you come. I'll drop whatever I'm doing and pick you up at the airport... A mill!... Jesus!"

The next morning Bryce called back:

"Andrew, Bryce here. I went to Miami and talked to the Cuban consul. He says in some special cases such an arrangement might be considered. I'll need you here though for the details. And I'm thinking we'll need about twenty-thousand for palm grease."

"Great news, Bryce. I'll be down as soon as I get a flight to Lauderdale. I'll call you as soon as the plane lands."

MacCrimmon's flight from SFO didn't arrive in Fort Lauderdale until after eleven. Rather than bother Bryce he took a cab to his condo. Bryce was shocked at what he called MacCrimmon's "supernatural" transformation, though he exaggerated his reaction for comic effect. The two men retired to his living area with snifters of peaty, iodine-tasting Laphroaig 18-year old. MacCrimmon fended off all questions about his personal life, saying everything was up in the air. He suggested they get down to business.

"Okay, Andrew, here's the deal. The official we'll be negotiating with is the assistant Consul, an aristocratic dude named Javier Bermudez de Cabrera. The Consul himself has to keep his hands clean, well, other than the grease on his palms."

"And how much will that be?"

"What I'd offer is a thousand to each for the inquiries and another nine apiece if the deal goes through. As for the ransom itself, start off at about a hundred K. I'll guide the bargaining from there as your agent—that's what I told them I was."

"Your cut is fifty K, minimum, Bryce, no matter the outcome, up to a million if we get Ramon out. In case you're wondering, I'd do the same for you if I had to."

The talk turned to the gold. Bryce said he had three interested parties if the ransom plan for the colonel fell through but no details had been discussed.

At midnight, Bryce said it was past his bedtime and toddled off, yawning. MacCrimmon, still on Pacific daylight time, was wide awake. He picked up the bottle, turned off the lights, and went out to the balcony. The memory of the night he learned Karen had married Ohrman hung in this place like a greasy fog. He drank several Scotches until he was sleepy.

At ten the next morning, MacCrimmon and Alberti were shown into the ornate Villa Paula, home of the recently resurrected Cuban consulate on North Miami Boulevard. A male secretary led them back to a large equally ornate office and introduced them to the consul, a distant arrogant old man whose name MacCrimmon didn't catch, and the more affable Bermudez de Cabrera.

Their first question was why they would go to such expense to ransom someone. "He's a man who once did me a great kindness," MacCrimmon said.

"And who is this person, this benefactor?"

"Colonel Ramon Ximenez, the assistant commandant of the Holquin prison."

Bermudez de Cabrera and the consul huddled and spoke in Spanish, assuming neither MacCrimmon nor Alberti understood.

MacCrimmon whispered out of the side of his mouth, "Too bad you don't speak Italian. I'd share what they're saying."

"I *do* speak it, thanks be to Benito and Sofia Alberti."

"You look so WASPY it never fully clicked you were Italian."

"Northern, *Piemontese.*"

MacCrimmon whispered, "*Sospettano che il colonnello Ximenez di intrappoli in facendo qualcosa di corrotto.*" ("They suspect Colonel Ximenez of trapping them into doing something corrupt.)

Bryce whispered back, "*Devi dire loro cosa ha fatto Ximenez per te. Va bene?*" ("It's time to tell them what Ximenez did for you, okay?")

When Bermudez de Cabrera looked up and smiled, MacCrimmon said, "I may have been a little vague about the Colonel. Due to a misunderstanding I was improperly imprisoned in Holquin. He saw to it that this mistake was, shall we say, rectified."

Bermudez de Cabrera glanced at the consul and said this was useful additional information. But contacting the proper people, he said, was time consuming and could even be dangerous.

Bryce said both he and the doctor were sympathetic and suggested a thousand dollars apiece might assist their early inquiries. As soon as the colonel was released there would be another nine thousand apiece. The consul said in Spanish to Bermudez de Cabrera that, if these gringos wanted to throw money around like water, let them.

MacCrimmon suggested a ransom of one-hundred thousand dollars. Bermudez de Cabrera laughed at this sum. If that amount were satisfactory, he said, the island would be emptied in two-weeks.

Alberti said, "Payment in gold, of course."

Bermudez de Cabrera again glanced at the consul and said, "You've climbed from the ridiculous to the interesting."

"What sum would take us from the merely interesting to the possible?"

"Five-million in gold can work wonders."

Bryce smiled indulgently. "That is far beyond what Dr. MacCrimmon can pay. One-million, perhaps—in gold."

Bermudez de Cabrera whispered something to the consul MacCrimmon didn't catch. "*Two*-million would be satisfactory," he said. Bryce looked at MacCrimmon, who agreed. "Be advised," Bermudez de Cabrera said, "the price may rise as we go up the line.

Leave your contact information with the secretary. Come back tomorrow at the same time."

The next morning, after pleasantries, Bermudez de Cabrera asked, "How would the transfer work?"

"We will give you a binding contract stating once the Colonel and his family are safely on American soil, Dr. MacCrimmon will deliver the agreed upon amount of gold to a place of your choice. You may weigh and assay the gold and any adjustments can be made."

Bermudez de Cabrera looked at the consul. He nodded agreement. Bermudez de Cabrera said the initial contacts were promising. With this agreement, additional negotiations could now proceed. "We can expect a definite answer in a day or two. We will call you."

That night MacCrimmon treated Bryce at Timpano, an Italian steakhouse on Las Olas, a few blocks from his condo. They had worked through a first bottle of Cabernet and were congratulating themselves on their negotiating skills when Bryce got a call. He answered in his usual irritating, "Hell-*ooh*!" Bryce listened. His face fell. He thanked the caller and hung up.

"What is it, Bryce?"

"I'm sorry as hell, Andrew."

"About what?"

"That was Bermudez de Cabrera. Colonel Ramon Ximenez was tragically killed in a car accident three weeks ago. Whoever he talked to assured him his wife and two children will be cared for by the government."

"'Car accident,' my ass! Those psychos murdered him!" He bit his lower lip and pounded his fists together.

"Easy, big boy, I'm only the messenger."

MacCrimmon looked up. "What?... Oh, no, Bryce, I'm not mad at you. I was thinking of Thomas Padgett."

Both men went silent, waiting, as the waiter opened and poured the second bottle of wine Bryce had ordered. MacCrimmon took an appreciative sip but banished the glass to arm's length as if it were responsible for this outrage. "When there's a killing, people seldom consider what the military calls 'collateral damage.' Oh, yeah, the news shows the spouse and kids weeping, but it ripples out so much further than that. Look at Thomas Padgett's scorecard to date. He killed Tamara, his wife; he killed poor old Mr. Jeliksen so his wife's life is ruined; he damn near killed me; he might as well have—my wife married another man; my kids have been in turmoil; Colonel Ximenez is dead and his wife and kids will suffer; and Vera's son, Brian, thinks his mother is dead. What punishment is severe enough for this piece of shit?"

Bryce suggested several possibilities, some involving such medieval implements as chain saws and propane torches.

MacCrimmon said he had something better. He punched numbers on his phone. Vera Snead answered:

"Vera, this is Andrew MacCrimmon."

"Yes. I recognize your voice. What do you want?"

"You will now pay *two*-million dollars to the San Antonio United Way. You have two days."

"That's impossible. We—"

"If the third day I don't see an announcement in the *San Antonio Express-News* I will go to the FBI field office here in Fort Lauderdale and report Thomas for the murders of Hans Jeliksen and Tamara Padgett and my attempted murder. I'll also suggest they check your fingerprints."

"Wait, wait!... You're going too fast... Say we do pay. You'll keep bleeding us."

"No, what's done is done. I'm better off now than before it happened. And I'm guilty of certain irregularities I'd rather law enforcement didn't get wind of. Two-million is adequate compensation. Our business will be finished."

"We can't—"

"Two days, Vera."

"Hard core," Bryce said. "But what was that crap about being better off?—and 'certain irregularities—and 'two million being adequate compensation'? You're not going to let these scumbags off the hook, are you?"

"I lied to her, Bryce. I don't like to lie, it puts one in bad company—politicians, lawyers, celebrities, corporate bigshots— but some people don't deserve the truth. If they do pay the two-million, I'll demand another two, and I'll turn them in anyway. In the meantime, the press and the politicians will make their lives miserable."

"So, you're not going to do them in yourself?"

"Nah... With my luck I'd get caught and I'd be the one going to prison."

The next day Dr. MacCrimmon closed the "Malcolm Sutherland" account and paid Bryce back both the fifty-thousand he'd loaned him and another three-thousand for the things he had bought him—the laptop, clothes, and dental care, among others. Bryce refused any payment for the ransom attempt because of the sad outcome. He said the pleasure of his company was compensation enough.

MacCrimmon flew home that evening. The Grant was full up but the Cornell, a French-style B and B next door, had a room.

Saturday, a day when Ohrman would likely be home, MacCrim-mon drove out to the Richmond District to talk to Karen. He turned south on 30th Avenue from California. In the middle of the block he drove slowly past Ohrman, carrying Maddy on his shoulders. Karen strolled beside him; she and Ohrman were talking and paid no attention to him. But Alex, who had skipped ahead, made eye contact for a full two seconds.

Seeing the happy family, the blow was almost as bad as that night in Bryce's condo when he first heard Karen had remarried.

If one compared mental anguish to physical suffering, what would be the equivalent of how he felt?—being burned at the stake?—having his eyes poked out? Whatever it was, it was bad enough he had to stop in the market parking lot for twenty-minutes until he could face the drive back downtown.

He had called ahead, so Isabella was waiting for him when he arrived late Sunday afternoon. Her tentative hug was of the sort one might give a second cousin with body odor. "What's up? I showered this morning."

"You look awful… Did you talk to her?"

"No, I saw the happy couple walking with the kids on the sidewalk. I would have been intruding in the worst way."

"You look stricken, like you did when you first came here."

"I'll get over it."

She pushed away from him. "Andrew, I know it's a bad time for you but we have to talk."

He glanced at the ceiling, but heavenly intervention was not forthcoming. "Those are the four most awful words a man can hear. 'You've got cancer,' is worse, I guess." He forced a smile. "Okay, tell me what we have to talk *about*."

She dragged him to the living room couch, impressing him once again with her strength. She sat next to him, holding both his hands. "You're still obsessed with Karen; it's written all over you."

"That's the clinical term for it, I guess."

"Do you know why I went crazy the night you left?"

"You said I'd never come back."

228

"That was it partially. Mostly it was because I knew how hopeless it was to think we'd ever have a life together. After the sex wore off you'd be miserable, stuck with someone you didn't love but were too honorable to leave. The life you described with me is probably the life Karen has with her psychiatrist. The thing is, I'm a proud person. I won't play second fiddle to anyone, and you have to admit, if there were ten Karens, I'd be number eleven below even the nastiest, ugliest one."

"Not true. If you and I were together you would be concertmistress, that's *first* fiddle."

She plowed ahead, ignoring him as if he had babbled something in Sanskrit: "You may wonder why I'm not more broken up about us not being together."

He looked at her blankly. "Not being together" was her idea so he elected not to speculate.

"It's because you gave me the greatest gift any man can give a woman. That's why I'm not sadder about losing you."

He assumed she was referring to his decision to give her his share of the estate. But he had only thought of it on the drive down and he hadn't told anyone. "How do you know about that?"

"Dr. Lacey told me yesterday."

"Who's Dr. Lacey?"

"My Ob-Gyn."

"Ob-Gyn," he mouthed to himself. The realization hit him like a slap to the face with a cold fish. "Oh, Gawd... N-o-o-o!" he howled. "It can't be!" He jumped up and marched in a circle, punching the side of his head. "You can't be *pregnant*!... You said you'd stopped cycling, Isabella!"

"I thought I had."

He turned away and said to the fireplace, "It's like I have a giant saltshaker, sprinkling the Earth with little bastards. This will make, what, five kids? And only one is legitimate?" He walked over to the French doors and looked out at the pool, his hands clasped behind his back, rocking on his heels until the shock of her announcement passed. But what she had said about not being together was hogwash—it was her way of releasing him from the responsibility of taking care of her and the child.

"Andrew, what 'gift' were *you* talking about?"

He returned to the couch. "Yes, my gift. It fits in with your news quite nicely. I'm giving you my share of the estate, for helping me recover. I couldn't have done it without you. Now you'll have a home to raise the child. With this place and your share of Lena's money, you'll be a wealthy woman. I have some business here first, but in a month or so I'll sign a quitclaim deed... Isabella, I don't know if we will ever be together or not, but I will never abandon you or the child."

25.

TWO DAYS after talking to MacCrimmon, Vera took a call from Enrico. She said she wasn't authorized to deal with him. She handed the phone over to Thomas, standing next to her, and mouthed a warning to control himself. Thomas took the phone, nodding and smiling to reassure her. He had already worked out a plan to deal with Enrico:

"Hoss, I need money."

"How much we talkin,' Enrico?"

"A hundred K. In five days or I go to the cops."

"We're leaving the country in two weeks, so we need time—"

"I'm not waiting no two weeks, Hoss."

"You didn't let me finish... We're flying to Puerto Rico anyway. The cops want to talk to us about Tamara's death. We can bring the money. You can meet us in a public place, we'll leave the bag on a table, whatever you want. But this is it. After this we're gone."

"You don't sound too pissed about it—not like you did before."

"It's over, Enrico. You can't suck off us anymore... Sunday morning, we'll be at the Museum of Contemporary Art. You know where that is?"

"I do."

"As soon as we see you, we'll leave the bag with the money and drive off in a cab. Agreed?"

"You fuck around with me, Hoss, I go straight to the cops."

"It'll be worth the hundred K to be rid of your sorry ass, you miserable lying piece of shit."

Thomas turned to Vera and said with his nicotine-stained, gap-toothed grin, "Start Packing, Vera m'dear, we're going to Puerto Rico in two days."

"You're going to pay the scumbag?"

"Of course not." He explained the essentials of the plan to Vera but left out until later her participation and the gorier details.

Thomas spent the rest of the day arranging flights, a hotel room, and a rental car. To cap it off, he went to the Enrico's Limo Service website and booked a limo for Saturday morning, October 6th, for a trip to Playa Vacia Talega for a "Magdalena Castro." The booking agent replied by email. The trip and sticking around for two hours would cost Ms. Castro three-hundred dollars, exclusive of the tip. "Ms. Castro" agreed.

Late Thursday afternoon, October 4th, Thomas and Vera presented Maltese passports in the names of Randall and Mary Petersen to the clerk at the Hotel Plaza Des Armas in old San Juan.

The next day they drove out of the city, east on route 187. Twenty miles out, Thomas stopped at a spur road he said was perfect. "I'll be parked on the side of this little road. Have Enrico pull in, say you recognize your sister's car—this car. Tell him she must have had mechanical problems. As soon as he stops, hit him in the head with that hammer we bought."

"I have to hit him?"

"Yes. Just hard enough to daze him—you don't have to kill him. I'll take care of the, uh, messy part. Afterward, we'll drive directly to the airport—we'll already be checked out of the hotel."

Saturday morning, October 6th, "Magdalena Castro," AKA Vera Snead, in her gaudy Kansas City hooker make up, wearing a floppy hat that covered her face, and a D-cup bra stuffed with toilet paper, presented herself to EN Limo Service on Las Palmeras, two miles from their hotel. She told the receptionist she was here for the trip to her family gathering at Playa Vacia Talega, twenty-five miles east of San Juan.

Enrico was quiet on the drive out of town. To break the silence Vera told him in her exaggerated New York accent that she had moved to New York twenty-years earlier and had done well in the fashion industry. Enrico was nervous and confined his responses to grunts and monosyllables. She guessed he was anxious to get his money the next day. He showed no sign of recognizing her in spite of having seen Tamara closeup when he buried her. He didn't recognize her voice either, even after talking to her several times on the phone—that had been their greatest concern.

Half an hour later, "Magdalena" spied a dark blue Toyota SUV in a side road. "Stop!... That's my sister's car. She must have had mechanical trouble. Please back up."

Enrico glumly nodded and backed up into the mouth of the side road. Vera slipped the wooden mallet Thomas had given her out of her purse and waited. Enrico stopped. She hit him hard on the top of the head. It didn't knock him out—the blow was delivered clumsily—but it stunned him, giving Thomas, hiding behind the SUV, enough time to rush to the car. He unbuckled Enrico and dragged him out on the ground. Enrico came around enough to recognize him. He saw the ten-inch chef's knife Thomas was holding. "No, please."

Thomas, holding him by his necktie, said, "Was it worth it, you cheating lying sack of shit?!" Getting no answer, he cut his throat with a single hard sweep.

Vera had not wanted to see any of this but her seatbelt had stuck, and by the time she got it free, had opened the heavy door, and had climbed out of the back seat, Enrico was clutching his throat, gurgling, as blood pulsed out of his severed left carotid artery. Vera hurried to the SUV, knelt out of sight, and vomited into the weeds on the side of the road.

Thomas slammed the door to the limo, but seeing cars coming, he put on Enrico's chauffeur's hat and pretended to be taking a piss. He waited until the cars had passed and dragged the body off the road and down an embankment. Lumbering back to the SUV he stopped to kick some dirt over the pool of blood next to the limo. "Get in, Vera. Hurry!"

Thomas hung a U-turn and headed west, back toward San Juan. He glanced over at her and did a double take. "Good God, Vera, you're white as a sheet."

Vera finished wiping vomit from her mouth and threw the dirty handkerchief out the window. She signaled with her fingers she was too upset to speak.

Five miles down the road Thomas stopped and waited for three cars to pass. He got out and threw the chef's knife to the north into some bushes and the hammer over the road to the south. Two miles further down the road he threw his bloody gloves out the window.

They drove directly to the airport. Thomas returned the rental car and they took the shuttle to the terminal.

Vera hurried to a lady's bathroom and locked herself in a stall. She sat on the commode, hunched over, weeping silently into her hands at what she had seen: Enrico, writhing in the dirt, wide-eyed, grabbing at his neck, and a minute later, lying still in a muddy pool of blood. Would the image ever fade? She closed her eyes and took deep breaths until she was calm enough to be seen in public. She unzipped her dress and slipped her arms out so as to remove the oversized bra. She used the wads of toilet paper from the cups to blow her nose and wipe her eyes and to wipe away her gaudy makeup. She slipped back into her dress, hoping her bralessness wasn't too obvious. She took a last deep breath, squared her shoulders, and left the stall. At the sink she finished removing the last smears of makeup. Without it, as white as she was, she looked twenty-years older. A woman next to her asked her if she was all right. She smiled wanly and said she'd eaten a bad oyster. On the way out she stuffed the bra, the hat, and her gloves in a trash can.

Thomas led her to a café and ordered a roast beef sandwich. She told him she wanted nothing to eat and might never eat again as long as she lived. They sat in tense silence until his sandwich arrived five minutes later. She turned away in disgust. He was gobbling it down without washing his hands, as he had that day, eleven months ago in that little café near the museum, minutes after killing Tamara.

Thomas Padgett was a vile, repulsive, very dangerous man. Seeing him kill Enrico had stripped away those few qualities she had found even remotely attractive in him. She vowed she would never again allow him to touch her, no matter how badly she wanted it.

Their 3:35 flight on American didn't reach San Antonio until 11:00. By the time they retrieved their luggage, got the car from the lot, and drove home, it was midnight. Thomas took a half glass of Bourbon out to the patio to relax. Vera, too tired to unpack, brushed her teeth, stripped to her panties, and crawled into bed.

Some time later—she didn't know how long—Vera was awakened from a deep sleep by Thomas pawing at her. "What are you doing, Thomas? What time is it?"

"Fun time."

"No, Thomas, not tonight."

"Yes, tonight. When you were on the plane I saw when you leaned over you weren't wearing a bra. I couldn't get it out of my mind." He crawled on top of her, holding her thin arms over her head, and spreading her legs with his knees. "Stop it, Thomas!" she shrieked. "You're hurting me!" In spite of her screaming and struggling he entered her. Being completely helpless she closed her eyes and went limp to keep him from hurting her even more.

Thomas took longer than usual as he often did when he was drunk. He finished and rolled off her and lay on his side, panting. She waited. When she heard him snoring regularly, she slipped out of bed and tip-toed to the kitchen for a glass of Bourbon she took to the living room. She lay on the giant leather couch and adjusted a plaid over her. Sipping her drink she finalized a plan that had been percolating for some time.

The next few days Thomas left her in peace, even seemed contrite, but she ignored him, other than tersely answering direct questions. He had no complaints—she continued cooking for him and attending to her other household duties—but she had moved to the guest room where she had stayed when she first came. Thomas so far hadn't bothered her there, and not wishing to anger her any more than he already had, he didn't question her about the "shopping" trips she said she took each day,

She *had* been shopping. Over the past four days she had stockpiled underwear, clothing, cosmetics and other essentials in suitcases in a public locker off I-35, ten miles from home. She had put off the larger purchases until the last minute lest Thomas got suspicious.

The next two days she didn't go out at all and behaved as if everything had returned to normal. This changed abruptly late afternoon, Friday, October 12th. Vera took a phone call, as was still their custom:

"Vera, this Andrew MacCrimmon."

"Yes. I recognize your voice. What do you want?"

"You will pay *two*-million dollars to the San Antonio United Way in two days. I've been way too flexible. That stops today."

"That's impossible. We—"

"It's the same deal we talked about earlier. If I don't see an announcement in the *San Antonio Express-News* I will go to the FBI field office here in Fort Lauderdale and report Thomas for the murders of Hans Jeliksen and Tamara Padgett and my attempted murder. I'll also suggest they check your fingerprints."

"We can't—"

"Two days, Vera."

Thomas came in from working outside as she was hanging up. "Who was that, Vera?"

"Sales call. They said it was an important survey. Sucked me in once again."

Thomas blustered something about gutting one or two of those jerks as a way of discouraging so-called sales calls. That out of his system, he lumbered on back to take a shower.

Two days, MacCrimmon had said. Monday, he would turn Thomas in. It couldn't have worked out better.

Saturday morning Vera, dressed casually in jeans, sandals, and a loose white shirt, told Thomas, fiddling with the lawn mower in the garage, she was going out to buy replacement glassware so they would no longer have to drink Bourbon out of plastic glasses. He mumbled something without looking up.

At their bank Vera emptied their joint checking account— forty-six thousand dollars. At a Best Buy a mile away she bought a Dell laptop. As much as Thomas knew about her movements she thought her old one might have some way of spying on her. She stopped off at the storage locker on I-135, loaded her suitcases in the back of the Mustang, and sped off. She took the I-10 turnoff and headed west.

At eight that night, Vera still hadn't returned. Thomas made a call:

"Did you find her, George?"

"Fort Stockton."

"So she's heading west. That's about, what, two hundred miles?"

"Three-hundred and change."

"What's the range on that tracker thing?"

"No limit. It's GPS, hooked into her car's electrical system so it don't need batteries. Sends an update every fifteen-minutes."

"How about the one in her purse?"

"Same deal, but I only get updates every hour, to save battery life. Should be good for a week or so…Where's she going, Boss?"

"Beats hell out of me."

"You going to follow her?"

"No. I'll wait 'til she settles down."

That evening, sitting by the pool, drinking Bourbon, first out of a plastic glass, later out of the bottle, Thomas Padgett wept for the first time in what he estimated was twenty-years. If anyone had ever told him a man could miss a woman this much, he would have called him a damn liar.

26.

SATURDAY afternoon, Karen grabbed her purse and called to Arnold she was going shopping. Alex, waiting by the front door, asked to go along. This was unusual—he seldom showed any interest in shopping—but he'd been acting strangely all morning, following her around, looking at her funny. She said, sure, he could come.

Karen pulled out of the driveway, turned south, and was approaching Clement when Alex said, "I thaw Da-da."

"What?!" She slammed on the brakes, getting a honk and a vulgar gesture from the man behind them who had come within inches of smashing into the back of the SUV. She pulled over to the side and parked. She unbuckled her seat belt and turned back to face him. "Where did you see him, Alex?"

"When we were walking thith morning. He drove by in a blue car."

"How can you be sure, Alex?"

He said with his stubborn bulldog glower, "Becauth it wath *Da-da*!... I *thaw* him!"

She put her hand on his cheek and said gently, "Sometimes we don't really see a person we miss—we *think* we see them, because we want so *much* to see them."

Lacking the rhetorical skills to convince her, the little lad wept in frustration. "It *wath* Da-da, Mama! He'th *not* dead!"

"Why didn't you tell me earlier?"

"I don't want Arnold and Mirah to know."

She mumbled to the windshield, "Could it be? Is it possible?... Okay, Alex. This is our secret. We don't tell Arnold, we don't tell anyone, okay?" She reached back. "Hook pinkies." He grinned and hooked his grubby little pinky in hers. "I'll ask Cam and Dre, everybody, if they've seen him."

That night in bed, Arnold skooched over to her and cupped her breasts. She pulled his hands away. "Not tonight, Arnold. I'm not in the mood."

"Why, Sweetheart, it was a nice day?"

"I don't feel like it." She rolled on her side away from him. "Go to sleep, Arnold."

Monday, after Karen left Alex off at school, she parked in the garage at 818 Mason, next to Andrew's fancy BMW that no one had touched in the eleven months since they left on their cruise. At the corner she caught a cab to Bruce Solomon's office in Embarcadero two. The receptionist sent her right in. "Karen!" Bruce cried, "What a surprise. You're looking well."

"For an old lady, you mean."

"If only old ladies looked half as good. But what brings you here?"

She ignored his invitation to take a seat. "I won't beat around the bush, Bruce. Is Andrew alive?... Alex swears he saw him."

It's an appropriate coincidence that lawyer and liar sound alike, and Bruce was the epitome of both. Standing in front of her, looking her straight in the eye, he said, "Karen, we've been through this a hundred times. The death certificate would not have been issued unless there was absolute proof he was dead. I'm sorry."

"So you haven't seen him since he was lost?"

"Of course, I haven't seen him. I hate to put it in such harsh terms but he's dead."

Karen's next stop was the corner of Bush and Montgomery where Martin Wrassle had his offices. Martin was as incapable of telling a lie as he was of telling a joke. Standing in front of his desk, she asked him, "Martin, is Andrew alive?" She had to bite her lip to keep from smiling at his embarrassed grimacing.

"There was a death certificate, Karen."

"You're not answering the question, Martin."

Martin looked at a far corner of his office and mumbled, "Death certificates have been wrong before so I can't say positively he *isn't* alive."

"But have you *seen* him, Martin?"

Martin said with the most sheepish expression she had ever seen on a living human being, "Why would I have occasion to see a dead man?"

So far Bruce had said no, he wasn't alive, but Bruce was a lawyer—his opinion would only have counted if he'd said he *had* seen him. Martin refused to say outright he hadn't seen Andrew, so him she took as a strong maybe.

That evening she called Dre, Andrew's daughter:

"Dre, Alex says he saw Andrew."

"It's really strange you would say that, Karen. I took a call from someone looking for Gino whose voice was exactly like Daddy's. I haven't seen him, of course. And the man never called back."

"I talked to both Bruce and Martin and couldn't get anything definite out of either of them."

"Have you talked to Alan? He and Daddy were close."

"Good idea."

That night she again rebuffed Arnold. She couldn't possibly have sex with this man if there was even a remote possibility Andrew was alive.

"What's with you, Karen? It's been two weeks now."

"I know, Arnold. I have a lot on my mind."

"What's on your mind that's so important? Your dead ex-husband again?"

"I *have* been thinking of him a lot. That always takes me out of the mood."

"How long before you lay him to rest, Karen?"

"I don't know. A big part of me will never lay *him* to rest until *I'm* laid to rest."

Thursday evening she called Alan. She hadn't spoken to him since the memorial service in January. He had separated himself from the family for reasons he had never explained so she wasn't even sure he would take the call. And he didn't—the housekeeper said he was not available. She left a message saying she would be down on Saturday morning to talk to him about something of vital importance. She said she expected him to be there.

She and Alan had always been close. At sixteen he had found living with his tyrannical father and a succession of nasty stepmothers impossible. Having nowhere else to turn he had shown up at the front door of his Uncle Andrew, a man he had never met and knew nothing about. Andrew wasn't at home—he had gone to the hardware store—but Karen let Alan in, thinking he was a workman come to move the old water heater. He in turn, having come from Paso Robles where he had had no experience with Asians, assumed she was the maid.

Andrew, after hearing Alan's story and after consulting with Karen, agreed Alan could stay as long as he promised to abide by basic standards of good behavior—no drug use, no profanity, helping around the house, and studying hard.

Alan agreed. He was lazy and an incorrigible prankster, but he was very bright so he did well in school.

Cameron, his brother, a year younger, hearing how well Alan was doing, showed up the next year. He had sinned in his father's eyes by being gay and by wanting to become a professional tuba player. Andrew had assured him he had come to the right place— San Francisco welcomed both idiosyncrasies—and they had absorbed him also into the *ménage*.

Both lads thrived. Andrew and Karen taught them manners, proper English, the finer things in life, educated them (at great expense) and, most important, taught them what it was to be a family.

They had only been married a few years so it hadn't been easy taking in two teenage boys, but they came to regard Alan and Cameron more as sons than nephews, and the boys reciprocated, considering them incomparably better parents than Matthew and whichever wife he was with at the time had ever been.

That evening Karen told Arnold she was driving to Paso Robles on Saturday to talk to her nephew Alan. She said she had asked Mirah, their housekeeper, to look after Alex and Maddy.

"Why are you driving to Paso Robles, Karen?"

"If Andrew's alive Alan might know."

"But Andrew's *not* alive, Karen. The DNA evidence proved that."

She smiled and patted his cheek. "You're probably right, Arnold. Bear with me. If Alan hasn't seen him I won't say anything more about it."

"Promise?"

"Promise."

"And we can get back on schedule?"

"Schedule," was Arnold's code word for sex. "We'll see."

Saturday morning, Karen arrived at the MacCrimmon mansion on the hill west of Paso Robles and was admitted by Carlotta, the Mexican maid. Alan's father, Matthew, Andrew's brother, greeted her. He said Alan was at the factory handling a personnel emergency. An armed security guard had come to work staggering drunk. He led her to the massive Spanish-style living room, seated her, and had Carlotta bring coffee.

Matthew was a big man, six-feet five or so, balding, and tending to fat. He was coarser featured than Andrew, taking after their father. Andrew looked more like their mother who was by all accounts a beauty. Matthew and Andrew hadn't spoken in decades due to unforgotten festering slights on both sides, but Matthew had always been polite to her, even courtly, as he was today. He said how sorry he was that he and Andrew hadn't worked through their differences.

After coffee and chit-chat about the children, whom he said he was sorry not to have seen, he had Carlotta show her to her room overlooking the pool, the largest of the five guest rooms. She was not ready to wear a bathing suit but she did change into shorts and a sleeveless top.

Ten minutes later Alan roared up in his fancy Italian convertible. She reached the base of the stairs as he thundered through the front door like a bull elephant, his entrance of choice for as long as she had known him. But instead of engulfing her in his arms and swinging her around as he had always done in the past, he smiled weakly and shook her tiny hand with his thumb and first two fingers. She assumed his coolness was because she had married Arnold, an act of betrayal in his opinion.

He led her out on the west side of the pool to heavily padded chairs arranged around a teak table, shaded from the morning sun by a large overhang. He said he'd be out in a minute, he had to change and order lunch.

He returned in shorts and a T-shirt, holding a beer. He flopped down across the table from her in a chair that creaked its annoyance at his weight.

Karen said in a shrill tone of urgency, "Is Andrew alive, Alan?"

Alan looked down at the beer bottle he was twirling and said brusquely that, before they got into any speculation about whether he was alive or not, he wanted to hear her story from the very beginning, especially the part where she married "a goddamned *psychiatrist.*"

"It's nothing like you think it is!" she shot back at him. "We'll get to that in the proper time... The whole fiasco started on a cruise we took last November. We went ashore in Puerto Rico. At a museum I saw a couple from the ship walking toward us, a giant named Thomas Padgett and his sour wife. But this woman was not the one he left the ship with. Her earrings, shoes, walk, hair, were all different, the things a woman would notice. We looked into it and decided they must have done away with the wife and replaced her with the twin sister."

"Why would they do that?"

"We didn't know. Andrew must have found out and challenged the man. The morning he disappeared the woman sent me a note threatening the children if I said anything. This pretty much proved they had done something awful."

"Do you still have this note?"

"I do. I had thrown it in with a pile of papers and had forgotten about it, but when we moved the belongings at 818 into storage I found it in a box. I had put it in a plastic bag in case it had fingerprints. I was going to show it to Andrew when he came back that morning. But he didn't *come* back."

She looked down, biting her lip. She shook off the memory, braced her shoulders, and continued: "The woman must have known before she sent the note that Padgett had thrown him overboard. Anyway, we searched the ship, but couldn't find him. That's when the safety officer said he and another man, an old man named Jeliksen, had gone overboard. He said a life ring was missing. Everybody assumed the old man had seen Padgett throw Andrew over the side and had thrown it to him.

"The first day I was hysterical, as you can imagine, but Selma, the old man's wife, comforted me, and by the second day I had calmed down enough to take care of what had to be done. The officers of the ship suspected Padgett—he even admitted he and Andrew had had 'words'—and they asked me over and over what the problem was between them. I said I didn't know. One officer,

Dawson, knew I was lying, but I stuck to the story because I was afraid for the children.

"When I left the ship Cam and Roger joined me. They'd flown to Fort Lauderdale to help. Two days later two FBI agents came to our hotel to interview me. The big African-American told me the FBI investigates crimes against American citizens on American ships, even if they're not in American waters. The way they talked, they also thought Padgett was guilty but they had no proof and no motive. They badgered me, trying to make tell what I knew, but I lied to them too. Cam was mad at me for not telling them but, like I said, I was afraid for the kids.

"On Thanksgiving Day—I was still in Fort Lauderdale—the Coast Guard called and said they'd found the life ring. That was good news—Andrew had probably had it—but also bad news—he was no longer with it. There wasn't any point in staying so I gave up and flew back to The City.

"I was already a wreck. Then in early December the FBI brought the evidence of Andrew's death."

"What evidence?"

"The electronic key to our suite, his Swiss Army knife, his wedding ring, the ashes, and the exact DNA match. I went berserk and tried to kill myself with oxycontin. Roger found me and called 9-1-1. That saved my life."

She took a sip of water and, fighting back tears, she looked down at her hands patting the table. She apologized for her weeping; the memories of that time were still very painful. "I was crazy as—well, really crazy. But even so, in spite of the so-called evidence, I knew he wasn't dead—he couldn't be, we are too perfect together... I talked to him as if he was right there with me. I waited for him, begged him to come home. But my craziness was too much for Roger and Renata to handle. I wasn't dressing myself, I didn't eat, I wandered the house at all hours—the kids were terrified. So they put me in a mental hospital in Marin. By the time I came home for Christmas I was better, even well enough to help with the memorial service."

She said to give her a minute, her mouth was dry. She poured another glass of water and took a tiny sip. "January, February, I wasn't getting any better. I was still neglecting the kids and myself. I was too much for Renata, so she, and Cam and Roger too, said I had to see a psychiatrist. That's when I started seeing Arnold Ohrman."

Alan asked, "Isn't it unethical for psychiatrists to hit on patients?"

"Be patient. I'll get to that... In the meantime, week after week went by and not only was I not improving, I was getting worse because I saw there was no hope—nobody could understand, certainly no psychiatrist, how much I missed Andrew. Arnold said my sorrow and longing was a disease. He called it an 'Exaggerated Grief Reaction.'"

"Yeah, this all interesting," Alan said, drumming the table, "but how did you come to marry him?"

"Good grief, Alan MacCrimmon, be patient! Go get another beer, get *six* beers. I'll *get* to it!"

She calmed down when she saw him hiding a smile at her outburst, but she still shook a finger at him, warning him to behave, as she had done when he was a mischievous teenager. "I guess it was April I first noticed he was attracted to me. Why anyone would find a skinny, greying old hag attractive I had no idea, but he's a man, and who knows what goes on in *their* heads."

Alan clapped his hands and laughed outright at this.

"We started out having coffee together. He is a nice man and was a good friend, a better friend than psychiatrist. That's when he said we'd do better with him treating me as a friend. From that point on I wasn't his client anymore, and he didn't charge me."

"Clever way to get around the ethics breach. Unscrupulous but clever."

"In May he invited me to dinner. I said absolutely not. He's good looking and smart and very nice, but I had no interest in him as a man. But Renata said the kids needed a father and threatened to quit if I didn't at least give him a chance. Cam and Roger, as usual, backed her up. So—I went to dinner with him, but with a strict no-touching rule which he obeyed. In June he invited me and the kids to his house. Again I refused and again Renata and Cam and Roger pressured me."

"Wait, wait, wait!" Alan shouted. "Why were Roger and Cam so damned anxious to get you married off?"

"Partly because they were worried about me, what crazy thing I'd do next. And partly because they were tired of coming over five or six times a week, every time I went nuts or there was some catastrophe."

"Okay, this guy invited you to his house. What happened next?"

"He has a lot going for him, like I said. I don't know why he was still single. His house is nice too with a big back yard. He made a barbeque for us and he was good with the kids. I saw him again a few times, but only so the three of them would stop badgering me.

"But when Renata fell down the stairs and broke her hip I was alone. Everything went wrong. Her son threatened to sue me, Alex was in trouble at school, the kitchen drain plugged up, I was behind in the bills, and all the time I was mourning for Andrew." She blushed and said, looking down, "I was lonely, Alan. And I have drives like any woman. And I had finally, *finally*, accepted that Andrew would never come home."

She again wept at the painful memories.

Alan said gently, "I'm sorry, Aunt Karen. It's not like I thought it was."

She looked up and wiped her eyes. "If I had never met Andrew, Arnold and I might have had a regular marriage, like most people, but I *had* met Andrew. All the other men in the world are like ants in comparison... I can't stop *thinking* about him, I can't stop *missing* him. I do what I have to do as a wife with Arnold but I feel guilty about it, as if I'm betraying Andrew's memory. Half the time I lie there like a dead fish. At least I don't cry anymore while does it. He might as well use one of those plastic dolls you blow up—like the one you had when you were in high school."

Alan blushed sunburn pink. "How did you know about that?"

"I found it in your closet when I was cleaning."

She blew her nose and wiped her eyes. Both went silent as Carlotta served the lunch Alan had ordered—chicken salad sandwiches, a beer for him, a glass of white wine for Karen—and shuffled back to the kitchen

Karen leaned over the table to him and demanded, "Where is he, Alan? And don't lie to me like everybody else has!"

He took a deep swig, emptying his bottle, and belched lightly. "What would you do, Aunt Karen—if he *was* alive?"

"We'd get back together, of course."

"You'd leave this new husband"— he snapped his fingers— "like that?"

"Tomorrow."

"You promise this on the lives of your children?"

"Do you seriously think I could ever be with another man if Andrew was alive?"

Alan looked off toward the pool and exhaled with a horse flutter.

"Alan, talk to me!"

"I'm breaking a sacred promise, Aunt Karen."

"He'll thank you for it."

"Okay!" He banged his beer bottle on the table to finalize his decision. "Yeah, he is alive! But when I saw him, he looked awful—skinny, a big beard and a ponytail. He'd been through hell."

"Oh, thank God!" she shrieked, pressing her fists against her chest. "Thank you, God!" She leaned over and grabbed his forearm with both hands. "Tell me all about him, Alan! Hurry! Tell me!"

He told her the story in as much detail as Andrew had given him. At various points Karen interrupted and repeated what he had said, as if it were too awful to believe—"He floated in the ocean for two days, at night in the dark?" and, "He was in prison and they beat him?" When he came to the coffin episode, Karen saw no humor in it whatever, in fact buried her face in her hands and sobbed at what might have happened if this Eddy hadn't removed the coffin lid in time. At the end she begged God to bless the man in Fort Lauderdale who had helped and befriended him.

She asked, sobbing, "Why, in heaven's name doesn't he contact me?"

"You're married to another man. He assumed you were happy and didn't want to upset you."

"God in heaven," she shrieked, "how could he possibly think any other man could mean anything to me."

"He meant enough to you to marry him."

"I was crazy, Alan... Andrew must be suffering terribly, thinking I wanted to marry Arnold."

"Yes, he is. He's bereft, he's in agony."

"Where is he, Alan? *Please!* I have to find him."

"I don't know where he is, Aunt Karen. I swear to God I don't know. He wouldn't say."

"But he must have said *something*, Alan, where he was going, what he was going to do."

"The only thing he said specifically was, he had to get himself in shape, to get Maddy back. He mentioned something about a place in Palm Springs."

"Palm Springs! Of course!" Karen cried. "That's where he is!" She fumbled around in her purse for her phone. Scrolling down she murmured, "I hope they haven't changed the number." She dialed:

> "Isabella speaking."
> "Isabella, this is Karen. Is Andrew there?"
> "'Andrew'?... Of course not, Karen. Andrew's dead."
> "No, he's not. Alex saw him and so have several other people."
> "They're seeing things, Karen. He's dead."

She didn't believe Isabella. Andrew had probably told her to deny he was there, as he had the others. That's where he was, she had no doubt about it.

27.

SUNDAY afternoon, Arnold called to Karen, grabbing her car keys from the table in the entry, "Where are you going? You just got back from Paso Robles two hours ago." She said with a sweet enigmatic smile she had business to take care of downtown.

At a stoplight on Clement she called Avni Gill, the tenant at 818 Mason, to tell her she would be dropping by. Twenty minutes later she opened the garage door in the alley behind the house and parked next to Andrew's BMW. She knocked at the door at the top of the basement stairs to announce her arrival and let herself in with her key. Mrs. Gill, accustomed to her eccentric landlady's spur of the moment visits, asked her to join her at the massive kitchen table. She asked why she had come.

"You are saving for a move to a nice apartment, is that true?"

Mrs. Gill said, yes, that was true.

"If I gave you ten-thousand-dollars—*gave* it to you, no strings attached—and returned your first month's rent and cleaning deposit, could you be out in ten days?"

"Such a short time, Missus. Where would we go?"

"A hotel for a while, maybe put your things in storage. With that much money you could find a place quickly."

"I'll talk to my husband."

Karen thanked her and rose to leave. Mrs. Gill said, "Missus, do you know a man named Sutherland?"

Dad Sutherland. Andrew's maternal grandfather. "I might. What did he look like?"

"Thin, heavy beard, a ponytail. He looked ill."

Exactly as Alan had described him. "When was this?"

"Six or eight weeks ago."

"What did he say?"

"He said he had once lived here. And he asked what became of all the furnishings."

"What did you tell him?"

"I said you must have sold them."

"Oh, good grief!" she cried. "Now I *have* to find him!"

Karen helped Mirah with dinner and clean up afterward, so Arnold wasn't able to talk to her until Alex and Maddy were asleep. He cornered her in their bedroom room and had her sit beside him on the bed. "I was worried about you this afternoon, Karen. Now, like magic, you look better than I've ever seen you. You're smiling."

"Andrew's alive. He's back, Arnold. Alex saw him. Alan and Avni Gill both talked to him. I decided, even if he doesn't want me—you know, for marrying you—knowing he's alive is enough. I feel like whatever it was that got ripped out of me has been put back in place."

Arnold said, patting the back of her hand, "Karen, Sweetheart, you can't rework your entire life based on the questionable observation of a bright imaginative little kid. And if Andrew really did come back why didn't he contact you? And what was he doing out here in this neighborhood?"

"He was checking up on us, to be sure the kids and I are okay."

"And why haven't the news outlets publicized his return? It would be a big story."

She shrugged. "Maybe he doesn't want the man who threw him overboard to know he's alive."

He hissed in anger and let the matter drop. She was relieved. Her crisp tone must have convinced him he couldn't break through, and if he tried, she would erupt in a shrieking rage as she already had several times when he had brought up Andrew.

At bedtime, Karen announced from the doorway of their bedroom she would be staying in the guest room from now on. She closed and locked the door before Arnold could respond.

The next morning Karen laid out, museum-like, all the mementos of Andrew she had brought from 818: several of his pictures, including the studio portrait anyone would swear was a of a movie star; a couple of his books—a Beowulf, and his Shakespeare tragedies that had such a nice leather smell; several of his shirts she used as nightgowns and wore around the house; and the last polo shirt he had worn on the cruise before he was lost. She had sealed it in a plastic bag to preserve his woodsy spicy scent.

Over the next days, to avert suspicion, Karen played impeccably her role as dutiful housewife, cleaning, doing laundry, cooking, and shopping. Arnold tried to reason with her but she said with adamantine stubbornness the new arrangement was permanent, there was nothing further to discuss. He asked her if this meant there would be no intimacy between them. She said that was exactly what in meant. That kind of contact would be adultery.

"Touching your husband is adultery?"

"Yes. My husband is alive. I'm not a widow anymore."

Saturday afternoon Karen took Alex and Maddy to Huntington Park. They hadn't been in a long time and all three missed it. While Alex romped around with his buddies from school, and Maddy toddled after one dog and another, Karen closed her eyes, folded her hands in her lap, and sat still. She could almost feel Andrew returning, hear the bench creak as he settled in next to her, feel his strong arm over her shoulders; she could almost smell his scent, and hear him saying something goofy, making her laugh.

Laughter. How different her life had become. She could count on one hand the number of times she'd laughed in the eleven-months he had been gone.

For a nostalgic dinner that evening Karen took the kids down the hill to Uncle Vito's for pizza. She had to smile at the people looking at Maddy, probably thinking this beautiful little girl in her nice dress with her perfectly symmetrical pigtails was a fastidious little lady. What a shock they were in for: she was a worse slob than Alex had been. Alex was still pretty much a pig but seeing his little sister smearing sauce over her face, on her pretty dress, and in her hair, he echoed his mother's comment: "Dith-*guth*ting!"

She remembered a time when Alex was Maddy's age and had looked much the same, and a childless couple next to them had asked how they would ever get him clean. Andrew said they ran him through the pots and pans cycle in the dishwasher a couple times—that usually cleaned him up pretty good. How they had laughed on the walk home at the looks on their faces. She had never appreciated how funny Andrew was. She missed laughter terribly.

Late that night, both kids bedded down and asleep, Karen went to her room to go to bed. The instant she turned the light on she saw what he had done. Every reminder of Andrew was gone—his pictures, books, even his shirts.

She ran downstairs to the living room where Arnold was watching PBS. "Why did you do it?!" she shrieked. "Where are Andrew's things?!"

"In the attic, Karen—they're safe. We'll discuss this upstairs." He clicked off the TV and guided her by her elbow upstairs to her room. He closed the door and stood, facing her.

She stamped her foot and demanded, "What right do you have to come in *my* room and take *my* things?!"

"You have to get over your obsession with a dead man, Karen. You're already making my life unbearable. Keep up this delusional behavior and you'll damage the children."

"I know what's best for *my* children!"

He sagged down on the bed, his hands between his thighs. "What happened, Karen? You were doing better, adjusting day by day. We even had a sex life of sorts."

Her sour chuckle suggested otherwise. "Lying under you like a slab of meat is not a 'sex life,' at least for me. It was like you were one of my clients at the Honolulu Sun!"

"'Honolulu Sun'?—what are you talking about?"

She rose and walked to the window. An old couple walking by on the sidewalk was holding hands. Would she and Andrew look like that some day? She said without looking back, "The Sun is a massage parlor on Geary. You may have seen it. It's between Polk and Larkin."

"Never had the pleasure. What's your point?"

She turned back and crossed her arms. "It's one of the many things I never told you during our sessions, Arnold. I was a prostitute there for a year and a half—until Andrew rescued me."

Arnold looked at her in stunned silence. Being a psychiatrist, she thought he would have heard every story in the book. He said he refused to believe it—there was no way his wife could have been a prostitute, especially in a sleazy massage parlor like that one. He said this was yet another delusion or perhaps even a conscious fabrication to hurt him because she was angry at him. She agreed she was angry at him—very angry—but she assured him it was no fabrication. Her father had run up gambling debts and with no means to pay, the gangsters he owed the money to had cut off a finger with garden shears. When they threated to decapitate him, she had done what she had to do.

"Let's assume for the moment you're telling the truth. You say I'm like one of your customers?—like you were doing it because I paid you?... I thought you enjoyed it."

"I did enjoy it sometimes, Arnold—you're a good and sensitive lover. But it's like I enjoyed it once in a while in the massage parlor. I have needs like anybody else. But there's so much more to marriage than sex and whatever it was that made you want to marry me... What do we have in common, Arnold?" He looked at her in blank bafflement. "I'll tell you what—*nothing*!... You have your political causes, and your diet with no gluten or GMO's and no alcohol and no red meat, and your Buddhism, and your political correctness that makes me feel guilty about laughing at anything, not that there's anything to laugh about anyway... Andrew and I are different, Arnold, we're common people, we're not like you."

"Andrew's dead, Karen. And he was never *common*. Neither were you."

"That rude man playing with his phone who bumped me on the sidewalk—you're bigger than he was and in better shape, but you did nothing."

"I suppose Andrew would have beaten him up."

"No, but he would have bumped him back and told him to watch where he was going." She added, smiling, "He might have beaten him up if he didn't apologize."

"Andrew's dead, Karen."

"There's no fun here, Arnold. There's no play, no laughter."

"There hasn't been all that much for me to laugh about either, Karen."

"I know, Arnold. I'm not blaming you."

"Tell me, for the sake of discussion, what would you do if he did return?"

She said without a second's hesitation, "I'd go back to him. I told you that over and over."

"But Andrew *can't* return, Karen. He's *dead*... Croaked... Corpsified... Departed... Expired... Deceased... He's *extinct*! Can't you get that into your head?!"

Mrs. Gill called Karen the next day. She said Mr. Gill had agreed to her proposal. They were moving out on Tuesday, the 23rd of October. Karen dropped by the next day to give her the check for the amount she had promised. That same day she called the moving and storage company on Battery where their goods were stored and arranged for everything to be delivered on Wednesday, the 24th, the day after the Gills left.

In the meantime, she arranged interviews with the four most promising applicants of the thirteen who had answered her ad requesting someone to help with housekeeping and childcare. The choice proved to be easy: a husky Austrian widow named Uta Hofer. Frau Hofer was in her mid-fifties, had forearms like Popeye, and wore her coarse lacquered blonde hair in a bun that reminded Karen of coiled baling wire. Frau Hofer spoke good English but with a heavy accent. She said she also spoke French passably— until recently she had taken care of the three children of a French diplomat who had been recalled to France—and she played the piano well enough to supervise the piano practice of two of the French children. She agreed to do light housework, even heavy housework, floors and windows, if paid accordingly. Karen readily agreed. Uta said she had a small apartment in the inner Sunset, but she would gladly stay over in one of the third-story bedrooms whenever necessary. Karen said they would plan on starting the day the furnishings were delivered.

Wednesday, October 24th, Karen left Maddy with Mirah as usual, and left Alex off at school. But instead of returning to Arnold's home she drove to the Mason Street house. Later that morning the movers brought back everything she had put in storage eight weeks earlier: the furniture; the carpets—which she had had cleaned; the paintings, which, at unconscionable expense, she had had cleaned and rehung; the thousands of books, each of which she or Uta dusted and returned, as best she could remember, to its original place. The kitchen ware; the piano; the list went on and on. The movers, a crew of Irishmen encouraged by a promise of heavy tips, placed the furniture and set up the beds. But the two ladies arranged the bedrooms exactly as they had been the day they had left on their cruise, down to leaving Andrew's wallet and his keys—which she'd brought back from the cruise—in the dish on the dresser where he always left them.

Frau Hofer, a reasonably sophisticated woman, realized what a mammoth expense all this had been. She asked Karen how, she, a single woman, could afford it. Karen set her straight on two points: She wasn't single—she had *two* husbands. And she was rich—her real husband, who would one day be coming home, the one whose clothing they had put in the closets and dressers, had given her five-million dollars to use any way she wished.

Three days later, Saturday, October 27th, a day she knew Arnold would be home, she called him into her room and said she had something to tell him. He said he hoped it was good news for once.

She had him sit beside her on the bed. "Arnold, the renters from the Mason Street house have left. The children and I are moving back. I had all our belongings returned and I hired a woman to help me with the house and the children."

Arnold stared at her a moment, unblinking, his mouth open. "I assume you're doing this because you think Andrew is coming back."

"He *is* coming back."

He asked what she would do if Andrew never came home and would she ever accept his death, which every person with even a pinch of good sense knew was a virtual certainty. His death, she said, she could never accept. If he didn't come home, she would never be completely happy, but she could live with it as long as she had his children. In answer to his unasked question, she said there might be other *men* but there would never be another *man* in her life.

"But Karen, we're legally married."

"No, Arnold. Andrew is alive so I think they call this bigamy. Once his return is official we can get an annulment."

"I'll never see you again?"

"Oh, I'll be in and out. I'll hire someone with a truck to help me move the things we have here."

They both rose. She kissed him on the cheek. "I'm grateful, and I'm sorry to have hurt you."

"I was good to you, Karen. How can you treat me this way?"

"Yes, you were good to me. I guess if I seem cruel it's because I resent you for marrying me in the first place. You knew all along I didn't love you and you knew I was hurting. You took advantage of me when I was desperate. Because of you Andrew may not want me anymore."

Arnold gritted his teeth and slapped the sides of his thighs. "Now I have some observations of my own, Mrs. *MacCrimmon*—or *Ms. Ting*... It always seemed odd," he said, addressing the closet door. "If she loved this man so much why would she use her maiden name." He moved closer and looked down at her. "Now that you're leaving, I can tell you frankly that, whatever your connection to this man is, it sure as hell isn't love!... It's some kind of—" he shook his hands in frustration looking for the right words, "oh, some kind of perverse bondage or obsession, a mix of infantile dependence, a whole hell of a lot of fantasy, some guilt, a lot of insecurity, and psychopathic indifference to the people you hurt very badly in this maelstrom you call a relationship."

Karen, unfazed by this outburst, said she agreed with him. This was much the same way Andrew described it. "He said it's like a rose growing out of a manure pile—"

"Typical delicate phrasing."

"—a beautiful flower with a lot of thorns. But a different way to look at it is the way Ms. Wu at Pine Hills Retreat said it. Andrew and I—who knows why?—have grown together so closely that separating us would be like tearing apart Siamese twins with elephants."

Karen turned to go, but Arnold clutched her arm to stop her. "One last question... I know this man is handsome and smart, all the usual, and God knows he's colorful. But it's what happens day to day, hour by hour, that's the strength of a relationship. I've had several clients, attractive wives of powerful men, who said they married the glamor and status, but for all their diamonds and fancy cars, their marriages were empty, loveless. What was it like for you, say, on a Monday morning or a rainy Thursday?"

Karen pried his fingers loose and backed away. "You're right, what you said about everyday stuff... Each day with Andrew was like being at summer camp. Every morning when I woke up there was the smell of fresh ground coffee, something going on with him and the kids, some noisy game they made up, somebody laughing. And he's so funny and playful, the goofy things he does, like when he plays 'Ragnar the Reprehensible,' a sensitive Viking who likes flower arranging and interpretive dance, or when he chases me through the house on crutches—once he even managed to corner me in a bedroom. He even makes *sex* fun."

"Did I mention infantile?" Arnold said with a chilly smile

Karen was sorry she had pushed this kind good man into uncharacteristic meanness. She conceded with a weak smile. "Well, childish maybe. Andrew is very smart but he comes down to my level because he loves me and he knows it makes me happy. Like I told you, Andrew and I are simple people."

"'Simple people'?" He rolled his eyes. "Good God! How deluded can one person be?"

"You should watch 'Seinfeld,' Arnold , you might laugh. Come to think of it, I've never seen you laugh out loud. I guess laughing's not politically correct—Oooh! You might offend some one."

"Common courtesy is not political correctness."

"The hardest I ever laughed was the time Andrew sang 'Mona Lisa' in a fake Chinese accent. Somehow I can't imagine you saying 'Mona Risa'—or *singing,* for that matter.

"I laugh—but it's usually at something a little more subtle than somebody pretending to be a Viking."

"Oh, Arnold," Karen said, ignoring him, "if you only knew how yummy a rib-eye steak is once in a while. It hasn't hurt Andrew's health—he's healthier than you are. Or was."

"There's more to it than just the meat, Karen."

"And what's the matter with gluten?"

"'Gluten'?"

"It's what makes bread bread. Anybody who doesn't like chewy Acme sourdough should come to you for help."

He closed his eyes and shook his head

Karen asked him with a quizzical look, "And what do you have against wine, Arnold?"

"'Wine'?"

"Yes... Andrew and I had a glass of wine or a cocktail every evening before dinner. It was a happy ritual. If it was a good day, we'd celebrate; if not, well, we had each other, and there was always tomorrow. Maybe if you drank a little wine we would have gotten along better."

"Enough of this nonsense, Karen."

"Okay, but one last question... Why would an attractive eligible man like you want to marry a crazy middle-aged ex-prostitute in love with another man, a woman you have nothing in common with... Am I that beautiful and sexy?"

"Yes, you are, Karen."

That weekend the autumn rains came. It was a good time for the kids to acclimate to the new arrangement. Arnold had been fabulous with both of them and they both missed him, Alex not as much as Maddy because he had seen his father and he knew he would be returning.

Saturday, for lunch, as a special treat she made mac and cheese which both of them loved, and after their naps, they watched the "Lion King" for the umpteenth time.

Arnold called late afternoon and asked if they were all right. There would be a time of adjustment, she said, and the kids missed him. He asked if he might come to see them. She said that would be a bad idea. She again thanked him for taking care of them and apologized for what must have seemed her cruel way of leaving. "If we had met before I met Andrew, we probably would have been happy together."

"That's a kind thing to say. Has he returned?"

"No, he hasn't."

The next morning, Uta arrived on schedule to take care of Maddy. When Karen returned from walking Alex to school she and Uta had a cup of coffee at the kitchen table. "We're home, Uta. It's like we never left, except everything is cleaner. Still, without Andrew, it's like living in a big empty box."

"He'll come, Karen. With such a beautiful wife and cheeldren, he'll come."

Later that morning, for the first time in almost a year, Karen went to her gym. Even as light as her workout was, she felt much better, enough better that she dyed her hair, also for the first time in almost a year.

Tuesday morning she walked Alex to school as usual, but she continued on down to Embarcadero two and the 17th floor offices of Bruce Solomon.

"Andrew's alive, Bruce. Alex saw him, and his nephew talked to him. You lied to me."

Bruce guided her by the elbow to one of the sumptuous leather chairs facing his desk. He took the one next to her and turned to face her. "I had no choice, Karen. Andrew made me promise I wouldn't tell anyone he was alive."

"Where is he?"

Bruce spread his hands in the universal expression of ignorance. "That I don't know, I swear it!"

Karen said she believed him. "I've moved back to Mason Street. I left Arnold. But I have to know which man I'm married to."

"You're married to Arnold, at least for the time being. It's called the Enoch Arden rule."

" I want to divorce him."

263

Bruce advised her to wait until there was a decision on a petition he had filed with the court to have Andrew's death certificate ruled invalid for reasons of fraud. If the court ruled favorably, Andrew should never have been ruled dead and her marriage to Arnold Ohrman would be annulled.

She agreed to wait.

28.

THOMAS PADGETT picked up after the sixth ring. He was out of breath, he'd had run to the phone from the shower:

"Vera?"

"No, Mister Padgett, It's Andrew MacCrimmon."

"Well, I'll be a son-of-a-bitch! You *are* alive. What do *you* want?"

"Didn't Vera tell you? You were supposed to donate two-million dollars to the United Way."

"When did you talk to Vera?"

"Friday. I told her you had two days. If you didn't pay, I'd go to the FBI with everything. But I got sidetracked. Odd she didn't tell you, don't you think?"

"She left Saturday."

"Good for her. Anyway, I've decided to give you until Friday, Padgett. Two-million dollars to the United Way. I'll check the webpage of the *San Antonio News-Express.* There'd better be a notice there."

"And if I do pay, what—"

MacCrimmon had hung up.

Vera, the miserable bitch, hadn't told him about MacCrimmon's call because she *wanted* the bastard to go to the FBI. He lumbered into the kitchen, poured a full glass of Bourbon, and took it out to the one surviving padded chair by the pool.

Vera must know she'd be charged as an accomplice in at least two murders, good for a life sentence. Was he so awful she'd rather go to jail for life than be with him? He took a deep swig and set the glass aside. What was she up to? Was she making a deal with the feds? No matter how she cut it she'd still get hard time... Or had she left the country?

He called George:

"Any change, George?"

"She's still in Tucson."

"What the hell is she doing in Tucson for two days?"

"She's staying at a motel. I thought she might have found the trackers and left them, but she's been driving and walking around... Look, Boss, it'd be a lot easier if you tracked her yourself. It ain't that hard."

"I'm an idiot with computers, George."

"I could show you how—you'd catch on. If five-year old kids can do it, you can."

"Aw, hell, come on over. I'll give it a try."

Thomas drained the Bourbon and set the empty glass on his thigh. He looked out at the pool, imagining Vera swimming laps nude.

He had until Friday before MacCrimmon called in the feds, not much time to arrange his escape, especially since Vera had drained the checking account, leaving him only a few thousand dollars. His credit card would be good for another nine-thousand, and he scrounged another eight-thousand by pawning what was left of Tamara's jewelry and three of the ugly paintings she had bought.

He couldn't get into the investments—they were community property and demanded "Tamara's" signature as well as his own. That was another question: why had she left behind the five-mill that was her share? It made no sense.

George showed up half an hour later. He explained again the car tracker was plugged into the Mustang's OBD port and had a backup battery for when the engine was turned off. It was set to give updates every fifteen minutes and reported both co-ordinates and street addresses. The personal unit was hidden in the lining of her purse and had a battery life of about ten days if it only updated every hour. He had long since taken care of the setup for both trackers. He showed Thomas how to log onto the GPS websites with his phone and gave him the usernames and passwords. Thomas hadn't realized how easy it was. He suspected George hadn't told him earlier so he could keep charging his outlandish fees.

George, as if reading his mind, said, "I'll need my money, Boss, 1152.27 by my last count. That includes keeping the GPS websites open for three more months." The implied threat was, he'd shut the websites down if he wasn't paid. A hard luck story was wasted on a private investigator. He paid him, in cash.

The next day, succumbing to the inevitable, he packed to leave for good. His aim was to find Vera, retrieve their assets, and convince her to escape with him abroad to some country without an extradition treaty, like Croatia. If he found her before the feds got involved they could still salvage their funds. If she refused both, well, maybe she would join her sister and Enrico.

Thursday, October 17, Thomas Padgett left the home he had lived in for the past twelve-years. The last with Vera had been choppy as hell, but there had been happy moments.

Merging onto I-10 from I-35, heading west, he remembered he hadn't locked the front door. He didn't turn back.

Vera had spent her first night away in a dumpy motel on the outskirts of a place called Fort Stockton. She hadn't slept all night, thinking each noise was Thomas coming for her. Sunday night she'd stayed in Las Cruces, New Mexico. Monday afternoon she reached Tucson where she planned to rest a couple of days and get her bearings. This time she'd elected to stay in a nice downtown motel.

Until now she had been too nervous to eat much other than packaged junk food at gas station minimarts, but in Tucson she had a decent dinner. On the way back to the motel she stopped in a liquor store and bought a fifth of Jack Daniels.

She opened the curtains of her room and dragged a chair to the sliding glass door looking out on the pool. Sipping JD out of the motel water glass she considered her options. Her share of the nine million was irretrievable—it required Thomas's permission to sell. She felt a certain purity in not taking blood money but without funds, flight abroad was out of the question. What would she do once the money ran out?

She could last almost a year if she lived frugally in some little out of the way place, maybe even get a job. But it was a matter of time until the FBI arrested her or, worse, Thomas found her.

With her second drink a plan formed. She would go to prison, possibly for the rest of her life—this was inevitable. Her only hope was reducing her sentence by giving evidence against Thomas. But she needed advice about it—if she were sentenced to life anyway there was no point in aggravating Thomas. She had no friends, no acquaintances. If she went directly to the FBI they would arrest her and she would be in no position to bargain. There *was* someone, however, who might help. He was about as unlikely a "friend" as she could imagine, potentially even dangerous, but she had no alternative. From what she had read about him on the internet there was a good chance he would welcome getting a shot at Thomas before the FBI caught him.

She took a deep breath, crossed her fingers, and made a call:

"Dr. MacCrimmon?"

"Yes. Who is this?"

"Vera Snead."

"What the hell do you want? And how did you get this number?"

"You should be more careful with caller ID... I'm calling because I want to give myself up. I escaped from Thomas and I'm willing to testify against him. You're the only one who could intercede with the FBI to get my sentence reduced."

"Why would I do that?"

"Can we at least talk?"

"Where are you?"

"Tucson. I can meet you in San Francisco."

"I'm not in San Francisco, I'm in Palm Springs."

"Will you meet me?"

"I suppose so, if you come alone... I'll be in the parking lot of the Palm Springs tramway. You'll pardon me for not trusting you. I'll be armed. Call me when you're about an hour away."

At 1:13 p.m. Wednesday, six hours after leaving Tucson, Vera Snead pulled into the parking lot at the base of Mt. San Jacinto for her meeting with Dr. Andrew MacCrimmon.

MacCrimmon, watching from the entrance, approached cautiously. Vera got out of her Mustang and held her hands up. "Put your hands down, for God's sake. People will think I'm robbing you."

"Can we sit down?" Vera said. "I'm so tired I'm about to collapse. You'll like to hear what I have to say."

He slid into the passenger seat of her red Mustang and looked her over. She had changed since he last saw her. She was still no beauty but she had gained a few much needed pounds and, beyond her fatigue, she looked softer, less sour, than when he saw her in that suite in the Miesterdam. He said he was surprised she would approach him like this. "Why me, of all people?"

"I've been a party to some awful things, Doctor. I haven't personally hurt anyone, but that's no excuse. My only hope to have my prison time reduced is by cooperating with the authorities and testifying against Thomas. To do that someone has to intercede with the FBI and no one is in a better position to do that than you."

"It's possible, I guess. If you tell me the exact story, no lies, I'll consider it."

Vera said that was all she had a right to expect. She told the story from the beginning, from the first time Thomas approached her in a freezing cold Buffalo park, to the end, fleeing from him a few days earlier.

"This *is* good stuff," MacCrimmon said, "the motive we only guessed at!... Now it all makes sense. The reason Thomas didn't do Tamara in directly is because he would be closely scrutinized. But there'd be no link to an obscure tourist from Buffalo."

"Exactly," Vera said. "Thomas killed Tamara the day you saw us at the museum. We knew from Mrs. MacCrimmon's look she knew I wasn't the woman who left the ship with Thomas. The plan was already collapsing, two hours from when it began."

"But you stayed with Padgett."

"I did. But after he killed Enrico, the limo driver who buried Tamara's body, I had to get away."

"Ah, yes, the limo driver. Another puzzle solved! But why kill him a year after the fact?"

"He was blackmailing us."

"Blackmail—of course... About Tamara... Didn't it bother you being a party to your own sister's murder?"

"I didn't see it happen but, as you say, I was a party to it. To answer your question, no, it didn't bother me. She was horrible. But I'm horrible, too. We always *were* horrible, both of us."

MacCrimmon smiled at this harsh self-assessment. "Where is Thomas now? The San Antonio phone is disconnected."

She said she didn't know.

"Could he have taken all the money and fled?"

"No, he can't get at the money. It's community property. It takes both of us to access it. I tried to get it all, but he knew everything, even the number of the accounts I set up, even where I was driving and walking. It was uncanny."

"No, not uncanny, not at all. He probably put a keylogger in your computer and a tracker in your car."

As the implications set in, Vera said with a look of panic, "He could be following me now?"

"Yes, he certainly could be." He had her get out. He checked under the dash and found a GPS tracker plugged into the OBD port. He pulled it out and showed it to her. She asked, "But would that tell him where I was walking?"

"No, it wouldn't. He'd have to have another one planted in something you carry with you."

"Like my keys and dark glasses and purse?"

"Purse, most likely." MacCrimmon had her hand over her leather bag. He felt around in it. Inside the lining he found a second, smaller, GPS tracker. He grinned and held it up for her to see. "Now let's have a little fun with Thomas, assuming he *is* following you. We're need something sticky." He looked up from the glove box he was rummaging through and called from the open window to three girls walking by, "Excuse me ladies. Do any of you chew gum?" A pudgy dark-haired sixteen-year old said she did. "I'll give you five-dollars for a pack of gum." She jumped at the offer and said he must like gum an awful lot. She warned him there were only three sticks left. He said he didn't care.

He chewed all three sticks until the sugar had leached out and divided the wad into two pieces and stuck one piece on the back of each of the two trackers.

Two lanes over he found an SUV with Oregon plates. A luggage rack on top was covered by a blue plastic tarp. "This'll do." He slapped the trackers onto the roof of the car and pressed and rotated them to assure a firm hold. The trackers were out of sight of the driver but in a position to pick up and send strong signals from the satellites. "That ought to keep Thomas occupied for a while."

That out of the way he had her follow him in her Mustang to the estate where he would introduce her to Isabella.

Thomas reached Las Cruces at five Thursday evening after a hard nine-hour drive from San Antonio. He checked into the same motel Vera had used. The next day he drove eight-hours covering 550 miles of desert before stopping in a dusty little California town called Blythe. Even as easy as the big Mercedes was to drive, he was too tired to continue.

At six Saturday evening Thomas Padgett reached Livermore, forty miles east of San Francisco, a city of 90,000 people, and checked into a motel. He had driven nine straight hours from Blythe, 1700 miles in three days since leaving San Antonio. He was in no mood this night to work his way through the maze of Bay Area towns and streets.

Vera had stopped three hours at a place outside of Palm Springs on Wednesday but had headed north to San Francisco where she had stayed in a motel on Lombard Street until earlier today. From San Francisco she had taken US-101 two-hundred miles north to a town called Garberville.

At six Sunday morning Thomas worked his way through the various East Bay freeways across a bridge to US 101 and headed north, chasing her. Fortunately, traffic was light. At ten he passed through tiny Garberville where he checked her progress on his phone. She was now in Gold Beach, in Oregon, another four hours north. He followed. Again exhausted, he stopped for the night in Gold Beach. At nine, when he checked, she was fifty miles north, in Bandon, another Oregon coastal town.

The next morning she was still in Bandon. This was his chance to catch her—she had to be as exhausted as he was. And what in the hell was she doing in Bandon, Oregon? She had told him that, before she came to Texas, she had never been west of Pennsylvania. Could this be a hideout she'd rented in advance? Could she have met someone, a man, or maybe an old lady who needed a companion? Could she be staying with a relative she'd never told him about?

He followed the tracker north to Bandon to a nicely landscaped, stuccoed two story house on Bluff Avenue, not far from the coast. A Honda SUV with a luggage rack on top was parked in the drive. Thomas took his Sig-Sauer 9 mm from the glove box and slipped it into the waist band of his slacks. He marched to the door and rang the bell. A fat kid wearing glasses who looked to be about eleven years old answered.

"You live here?" Thomas said. The kid said he did. "Is Vera here? All I want to do is talk to her."

"What does she look like? Some ladies came earlier."

"She looks like a rat."

The kid turned and yelled, "Hey, Dad! Did a woman who looks like a rat come here today."

A man bellowed back from deep in the house, "A Jehovah's Witness who looked like a penguin came, but no rats."

Padgett barged past the kid into the house, through a nicely furnished but messy living room, into a large kitchen smelling of burned toast and bacon grease. "Where's Vera?"

A stocky amiable looking blond man in his early thirties, sitting at the kitchen table drinking coffee, asked, "'Vera'? Who the hell is Vera? Who the hell are *you*?"

Thomas pulled his pistol. "Where is she? Don't lie—I followed her here."

The man stared at the pistol. "Followed her? How?"

"GPS trackers in her car and purse."

The man laughed and motioned for him to put the gun away. "Come with me." Thomas slipped his pistol back into his waist band and followed the man, the boy, and a toddler with a suspiciously full diaper who had materialized from somewhere. They trooped out the front entrance around to the garage door. Stuck to the side trim were the two trackers. The man pulled them loose and gave them to him. "You mean these?" Thomas turned them over in his hand, examining them. He shook his fists and cursed Vera.

"We found them when we unloaded last night. Stuck on with chewing gum. We wondered if we'd get visitors. Wife run off?"

"Yeah."

"She's the one who looks like a rat?"

"On her best days... I'm not going to shoot her. I don't even want her back. I only want the money she stole."

"You look about done in. Want some breakfast?"

"That's good of you, but, no, no thanks, I've gotta hit the road. How far to San Francisco?"

"We just came from there. Four-hundred and fifty miles, nine or ten hours alone—fifteen with kids."

"Sorry about the gun."

"To tell you the truth, I thought it was fake. I'm a bank clerk so I see one like that every once in a while. Anyway, good luck to you."

Padgett tapped the man's shoulder. "Wait a second. How long were you in San Francisco?"

"Three nights, two days."

"And before that?"

"Palm Springs. Too ritzy for the likes of us, but we took the tram up Mt. San Jacinto."

"Before that?"

"San Diego... You're tryin' to figure where they switched the trackers?"

"Yeah... I'll Have to think about it. Thanks again."

"No, thank *you!*... What a story to tell at work."

Nine-hours later Thomas stopped for the night in a nice town called Santa Rosa, fifty-miles north of San Francisco.

The next morning, eating breakfast in a diner south of town, he went over the five places Vera had stopped since Tucson: Palm Springs, the San Francisco motel, the parking lot of the Golden Gate Bridge, Garberville, and Gold Beach. But where had she switched the trackers? This in turn begged the question—how did she *find* them? Other than word processing software she was almost as technologically illiterate as he was.

Out of the fog it came to him, what she'd said on the ship after looking MacCrimmon up on the web—he lived on Nob Hill in San

Francisco. That was it! The nasty bitch was reaching out to MacCrimmon to make a deal. Maybe she had sounded him out when she talked to him about the demand for two million. He remembered Vera had said he lived on a street called Mason and he thought she had mentioned an 800 number. But Vera hadn't stopped anywhere close to that address.

She, or the trackers, had stayed three nights and two days at the tourist motel on Lombard. The purse tracker hadn't moved, so either she left her purse in the car, which was unlikely—she hung onto her goddamned purse like it was a body part—or the trackers had already been switched. On the way out of town it was unlikely she would have stopped two hours at a tourist place like the Golden Gate Bridge, so the switch had to have already been made. She had probably met MacCrimmon at the motel and that's where he had found the trackers and stuck them on the Oregon tourist's SUV, parked there in the same motel.

But what about Palm Springs? She was on the run. She wouldn't have stopped there either unless it was to meet someone. But who? He had nothing to go on there. His only hope was the MacCrimmon place in Frisco. MacCrimmon was his only lead.

He left the diner at 6:20. An hour later, cursing and bellowing his rage at San Francisco's traffic, ubiquitous roadwork, and illogical one-way streets, his phone directions led him to California Street and right on Mason. Halfway down the giddily steep hill he found a perpendicular parking space facing the Mark Hopkins. The hotel took up the entire east side of the block so, if he remembered the address correctly, MacCrimmon's place had to be along there on the other side of the street. All he could do was watch and wait.

At a quarter to eight, as if in answer to a prayer, Mrs. MacCrimmon left the house directly across from him holding the hand of a little boy in a school uniform. Padgett crossed over to 818, the three-story Victorian she had left, and checked the entry. A CCTV camera looked down. He would never get in by knocking. They'd recognize him and call the cops.

Ten minutes later Mrs. MacCrimmon returned. She put her key in, entered, and closed the door too quickly for him to even think about getting across the street and barging in after her.

He waited.

At 9:10 a husky middle-aged blonde woman in what looked like a maid's dress wheeled a little girl in a stroller up the steep hill. He had to laugh—the woman had calves like a weightlifter.

29.

MACCRIMMON led Vera through to the kitchen where Isabella was making a pie. "Isabella, this is Vera Snead."

Isabella wiped her floury hands on her apron and shook Vera's hand. "You're the one who—?"

"Yes, I am."

Isabella said with a chilly half-smile, "And here I thought I was a killer with a measly two."

"Play nice, Isabella."

"No, it's okay, Doctor," Vera said, "I deserve it."

"Vera is going to give herself up," he said. "I want to see if I can get her a deal. Her testimony against Thomas should go a long way in that direction... In the meantime I think Ms. Snead could use a drink. I have a call to make."

MacCrimmon found the number for the FBI's Miami Field Office on the FBI website. He called and asked to speak with the agent in charge of the murders on the cruise ship, Miesterdam. The person at the desk asked the nature of his information? "I'm Andrew MacCrimmon. I'm one of the men thrown overboard."

Half an hour later Agent Whitley returned his call and introduced himself:

"*The* Doctor MacCrimmon? You survived."

"Technically."

"Why did Padgett do this? He said you'd had words because he'd stared at your wife."

"Nope… I uncovered his plot to replace his detested wife, Tamara, with his more compliant sister-in-law, Tamara's twin sister, Vera Snead. The body in Puerto Rico is Tamara Padgett. Vera Snead is alive and well. Tamara controlled the couple's fortune and she was going to divorce Thomas Padgett, leaving him with nothing. If he killed Tamara outright, the law would have been all over him. But who would worry excessively about her obscure sister, killed by a robber in Puerto Rico?"

"Damn! It was in front of us all the time. If we'd had access to their financial records we could have figured it out, but no judge would give us a search warrant based on the flimsy circumstantial evidence we had. This ties everything together. We were wracking our minds for a motive. With your testimony we have the guy. Incidentally, PR police found a body on Route 187 east of San Juan, a limo driver named Ricardo Nelson. His throat had been cut. His prints matched those on a letter he supposedly forwarded to Ms. Snead's son. We showed Ms. Snead's photo to the receptionist at the limo place and she identified her unequivocally."

""Now, about Enrico Nelson. He drove Padgett and Tamara; Padgett killed her in the car; Enrico drove Padgett back to San Juan, turned around and drove to that nature preserve and buried Tamara's body. Meanwhile, Vera took over the role of Tamara. My wife knew right away she was a different woman."

"Information she refused to share with us... Now, why did they kill Enrico Nelson?—I'm assuming it was them."

"It was. He was blackmailing them.... What's next Agent Whitley?"

"I'll send a team out to Padgett's house post haste."

"He's gone. His phone is disconnected."

"You've called him?"

"Several times."

"Why in the name of all that's holy didn't you let us know?"

"To torment him, Agent Whitley. I'm entitled. Now, in return for all this, if Vera told her whole story and testified against Thomas Padgett, could she get a break?"

"That'd be up to the prosecutor. She has to understand she's an accomplice in three homicides and an attempted homicide. An accomplice is considered a principal, same as the trigger-puller. You probably confused her with an accessory."

"Something short of life in prison?"

"I'll go out on a limb here and say something along those lines might be arranged."

Later that afternoon Whitley called back:

"Doctor, we had a team in San Antonio go through Padgett's house. He left in such a hurry, he didn't even lock the front door. We found a sandal that matched the footprint on the envelope of the letter to Vera's son that was supposedly dropped or lost."

"Padgett must be panicking."

"The next question, Doc... Where are these two?"

"I know where Vera is. She's hiding out from Thomas."

"I'm sympathetic, Doc, with all you went through, but you'd best tread carefully if you're harboring a fugitive."

"I'm not harboring anybody. I know where she is, but she'll only be there until she gives herself up, which she will do. Think of it not as 'harboring' but a sort of private protective custody, saving you the trouble."

"I assume you don't have Thomas tucked away anywhere in 'private protective custody'?"

"Nope. But he'll show up. He needs Vera to get the money. Worse than that, he's in love with her."

"Motives one and two on anyone's list of murderers."

Bryce Alberti called MacCrimmon that night to say he had a buyer for the gold, a Saudi prince, Khalid bin Ahmed Al Sudairi, a nephew of King Salman. "You'll have to fly to Lauderdale to meet him, give him your *bona fides.* Wear your best suit—they put a lot of stock in such formalities."

"I'll fly out tomorrow."

Bryce picked MacCrimmon up at the Miami airport the next afternoon and drove him back to his condo. MacCrimmon showered, shaved, and arrayed himself in a medium grey three-piece Armani suit he'd picked up the day before at the Armani outlet outside of Banning. He pronounced himself ready to meet the prince.

Bryce drove them in his Cadillac to Pier 66, a large garden hotel and Marina complex where the prince's yacht was anchored. At 350 feet in length MacCrimmon muttered to Bryce it should more accurately be called a liner. The tender on the stern was larger than most private yachts.

A young man in a suit led them through the cavernous ship, fitted out tastefully in a blend of modern and traditional styles, to an opulent office. The prince, a distant, dignified, portly man in his sixties wore the traditional robes; the four men with him—at least two of whom were bodyguards—wore suits. All wore the gutra and igal (head dresses). MacCrimmon complimented the prince on the imaginative design of the yacht. The prince responded with the single slow nod and cool smile of a man so used to sycophancy he couldn't recognize a true compliment when he heard one. In the eastern manner, only after tea was served and small talk and pleasantries were exchanged did the men ease into business.

The prince asked what form the gold was in. MacCrimmon said it was in irregular bars and rods but he would smelt it into a single block if that was what the prince preferred. One of the advisors said that was exactly what the prince would prefer. MacCrimmon said it would be twelve inches square and five-inches high, about the size of two shoe boxes side-by-side. The chief negotiator asked how the doctor would like payment. MacCrimmon said a check or cash transfer to one of his investment accounts would be satisfactory. He made it clear the transaction was entirely aboveboard—he intended to declare the sale to the IRS which would eat up half the value. Alberti said he would be responsible for picking up the gold at a place of Dr. MacCrimmon's choosing, as well as shipping, safeguarding, and delivering it. Upon delivery, the prince's own metallurgists could weigh it and assess the purity of the gold and, if necessary, adjust the price, which would be that day's spot price. The main advisor produced a contract which specified the points they had discussed. The prince and two of the advisors signed it. MacCrimmon said he would have his attorney review it and return the signed copies by overnight delivery.

To celebrate the sale, Bryce and MacCrimmon had dinner at the steakhouse on Las Olmas they had gone to the first day he was back in America. "You look a little different than the last time we ate here."

"I did what amounted to boot camp in Palm Springs for six-weeks with a very remarkable woman."

"Dare I ask how you and your wife are getting on?"

"She's happily married to her psychiatrist."

"I'm sorry to hear it, Andrew. *Le Donne sono mobile, no?*"

"I never would have guessed it."

Bryce, detesting melodrama, jumped away to the matter at hand. "How long will it take to smelt the gold and get it ready for shipment?"

"Give me a week."

He said that would work.

The next morning Bryce drove MacCrimmon to Miami for his early flight. He arrived in Palm Springs a little before noon.

This warm autumn day he found both Isabella and Vera sunbathing nude. He checked them both out carefully enough to partially revise his opinion of Vera's charms—she had a surprisingly nice *derriere*—but voyeurism not being his thing, he returned to the front door, gave it a hearty slam, and bellowed, "Honey, I'm home!"

He returned to the French doors. Neither had budged. Isabella must have explained to Vera that Andrew, being a doctor, had seen it all.

He repaired to the kitchen and poured a glass of the Chardonnay in the fridge. Maybe they hadn't heard him. He sauntered out and sagged into one of the padded chairs at the glass table. If he expected squeals and a flurry of towels he was to be disappointed: nothing; neither budged, though Isabella did call over to him, inviting him to join them. There was a time when he might have taken them up on that but he declined.

That evening he remembered to call Alan to tell him he didn't need his million dollars. Alan, as usual, wasn't available. He left a message thanking him, but said the Cuban authorities had murdered Colonel Ximenez before he could escape. He said he would call him later with an update.

Early the next morning, after MacCrimmon left on his five-mile run, Isabella took this call:

"Isabella? This is Karen. I need to find Andrew. Please don't say he's not there. My nephew phoned. He said he got a call from Andrew last night from this number. Let me speak to him."

"He *is* here, Karen. He left on a run. He'll be back in about an hour."

"Please tell him I left Arnold as soon as I heard from his nephew he was alive—this was two weeks ago. We moved back to the Mason Street house... Is he all right, Isabella?"

"Physically, yes, maybe better than ever. But you hurt him badly, like you always do."

"I'm flying down there, to talk to him."

"No, Karen! He's got that woman here, Vera, who's running away from her husband, the guy who threw Andrew overboard. Let him take care of that business first."

"Please, Isabella, tell him I love him. There was never anyone else. It was all a big misunderstanding."

"For God's sake Karen, you married another man! It's a helluva lot more than a *'misunderstanding.'* You betrayed him!"

30.

AT 10:32 the big blonde woman reappeared at the top of the hill. She walked slowly, leaning back to counter the steep gradient, holding the little girl by one hand and guiding the stroller with the other. Padgett ambled across the street, praying she hadn't been told about him. He adjusted his stride so as to pass as she opened the front door. She looked up at him as she fumbled with the key. He wished her a good morning and thoughtfully held the stroller for her, freeing up her other hand.

She opened the door and turned to thank him. Padgett stuck his pistol against her cheek and grabbed her muscular forearm. "Don't make a sound. Is MacCrimmon here?" She said, no, he wasn't. "Is Vera here?" She said she didn't know anyone named Vera.

"Mrs. MacCrimmon?"

"Yes."

"When we get in, call Mrs. MacCrimmon. If you try any funny stuff I'll kill the kid."

"Don't hurt her, please! I von't make any trouble."

"Call her."

Uta shouted, "Karen. Can I see you!"

Karen came out of the kitchen, wiping her hands on a dish towel. She inhaled with a sharp squeak when she saw Padgett pointing a gun at Maddy.

"Come here, Mrs. MacCrimmon. Don't scream!"

Karen edged over to Padgett and tried to grab Maddy, but he straight-armed her away. "Where is Vera?"

"I don't know."

Padgett hit her with a backhand slap to the face that knocked her backward. He leaned toward her and said, "I count to three. If you don't tell me where Vera is, I kill the kid."

Maddy, seeing her mother struck, howled.

Karen rubbed her right cheek where he had hit her. "She's in Palm Springs... Please, don't hurt her!"

Padgett shouted above Maddy's shrieking, "Was she here?" .

"Vera, you mean? No, she wasn't!"

"Is she in a house, a hotel, what?"

"An estate. There's nobody around, no neighbors."

"Where's your husband?"

"He's at his office."

"Where is that?"

"In the Richmond District. It's toward the ocean."

Padgett waved his pistol as permission for Karen to pick Maddy up. She comforted her and turned away, shielding her with her body.

"How far is it to Palm Springs?"

She said it took seven hours to drive but she didn't know the distance. Padgett said they were going to drive there. He told Uta if she called ahead, or if Vera was gone when they arrived, or if cops were anywhere in sight, he would kill Mrs. MacCrimmon.

Padgett confiscated Karen's phone and checked her purse for anything that could be used as a weapon. At her request he let her use the bathroom. When she came out he prodded her at gunpoint toward the entry. Karen knelt and kissed Maddy. "Mama's going bye-bye, Sweetheart. You be a good girl." Maddy whimpered she wanted to go bye-bye too. "Not this time, Sweetie."

Karen begged Uta to look after the kids. She said she would, of course.

Padgett watched Karen buckle herself in and reached across to test her seat belt, more to insure she wouldn't jump out at a red light than from any concern for her safety. He backed out and headed slowly down the vertiginous hill. "How do we get there?"

"Turn left on Bush, the next street." From there she guided him street by street to the Bay Bridge.

Stuck at the intersection of Bush and Battery, progressing one or two cars per signal cycle waiting to cross Market Street, Padgett pounded the steering wheel and bellowed, "How does anyone get anywhere in this goddamned city? It's a nightmare."

Karen, looking out the window, said nothing.

Once over the Bay Bridge, on I-580 heading east out of Oakland, Padgett relaxed. "Sorry about hitting you. It was an act I put on for the Kraut woman. I'm not going to kill you, no matter what happens."

Karen, looking straight ahead, said, "The kids are safe. That's all I care about."

Padgett glanced over at her, surprised by her calm courage. He remembered back when Vera had said she was "all fluff and no fiber." How wrong she was. "How do you know Vera's in Palm Springs, Mrs. MacCrimmon?"

"The housekeeper down there told me."

"Why did she go there?"

"Andrew must have sent her there."

He mumbled to himself, "Probably when he called her, just before she left." He said to her, "I'm not going to hurt Vera, if that's what you're worried about."

"I'm not worried. I don't care one way or the other what you do with her."

"I need her to gain access to some funds... Did she say what she was up to?"

"I already told you, I haven't seen her, haven't talked to her. You'll have to ask the housekeeper... Why are you taking *me* to Palm Springs anyway?"

He said with a gap-toothed grin, "You're my hostage."

"Oh."

Two hours of stultifying boredom later, driving down I-5 through the great San Joaquin Valley, Padgett asked, "How did your husband survive?"

"If you mean Andrew, he's not my husband."

He asked for clarification.

"When Andrew didn't return we assumed he was dead. I married another man because my kids need a father. Andrew survived because of the life ring. He was rescued by Cubans. They kept him in jail for nine months but he escaped."

"So, your husband at his office out by the ocean, this is not MacCrimmon."

"No, my husband's a psychiatrist. I already told you, no one knows where Andrew is... Speaking of Andrew, why did you throw him overboard, Mr. Padgett?"

He snapped a look at her as if she were mocking him. "Why do you think? He knew about Vera. He said he was going to tell the cops."

"But he was only guessing. We didn't know anything for sure. We agreed it was none of our business."

"Your husband, well, ex-husband, knew. The previous afternoon he talked to Vera. He tricked her. He said he was a ship's officer with a telegram about her son. She was drunk and fell for it."

Karen gasped and looked out the window.

Padgett, hearing her weeping, Said, "I'm not going to hurt you, Mrs. MacCrimmon, honest to God!"

"I'm *not* 'Mrs. MacCrimmon'—I'm Mrs. Ohrman... And it's not you—I'm not afraid of you. A horrible man lied to me. He swore he would never get involved in things like this but he did anyway and he ruined my life."

"What 'horrible man'?"

'It doesn't matter."

A mile further down the road, Padgett said, "I hope I'm not out of line asking, but do you still love MacCrimmon?"

"No! I *don't* love him. I hate him! Because of him poor Mr. Jeliksen was killed and God knows who else!"

Padgett's role in these deaths was somewhat greater than MacCrimmon's but he didn't question her line of reasoning.

Three hours after leaving San Francisco Padgett pulled off I-5 into Kettleman City, a tiny valley town, and stopped in a Chevron station so Karen could use the restroom. He waited outside to be sure she didn't pull any tricks. She had promised she'd give him no trouble and so far she hadn't. He bought a prepackaged sandwich, but Karen said she wasn't hungry.

Thomas Padgett, a blustery, profane man of monumental rages could think of few things he was afraid of but he admitted he was intimidated by this small woman. He had never been in the presence of anyone, man or woman, of such exquisite beauty. To this she added courage and sad dignity. What would it be like, he wondered, to touch this woman, kiss her, sleep with her. Would she scream and writhe around like Vera, or would she lie there like a cool statue? No wonder MacCrimmon survived, if he had her to come home to. He was probably mad as hell when he found she was married to someone else. That explained why he'd tormented them so relentlessly.

Sneaking another look at this beautiful woman he felt a burning resentment that, not only was a person like this as unattainable as someone, say, on Mars, but he was lucky to have had, even briefly, a creature like Vera Snead. Too bad, he thought not for the first time, there wasn't an option never to have been born.

He broke another two hours of silence. "Your little girl's beautiful. I wouldn't have hurt her for the world."

"Yes, she is beautiful. Thank you."

"And I wouldn't harm a hair of your head either."

"I believe you, Mr. Padgett. Other than hitting me, you've been a perfect gentleman. Now I'd like to rest if you don't mind." She reclined the seat, crossed her arms and closed her eyes.

North of palm Springs, seven hours after leaving San Francisco, Karen had Padgett take the 111 offramp. She explained it was about ten miles to Palm Springs and another five on South Palm Canyon Drive.

Padgett asked, "Once again, is there a man at this place?"

"No, only a housekeeper." She closed her eyes and prayed Andrew kept out of sight.

Karen, recognizing the area, told him it was about a half-mile up ahead. A minute later she pointed to the drive. He slowed and turned onto the fifty-yard lane leading to Lena Montoya's estate. He drove slowly and stopped next to Vera's mustang in the large gravel parking area in front of the garage, out of sight of the front door. "Lead me to the entrance. Act normal." He pulled his gun out of the glove box and held it against the side of his leg. "Ring the doorbell."

Karen rang. Isabella opened. "Karen! What are you—" Thomas rushed in, pointing the gun at her head. "Where's Vera?" Isabella backed away holding her hands up. Padgett bellowed, "Tell me, Goddamn it! Where is she?"

"I'm here, Thomas," Vera said from the kitchen door at the end of hallway, thirty feet away.

Thomas dropped his pistol to his side and shouted to her, "Vera, you have to come with me. I'm not going to hurt you. Once we sell the assets and divide the proceeds you're free." He lumbered down the hallway toward her, still holding the gun at his side. From an open doorway on his left MacCrimmon hurtled out and tackled him. The two went down, rolling and thrashing.

MacCrimmon, not as big as Padgett but stronger, turned him and straddled him. He hit him hard with a right to the jaw that stunned him. "That's for Karen;" a left to the side of his face, "for my kids;" a pile driver punch to his nose, "that's for Colonel Ximenez;" and a roundhouse to his left ear, "and that's for everybody else you hurt."

Padgett, bleeding heavily from his face, braced his foot against the wall and bucked MacCrimmon off to one side, far enough to swing his pistol around. MacCrimmon grabbed his arm. The pistol went off, Vera screamed. MacCrimmon grabbed the hand holding the gun and bit Padgett's thumb. Padgett bellowed and let the gun fall to the right of him. MacCrimmon rose, but Padgett tripped him and kicked him in the side. Both crawled to the gun, but Padgett rolled toward it and got there first. He clambered to his feet, quickly for a large clumsy man. MacCrimmon had stumbled trying to get up. He rose to his knees. Padgett aimed the Sig-Sauer down at him. "Now I'll finish the job."

A thunderous report. Padgett fell to the floor, squealing and writhing in agony. Isabella, overlooked in the fray, had drawn her .45 from the waistband of her jeans and had shot Padgett in the back of his right knee.

MacCrimmon, kneeling next to him, jerked the pistol out of his hand and jumped to his feet. He aimed at Padgett's forehead. "Now, *I'll* finish the job, you motherfucker!"

"*NO*, Andrew!" Isabella screamed. "Don't do it! He's not worth it! Killing him lets him off too easy!

MacCrimmon bellowed in spittle-spraying rage, "This miserable piece of shit has to die!"

"No, Andrew, please! For our unborn child!"

MacCrimmon looked over at her. He glared again at Padgett but sighed and pointed the gun off to one side. Isabella came closer and held her hand out. "Give me the gun, Andrew. Please."

He pounded the butt of the pistol hard on the top of Padgett's head and handed it to her, butt first.

Isabella shouted to Karen, staring in open-mouthed shock at Padgett, "Call 9-1-1, Karen. Tell them two people have been shot. Have them send the police and an ambulance. Hurry, Karen!"

MacCrimmon, seeing Vera lying in the hallway, moaning, trotted back to her. The shot had hit her in the left upper chest below the clavicle. The bullet had missed the subclavian artery, the brachial plexus, and the large vessels in the lung. He gently raised her and checked her back. The bullet had exited through the scapula. There was little bleeding. "Through and through wound, Vera. You're lucky. You won't even need surgery, only bed rest for a while."

"Why didn't you kill him?" she screamed. "He's evil!"

"He is that, but a cooler head prevailed… Now lie back and take shallow breaths."

Karen returned from making the 9-1-1 call. Seeing Padgett groaning in pain and clutching his leg above the knee, rolling back and forth in a widening puddle of blood, she mumbled, "Oh, Jesus God!" She scrunched her eyes shut and turned her head away.

MacCrimmon, breathing heavily, his heart pounding, strode over to the two ladies. Isabella asked, "Are you okay?—are your hands broken?"

"I don't think so." He turned to Karen.

She crossed her arms, corpse-like over her chest, and screamed, "Don't come near me!"

Isabella, holding "Baby" at her side, looked at him for a reaction. He shrugged and turned his back on Karen and said to Isabella that, as profusely as Padgett was bleeding, she must have hit the popliteal, the big artery that runs behind the knee. He had her fetch a towel and had Padgett press it hard against the entrance wound. In the meantime, he retired to the kitchen to ice his hands while they waited for the ambulance and the cops.

The ambulance arrived seven minutes later. Padgett was now in deep shock from blood loss. The EMTs, with MacCrimmon's help, loaded the giant on a gurney. One placed a tourniquet around his leg and fixed an oxygen mask over his nose and mouth while the other started an IV. They helped Vera on to a second gurney, loaded both into the ambulance, and hauled them away, code 3.

Two squad cars and an unmarked sedan arrived two minutes later. The uniformed officers came in, guns drawn, followed by Lt. Dave Harrington and another plain clothes cop. MacCrimmon had had dealings with Harrington before, both in the kidnapping of Maddy and the deaths of Father Gus and Lena Montoya. Harrington, seeing Isabella, said, "You again! You shot him with that?" He pointed at the .45 and the clip Isabella had put on a side table.

She said, yes, she had, but only after he burst into the house, threatening them with the Sig-Sauer, also on the table. MacCrimmon confirmed this.

Harrington asked her, "How did you happen to have it on you?"

"Vera—the lady the ambulance hauled away—warned us he might show up. And Karen's housekeeper called to warn us he was coming."

Karen added, "He kidnapped me from my home in San Francisco and drove me here."

"Who are you?" Harrington asked.

"Karen Ohrman. I used to be married to *him*." She pointed her pinky at MacCrimmon.

"Of course. I remember you from last year when your husband was in the hospital. I should've known he'd be mixed up in this somehow... Who *is* this guy?"

"Thomas Padgett," MacCrimmon said. "He threw me and another man overboard from the cruise ship."

"This is *the* guy?"

"He is. I survived. The other man didn't. And he killed a limo driver in Puerto Rico."

"Who was the other woman?"

"Vera Snead, his accomplice."

Harrington and the other policemen excused themselves and looked around the house while Isabella and MacCrimmon mopped up most of the blood with bath towels which Isabella threw in the trash. She said she'd mop up the rest later.

Thirty minutes later, their check of the house complete, Harrington drove Karen and Isabella to police headquarters to give their statements. MacCrimmon went in a squad car to the Desert Medical Center ER up the road to have his hands checked for fractures. An hour later he took a cab to police headquarters.

Harrington told MacCrimmon he had notified the FBI that their guy was in custody. He assured him Isabella wouldn't be charged for shooting Padgett. Convicted felons weren't allowed to own guns but there was an exception for self-defense which this clearly was. MacCrimmon was "Baby's" official owner anyway, a maneuver he and Isabella had come up with to allow her to keep Baby in the house.

•

31.

AT 9:30 that night, a policeman drove the two ladies back to the estate. Isabella joined Karen at the kitchen table. "I'm sorry for saying Andrew wasn't here when you called two-months ago. He didn't want anyone to know he was alive."

"It doesn't matter. The result would have been the same. We would have been apart anyway."

"What?... I don't understand."

"I can't be with Andrew. I'm going back to Arnold."

Isabella leaned toward her, staring at her in disbeief. "You're going *back* to Arnold? You told me you left Arnold a few days ago. And I told Andrew."

"Yes. We moved back to Mason Street as soon as I knew Andrew was alive."

"And now you're going right back to your headshrinker? Why in the name of all that's holy would you do that?"

Karen looked down at her shaking hands. "I can't trust Andrew, Isabella. He swore he wouldn't get involved with this Padgett person but he did anyway. He broke his promise—that's why he got thrown overboard. And that's why that awful man kidnapped me and pointed a gun at my two-year old daughter! We're not safe around him, none of us is... His daughter Dre was shot and kidnapped because of his meddling... Alan, his nephew, was shot... A man almost cut my throat and Alex's and Dre's because of him. He killed the man right in front of us. It was the most awful thing I ever saw, well, until, tonight."

"Killing him sounds like the right thing to do if the guy was going to cut your throats."

Karen continued in a hysterical rush of words, "That doesn't even include all the times he's been shot or shot at or stabbed or beaten up—I have to think of the safety of the kids... Playing around with these things that are none of his business is more important to him than me and Alex and Maddy!"

"If you think that, you really *are* crazy!"

"Tonight we hadn't shared a single word and already he was in another fight, people were getting shot, there was blood everywhere, and he would have killed that man if you hadn't stopped him."

"Of course he was in a fight, Karen, you unbelievably stupid broad!... What was he supposed to do, let that monster kill us all?" Isabella rose and slammed her chair back under the table. She said with a sneer, "I'm glad to hear you're going back to *Arnold*. You deserve each other. And Andrew deserves a better wife than some flaky looney who leaves him every two months. He'll hurt—hurt like hell—but he'll get over it and he'll find a woman a helluva lot better than you!"

Karen, now angry, cried, "You, maybe?"

"Maybe. We discussed it. I do know I'd be ten-times a better wife than you ever were and a good mother to Maddy."

Karen inhaled sharply.

Isabella leaned down to her. "That's right, dummy! Maddy is Andrew's daughter. If I have anything to say about it, we'll drive up tomorrow and get her!" She glared at Karen, waiting for a response, but she was speechless. "God, what an idiot!" She stalked off to the sink to wash her hands.

Ten minutes later, when the cab arrived to take Karen to the airport, Isabella joined her in the entry where she'd been waiting. "You've made a whole pot-full of dumb decisions in your married life, Karen, but this is the cruelest and the stupidest."

Karen said with a chilly smile, "I hadn't appreciated how nice it felt just to be safe. I'm moving back with my real husband—where I belong."

Isabella chuckled and said, "Truer words were never spoken."

Two hours later, Isabella paused mopping up the last of Padgett's blood from the terra cotta tiles and looked out the front window at a cab that had just arrived. MacCrimmon disembarked from the front passenger seat, handed some bills to the driver, and marched into the house.

Isabella leaned the mop against the wall. "Come inside, Andrew." She led him by the elbow to the kitchen table, poured him a glass of wine, and took the chair next to him. "How are the hands?"

"Bad bruises, ligament strains, no fractures." He looked around. "Where's Karen?"

"She went to the airport... You'll find this hard to believe."

"There's not much I find hard to believe, Isabella."

"She's going back to her shrink." She filled him in on what Karen had said.

He closed his eyes and chuckled silently. Isabella leaned toward him and grabbed his uninjured left hand. "You'll be okay?"

"Yeah, I will... I didn't see the Karen I knew anyway—I saw a strange woman who belonged to another man. And there wasn't much love in the way she looked at me." He looked down at the wineglass he was holding at arm's length. "This is just the last stage of what began as a true Aristotelean tragedy."

"Which is?"

"A man forced by his tragic flaw to fight the Gods for his survival. It degenerated into sloppy melodrama, like one of those supermarket romances where the heroine ups and marries another man. Today it putrefied into low farce. It would take someone weaker and stupider than me—if that were possible—to waste any more time and emotional energy on this woman."

At bedtime Isabella, waiting in the hallway, grabbed his hand as he came out of the bathroom. She said she was upset about shooting Padgett and didn't want to be alone. He said that was understandable. She asked if she could sleep with him, not to do anything, just to be with someone. He said he could use a little friendly human contact himself.

Lying in bed with Isabella spooned against him, he ran his hands over her bare belly. "You're getting a baby bump."

"Not only that, this morning I vomited from morning sickness. But it's not all bad." She slid his hands up to her breasts. "Wouldn't it be nice if they stayed this size?"

Afterward, lying side-by-side in blissful post-coital torpor, Isabella said, "Seeing Karen didn't affect your, uh, enthusiasm."

"She's a stranger. I was an idiot to go all crazy over her."

"An energetic idiot."

"Surprised even me... Remember last year about this time, when you were drunk and you said you wanted a child fathered by me?"

"Vaguely," she said, vaguely.

"Did you plan to get pregnant all along?"

"Would you be mad at me if I did?"

"I would have been mad as hell if I'd known you were deceiving me, but now, well, it seems to have worked out all right."

She rolled on her side to face him. "I love you, Andrew, and I always will. No matter what you say, you'll go back to Karen—the two of you are like magnets—but now a part of you will always be with me. Without this child my love would have been wasted."

"If I'm not around—I'm not saying that'll be the case—but if I'm not, will there ever be another man?"

"No!" She slapped his chest, hard. "You know very well I *hate* men!... No, I'll hire somebody like me or Consuela to help out with the estate and the child."

Two days later Agent Whitley called MacCrimmon. He said he was in Palm Springs and asked if they might meet. MacCrimmon said he looked forward to it and gave him the address.

The two agents arrived a little after ten. Whitley, a large, heavy African-American, and a younger, slender Hispanic man named Andrade, flashed badges and cards identifying themselves. MacCrimmon led them back to the kitchen. Pleasantries exchanged, he told the men the story, from first seeing Vera at the museum in San Juan, to Padgett being shot by Isabella.

"And you'll be willing to testify to all this in Court?"

"Of course... A question, Agent Whitley. Why is the FBI involved in a cruise ship crime? Don't they have police on these ships?"

The question hit a nerve with Whitley. "It's a serious problem, Doctor." Cruise ships, he said, little floating cities offering a week or two of over-feeding, over-entertaining, too often over-drinking, and general coddling. Any unpleasantness likely to affect the holiday atmosphere, and thus adversely affect business—like passengers going overboard—is quickly suppressed. Crimes perpetrated by passengers and staff on cruise ships—rape, assault, battery, and theft being the commonest—are investigated desultorily, if at all, and frequently are swept under the carpet. Even when culprits are identified, prosecutions are rare. Andrew MacCrimmon and Hans Jeliksen, and their likely murderer, Thomas Padgett, had been forgotten as soon as the Miesterdam left Port Everglades on its next cruise.

Whitley said the ship's brief and incomplete investigation may have satisfied the weak standards of admiralty law, which prevails on the open sea outside the territorial waters of any country, but it could only be described as negligent and incompetent by the standards of most land-based jurisdictions, and laughable by FBI standards. The murder of Mr. Jeliksen and the attempted murder of

Dr. MacCrimmon had involved U.S. citizens on an American-based ship, so even though the crimes occurred in international waters, the FBI had jurisdiction.

"Why did it take so long? Wasn't there evidence?"

"It was all circumstantial, Doctor. We had no bodies, no witnesses, no physical evidence, and a motive we could only guess at."

"What about the blood and the brain matter from the railing Jeliksen hit?"

"As described by a ship's doctor who was once suspended from practicing for incompetence and who has a problem with alcohol. His description is vague and neither he nor anyone else thought to take samples for analysis before it was hastily cleaned up. We'd be laughed out of court."

"How's Padgett doing?"

"He lost a lot of blood, and his face is battered up real bad, but he'll live—and limp for what's left of his life. He'll get the death penalty."

"And Vera?"

"She'll recover. She told us everything. Still, being an accomplice, she's looking at probably twenty-years, twelve with good behavior."

"What will happen to Padgett's cars and house and all the money he was after?"

"We'll impound the Mustang and the Mercedes. They'll be sold at auction. Vera's kid may come into some of the money, being the only relative of any of the three. Most of it will probably go to the state."

MacCrimmon leaned back and laced his fingers behind his head. "It's too bad he'll only die once, painlessly at that. He killed Tamara, Jeliksen, and Ricardo. He damn near killed me. My wife, Karen, is legally married to another man because they thought I was dead. Her husband's life is damaged, *our* lives are damaged; the colonel of the Cuban army who saved my life was killed so his wife and kids will suffer, all because of Padgett. And in another week it will be exactly a year since all this began, a completely wasted year of our lives."

"Collateral damage, Doctor."

The following Monday, as MacCrimmon was leaving for San Francisco, Isabella, fresh from the shower, hugged him at the open front door and whispered in his ear, "If you want to come back here with Maddy, I'll be your housekeeper, no strings attached. You could do a lot worse."

He kissed her hard on the mouth. "A *hell* of a lot worse. Let's see how things play out."

Mid-afternoon he checked into his usual room at the Grant Hotel. He was tired after the long, boring drive he'd made many times in the past months, but he put off taking a nap until he had checked out his house.

He hiked up the hill to Vine Terrace, the alley in back of 818 Mason. He found the spare key he had hidden in a crack in the garage door frame two years earlier. He let himself in the alley door—which still had the bullet holes from the time he shot at Pavo Makkonen—and trudged up to the basement door at the top of the stairs.

In the kitchen he came face to face with a stocky middle-aged blonde woman. Both started. "I'm sorry," he said. "I thought the place was empty."

She grinned, showing large, white teeth, and said in a German accent, "You must be Doctor MacCrimmon."

He shook her hand, bowed his head in the European fashion, and formally introduced himself in German. She said she was Frau Uta Hofer, Karen's housekeeper. She said she was Austrian; she came from Innsbruck. Hearing she was Tyrolean, MacCrimmon treated her to a couple lines of the thick near incomprehensible Tyrolean dialect:

Tyrol isch lei oans
Isch a landl a kloans....

Uta laughed heartily and said he could pass for *Ein echter Tiroler*. He said, as a young man, he had spent many happy days in the Tyrol, climbing in the Dolomites and the Stubai Alps.

He liked Uta immediately—he liked all women who laughed. There was even a time when Karen had laughed, a hearty, breathy contralto laugh she hid behind her hand.

Returning to business, he said, "Karen's still here?... I thought she was moving back to Dr. Ohrman's house."

"Doctor, you must understand, she vas very upset, being kidnapped, and vis all zose horrible things that happened down there, she vas very angry wiss you."

"I understand, Frau Hofer. I'm sure she'll be much safer and happier with Dr. Ohrman. I came to get some clothes and personal things. Where *is* Karen?"

"She is talking to Dr. Ohrman. Alex and Maddy went with her."

"Tell her that over the next few days I'll be putting the house up for sale and making arrangements to take Maddy to Palm Springs. Karen will have to move again."

"You vould take Maddy away?"

"She's *my* daughter, Frau Hofer. Karen is not her mother." Frau Hofer had much more to say on this topic but Dr. MacCrimmon held his hands up in a way that left no doubt the subject was closed. He excused himself and bounded up the stairs.

He returned with a suitcase and a suit carrier. His wallet and his keys were in the pewter plate on the dresser, exactly where he would have found them before going to work a year ago. Passing through the living room, he stopped and looked around. The house, empty the last time he saw it when the Indian couple lived here, now looked the same as it had the day they left on their ill-fated cruise, other than some of the books being out of alphabetical order.

At the front door Uta offered to call him a cab. He thanked her but said he was staying at the Grant Hotel, only two blocks away.

At noon the next day MacCrimmon met Bruce Solomon at Gaspar, an upscale brasserie on Sutter, in the financial district. Over a bottle of Kenwood Cabernet he told him of recent events.

Bruce listened and reiterated: "So, you beat the shit out of the guy that threw you overboard, and the quote *housekeeper* you got pregnant shot him in the leg, and to top it off, the guy's lady partner in crime was shot in the chest?"

MacCrimmon said that was a fair summary though told with a typical lawyerly trick to make it sound more sordid than it was.

Bruce looked up and told the hovering waiter they'd share an order of charcuterie. "And Karen said she was so upset with you for what happened down there she was going back to Ohrman—after moving to Mason Street only the week before?"

"That's also a fair assessment."

"I never thought I'd say this, but you may be better off without her. She's nuts!"

"I often wondered if I stayed with her more to avoid the pain of separation than for the pleasure of her company."

"And Isabella, this housekeeper—she's the one I got out of prison, the tall slender beauty with the big brown eyes?"

"Twice she's shot miscreants, and twice saved my life."

The waiter, refilling their glasses, raised his eyebrows at this.

"If it were me," Bruce said, "I'd count myself lucky to have Maddy and Isabella and Palm Springs. If you can rule out a relationship with her you must be one choosy son of a bitch."

"I'm not ruling out anything... Now about my legal issues."

"Yeah... Probate was terminated. All your assets are as before. 818 Mason belongs to you and you alone. Karen is there at your forbearance. She is legally married to this Ohrman cat, so you're a free man. Karen is responsible for paying back the life insurance, five-mill. Maddy is all yours, though a court may grant visitation if Karen pushes it. And you'll get joint custody of Alex once you've settled down, say, with your quote *housekeeper*."

"How about the voiding of the death certificate?"

"I already filed it with the court. It all hinges on whether Karen wants to be married to Ohrman, and from the way you tell it, she does. I can withdraw it any time. But the ways things flip back and forth between you two, let's leave it be for now."

That evening MacCrimmon called Bryce and cancelled the gold sale. He said he had too much on his plate at the time and didn't need the money anyway. Bryce, mightily annoyed, said this was a major inconvenience and embarrassment to him, having already set everything up with the prince. MacCrimmon assured him he would sell the gold at some later date. He upped Bryce's commission to seven-and-a-half percent, a fifty-thousand dollar raise, which mollified him somewhat.

32.

LATE THAT afternoon a small Eurasian boy in a school uniform approached a nicely dressed young African-American woman waiting on the corner of Pine and Mason and tugged her sleeve. She looked down and asked him what he wanted.

"Whereth the Grant Hotel?"

She said she didn't know. "Why, do you want to go there, little boy?"

"That'th where my Da-da ith. Can you find it on your phone?"

Warming to the little chap she said she'd give it a try. She tapped and scrolled and found an address on Bush. "It's only a block and a half away. C'mon, I'll take you." The woman, who said her name was Brittney, took his hand and walked him down the steep hill to the hotel, a half-block east on Bush. She said to the elderly desk clerk, "This young man is looking for someone."

The clerk leaned over the desk and asked, "Who are you looking for, young fella?"

"My Da-da."

"What's his name?"

"Da-da."

"He meant, what does your mama call him," Brittney said.

"Andrew."

The clerk asked, "But what's his *last* name." This stumped the young searcher. "Do you know *your* last name?"

"Yath."

"Well, what is it?"

"MacCrimmon."

"Ah, yes, Dr. MacCrimmon is staying with us. Jim will take you up."

Alex shook Brittney's hand and thanked her, as he had been taught, but she said that wasn't good enough. She knelt down and pointed to her cheek. Alex had been in this position many a time with many a woman; he knew what was expected of him. He draped his arms around the young woman's neck and gave her a light, little-boy kiss on the cheek. "Your Da-da is a very lucky man, Alex." Brittney, watching the bellman take Alex over to the elevator, said to the desk clerk that Alex was about the cutest little boy she'd ever seen. The desk clerk said he couldn't disagree.

As soon as the bellman closed the room door behind him Alex blubbered to his father, "Why aren't you home?"

MacCrimmon knelt for several moments hugging the little son he hadn't seen in almost a year. When he got his voice back he asked, "What are you doing here, Alex?"

Alex, crying even harder, shouted, "Why aren't you home?"

Unable to answer to this reasonable question, the little boy's father resorted to redirection. "How did you find me?"

"I heard Uta tell Mama." Not falling for this diversion, Alex said with his bulldog scowl of anger, "It ithn't fair! You went away, and you came back, but you're *thtill* not home!"

"You're right, Alex, it isn't fair... Does your mother know you're here?"

"No. I thneaked out."

Dr. MacCrimmon powered down his laptop, turned off all the lights, and grabbed his little son's hand. "C'mon Alex. I'll take you home. Your mom's probably frantic."

His mom, of course, *was* frantic. She knelt and grabbed Alex's arms. "Alex MacCrimmon, where have you *been*?! I was about to call the police!"

"I went to thee Da-da at the Grant Hotel. Brittney helped me."

Karen whispered to Andrew, "Who's Brittney?"

Da-da shrugged and said he had no idea.

She shook her finger in Alex's face. "That was a naughty, *naughty* thing to do!"

Alex grabbed his father's sleeve and looked up at him. "Pleath thtay at home now, Da-da."

Unlike adult pain, so often mixed with anger and jealousy and denial, Alex's child pain was uncontaminated—and infinitely more touching. It was as if all their suffering had been concentrated in the sad beseeching look of this little boy. MacCrimmon tossed a quick glance at Karen and turned away. He said in a shaky voice he had to go to the library.

Alex, watching his father hurry off, asked, "Wath Da-da crying, Mama?"

Karen knelt down and took his hand. "Men don't like to call it that, Alex. Da-da has been sad for a long, long time and Mama hasn't been very nice to him. But he's home now, like I promised you, and we're not going to let him go away again. If we have to, we'll tie him with ropes to the piano."

Alex, satisfied with this plan, brightened, and suggested the prisoner should be forced to eat gruel.

Late that evening, after the kids were bedded down, Karen tapped on the library door and entered. She had changed into tan slacks and an emerald green silk blouse, one of his favorite outfits. Andrew was leaning back in his office chair, his feet on the desk, his eyes closed, listening to the Bruch, *Scottish Fantasy*, a pretty piece for violin. He put the player on mute. "Sorry for that little show. Everything sort of flooded out. But it *was* cathartic."

"The kids wanted to see you before they went to bed, but I said you weren't feeling well."

"Yeah. I am a little shaky."

"You must be hungry. I can fix you something."

He jumped up and straightened his shirt. "Thanks, but no. I'd better get back to the hotel."

"Come out to the couch, Andrew. Maybe at last we can talk like adults." She took his hand and led him to the living room. She had set out a bottle of cognac and two snifters. They settled in, shoulder to shoulder, on the old palomino-colored suede couch facing the fireplace as they had several thousand times over the past thirty years, and kicked their stockinged feet up on the coffee table.

"After being apart a year," Karen said, "you'd think we'd be in each other's arms... There's a barrier between us."

"Barbed wire."

"You have to understand, Andrew, I was terrified, I was in shock. That horrible beast of a man pointed a gun at Maddy and kidnapped me. The first time I'd seen you in a year, you're yelling like a maniac, beating that man up, he was going to kill *you*, you were going to kill *him*, there was shooting, there was blood everywhere."

He repeated what Isabella had said, about it being better than letting Padgett kill all of them.

"I went to see Arnold yesterday, about some business things, not about going back to him. That was so silly. Sometimes I don't think things through very carefully."

MacCrimmon forced back a hundred comments that came to mind and said nothing.

"I asked him how you could change so much, be so cold and violent, why you never contacted me. He said he didn't know the details, but you might have a kind of posttraumatic stress disorder."

"No, Karen. There were a lot of prisoners worse off than I was."

"He didn't mean being in the ocean or in prison; you're too strong for that. He meant that, when you saw our wedding announcement, being a physical and emotional wreck with no defenses, it hit you extra hard. You're angry and hurt because you think I betrayed you."

"Yes. That's a fair statement."

"That's why you had your thing with Isabella. You don't love her so she couldn't hurt you. She told me all about it."

"My affair with Isabella was part gratitude, part lust, a lot of affection, a rebound thing. I'll always be grateful for all she did to help me get back in shape. Much of my recovery is because of her. She was there for me when you weren't. And she would be a good wife and good mother for Maddy."

Karen closed her eyes and shuddered. "Good God, Andrew! Don't even say the words! I'd die for sure."

He looked away and mumbled, "There was a time I would have believed that."

Karen let this bitter remark pass. If the acrimony escalated and he left, she doubted he would ever return. She waited until he looked back. "While we were at the police station and you were in the ER, I asked Isabella what she had meant when she said something about your 'unborn child.' She told me she's pregnant. And she said you're giving her the estate. "

Karen had said this as simple declarative sentences—no anger, no disgust, as if it were another distasteful but not particularly important element in the on-going calamity.

He said that was true on both counts. "Father Gus left the money he inherited from Lena to both her and me. She'll be a wealthy woman once probate is finished—her share is somewhere around four-million dollars. I promised her I'll be there when the baby is born. I'll file a declaration of paternity so I'll be listed as the father on the birth certificate."

"Are you going back to her?"

"I will, definitely, if you go back to Ohrman, and I'll take Maddy with me."

"I'm not going back to him. Ever."

"We'll see what happens."

Karen turned to him and laid her hand lightly on his bare forearm. "Oh, Andrew, no matter how awful you've been, every time I see you after you've been gone awhile it's the same. My throat chokes up and I can hardly breathe, and my insides are churning, and I feel like crying... I can't understand how one person can make another person feel this way."

He was having his own trouble breathing, and her touch on his bare arm, as it always did, sent galvanic tingling through his entire body. He too thought it strange a simple physiological reaction that had probably evolved sometime around the Devonian period, 650-million years ago, trumped the jewel in evolution's crown, the human mind. A lump in his throat, an electric thrill, and all the hurt and anger, even the legitimate reasons he should rid himself of this woman, evaporated as if they had never existed. It had always been this way with Karen: logic and reason had never been anything but squeaky voices in the wilderness.

She whispered in his ear, "Will I ever not be crazy?"

He gently brushed her cheek with the back of his hand and whispered back, "No. If there's one thing certain in this world it's that you'll never not be crazy."

"Could you still love me after all this?"

He chuckled into his snifter at the question. "Karen, calling what I feel for you 'love' is like calling a lily or an orchid a vegetable. It's much too complex a phenomenon for one simple word... But there is one major change—I can move on without you, love or no love."

They each took a sip of cognac. Karen leaned back and rested her snifter on her chest. "You'll be staying here now, won't you?"

"I hadn't planned on it, but I'll try it a while."

"Will you ever sleep with me again, you know, because I was with Arnold?... You always said if I ever slept with another man, you wouldn't—"

"You were—are—married to the man, Karen. What were you supposed to do? At least no pregnancy resulted. That's more than I can say for my adventure in rebounding. The question is moot— you're a married woman. I'll be sleeping alone anyway. I have nightmares and I thrash violently and I wander around at night when I can't sleep."

Karen drew her legs up and sat cross-legged, facing him. "I need to hear the one-hour, adult version of what happened, Andrew, from the time you confronted that creature on the Miesterdam until you, well, did what you did to him in Palm Springs. Don't leave *anything* out, I don't care how trivial or awful or disgusting it is. I *have* to know."

He took a slow sip of cognac, set the snifter on the coffee table, and turned to face her. "Agreed. If you'll tell me why you married Arnold Ohrman. Not 'the kids needed a dad' stuff—the real reason why after only a few months you married another man. That's what *I* have to know."

Karen blushed and looked down at the piece of non-existent lint she was plucking off the leg of her slacks. "Tomorrow. We'll go up to Huntington Park, it's neutral ground. I'll tell you everything."

He said he would take her at her word.

She looked up and said in a tone that allowed no refusal, "But tonight, you're going to tell me where you were all those months and what you were doing."

Over the next forty-minutes he did exactly what she'd asked— he spared her nothing. She shrieked in horror when he told her about the shark biting him, and she seethed at Abrantes and Thuggo for beating and mistreating him. She shivered in revulsion when he told her about Teofilo, the rat. She laughed at the chess game he'd had with Ramon Ximenez and wept when he told her he had lost forty-five pounds and was worm infested when he washed up on that Key West beach. She blushed and shuddered when he described reading her wedding announcement in Bryce's condo.

"Mid-August I came back to The City. I came here, to this house. All my books and paintings were gone. The lady said you must have sold everything."

She said angrily, "How could you possibly believe I would do such a thing?"

"What else was I to think? Anyway, the next day I drove out to Ohrman's home to check on you. I followed you to that market on Clement. I walked right by you, looked right at you, but I was such a scrawny mess you didn't recognize me."

She grabbed his arm and said in a muffled shriek, "Good grief, Andrew, why didn't you say something? I would have left him that minute!"

"You looked fine, content, like you'd adjusted. I didn't want to upset you. You were—are—another man's wife... From there I went to Palm Springs to recover." She clenched her lips and tapped her thighs as he described his recovery regime and Isabella's role in helping him. He reminded her she'd said she wanted to hear everything. Having come to the end he spread his hands and announced, "That's it."

Karen sniffled and wiped her eyes with a hanky. "It's a miracle, isn't it," she said, smiling weakly, "that after all that's happened we're sitting here together.

He said coolly, "No, the miracle will be us sitting here together six-days or six-months from now.

33.

MacCRIMMON woke at nine. He made the bed in the guest room and threw on shorts, sandals, and a T-shirt he found in what had been their bedroom. He shuffled down to the kitchen and Karen handed him a mug of coffee. He kissed Maddy on the top of her head and said good morning to Uta Hofer. Uta excused herself and hauled Maddy off to be dressed. Karen kissed him on the cheek and took the chair next to him. "Did you sleep, Andrew?"

"Best night's rest in eleven months. I only roused a couple of times. My spell in the library must have washed away a lot of bad stuff—like lancing an abscess."

An hour later Karen stuck her head in the library where MacCrimmon had begun the Herculean task of untangling all the business and book-keeping matters neglected over the past year. She suggested they go to Huntington Park first and go to lunch afterward. As usual, she was stunning—tan slacks, a white blouse and a loose navy-blue silk sweater, set off by a light blue silk scarf. She pointed in mock disgust at his T-shirt and baggy shorts.

He reappeared ten minutes later in dark grey slacks, a dove grey shirt, maroon tie, and navy blazer. He spread his arms and pirouetted. She laughed and nodded her approval.

In the park this cold fall day the brisk breeze had driven away all but a few hardy souls. They took a bench on the north side of the plaza facing the grey-shrouded sun.

"I can't start out with my time with Arnold," Karen said. "That would make it sound like I wanted to be with him. There were awful things that led up to it."

MacCrimmon said he had assumed as much. He told her to start from the beginning.

"On the ship, before I even knew you were missing, that horrible woman sent me a note threatening to hurt the children if I said anything. When they told me you went overboard I was hysterical, naturally. My only consolation was the missing life ring. When I left the ship Cam and Roger flew to Fort Lauderdale to be with me. That's when I talked to the two FBI agents. I lied to them and said I didn't know anything about Padgett and that woman but they didn't believe me.

"After I got home I waited for you, still thinking you'd be picked up. In early December two other FBI agents came and said they had proof you were dead—your ring, room key, pocketknife, and a positive DNA test that matched the stuff on your toothbrush I'd given them earlier."

MacCrimmon punched his palm and muttered a curse. "That was the work of that miserable Teofilo Abrantes, the cop in Mariendo, his revenge for me punching him in the nose."

Karen suggested in future he should be more careful whom he punched in the nose.

He admitted Abrantes wasn't one of his more prudently chosen punchees.

"After I heard you were dead I went really crazy. I was in such agony I tried to kill myself with pain medicine, but Roger found me in time. After I got out of St. Xavier's Rog and Cam sent me to a mental clinic in Marin for two weeks. I got better, but I still spent hours on the window seat in our bedroom watching for you to come home. And I had long conversations with you."

"Did I ever answer?"

"I heard some murmurs a few times, nothing distinct, but it was enough to convince me you were still alive. Even after a judge approved the death certificate I was still certain you weren't dead so I took all the so-called evidence over to Stockton to Dr. Crenelaw

312

to look at. He said it all could easily have been faked. He said they never should have issued the death certificate."

"Bert Crenelaw deserves a bottle of cognac for that."

She told him everything she had told Alan up to the point she'd reached the end of her rope. "I told Cam and Roger I couldn't stand it anymore, that I wanted to put the kids up for adoption."

"'*Adoption*'!... Good God! What were you thinking?"

"It never would have happened, of course, but that should tell you how crazy and desperate I was. That's when Arnold came to the house and proposed again. He'd been put up to it by Cam and Roger. They were fed up with my craziness too. I was so frantic I said I'd agree to marry him. He's good-looking and very nice and he's fabulous with the kids, and by that time I was convinced you were never coming back. I warned him over and over I didn't love him. He said he understood. He promised love would come in due course."

She looked at him as if she had forgotten what to say.

"Go ahead, Karen."

She took his hands in hers. "Love never came and it never would have come... But you must know what *did* come. We *were* married."

"I know what you're saying, Karen. I get it. You don't need to explain."

"No, Andrew, you have to hear this. You would always wonder... I enjoyed it a few times, Andrew, really enjoyed it."

He ignored the sharp pain in his guts and, fighting down his ridiculously inappropriate anger, he said, "Of course, you did. He's an attractive man and you have needs. And I'm in no position to judge considering Isabella and I went at it like honeymooners."

She laid her head against his shoulder and said through her soft weeping, "You would never have said anything that cruel unless you were angry."

313

"It's like the waves that hit me in the face when I was in the sea. They came, they were gone, I wiped the salt out of my eyes, and I thought no more of them." He rose and helped her up with both hands.*/

"You don't hate me? You won't leave me?" she said.

He tilted her chin up with his forefinger and kissed away her tears, and for the first time in eleven months, he kissed her on the mouth. "C'mon, Love, let's go have lunch. I could use a glass of wine."

In spite of what he'd said, it took many days and many glasses of wine before he moved beyond the words, "I really enjoyed it," and all the lurid activities the words implied, the same activities, he assumed, he and she had enjoyed during their marriage, perhaps even more. This was the first time in all the years they had been together she had voluntarily slept with another man, let alone admitted enjoying it. The Reverend Pete, Pavo Makkonen, the Count of Bassigny had all raped her one way or another—with them she had been anything *but* a willing participant. What bothered him even more was his own reaction, the irrationality, the unfairness of blaming her for having sex with her legal husband, and he *was* blaming her, as idiotic as that might have been. He lamented, not for the first time, that it wasn't easy being a hopeless neurotic, hagridden by insecurities.

The next days with Karen passed in platonic amiability. He gradually re-acquainted himself with the kids, especially Maddy, who had forgotten him. Each night he read to them and sang to them, as he had before he left.

Friday afternoon, a week after he returned, Karen tapped on the library door jamb. He looked over and motioned her in. "It's a mess, isn't it?" she said, referring to the unpaid bills, lapsed insurance policies and the like he'd spent hours working on. He agreed—it *was* a ghastly mess. She ambled over and sat on the corner of his desk.

Karen was wearing shorts. On the long list of Ms. Ting's charms, her legs, especially her firmly rounded, ivory smooth thighs, were near the top. Being home, resuming his routine, his distress of the past months had lessened considerably, and as he and Karen had become less wary of each other, he was again sensible of her charms. Loath to show it—she was, after all, the wife of another man—he forced himself to look at the unpaid water bill he had opened so as not to stare at her legs. She slid off the desk and looked over his shoulder at the bill. She leaned closer, pressing her breast against his shoulder. "Forty-two dollars! Good grief!" Her hair brushed his cheek. He caught the aphrodisiacal scent of her lavender shampoo. She said breathily in his ear, "Who would have thought it would be so much."

Her sudden concern about a utility bill was unusual. In all the years he'd known her she had never shown the slightest interest in how much they paid for water. When she left the library, mumbling something about conserving a precious resource, he could have sworn she was swinging her hips. But it couldn't be.

That night he had stripped to his boxers preparing for bed when Karen bustled into the guest room waving a document. She was wearing short shorts, one of his white dress shirts, and the black-rimmed reading glasses she now admitted she needed, and her hair was fluffy, as it always was when she was fresh from the shower. She ordered him to sit on the edge of the bed, and sat next to him, so close their bare thighs touched.

"Now that we have some peace and quiet you have to see Alex's progress report. He was acting up in class."

It was the usual—"Alex is a bright engaging child whose academic skills are superior, but he has trouble relating to others." It could have been copied verbatim from one of his own report cards from grade school. Karen had already reviewed and signed it a month earlier, so he didn't understand the urgency. He suggested there had been a lot of turmoil in the past months, that giving him some readjustment time would be the best plan.

Karen agreed. She set the paper aside and, looking up at him, she traced the scar on his left cheek with her fingertips. "Andrew, do you love Isabella?"

The question, asked so abruptly, caught him by surprise. It took him a moment to frame an answer. "No," he said. "It's something better than love—I like her very much... She deserves all the credit for my recovery. She cleaned, cooked, shopped, allowed nothing to interfere with my diet or exercise regimes."

"But could you be with her, I mean permanently?"

"She would be a devoted wife and mother. I would be happy with her, yes."

"But you're home now."

"There are still a lot of loose ends to take care of but, yes, I am home."

"What loose ends?"

"You're married to another man."

She ignored this as an irrelevancy not worth considering. "But you'll be staying?"

"Let's see how things work out."

The next morning MacCrimmon returned from walking Alex to school to find burly, balding Emmett Sanderson, a columnist for the *Chronicle*, sitting at the kitchen table drinking coffee with Karen. MacCrimmon disliked the press—a sentiment they enthusiastically reciprocated—but he made an exception for Emmett. Emmett had defended him consistently when the media was hostile and the police, many in city government, and many in the public wanted his head. More recently, he had written MacCrimmon's obituary and had spoken at his memorial service. Emmett started to rise but MacCrimmon pushed him back down by his shoulders. Emmett had a bad limp from a horrendous auto accident when he was a teenager.

"Making time with my girl, are you, Emmett?"

"None of your evasions, Andrew," Karen said.

"It's time to write your story, my friend," Emmett said.

"And don't you dare try and weasel out of it," Karen warned, shaking a finger at him.

MacCrimmon detested opening himself up to public view but better Emmett than one of the many reporters who disliked him. "Collusion, I say. Dastardly collusion… Where? When?"

"Here. Now."

"Okay," MacCrimmon groaned, "let's get it over with."

Emmett clicked on a voice recorder *and* pulled out a notebook—he was a belt *and* suspenders man. "Karen gave me the basics. We'll start with the first time you saw this giant on the cruise ship—be sure to spell all the names for me. We'll build up from the time you were in the water and in prison and your escape. Beating the guy up after he kidnapped Karen will be the denouement." He said to Karen, "God, what a book this would make!"

She said, addressing Emmett but looking at MacCrimmon, "If anyone writes it, it will be you."

"Let's get on with it, if you don't mind," MacCrimmon said.

An hour and several cups of coffee later, Emmett wrapped it up. He clicked off his recorder and said, laughing, "You have to admit that thing with the coffin was hilarious."

Karen, who didn't think it was funny in the slightest, glared at him. "Emmett Sanderson, there was nothing 'hilarious' about it!"

Limping with MacCrimmon to the front door Emmett whispered, "A fat little guy with a gold tooth listening to salsa

317

music while you're banging on a coffin lid—how can you *not* make it a comical scene?"

MacCrimmon, who didn't care one way or the other, shrugged, but warned him if he did make it humorous he'd better stay out of Karen's way for a while.

MacCrimmon saw Emmett out and returned to the library to resume clearing up the mess his financial affairs had gotten into. He was now dealing with unpaid bills going to collection, investments going south he would have to unload, and problems with his rental properties.

He'd been there about ten-minutes when Karen called him to see something in the upstairs bath. He hurried up, assuming it was a leak or an act of vandalism perpetrated by Alex. But no. On the floor was an air mattress Karen had found somewhere. He had been tense lately, she informed him in her crisp sensuous contralto, in serious need of a massage. Uta had taken Maddy shopping so it was a perfect opportunity. She ordered him to strip and lie face down. He obeyed but was dubious—her massage skills when she was at the Honolulu Sun were average at best—but he was soon proved wrong, *very* wrong. She stripped off her white shirt—her only garment—and covered both their bodies in a fragrant oil she had warmed under the hot water faucet. Several minutes she massaged him with her entire body as he lay prone. She whispered, "Turn over." He obeyed. She straddled him and impaled herself. Seconds later he bellowed his release. The next more leisurely twenty-minutes he attended to *her* needs and wants.

They hurriedly cleaned up the mess and showered together. When Uta returned they were drinking coffee at the kitchen table. He said he had officially enshrined this episode in the pantheon of their erotic high points. He asked her where she got the idea— something she'd learned from Arnold?

She slapped his arm, hard, and said that was an insulting question—she'd never allowed Arnold anything beyond what the strictest of missionaries would have allowed Pacific Islanders, and the times she *had* enjoyed it, she'd had her eyes closed, thinking of him. "No," she said. "I found the idea on a naughty website I went to for inspiration."

He smiled at the way their intimacy had evolved after he returned home. At first, when she was defensive about marrying Arnold, she had overlooked his snarky crack about honeymooning with Isabella. But as he again succumbed to her charms, and she was again on the erotic high ground, so to speak, she took him to task for bragging about having wild sex with another woman. Now, the third stage, was the arousal of her competitive spirit. What Isabella could do in the area of honeymooning, Karen figured, she could do much better. He thought it best not to share with her that an oily massage like this was exactly how his "honeymoon" with Isabella had begun.

34.

SEARCH AND DESTROY, a game Alex and his father had devised, entailed running from room to room and up and down the stairs, throwing nerf balls at each other, trying for a head shot, which signaled victory. For Maddy it was frustrating as she had trouble negotiating the stairs—for an adult the equivalent would have been climbing on and off the dining room table. This morning's game she had been left behind in the kitchen by her father and brother, so in her infantile innocence she had chucked her nerf ball at an easier target—her mother. MacCrimmon returned to the kitchen, sweating and panting. Karen had perched Maddy on a kitchen chair and was making it clear that, while she could do what she wanted with those other two savages, as a target her mother was strictly off limits. He knew Karen took this seriously—both he and Alex had suffered twenty-minute timeouts for hitting her with nerf balls, in Alex's case, accidentally—but from the way she was unsuccessfully hiding her laughter behind her hand, he guessed this offense was low on the severity scale.

"How can you reprimand her, Andrew?" Karen said, now laughing openly, "when she looks up at you with those intense blue eyes?"

He knelt next to the miscreant's chair and asked, "Well, young lady? What do you have to say for yourself?"

Maddy poked his cheek with a chubby forefinger and said, "Da-da Ting a tong."

"'Sing a song,' of course. Diversion. Alex's tactic."

Realizing from her parents' laughter she was off the hook, she clambered down and toddled off in search of her brother.

MacCrimmon had settled in with a cup of coffee when Karen took a call. She listened a moment and handed him the handset. The caller identified himself as Arnold Ohrman. He asked if they might talk, man to man. MacCrimmon agreed.

Shortly after noon Dr. MacCrimmon pulled into the driveway of Dr. Arnold Ohrman's home in the outer Richmond District. He pressed the doorbell button and waited several long moments, tapping his foot and fiddling with his fingers, wondering what the man wanted.

Dr. Ohrman welcomed him in a soft, warm baritone, a voice his patients must find comforting. He wondered how Karen could not love this strongly built handsome man with his kind face and gentle pale blue eyes. Probably the same reason *he* didn't love Isabella. "You *are* alive, Dr. MacCrimmon! We all thought Karen was delusional."

MacCrimmon shook his hand and said he was comforted a licensed psychiatrist had confirmed he was alive—there had been times the past year he'd had his doubts.

Ohrman stepped back and invited him in. MacCrimmon passed through the short hallway into a cluttered living room, sparsely furnished bachelor fashion: a couch covered with a tattered brown corduroy slipcover, a floor lamp next to an overstuffed easy chair, and a wooden coffee table. A bookcase along one wall was untidily stuffed with books and journals. "Not much furniture, I'm afraid. My ex-wife took most of it. Five years and I never got around to replacing it." Ohrman had him take the easy chair while he took the closest end of the sagging couch. MacCrimmon was surprised that Karen would allow such shabbiness. She never would have in *their* home. She must never have felt at home here, must never have intended to stay.

"I wanted to talk to you to see where matters stand," Ohrman said. "I'm legally married to Karen so I have a legitimate interest."

"Yes, you do have a legitimate interest."

"Before we get into that may I ask where you've been the last year?"

MacCrimmon gave him the five-minute summary. Dr. Ohrman interrupted at several points asking for details, as everyone else had. He was especially interested in the hallucinations he had suffered that last night he drifted in the ocean.

"In the beginning," Ohrman said, "when you were first reported as being dead, when Karen was most seriously disturbed, she said she talked to you. Did you, uh, by any chance hear her— talking to you, I mean?"

"No, I didn't hear her, but I saw her—her image was always before me, as if plastered against my retinas. That's what kept me going, why I would put off for another hour drinking sea water, why I would force down food crawling with insect larvae, why I would paddle another five yards when all I wanted to do was sink into exhausted oblivion, why I never lost faith, why I survived. So, when I was safely back in Florida, ready to come home and surprise her, and I saw the announcement of your wedding on the net, it deflated me, you might say, set me back—it came at a bad time."

"It's hard to imagine anything worse."

"A blow like that leaves wounds that will never heal... Karen, as she always does, says we'll be together until death. She likes to think our marriage will be exactly like it was before this fiasco, that nothing has changed. But much *has* changed."

"You mean because she married me?"

"I don't claim it's rational—that's why they're called feelings, not thinkings... There's another complication as well."

"And what is that?"

"Everything we say will be held in confidence?"

"Of course."

"I assumed Karen had married you out of love. In fact if anyone had told me she had married out of convenience or desperation I would have called him a damn liar!... Mid-August I came out here to watch, to assure myself she and the children were all right. I saw the kids, and they looked fine. I followed Karen into a market. I was a mess so she didn't recognize me. She seemed happy and well-adjusted—I didn't know the, uh, real situation." He paused and looked down at his twiddling fingers. "All I had to do was say to her, 'Karen, I'm home,' and all of this could have been avoided."

"All of *what* could have been avoided?"

"There's another woman. I spent six weeks in Palm Springs getting myself back in shape. Isabella took care of me in a way no one else could have, including Karen."

"This other woman, Doctor, do you love her?"

"Love is a young man's sport, Dr. Ohrman. The upside can be ecstatic, sure, but the downside is probably where the concept of hell originated... Isabella would be—is—a fine companion and would be a fine mother for Madeleine. And she wouldn't leave me every six-months over some real or imagined offense, nor would she end up in some man's bed, as Karen has done several times. Not that she betrayed me consciously, of course—it was always some horrendous lapse in judgment. As an added complication, Isabella is pregnant—with a son she has already named 'Malcolm,' after one of my grandfathers. None of this would have happened if Karen hadn't married you."

"If things don't work out with Karen what will you do?"

"Take Maddy and move to Palm Springs with Isabella."

Ohrman asked MacCrimmon if he would like coffee. He declined. He wandered over and looked out at the back yard while Ohrman brewed his cup of herb tea.

Ohrman returned; the men seated themselves again. "Your relationship with Karen is unusual, Dr. MacCrimmon. How did you and she meet, if I might ask?"

"'Unusual' is a mild word for it. We met when I was a John and Karen, or 'Lola,' as she called herself, was a prostitute—I assume she told you about her life before we were married."

"If you mean the Honolulu Sun, yes, she did tell me about it. I visited it. It's a squalid place—unless it's changed."

No," MacCrimmon said, chuckling, "it always *was* squalid."

"Is her story about her father's gambling debts true?"

"Yes. Her sister, Kay, confirmed it."

"Karen described our love life, what little there was of it, as if I were a client and she was a prostitute, forced to do what she was doing out of necessity."

MacCrimmon poofed in disgust. "She *is* capable of that kind of cruelty, I know from bitter experience. I think it's more solipsistic than intentional but the hurt is the same. You have my sympathy— and no one is in a better position to give it... Along those lines, how would you describe your own distress in all this?"

"I was broken up, of course, but it was clear from the beginning Karen didn't love me, so my guard was up. When I found out about her time as a prostitute, and I appreciated the degree and quality of her attachment to you, I realized she and I weren't a good fit, that there would never be any closeness between us."

Ohrman leaned forward and said softly, as if to avoid being overheard, "But back to this massage parlor—why would a man of your obvious gifts patronize a place like that?"

"Good question... When I was younger I had many relationships, a hundred or thereabouts. Some lasted months; most, weeks or even less. They all had one thing in common: I didn't love the women, not a one. There is a strange quirk in the female psyche—they love men who *don't* love them more than they love men who *do* love them."

"That's an overly broad generalization."

"There are many exceptions, Karen, for one... But hurting so many women took its toll. For the good of the women I would never meet and thus never hurt, and to salve my conscience for those I *had* hurt, I satisfied my earthier needs where a lady's broken heart was not a concern.

"That's when I met Karen. If you think she is beautiful now you should have seen her then. But it wasn't only her beauty—it was her dignity, and the strength with which she faced the appalling degradation of that place and what she had to do. I knew instantly she was the only woman I would ever love. My obsession with her, which began seconds after first catching sight of her, grew over the next year, monopolizing my thoughts, interfering with my work, alienating my friends. She, on the other hand, treated me with cool indifference. At one point she even considered cutting me off—she suspected I was one of those freaks who liked killing whores.

"Our association, I guess you could call it, came to an abrupt end when she played an inhumanly cruel trick on me, so heartless it drove me to a suicide attempt." He waved away Ohrman's request for details. "A month passed, I'd neither seen her nor heard from her when much to my surprise she showed up one afternoon at my front door, grievously ill from a work-related injury."

"'Work related' at a massage parlor? Can you specify?"

"Yes. A drunken client had jammed a sex toy into her, tearing up her female innards."

Ohrman blinked hard. "Good God!"

"Yes. Sordid, disgusting, isn't it? Hard to imagine, knowing her now... Anyway, it had gotten infected. She only came to me out of end stage desperation, knowing I was a doctor. She refused to go to the hospital so I cared for her, gave her antibiotics, entertained her, and fed her—she was dangerously malnourished. Living in my nice home with me and seeing I was a completely different person outside the sleazy massage parlor, something clicked in her. From that point on, several psychiatric disorders, some individual, some shared, mashed together to form the now *mutual* obsession that persists to this day."

Ohrman laughed at a passion such as theirs being called a "mash of psychiatric disorders."

"At times it's been ecstatic, other times so agonizing I thought I only existed as someone for her to cruelly punish for misdeeds I never knew I'd committed. As a grand passion it suffers from being melodramatic, overblown, and, recently, ridiculous. Thisbe and Pyramus, Tristan and Isolde, Heloise and Abelard we ain't."

"But you do love her."

"If you consider what I feel for her a grotesque isotope of the word as it's usually understood, yes."

Ohrman mouthed "isotope" and laughed. Again serious he asked, "Knowing she was with all those men—doesn't that bother you?... It did me. Being treated as one of a hundred or so other faceless men effectively killed my ardor."

"Less than it used to, but, yes, it still does. In the beginning, when it seemed we were pretty much tied to each other, we made a pact of mutual monogamy. The only way I could put all those men behind me was by fostering the illusion that 'Lola the whore' had been reincarnated as 'Karen the pure.' Karen broke that pact when she slept with you."

"But we all thought you were dead, and, after all, we *were* married."

"My guts say 'yes,' she broke the pact; my head says, 'no.' My head is why she and I are now together."

"At the risk of being offensive," Dr. Ohrman said smiling, "it seems you have your own issues."

"A whole seething, writhing passel of 'em—deep insecurities, jealousy, an anachronistic moral code, among others... Speaking of 'issues,' may I ask what your treatment plan was for Karen?"

"I was of very little help to her. I knew from the beginning she had only come to me because her housekeeper and nephews forced her. She volunteered nothing. If I had allowed it she would have sat through the entire session without saying a word. She answered questions in monosyllables or not at all. She was delusional and depressed. What I got from talking to Roger, and what little I got out of her, fit with a diagnosis of 'Complicated Grief Disorder,' by far the worst case I've ever seen. She violently refused any kind of drug treatment—by that I mean she *screamed* her refusal—and she stoutly resisted psychotherapy, so there was little I could do for her. That's when I suggested we meet for coffee. She opened up a little outside the physician-patient relationship. That's when I fell in love with her."

"Why would you marry someone who was so obviously damaged?"

"As you said earlier in so many words, the head and the heart aren't always in sync. I naively believed once she was a mother and wife again, the cycle—the grieving, the depression, the delusions, the inability to function, the alienation and bitterness—might be broken."

A long moment of silence passed. "Doctor!" Ohrman said to get MacCrimmon's attention—he had been staring off into the distance. "You're not at all how I pictured you."

MacCrimmon looked back, blinking. "Sorry. I was, uh, reflecting... You mean I'm *not* the wild-eyed homicidal maniac you thought I was?"

"I hadn't expected someone so affable. I pictured you more as a brooding, menacing character in a Gothic novel, a Heathcliff-type."

"The degree of attachment between Karen and me, and our mawkish emotional excesses, must seem a little 'Gothic' in an age when people gird themselves in cool irony and change mates with about as much feeling as they change underwear. I have it on reliable authority it's not unusual for people to look at their phones, even text, while they're having sex."

"The price of promiscuity."

MacCrimmon, sensing the interview was at an end, rose and straightened the legs of his slacks. He grinned at Ohrman in mock despair and gave a long dramatic sigh. "This has been an unholy fucked up mess all around, hasn't it?"

Ohrman said with a flicker of a smile, "Your understatement does scant justice to the situation."

On the walk to the front door Ohrman said, "I never asked my most important question. What do I do about my marriage to Karen?"

"Yes, of course... She won't be coming back to you, even if she and I go our separate ways. Either you or Karen will have to file for divorce, though there is another possibility." He described Bruce's plan to have the death certificate overturned. Ohrman said he would support that wholeheartedly.

Three weeks later, the court did rule on Bruce Solomon's petition to void MacCrimmon's death certificate. Bruce's argument had been that the evidence purporting to prove MacCrimmon's death had been fraudulent. Bert Crenelaw had submitted a report detailing the reasons the death certificate should never have been issued in the first place. The ashes could have come from a burning garbage pile; the DNA only proved it came from MacCrimmon and in no way proved he was dead; and no photos had been submitted. He concluded the evidence was insufficient for proof of death. By voiding the death certificate, Bruce argued, Karen's marriage to Ohrman would be invalid, since her husband—MacCrimmon— should not have been declared dead. If the court accepted this reasoning, a long divorce could be avoided.

The judge conceded Crenelaw's report was informative but he dismissed it as legally irrelevant because it came after the fact. He said, at the time, the evidence presented had met the standards of reasonable proof of death. However, as there were no child custody issues, no property issues, nor anything other than the marriage, and as Dr. Ohrman, the second husband, had come out strongly in favor of the petition, the judge said he was willing to exercise a certain latitude in this case. He voided the death certificate. He said

Dr. MacCrimmon standing in front of him, very much alive, made the decision easier.

The upshot was, Andrew MacCrimmon and Karen Ting were again man and wife and had never been anything but. Ohrman, for his part, was no longer saddled with a wife living with another man and would be spared the bother of a divorce from a woman he never should have married in the first place.

That afternoon, in the library, MacCrimmon, heard Karen and the kids whispering. He figured they were up to something but paid no attention. On his way to the kitchen for a drink of water they attacked. Karen jumped on his back and each kid grabbed a leg. He dragged them, Frankenstein style, to the carpet in the living room and slowly collapsed on his back. Karen, now straddling him, told the kids to hold his arms while she tickled him. He was ticklish but he stood it for several moments, looking into the distance, expressionless. Unable to endure it any longer, he let out a lion roar and grabbed all three in a great bear hug.

Unlike their usual wiggling horse play, Maddy and Alex lay still in his arms for five seconds—five blissful seconds of contentment he hadn't known for a year and thought might never come again. The Lilliputians quickly tired of inert Gulliver and ran off, screaming. Karen, lying on him, kissed his neck and asked what he was thinking.

"How effective contentment is in clearing away mental debris."

"You mean me marrying Arnold?"

"Not only that. All the sadness and anger that swine Padgett caused all of us."

"I've gotten over it, Andrew."

He kissed her lightly on the lips. "Yeah. I'll get there too, sooner or later."

Late that night, MacCrimmon opened one of their treasured bottles of Perrier-Jouët to celebrate the court decision. The ebullience of the bubbly, as is it commonly did, led to vigorous lovemaking, on this occasion on a pile of quilts in front of a cheery fire.

Afterward, Karen said, "You were different, Andrew, looser, more fun, the way you used to be, before all these horrible things happened."

"The judge wiped the slate clean. It's as if all that bad stuff was a nasty dream."

He rolled onto his side and went over Karen's naked body with his fingertips, marveling as he always did at her porcelain perfection. When he reached her lips she grabbed his hand and nipped his fingers, a bit too hard for simple playfulness. She said with a teasing lift of her eyebrow, "How about the barbed wire you said was separating us?"

"Ah, yes, barbed wire. It's there all right, but I was mistaken. It doesn't separate us—it binds us together. When I was eleven and got trapped in a barbed wire fence I fought against it and it tore me up badly. I still have the scars."

"The ones on your back."

"Yes... There's a lesson there, about trying to untangle a person from barbed wire, wounds inflicted, all that."

Karen said through her low sultry laugh, "'Held together by barbed wire.' My romantic husband."

"Yes, 'husband.' I like the sound of the word." He clambered up, poured the last of the Champagne in their glasses, and settled back down next to her. "A toast." He clicked his glass to hers. "To never having been not married."

Made in the USA
Middletown, DE
04 December 2020